Winners & Losers

CATRIN COLLIER

ORION

First published in Great Britain in 2004 by Orion,
an imprint of the Orion Publishing Group Ltd.

Copyright © Catrin Collier, 2004

The moral right of Catrin Collier to be identified as the author
of this work has been asserted in accordance with
the Copyright, Designs and Patents Act of 1988.

A CIP catalogue record for this book is available
from the British Library.

ISBN 0 75285 315 5 (hardback) 0 75285 316 3 (trade paperback)

Typeset by Deltatype Ltd, Birkenhead, Merseyside

Printed in Great Britain by Clays Ltd, St Ives plc

All the characters in this book are fictitious, and any resemblance
to actual persons living or dead is purely coincidental.

The Orion Publishing Group Ltd
Orion House
5 Upper Saint Martin's Lane
London, WC2H 9EA

Winners & Losers

For my own 'winners', Ken and Marguerite Griffiths,
with love and more gratitude than I can ever express

Acknowledgements

I apologize for the length of this acknowledgement but I would like to thank everyone who helped me research this book and so generously gave of their time and expertise.

All the dedicated staff of Rhondda Cynon Taff's exceptional library service, especially Mrs Lindsay Morris for her ongoing help and support. Catherine Morgan the archivist at Pontypridd and Nick Kelland, the archivist at Treorchy library.

The staff of Pontypridd Museum, Brian Davies, David Gwyer and Ann Cleary, for allowing me to dip into their extensive collection of old photographs and for doing such a wonderful job of preserving the history of Pontypridd.

Professor Dai Smith of the University of Glamorgan for sharing his knowledge of the Tonypandy Riots with me and his account of the riots in Wales, in the chapter, 'A Place in South Wales' in the book, *Wales, A Question for History*.

Deirdre Beddoe for her meticulously documented accounts of women's lives in Wales at the turn of the last century.

The fascinating period photographs Gareth Williams has posted on his Internet site, 'A Tribute to the Rhondda', which also gives an in-depth account of the Tonypandy Riots.

The people of Tonypandy and the Rhondda, the friendliest, most hospitable people on earth, who are always prepared to talk to and listen to a stranger.

My husband John and our children, Ralph, Ross, Sophie and Nick, and my parents Glyn and Gerda for their love, support and the time they gave me to write this book.

Margaret Bloomfield for her friendship and help in so many ways.

My agent, Ken Griffiths, for his professionalism, friendship and inspiring imagination. And his wife Marguerite for her hospitality and warm friendship.

Absolutely everyone at Orion, especially my editor Yvette Goulden for her encouragement and constructive criticism, Rachel Leyshon my eagle-eyed copy-editor, Angela McMahon my publicist, Juliet Ewers, Sara O'Keeffe, Jenny Page, Dean Mitchell and all the editorial, sales and marketing teams.

And all the booksellers and readers who make writing such a privileged occupation.

While I wish to acknowledge all the assistance I received, I wish also to state that any errors in *Winners & Losers* are entirely mine.

Catrin Collier
October 2003

Chapter 1

JOEY EVANS turned the key that was left permanently in the lock of his family's front door, stepped inside and started whistling, '*A Little of What You Fancy Does You Good*'.

'Quiet! You'll wake Harry.' His eldest brother Lloyd walked in behind him and hung his trilby on the rack in the passage.

'Someone has to warn the lovebirds. You don't want to see anything that will make you blush, now do you?' Joey hung his cap and overcoat next to Lloyd's.

'Unlike you, Victor behaves himself around the ladies.' Lloyd opened the kitchen door. Their middle brother Victor was sitting at the table playing chess with his girlfriend of two years, nineteen-year-old Megan Williams. She was wrapped up in her cloak, Victor in his overcoat and both of them were wearing mufflers and woollen gloves. 'Disappointed, Joey?' Lloyd raised his eyebrows.

'With what?' Victor glanced up at his brothers.

'Joey was hoping that you and Megan would be doing something that would embarrass us.' Lloyd winked at Megan as he sat next to her.

Megan smiled at Lloyd but scowled at Joey. At the age of thirteen she had been sent to housekeep for her uncle, who lived next door to the Evans, after her aunt had died in childbirth. Back then she had become besotted with Victor's younger brother, who was the same age as her. Joey had been, and still was in most of the local girls' opinion, the handsomest boy in Tonypandy, if not the whole of Wales. It had taken her three years to realize that he was as infatuated with his good looks as his admirers and capable of remaining faithful to a girl only for as long as it took him to catch the eye of another. It was then that she had discovered that

1

Joey's older colliery blacksmith brother, whose height and breadth she had always found intimidating, had a gentle side.

It had been difficult to determine who was the more surprised, her or Victor, when they found themselves in love after a year of outings based on 'friendship'. But it was a love fraught with difficulties, which they tried to put from their minds whenever they were together.

'It's cold enough in here to freeze the cockles of a man's heart without you giving me one of your frigid looks, Megan.' Joey dived out and retrieved his overcoat.

'We raked out the fire after Dad and Sali left for the meeting,' Victor explained.

'You would have been warmer playing chess on the picket line. At least we have a brazier going down there.' Joey pulled on his gloves and joined them at the table.

'But we wouldn't have been able to see to Harry if he woke up.' Megan moved her rook and took Victor's bishop.

'Poor kid's probably frozen to his bed.' Joey studied the board.

'Sali wrapped a couple of hot bricks in flannel and put them at his feet when she tucked him in. She also left a couple of egg sandwiches for you two in the pantry.' Victor moved his queen.

'You suicidal?' Joey demanded.

'Victor's conceding the game because he knows my uncle and his brothers probably walked up from the picket line with you and they'll be wanting something to eat.' Megan wrinkled her nose. 'Not that I've much to give them.'

'Can't a man make a bad chess move?' Victor protested.

'Not when he doesn't usually.' Megan took Victor's queen and put his king into checkmate. 'But then you don't always let me win. It was a draw until this one.' She left the table and blew Victor a kiss from the door. 'Night, all.'

Lloyd heard Megan talking to Sali and his father in the passage as he set up the board again. 'Thanks for babysitting Harry, Victor.'

'Megan and I didn't have anything else to do.' Victor left the table and went to the pantry. He was surprisingly light-footed for a man of his size. Six feet six in his stockinged feet, broad-shouldered, finely muscled and well built, he towered above most men in the valleys.

'You would have had plenty if it was summer and warm enough to sit on the mountain,' Joey suggested archly.

'That's my girlfriend, not one of your tarts you're talking about.' Victor spoke softly as he always did when he was angry.

'I didn't mean anything. You've been courting Megan for two years——.'

'And while her father withholds his consent, that's all I can do.' Victor set the sandwiches in front of his brothers and lifted a couple of plates from the dresser.

'Good meeting?' Lloyd asked his father when he came in.

'That depends on what you mean by "good". Just about every Bible-thumping church and chapel minister in the Rhondda has managed to wangle themselves a place on the Distress Committee. There's so many on it, I doubt they'll agree long enough make a single decision. Still, the amount of time they'll waste arguing amongst themselves shouldn't leave them with much spare time to bother any poor soul intent on committing a few harmless sins.' Billy Evans fished his empty pipe out of his pocket before he sat down. 'We would have been home half an hour ago if the Methodists and Baptists hadn't tabled a formal complaint about Father Kelly's soup kitchen.'

'They object to him feeding people in the Catholic Hall?' Lloyd asked in surprise.

'No, but they think he gets more donations than they do.'

'Of food or money?' Lloyd enquired.

'Both,' Billy Evans said drily.

'Now I wonder why people are happier to give to Father Kelly than the chapels.' Lloyd grabbed Sali's hand and pulled her on to his lap as she walked through the door.

'Because he feeds everyone who walks through the door without asking what denomination they are and because his volunteers work hard to bring in as many donations as they can?' Sali suggested.

'None of them works as hard as you, sweetheart. You look tired. You've been overdoing it in your kitchen lately.'

'I have not, and it's not my kitchen, it's Father Kelly's.' Sali had been the Evans' housekeeper for over a year and Lloyd's lover for eight months. It was a relationship that had been welcomed by his father and brothers, who already treated her as if she were one of the family, which she very soon would be as they had booked Pontypridd register office for their wedding. Lloyd insisted their marriage go ahead the Saturday before Christmas, despite his workload as one of the strike organizers. It was the earliest date possible due to circumstances they had kept secret from all but a very few people in Tonypandy.

'Without the food and money you persuade people to donate, Sali, all Father Kelly would have to serve is bread and water without the bread.' Mr Evans set his empty tobacco pouch on the table out of habit. He hadn't bought any tobacco since the onset of the strike. 'Is Harry asleep?'

'And before you say you don't know, we heard you creep up the stairs after Megan left,' Lloyd teased Sali.

Sali didn't rise to his bait. 'Harry's sleeping like an angel. He didn't give you and Megan any trouble, did he, Victor?'

'Unfortunately he didn't wake once. If he had, it would have given me an excuse to relight the fire.' Victor filled a glass with water.

Unable to resist a second gibe, Joey said, 'You and Megan could have kept one another warm.'

Knowing how sensitive Victor was about Megan, Billy Evans broke in sharply, 'Joey! Enough! Has Megan heard from her father lately, Victor?'

'Not that she's told me. But then she's hardly mentioned him since he refused to allow us to get engaged at Christmas.' Victor sat at the table and moved a white pawn on the board Lloyd had set up.

'Megan won't be under age for ever, Victor.' Sali moved to her own chair and watched Lloyd move out a black pawn to meet Victor's.

'I've some papers to go through for the committee, so I'll call it a night. Aren't you on early picket tomorrow, Joey?' Billy asked.

'Yes.' Joey made a face.

'Then go to bed and get some sleep,' Billy ordered. 'If I leave you down here, you'll only plague the life out of Victor.'

'What's a brother for, if not to annoy?' Joey answered smartly.

'Joey!' Billy said sternly.

'I'm going.'

'You two coming down to Porth magistrates court with me tomorrow?' Billy asked. Everyone in the town, collier and tradesman, was eagerly awaiting the outcome of an inquest on a miner who had died from injuries he'd received during the worse night of the recent riots.

'I'll walk down there with you,' Lloyd answered.

'Victor?'

'I have one or two things to do first,' Victor murmured evasively, concentrating on the game.

'If those one or two things involve working in the illegal drift mines the boys have opened up on the mountain, forget it,' Billy warned. 'A man your size is easily recognized, even by some of the idiots in the police. Try it and you'll end up in court facing a fine we won't be able to pay. Did you hear me?' Billy questioned when Victor didn't answer.

'I hear you, Dad.' Victor moved his knight and took Lloyd's pawn.

'Try to remember what I said, will you?' Billy shook his head as he closed the kitchen door behind him.

At half past eleven the following morning Megan tossed the stone she'd used to whiten the flagstone floor into a bucket of freezing water. The kitchen might be ice cold and gloomy, but it was clean. Not as clean as it would have been if she'd had hot water but it was too early to waste precious coals and paraffin by lighting the stove and lamp. She sat back on her heels and checked she hadn't missed any bits. Satisfied she'd done the job as well as she could, given what she had to work with, she climbed to her feet. Heaving the bucket into the sink, she tipped the dirty water down the drain.

The front door opened and footsteps echoed down the passage.

'Megan, you going to the shops?' Megan's neighbour, Betty Morgan saw the freshly scrubbed floor and stopped in her tracks.

The slightest speck of dirt carried on to a wet floor and made it twice as hard to clean the next time.

'Yes, Mrs Morgan, as soon as I've washed my hands and face,' Megan answered.

Betty Morgan was a grandmother six times over and, although she'd frequently asked Megan to call her by her Christian name, Megan had never plucked up courage to do so, despite the informality that was the rule rather than the exception between neighbours in the Rhondda.

'Then I'll wait for you.' Betty didn't need to explain her reluctance to walk into town alone. Most housewives had enjoyed visiting the shops in Tonypandy, regarding their outings as a welcome break from the drudgery of housework, but that had been before over a thousand police officers had been imported from all over Britain to control the striking miners who had brought the collieries in the valley to a standstill. The picket lines the colliers had set up around the pits had become battlegrounds. And now that the strike had entered its third month and two regiments of soldiers had been drafted in to support the police, fights between colliers, their supporters and the police frequently spilled over into the town.

Megan rinsed the bucket, placed it below the sink and washed her hands, arms and face under the running tap with a sliver of green household soap. She dried herself on the kitchen towel, rolled down her sleeves, untied her calico apron, draped it over a chair and tiptoed over the wet floor into the passage. Betty was leaning against the open front door, chatting to Jane Edwards who lived next door but one to her and on the opposite side of the Street to the Evans.

Megan lifted her black serge cloak and hat from the row of pegs and paused to stare at her reflection in the mirror. She was pale, her eyes unnaturally large. Weeks on a near starvation diet were beginning to take their toll on her just as they were on everyone else in her uncle's family. She pulled the brim of her hat low, fastened the button at the neck of her cloak, picked up her basket, and joined Betty.

'Cold enough for you today, Megan?' Jane asked.

'Freezing, Jane.' Megan had no compunction about calling Jane by her Christian name. A head-turningly attractive brunette, at seventeen Jane was two years younger than her. Gossips had labelled Jane as 'one for the boys' before she'd reached her fourteenth birthday, and she'd set every tongue in Tonypandy wagging when she had married Emlyn Edwards, a fifty-year-old collier, the day after her sixteenth birthday. The old wives in the town had watched her waistline ever since, and they continued to watch and wait. Because the baby everyone had assumed Jane was carrying had never materialized.

'I was just asking Jane if she'd seen Emlyn lately,' Betty commented.

'You of all people should know strike pay doesn't allow for luxuries like train tickets down to Cardiff, Betty,' Jane scoffed. 'I write to Emlyn once a week and he writes back. But he's not expecting to be let out early.'

'It's scandalous to jail men for withdrawing their labour in an effort to get a living wage.' Betty conveniently forgot that Emlyn had been given a year's hard labour for assaulting a police officer who'd been trying to escort blacklegs into the Cambrian Colliery.

'You two going to the shops?' Jane dropped the rag she was half-heartedly using to wash her windows into her bucket.

'Only to Rodney's,' Megan said, referring to the largest provision store in Tonypandy. 'Can we get you anything?'

'Plenty, but seeing as I haven't a brass farthing to my name and won't have until the strike money is doled out on Friday, I can only take what they're giving away.'

'I can guarantee fresh air and insults from the police but not much else. See you, Jane.' Betty led the way and Megan followed, leaving Jane to her window-washing, although she was smearing not shifting the dirt with her torn piece of old petticoat and cold water.

It took ten minutes for Megan and Betty to walk the short distance to the end of the street. No family had enough coal to keep the fires lit during the day, so the housewives were out in force, scrubbing doorsteps and the pavements in front of their

7

houses because it was warmer, and more companionable outside, than inside stone walls.

They heard shouts coming from the main street when they turned right down the hill. Murmuring a prayer for her uncle who was manning the picket line around the Glamorgan Colliery, Megan quickened her pace.

A crowd of women marched in parade formation down the centre of the road between the tramlines. A horse-drawn cart swerved to avoid them and a load of boots destined for Oliver's Shoes ended up in the gutter. The women were carrying a dummy dressed in a collier's helmet, red flannel shirt, trousers and hobnailed boots, and were shouting loudly, if not melodically:

> *The colliers will work for three bob a day,*
> *If colliers grumble, Leonard will say,*
> *Pick up your tools and clear away.*

'Betty, Megan, join us and show Leonard Llewellyn and the rest of his colliery management toadies exactly what we women think of them,' Betty's sister, Alice Hughes, who lived in Clydach, yelled from the front line of the marchers.

'We're busy shopping, Alice.' As they turned to leave, Betty glimpsed a constable heading for the women and deliberately stepped in front of him. He elbowed her in the small of her back and she cried out. Falling awkwardly, she caught her knees painfully on the kerb.

'Mrs Morgan, are you all right!' Megan crouched beside her. A police boot landed on her skirt, effectively pinning her to the ground.

The grinning constable stood over them. 'Obstructing a police officer in the course of his duty is a serious offence . . . ladies.' He spat out the last word.

'I saw that, officer.' Father Kelly pushed his way towards them. 'You hit that poor defenceless woman—'

'She was causing an obstruction,' the officer refuted sullenly.

'You are standing on this lady's skirt,' Father Kelly's companion pointed out coldly. It was the Anglican vicar, Reverend Williams of the mid-Rhondda Central Distress Committee.

'I wasn't aware that I was, sir.' A crowd began to form around them and the officer retreated to the pavement.

'Are you hurt, Mrs Morgan?' Reverend Williams helped Father Kelly and Megan raise Betty to her feet.

'I'll live.' Betty glared at the constable before dusting down her skirt.

'I was about to arrest those troublemakers, when this woman prevented me—'

'Troublemakers now, is it?' Father Kelly interrupted the constable. 'I see no troublemakers in this street. Do you, Reverend Williams?'

'None, Father Kelly.'

'What's the problem here, Shipton?' An officer in sergeant's uniform forced his way through the crowd.

Constable Shipton snapped to attention. 'This woman prevented me from making a lawful arrest, Sergeant Martin.'

'She did no such thing, sergeant,' Father Kelly contradicted. 'She was standing peacefully watching the parade, as we all were. Absolutely no trouble to a soul around her.'

'An illegal parade,' the sergeant stated tersely.

'Illegal is it?' Father Kelly crossed his arms across his chest and squared up to the man. There was something ridiculous about the short, fat priest confronting a police officer a full head taller than himself, but no one laughed. 'Tell me now, Sergeant Martin, when was the law passed that made it illegal for women to walk down the street of their home town in the middle of the day?'

'There are special circumstances—'

'I'll say there are.' Father Kelly refused to allow the sergeant to get a word in edgewise. 'Circumstances your men believe give them the right to provoke and torment the inhabitants of this town, just as you English do the poor souls in Ireland. You won't be happy until you have another riot on your hands. Then you can go to the London papers and say, "Look at those savages in Tonypandy" all over again. And that will give your Home Secretary, Mr Churchill, an excuse to send even more regiments of soldiers here.'

'The last thing we want is another riot, Father.'

Angry murmurs rippled through the crowd around them.

'Really? You could have fooled me with the way your men have treated these ladies.'

'Constable Shipton said they were obstructing him. And obstructing a police officer with the view to prevent him carrying out his duty is a criminal offence.'

'Given the high-handed way some of your men behave, Sergeant, you have to forgive us poor natives a bit of obstructing now and then. You see, obstructing is the only way we have left to show our feelings,' Father Kelly said caustically.

Sergeant Martin beckoned to a group of constables across the road. A dozen marched in formation to join him.

'Constable Shipton, officers, take the name of anyone who hasn't moved on from this unlawful assembly in the next sixty seconds.' Turning his back, he walked away.

Too many strikers had been fined for offences ranging from disorderly conduct to affray and assault for anyone to ignore the threat. Fines meant prison, since no striker had the means to pay them.

'Thank you, Father Kelly, Reverend Williams,' Betty said gratefully. She hooked her arm into Megan's.

'Glad we could help, ladies.' Reverend Williams tipped his hat.

'Go with God and go safely, ladies.' Father Kelly gave them a warm smile before continuing on his way.

Megan and Betty walked along the pavement until a group of uniformed Hussars blocked their path. When it was obvious that they weren't going to move, the women stepped into the gutter. Holding her skirt up to avoid the piles of horse manure and dog mess left by the strays turned out by the families of strikers who could no longer afford to feed them, Megan picked her way down the street, all the while sensing the officers watching them. When she saw a gap in the traffic, she crossed the road but there were even more police on the opposite pavement.

A queue snaked out of the door of Rodney's Provisions. Megan and Betty joined it. As the procession of women with their collier's dummy moved on out of earshot, an unnatural silence fell, thick and heavy, like a suffocating blanket over the town. When it was their turn finally to step inside the store, Megan started nervously. A sergeant and a constable flanked the door, their backs to the front wall, their hands clasped around the truncheons hanging from their belts as if they were expecting the customers to turn violent. Betty gripped Megan's hand briefly to give her courage, turned her back to them and looked to the counter.

Rodney's, along with every other shop in Tonypandy barring two, had been targeted by the incensed crowd on the night of the worst riot. The mob had only by-passed the chemist's owned by Willie Llewellyn, an ex-Welsh rugby international and local hero, and a pawnbroker who'd had the courage – or insanity – to fire a pistol in the air when they reached his door.

In comparison with some of the neighbouring businesses, the shop had suffered lightly. The mahogany counter that ran the full length of the back wall had been scarred by hobnailed boots, the glass cake case reduced to a metal frame, the marble cheese and butter slabs cracked, but most of the other shop fittings remained intact. And despite losing three-quarters of her goods to the looters and having to pay a carpenter to board her windows and doors until replacements could be made, Connie Rodney didn't bear a grudge against her customers. She couldn't afford to. Even if she put her business on the market, no one would buy it, leastways, not until the strike was settled and the miners started making wages again. So, like the other tradesmen in Dunraven and De Winter Streets, she'd ordered as much replacement stock as her suppliers would credit her with, which judging by her shelves, wasn't much, and opened for business.

'Half your usual weekly staples, same as last week?' Connie asked Megan when it was her turn to be served. Connie had stopped selling luxuries like jam, cheese, butter, tinned goods, sugar and dried fruit during the first week of the strike. Now that it was heading into the third month, some housewives were even dropping margarine, flour and potatoes from their shopping lists. Fires were needed to boil potatoes and bake bread, and without the rations of coal that were part of a miner's wage, there was no fuel.

'No, thank you, Mrs Rodney.' Megan lifted her empty basket

on to the counter. 'My uncle has asked me to buy what we need on a daily basis from now on.'

'Well, we're open six days a week.' Connie gave her a rare smile.

With her long red-gold hair tied back from her scrubbed freckled face and her bright green eyes, nineteen-year-old Megan Williams was an exceptionally pretty girl and Victor Evans also happened to be Connie's favourite cousin.

Megan pulled a scrap of paper from her pocket and glanced at it. 'I'll have your smallest scrag end of lamb, ten pounds of potatoes, a quarter of tea and three loaves of bread, please.'

'Would that be strikers' loaves?' Annie O'Leary, Connie's tall, spare, Irish assistant asked drily. The atmosphere instantly lightened as the women waiting their turn to be served burst into laughter despite the police presence. When the miners had withdrawn their labour, a local baker had produced a half-size 'strikers' loaf aimed at his newly impoverished customers, only to have his cart overturned and the contents vanish into the crowd, which dissipated as quickly as his bread. Even more mysteriously, his deliveryman failed to recognize a single person in the mob.

'The boy could deliver the goods for you, Megan. We'll be sending the cart out in an hour.' Connie handed Megan's basket to one of her assistants and sent him to weigh the potatoes from the sacks ranged against the wall below the counter.

'I'll take them with me. My uncle and his brothers will want their tea when they get home.' Megan took her purse from her pocket and lowered her voice. 'My uncle also asked me to settle up with you, Mrs Rodney. He doesn't want to put our goods on the slate any more while he only draws strike pay from the union.'

Connie was surprised but relieved. The colliers who were members of the union, unfortunately only slightly more than half of her customers, drew strike pay of ten shillings a week plus a shilling for each child. Larger families who hadn't found it easy to live on thirty-five shillings a week before the colliery companies had cut wages, were finding life during the strike desperate. And workers who weren't members of a union had been left destitute. No striker's family could afford to pay rent. At an average of ten shillings a week it would have left nothing for food. As it was, more and more of her customers were coming in every day asking for their credit to be extended until the strike was called off because they had come to the end of their savings.

An ardent Catholic, Connie had gone to mass and confession three times a week, but since the strike she had taken to walking the short distance to the Catholic Church every morning to pray for an end to the dispute before her own savings and credit with her suppliers ran out.

She pulled a massive leather-bound ledger towards her, checked the account and added Megan's purchases. 'That will be seven shillings and sixpence three farthings.' Anxious not to offend Betty who was being served by Annie, or any of her other customers who weren't in a position to settle their bill, Connie whispered. 'Tell your uncle that I appreciate his paying cash for as long as he can.'

'I'll do that, Mrs Rodney. And thank you.' Megan opened her purse, extracted three half crowns, a halfpenny and a farthing and handed them over. Taking her basket from the boy, she waited for Betty to finish placing her order, before making her way past the queue to the door. The police sergeant stepped in front of her. Megan glanced up, only to immediately look down again when he gazed coolly back at her. He was broad-shouldered, over six feet tall and there was a glint in his pale blue eyes that unnerved her. She was accustomed to living in a houseful of men but not one of them had ever made her feel as uneasy as this sergeant did. Struggling to lift her basket, she clutched her cloak around her, more to conceal than warm herself.

'I've seen you before, haven't I?' The officer's voice sounded rough, harsh in comparison to the soft Welsh lilt.

'I don't think so, sir,' Megan whispered timidly.

'You sure?' he persisted.

'Yes, sir.'

'You weren't out with the men on the picket lines around the Glamorgan Colliery yesterday afternoon?'

'No, sir.'

'Miss Williams was with me all yesterday afternoon, officer,'

13

Betty lied coolly. 'We were at the women's knitting circle.'

'And what was it that you were knitting, Mrs Morgan?' the sergeant enquired.

'Blankets for poor unfortunates, Sergeant Lamb.'

'Why is it that I can never believe a word you say, Mrs Morgan?' He turned his attention from Megan to Betty, just as the older woman had intended. Her husband, Ned Morgan, was a union official and Betty knew the authorities had marked her, along with all the members of the strike leaders' families, as a potential troublemaker.

The queue moved forward; Betty gave Megan a slight push. They sidestepped past the police and out of the door. A dozen officers had circled a crowd of collier boys on the pavement, three of Megan's cousins among them. A constable Megan recognized as Gwyn Jenkins, a local man, and before the strike a friend of her uncle's, was talking to them.

'Come on now, boys, no one wants any trouble. I'm asking nicely. Leave here and go up the mountain. You never know, if you take your dogs you may even find a rabbit or two to take home to your mothers for the pot,' Gwyn coaxed persuasively.

'Haven't you heard?' one of the wags answered back. 'The bunnies are on strike too. They won't come out of their burrows.'

'Then send the dogs down after them to draw blood.' Gwyn looked from the boy to the officers beside him. 'Please, do as you've been asked, son, and you have my word no one will get hurt.'

The boys gazed impassively back. But just as Megan expected her eldest cousin to do something stupid, the boys turned and headed up the nearest hill.

Betty took Megan's arm. Daring to breathe again, they walked on. It was a freezing, damp, grey November day, but that hadn't deterred a crowd of young men from playing football with a tin can on the only flattened area of mountainside high above the rows of terraced houses. Their whoops and shouts carried down towards them on the wind.

'I'm glad someone can forget the strike, if only for a few hours,' Betty said philosophically, as they crossed the road to avoid yet another group of police officers.

'I wish I could.'

'It must be hard on you, with your uncle not being able to pay your wages,' Betty commiserated.

'If it was up to me I'd be happy to carry on doing the housework and taking care of the family for my keep.'

'Your what?' Betty laughed.

'What passes for keep these days,' Megan amended. 'But ever since I started working for him I've sent ten shillings a week home to my father.'

'Your uncle pays you fifteen shillings a week, right?'

'He did until the strike started. It's the going rate for a housekeeper.'

'It was,' Betty nodded sagely, 'but it seems to me that your father's been getting a lot more than the going rate from a daughter. I used to count myself lucky to get ten shillings a month from my Annie when she was in service before she married.'

'Things aren't easy at home. It's hard trying to make ends meet on a hill farm and aside from Mam and Dad I've two younger sisters and brothers. I don't like to think of them suffering on my account. I know I should look for a paying job, but—'

'They're harder to find than gold in the valleys these days, especially for women,' Betty observed.

'And I'd hate to leave my uncle. Who'd look after his house and family if I didn't?'

'Now there's a job.' Betty pointed to a sign in the window of a large, square four-storey house on the corner of the street. They stopped and read the card propped inside the window:

GIRL WANTED TO HELP WITH DOMESTIC WORK. MUST BE
EXPERIENCED COOK, ABLE TO WASH, IRON AND DO GEN-
ERAL CLEANING WITHOUT SUPERVISION. ABOVE AVERAGE
WAGES OFFERED TO AN EFFICIENT PERSON. APPLY WITHIN.

'I've heard that Joyce Palmer is prepared to pay as much as a pound a week to the right girl.'

'Really?' Megan's eyes rounded in wonder.

'Not that I've spoken to Joyce myself,' Betty added. 'Well, not since the colliery company gave notice to all the miners in the

15

lodging houses they owned and made them over to policemen. No decent woman would have stayed on to wait on them.'

'Mrs Palmer had nowhere else to go.' Megan repeated an observation Victor had made.

'She could have found somewhere if she'd tried,' Betty dismissed. 'Mrs Payne in the Post Office told me that Joyce has taken one girl out of the workhouse to help her, but she's found her a bit slow, and she'd rather not take on another. I can't see any man in the town who sympathizes with the colliers' grievances, let alone the colliers themselves, allowing any member of their family to wait on police or soldiers.' Two officers headed towards them. 'Come on, time we were on our way.'

Megan gripped her basket and trudged on up the hill after Betty. Turning left, they greeted their neighbours again. Megan said goodbye to Betty and turned the key that was kept in the lock of her uncle's house and opened the door. Goose pimples rose on her skin when she stopped in the hall to take off her cloak and hat, but she was afraid of staining her cloak if she tried to do housework wearing it.

She carried her basket through to the kitchen, tied on her apron and filled the tin bowl in the sink ready to wash and peel the potatoes. The strike had made life cold, hungry and uncomfortable, but it had done little to change her routine. Her uncle and his brothers still rose at half past four in the morning, although they no longer had to be at the colliery gates before six in time to go down in the cage. But they didn't linger in the house. In an effort to eke out the last coal ration they had received from the pit, she lit the kitchen stove for an hour in the morning so she could heat water for washing and tea and raked it out until three in the afternoon when it was time to cook the evening meal. She found it hard to do housework in the icy temperature but she didn't doubt that her uncle and his brothers found it just as cold on the picket line.

She poured the packet of tea she had bought into the empty caddy and fetched a swede, half a dozen turnips and a bunch of carrots that her uncle had brought down from his allotment the day before and put in the pantry. She wouldn't have had to buy potatoes if theirs hadn't been struck by blight. She unwrapped the lamb from the newspaper. It was a very small portion of meat for so many people but the first her uncle had allowed her to buy in two months. At least they would eat tonight. There were plenty in the town who wouldn't.

She'd put the lamb in a pan of cold water to soak and picked up a knife to start peeling the potatoes when she heard someone walk up the stone steps that led from the basement to the kitchen. There was a tap on the door, then it opened.

Victor's massive frame filled the doorway. He smiled and his teeth gleamed startlingly white against his blackened face and filthy clothes. He held up a bucketful of coal. 'You can light the stove early. There's plenty more where this came from, I've just emptied a couple of sacks into your coalhouse.'

'You've been working in the drifts the strikers have opened up on the mountain!'

His soft grey eyes sparkled in vivid contrast to his dirty face. His grin widened as he held his finger to his lips.

'The police will arrest you—'

'They have to catch me first, and even if they do, I'll only get a fine. It's worth risking that to warm a few houses. Mrs Richards in the colliery cottages off the square didn't have scrap of coal and she has four under three years old.'

'If you are fined, no one will be able to pay it and then you'll be put in prison.'

'I wasn't caught, Megs.' He called her by the nickname he had invented for her and no one else used.

'This time,' Megan murmured fearfully.

'Love you.'

'You always say that whenever I'm cross with you.'

'Because it's the only thing that calms you down, Megs. Seeing as how I'm covered in coal dust I may as well light the stove for you. And if you lay newspaper on the floor I won't dirty your nice clean flagstones.'

Megan opened the cupboard in the alcove next to the stove where she kept old newspapers and sticks for the fire. She picked up a copy of the *Rhondda Leader* from the top of the pile and spread its pages in layers from the basement door to the hearth.

'You didn't go down to Porth to wait for the verdict on the inquest with your father?'

'I had more important things to do.' Victor raked out the remains of the small fire she had doused that morning, laid balls of newspaper over the iron fire basket, balanced sticks on them and arranged the half-burnt coals together with lumps of fresh coal on top.

'Like supply half of Tonypandy with coal?' she suggested.

'I only wish I could.' He brushed his light brown hair from his eyes, griming it even more. 'Your family and mine are lucky, Megs. Strike pay may not be enough to live on but at least we're getting some money. The men with the most children and the lowest wages couldn't afford to pay union dues, and now the pits are closed they can't work either. I can't sit back and watch them freeze and starve to death.'

'You and the others who are risking prosecution won't get enough coal out of the drifts to keep every kitchen stove burning in Pandy, no more than you can feed everyone in the town from what you grow in your garden.'

'No, but I can do my bit.' He struck a match, lit a newspaper spill the children had made and blew on it before touching the balls of paper at the bottom of the fire. They caught immediately, sending spirals of grey smoke curling up the chimney. 'There, you can start cooking that cawl you're making.'

She folded the rest of the newspapers she was holding back into the cupboard and closed the door. 'If you weren't so dirty I would hug you.'

'If there's no one else in the house you could give me a kiss.' His smile broadened in anticipation.

She stooped over him and when their lips met he couldn't resist cupping her face in his hands. As always, she warmed to his touch, instinctively leaning against him. The front door banged and they sprang apart.

Footsteps echoed in the hall, then the kitchen door opened and a short, wiry, middle-aged man glowered at them through piercing blue eyes. His cap was so grimy it was impossible to determine what colour it had originally been, his grubby brown moleskin

18

trousers were tied with twine in place of a belt at his waist and again just below his knees, his red flannel shirt was collarless and his tweed jacket more hole than cloth.

Megan stared at him. He was smaller, more wrinkled and older than she remembered. 'Dad?' she murmured tentatively.'

'So you do remember me, girl,' he lisped through yellow, broken teeth.

She felt that she should have hugged him, but the moment was over. 'What are you doing here?'

Ianto Williams removed his cap to reveal a shock of grey curls. 'I would have thought that was obvious.'

'How did you get here?' She was too taken aback to attempt to make sense of his answer.

'I left the farm at two this morning and rode into Swansea Market on Jones's cheese and cream cart. Then I got a ride on the fresh fish and cockle donkey cart that travels up here from Penclawdd. It'll be leaving before dawn in the morning.' He settled a hostile glare on Victor. 'Your uncle or his brothers in?'

'He and the other men have gone down to Porth,' Megan stammered.

'The children?'

'The younger two are in school, the older boys out playing.' Colour rose in her cheeks as her father continued to stare at Victor. 'This is Mr Victor Evans, Dad. He lives next door. He brought us some coal and laid the fire for me.'

'I remember the name. You've laid just the one fire?' He eyed Victor's blackened face and filthy clothes.

'I've been working a drift on the mountain, Mr Williams,' Victor explained.

'Isn't that illegal?'

'That depends on your point of view,' Victor replied easily. 'It is good to meet you after all this time, Mr Williams. Megan talks a lot about her family.'

'To you?' Ianto Williams enquired sternly.

'Sometimes.' Victor refused to be intimidated. 'Our families are close and Megan and I are friends.'

'Friendly enough to persuade her to write to me and ask my

permission to get engaged to you. And friendly enough for you to be left alone with her in the house after I wrote to her at Christmas expressly forbidding her to see you or talk to you.'

'Victor lives next door, Dad . . .'

'So you said, girl.'

Ignoring Mr Williams' outburst in the rapidly diminishing hope of winning him round, Victor said, 'I would offer to shake your hand but, as you can see, I'm covered in coal dust.'

'I wouldn't shake the hand of a Papist if it was disinfected.'

'I have to cook the dinner, Victor.'

Victor saw the pleading look in Megan's eyes and realized he was making a bad situation worse. Careful to step on the newspaper he retraced his steps to the basement door. 'I've a few more bags of coal to deliver, so I'll be off.'

'Thank you for the coal, Victor,' Megan called after him when he closed the door behind him.

'So that's the Catholic you've been making a fool of yourself with.' Ianto moved in front of the fire to warm himself.

'I haven't been making a fool of myself with anyone, Dad.' Megan gathered the dust-stained sheets of newspaper from the floor.

'No?' Ianto said. 'I suggest you look at yourself in the mirror, girl, before you say another word.'

Megan dropped the coal-smudged papers on top of the coal bucket, went to the sink and picked up the men's shaving mirror. Black imprints of Victor's hands covered both her cheeks and there were coal smuts on her lips. Dampening the corner of a tea towel under the tap, she scrubbed at her face.

'Have you anything to say for yourself?'

'As you said, I did write to ask you if I could get engaged to Victor at Christmas. And it's not as if it's sudden. We've known one another for over five years.'

'And I wrote back telling you that I'd prefer to see you dead than married to a Catholic. And I forbid you to see or talk to him again.'

'Victor's a good man—'

'I'll have no more said about him.' Ianto scraped a wooden chair over the flagstones and plonked it in front of the fire. 'You can make me a cup of tea and give me some bread and cheese to keep me going until tea's on the table.'

'I can make you tea and give you bread, Dad. But there's no cheese. With so little money coming into the house we've had to cut back.' Megan filled the blackened tin kettle, opened up a hob and put it on to boil. 'You still haven't said what you're doing here.'

'As I said when I came in, it's obvious. Your uncle's emigrating and I've come to take you home, not that we can afford to keep you there. You'll have to find another job – and quick.'

'Emigrating . . .' Her voice died to a whisper.

'To Canada. With no job or home to go to, your uncle won't risk taking his two youngest and he's asked your mother and me to take them in. We've room now that your brothers and sisters have left home. Tea, girl,' he reminded, as she stood, pale and trembling, beside his chair.

Chapter 2

'YOU LOOK exhausted. Sit by the fire and I'll make a pot of tea,' Victor offered when Sali walked into the kitchen with her four-year-old son, Harry.

'I am tired,' Sali conceded. She unbuttoned Harry's coat, then her own, carried them out into the passage and hung them away. 'And thank you for lighting the fire up here.' All the houses on the lower side of the terrace, including theirs, had a basement as well as an upstairs kitchen. Before the strike, the stoves in both had been lit every day, and the men had used the one in the basement to heat water to fill the tin baths they kept and bathed in down there. But since the strike they had economized by only lighting the stove upstairs and then, like all the other mining families, only for an hour in the morning and late in the afternoon to cook the main meal.

'I needed a bath and I heated the water up here.' Victor filled the kettle.

'You've been working in one of the drifts?' Sali's eyes rounded in alarm.

'Don't worry, no one saw me – no one who is likely to shop me, that is,' he qualified.

'That you know about. You heard your father yesterday.' Sali was more fearful for him than angry. 'You're so big, one glimpse of you covered in coal dust or carrying a sack, and the police will know it's you.'

'You sound just like Megan.'

'We've every right to be worried about you.'

'It's all right, Sali. I wasn't caught.' Victor smiled at Harry. 'The hens laid well today considering it's winter. Want a boiled egg for your tea?'

'Can I, Mam?' Young as Harry was, he knew food was in short supply. The teachers had organized 'feeding centres' in the schools, where they served breakfast and midday dinners to the children, courtesy of the crache the headmasters coerced into donating food. And every day since the strike had started, Sali had picked him up from his 'babies' class and taken him to the soup kitchen in the Catholic Hall. She also gave him a bowl of whatever was on the menu, but the soup had become noticeably thinner over the last few weeks, not because people contributed less, but because more and more colliers' families were setting aside their pride and arriving at the kitchen to be fed.

'You most certainly can have an egg, young man.' Sali gave Victor a grateful smile, knowing he always kept the largest egg for Harry's tea.

'And bread and butter soldiers?' Harry asked.

'Of course.' Victor set a pan of water on to boil and went into the pantry to get the margarine.

'Your father, Joey and Lloyd not back from the inquest?' Sali took the tea Victor handed her.

'They are now.' The front door slammed.

'Bloody coroner!' Joey strode into the kitchen ahead of his father and Lloyd.

'Language,' Victor reprimanded, carefully lowering an egg into a pan of simmering water.

'You didn't hear that, did you, butty?' Joey ruffled Harry's hair and sat at the table beside him.

'Mam told me not to repeat your naughty words.' Harry concentrated on spreading margarine on the slice of bread Victor had cut for him.

'Hello, love.' Lloyd stooped to kiss Sali's cheek before taking off his coat.

'I take it the inquest went as badly as you predicted?' Victor poured more tea for his father and brothers, lifted the egg from the boiling water, dropped it into an eggcup decorated with a picture of a fat red hen and put it on the table in front of Harry.

'The jury agreed that Samuel Rayes died from injuries received on the eighth of November nineteen ten, caused by some blunt instrument. The evidence is not sufficiently clear as to how he received those injuries,' Lloyd recited impassively, sitting next to Harry.

'If the court had allowed the miners as much leeway and time to give evidence as the police, the jury might have delivered a different verdict. But then again, given the weak-chinned, brainless crache who made up the jury, probably not,' Billy Evans pronounced scathingly.

'They even brought stones and railings into court as evidence,' Joey grumbled. 'They said the railings had been ripped out and used as weapons by the colliers and the stones had been gathered by the police after they'd been thrown at them during the rioting – as if anyone could prove otherwise. Then, they decided that a miner could just as easily have injured Samuel as a police officer – as if we'd hit one of our own. The police inspector from Bristol even had the gall to swear on oath that none of his men used their batons that night.'

'Will there be an appeal?' Sali asked. Joey was the most vociferous but she sensed that Lloyd and his father were more incensed by the injustice of the verdict.

Mr Evans shook his head. 'The authorities are writing the history books their way, Sali. They wouldn't overturn the verdict now, not even if we produced two dozen eyewitnesses who saw a police officer bludgeon Samuel.'

'The bloody police have organized a damned whitewash!' Joey exploded. 'A man's dead from a crack on the skull. Someone should swing for him . . .'

Victor kicked Joey's foot under the table and looked significantly at Harry, who was watching Sali cut the top from his egg.

'There's no point in talking about it. What's done is done,' Lloyd said abruptly. 'We have to move on and make sure that Samuel Rayes's death counts for something.'

Billy Evans gave Victor a searching look. 'And what were you doing that was so important you couldn't come down to the court to show your support for your fellow worker? And don't try telling me you were on the picket lines. I spoke to a couple of the boys on the way up. They said they haven't seen hide nor hair of you all day.'

Lloyd spoke before Victor could answer. 'If I was in Victor's shoes I wouldn't have gone to the court either. He and Megan have little enough time left together as it is.'

'What do you mean?' Victor poured milk into his tea and stirred it.

'I walked back from Porth with her uncle. Her father's coming today—'

'He arrived when I was there,' Victor interrupted.

'He's taking Megan and the two youngest children back to his farm in the Swansea Valley. Her uncle booked passage for himself, his brothers and his three oldest boys last week with Evans and Short. They're emigrating to Canada, sailing with the White Star Line from Liverpool tomorrow night.'

The blood drained from Victor's face. 'Megan never said a word to me.'

'She didn't know,' Lloyd revealed. 'Her uncle said he wanted to carry on as normal until the last minute because he didn't want to upset the children. It's my guess he also didn't want to give people round here time to have a go at him and his brothers for deserting the strike at a time when we need every man to show solidarity.'

'He told *you*,' Victor pointed out angrily.

'Half an hour ago and only because I'm his landlord.' Lloyd took the milk jug Sali handed him.

Billy Evans had encouraged his sons to save and invest their money in property. Originally, all he had hoped for was to give each of them a mortgage-free house when they married, but over the years he had bought a dozen houses, which he'd put in his own and his sons' names. When Lloyd had been left a legacy by his former employer, Sali's father, years before they had become friends let alone lovers, he had followed his father's example and used to it to buy several tenanted houses in Tonypandy, including the one next door. But as the strikers weren't in a position to pay their rents, their investments were worthless and were likely to remain that way until the dispute was settled.

'He asked if I'd take the furniture in lieu of the rent he owes. After he paid his debts and passage for him and his three oldest boys he only had thirty pounds left of his life savings. And Megan's father won't take the two youngest for less than twenty because there's no saying how long they'll be living with him.' Lloyd hadn't bought any tobacco for weeks but, like his father, he pulled his empty pipe from his pocket out of habit and set it beside his teacup on the table.

'I'm going next door to see Megan.' Victor pushed his chair back from the table.

'I wouldn't if I were you, not just yet,' Sali advised. 'If she didn't know that her uncle was emigrating, she'll need time to adjust to the news herself. And, as she hasn't seen her father in a long time they're bound to have some catching up to do.'

'They're doing that all right,' Victor concurred bitterly. 'When he found out who I was, he reminded her about the letter he wrote forbidding her to see me.'

'It's too late for them to start travelling back to Swansea today,' Lloyd said practically. 'Why don't you call round to see her later, or better still get Sali to do it? She's more diplomatic than any of us and Megan's father is likely to be more polite to a woman.'

Victor sank slowly back on to his chair. Considering Ianto Williams' venomous reaction when he'd found him alone with his daughter, Lloyd had given him good advice. But that didn't make it any easier to take.

'I'll go next door as soon as I've put Harry to bed. If I can, I'll bring Megan back here. I'll tell her father that I need her help to pin up a hem or something.' Disturbed by Victor's bleak expression, Sali laid her hand over his.

Victor gripped her hand briefly, then finished his tea. 'I'll shut the chickens in the coop and check the dogs before it gets too dark to see your hand in front of your face out there.'

'Can I come, Uncle Victor?' Harry asked eagerly.

'Not until you've finished your egg and drunk your tea.' Sali looked at Lloyd and knew he was thinking the same as her. If Megan's father had returned to take her home there was nothing any of them could do to prevent him. He was Megan's legal

26

guardian and until her twenty-first birthday Megan had no choice but to obey him.

Oblivious to the hungry looks the children were giving Megan when she lifted the stewpan from the stove a second time, Ianto Williams held out his bowl. 'It's not as good as your mother's cawl, but I've been all day on the road so I'll have another spoonful.'

Megan poured half a ladleful into her father's bowl.

'I'll have more than that, girl,' her father complained when she split most of what was left between the bowls of the three older boys, as seven-year-old Daisy and six-year-old Sam had been fed in school.

'Let your father finish the cawl.' Megan's uncle left his chair. 'My brothers and me have a few goodbyes to say down the Pandy, Ianto. You're welcome to come with us.'

'Into a Godless public house where they serve the devil's brew?' Ianto's face contorted in contempt.

'I should have known better than to ask a Baptist. We'll see you when we get back. Megan. I'm sorry I can't take you to Canada with us.'

'I wouldn't have wanted to go, uncle.'

'You may change your mind in a few years. There's opportunity out there, which is more than can be said for this valley the way the miners are being squeezed to sell their labour for next to nothing.' He looked at Daisy and Sam, who had been crushed by the news that they were to be left behind with an aunt and uncle they had never met and even worse, banished miles from everyone they knew. 'I promise you two, I'll send for you the minute I have a home for you to live in and someone to look after you.'

'Promise?' Daisy could barely get the word out as she struggled to choke back her tears.

'I promise. When you've finished your cawl, go upstairs, pack your clothes and toys into the cardboard boxes I brought up from the shop. Megan,' he addressed his niece's back as she carried the empty stewpan to the sink, 'don't forget to write to let us know how you are getting on.'

27

'I won't, uncle.' Megan turned and watched him walk out of the door ahead of his brothers. She knew he'd be back later that evening, but not before her bedtime. The cart was leaving for Swansea at three in the morning and she doubted he'd be up to see them off. It wasn't much of a goodbye after five years. He'd always been fair to her but he'd also been detached to the point of coolness, although the neighbours had told her he'd been a very different man when her aunt had been alive.

Ianto cut a hunk from the third and last loaf and dunked it into the cawl.

'Can we go round to Tegwen's and say goodbye to them before we pack?' the oldest boy asked.

Megan nodded, too heartsick to answer.

'And Sam and me?' Daisy added.

'There'll be no time to visit friends when you're on the farm with me and your Auntie Mary,' Ianto warned. 'You'll be too busy gathering the eggs, cleaning out the hen runs and looking after the vegetable garden. Just like Megan did when she was your age.'

'But Megan will be coming with us, won't she?' Daisy's bottom lip trembled.

'Only on the journey. Then she'll have to go away to earn her living.'

'Megan—'

'Go and see Tegwen, Daisy,' Megan said shortly. 'But I want you and Sam back here in half an hour. Have you already found me a job in the Swansea Valley?' she asked her father after the children had left.

'There's nothing going around Ystradgynlais, so I thought I'd take you up to Brecon. There's a hiring in Ship Street next week. Not many farmers will be looking for workers at this time of year, so don't go expecting too much. There's little enough choice in spring let alone winter.'

'I haven't done any farm work in five years.' She picked up the children's bowls and carried them to the sink.

Ianto wiped the last vestiges of cawl from his bowl with the bread and pushed it into his mouth. 'You've had it soft here, girl.'

'Soft! With four grown men, three working boys and two

children to wash, cook, clean and scrub for? Have you any idea how hard I've had to work to run this house?' A firm believer in free speech and the emancipation of women, Megan's uncle had encouraged her to voice her opinions.

'I have an idea from that outburst just how much your uncle has allowed you run wild. You're forgetting who you are talking to, girl.'

'If you give me a chance I might be able to find work around here, Dad,' she pleaded.

'So you can carry on seeing that Catholic I found you alone in the house with.'

'Victor was lighting the fire.'

'From what I saw, he was lighting a lot more than just the fire,' Ianto countered viciously.

Megan felt sick to the pit of her stomach. Her uncle had warned her that her ardent Baptist father would never approve of her associating with a Catholic. But he hadn't attempted to stop her from seeing Victor in the mistaken belief that if they encountered no opposition, their feelings for one another would burn out.

'I found work for your brothers last month on a farm outside Ammanford. Gwilym gets his keep and ten pounds a year, Owain five.'

Megan did a rapid calculation as she poured hot water from the kettle into the tin bowl in the sink. 'But Owain is only ten.'

'Which is why he gets no more than five pounds a year. Your sisters have it easier. They're working in Craig yr Nos as kitchen maids and from what I've seen of the carts going in there, the servants live off the fat and cream of the land. They get twelve pounds a year apiece without putting in a tenth of the work your brothers have to at the farm. But as they all keep half their earnings back for clothes, your mother and me only get eighteen pounds ten shillings a year from the lot of them. Not much gratitude for the effort we put into feeding and clothing them and bringing them up to be God-fearing Christians. Your twenty-six pounds a year just about kept us going. But I can see we're going to have to tighten our belts. And from that cawl you put on the table, a lot more than the miners in this valley. You'll earn nothing like as much in

Brecon. Be lucky to make ten pounds a year and your keep like Gwilym.'

'Supposing I found a job here that would pay me a pound a week,' Megan blurted breathlessly.

'Don't talk daft, girl.'

'There's a lodging house down the road that's paying that kind of money.'

'What kind of a lodging house?' he questioned suspiciously.

'One the police live in. The miners won't let their wives or daughters work there because of the fights that keep breaking out between the strikers and police.'

'You sure they're paying a pound a week?' His eyes narrowed.

'That's what people around here are saying. If I get it, I could send fifteen shillings a week home,' she promised recklessly.

Her father fell silent and Megan sensed he was weighing up the money against the risk of leaving her in the same town as Victor.

'Get your coat, we'll go down there now and see about this job,' he said finally.

'I have to wait for the children to come home so I can put Daisy and Sam to bed. And I'd be better off applying on my own—'

'Oh no you don't, girl. I want to see exactly what kind of a house it is. And meet whoever is running it. If you get the job, I need to be sure that they won't be like your uncle and allow you to run wild with Papists.'

'You have to undress for bed and you have to do it now!' Megan had never been impatient with Daisy and Sam before, but the thought of having to leave Tonypandy and more especially Victor, had driven every other consideration from her mind. The children were upset but so was she. And it had taken a mammoth effort just to get them to pack their clothes and few toys in the cardboard boxes their father had cadged from Connie Rodney.

'I don't want to go to bed because when I wake up I'll have to go away . . .' Daisy threw herself, face down next to Sam on the bed he shared with his brothers, and howled. Ashamed of herself for losing her temper, Megan struggled to hold back her own tears. Daisy and Sam had fought one another from cradle days and it

30

disturbed her more to see Sam slip his arm around his sister's thin shoulders in an attempt to comfort her, than the times she'd caught him pinching and kicking her when he'd assumed no one was watching them.

The front door opened and Sali called out, 'Hello, anyone in?'

Weak with relief, Megan left the children and ran down the stairs. 'You've heard?'

'Your uncle told Lloyd. I came to see if you needed help with packing. Harry's in bed, but Victor's offered to sit with him until I get back. He would like to see you. So, if I can take over here—'

The kitchen door opened and Megan's father joined them in the passage. 'I heard voices.'

Sali held out her hand. 'Hello, you must be Mr Williams, Megan's father. I'm Sali Jones, one of Megan's neighbours.'

'Not popish, are you?' he demanded.

Although Victor had discussed Megan's father's opposition to their engagement with her, Sali was taken aback by his directness – and hostility to Catholicism. 'No, Mr Williams.'

'Baptist?'

'My parents brought me up in the Methodist faith.' Sali omitted to mention that the only church that she had set foot in during the last year had been the Catholic Saints Gabriel and Raphael when Joey and Victor had invited her to attend Christmas Eve midnight mass with them.

'So you're not popish,' he reiterated, as if he hadn't quite believed her.

'No, Mr Williams.'

'Your husband?'

'I am a widow.' She blushed, as she always did, whenever she denied the existence of Owen Bull, the man her uncle had forced her to marry, who had raped and abused her before she had escaped him, and was now awaiting execution in prison for murder.

'I would like to go out and see about a job,' Megan interrupted before her father could interrogate Sali any further.

'You go. I'll put Daisy and Sam to bed and see to everything here.' Sali couldn't imagine what kind of a job Megan was applying

31

for at that hour, but the fact that she had something in mind looked hopeful for her – and Victor.

'I've packed their things and laid out their clothes for the morning. But Daisy's terribly upset.'

'I'll tell them a story. That will take their mind off tomorrow.' Sali lifted Megan's cloak and hat from the pegs and handed them to her. 'Is there anything else you'd like me to do?'

Megan shook her head. 'We won't be long.'

Ianto Williams, who hadn't removed his stained and creased jacket since he'd entered the house, pulled his cap from his pocket and followed Megan out through the front door.

Ianto didn't offer Megan his arm as they walked up the dark street and joined the gas-lit thoroughfare that led down the hill into the town centre. A fine drizzle needled the glow in front of the lamps and Megan lifted the hood on her cloak to save her hat. Despite the rain, the air was thick with the smoke and smuts that spewed out of the chimneys. Coal didn't burn clean, but tarred wood was worse and she recalled the colliery railings that had been ripped up by the rioters.

'Where's this lodging house?' Ianto enquired brusquely.

'Bottom of the street on the left.'

As they walked, the sound of voices raised in anger reached them. Megan began to run down the hill, past the lodging house into Dunraven Street, ignoring the shouts of her father behind her. A crowd of men, boys and women, a few nursing babies in shawls wrapped Welsh fashion around both mother and child, faced a solid wedge of constables and mounted police who were blocking the main thoroughfare.

A window opened above the police and steaming buckets of water were thrown over their heads. Agonized screams filled the air. The police lines thinned as officers helped injured colleagues limp away from the confrontation. An order was shouted from the front line.

'Hold firm! Draw batons!'

Gwyn Jenkins stepped forward and yelled at Joey Evans, who

stood, arms crossed, defiantly facing the police, but his voice was drowned out by the chants of the hostile mob.

'No blacklegs!'

'Right to picket!'

'Fair wages for all!'

'Fight or starve!'

Half a brick flew through the air from somewhere behind Joey. It smashed into the face of a constable in the front line. Blood poured from his head, he staggered and his fall to the ground signalled the end of police restraint. Batons flailing, they charged into the crowd as two officers carried him away. Megan watched helplessly, while people ran to avoid the blows being rained down on them. Men pushed the women, children and babies behind them. Sticks and stones appeared from nowhere as a few intrepid colliers attempted to fight back. But their makeshift weapons were no match for the solid police batons. A policeman knocked a woman to the ground and Megan ran forward. But when she extended her hand to help the woman, the constable turned his attention to her.

'Come on!' Joey appeared, grabbed Megan's arm and pulled her back up the hill.

Hearing footsteps, Megan glanced over her shoulder, expecting to see the police chasing them, but the woman she had tried to help and a crowd of boys were running behind them.

'Go home, Megan, before you get hurt,' Joey shouted.

'I don't see you taking your own advice, Joey Evans.' She stopped and rested her hands on her knees to catch her breath, as the woman and boys disappeared up the lane that cut behind the shops.

'They're bringing blacklegs in on the train to work the Cambrian pit. They won't allow us to picket the station and until they do there's going to be trouble.' Joey followed the others up the alley.

A dozen police rounded the corner and Megan joined her father, who had remained halfway up the hill, well away from the skirmishing.

'You see any colliers come this way, miss?'

Terrified of the officers, yet too afraid to tell a lie in front of her father, Megan remained silent.

Having always regarded miners as being overpaid in comparison to farm workers, Ianto Williams had no compunction about betraying them. He pointed to the entrance to the lane. 'They went in there.' He waited until the police ran after them before taking Megan to task. 'Fine place you live in, girl.'

'Tonypandy is a good place and most of the people who live here are wonderful. It's only like this now because of the strike.' Megan listened intently but all she could hear was the steady tramp of police boots. The garden walls behind the houses were high, but not too high for Joey and the others to vault over, and she hoped that they were all safely hidden in the houses by now.

'If colliers tried to live on farm wages they'd know what it is to go hungry,' Ianto sneered.

Wary of offending her father any more than she already had, lest he take it into his head to drag her back to the Swansea Valley even if Joyce Palmer did offer her a job, Megan didn't remind him that unlike the vast majority of colliers, farm labourers had gardens big enough to keep a few chickens and grow vegetables.

She led the way back down the hill to the side door of the lodging house and lifted the doorknocker, bringing it down on a polished brass lion's head.

'Do you know that boy who spoke to you?'

'He's one of the neighbours.'

'Related to that Catholic?' her father questioned sharply.

'His brother.' She was glad to see the door opening.

Joyce Palmer was a tall, thin woman, who wore her hair pinned back in a severe bun. It had changed colour, from a rich brown to white overnight when her husband and five young sons had been killed in the Wattstown colliery disaster five years before, along with a hundred and fourteen other mineworkers. With few savings and a widow's pension that didn't cover the rent of her colliery-owned house, Joyce had taken the position of lodging house landlady two days after their funeral. She had a reputation for plain speaking and most of her neighbours were wary of her, despite the fact that if anyone was in real need, Joyce was always the first on the doorstep.

When the miners withdrew their labour, the colliery company that owned the house gave the tenants notice to clear their rooms for police officers. Joyce's neighbours had expected her to leave along with the colliers, but she stayed. She knew that most people condemned her for her stance, but she was too busy catering to the needs of her new lodgers for the gossips' attitude to concern her.

'Can I help you, Megan?' Joyce asked with the air of a woman who had a great deal to do and a shortage of time to do it in.

'This is my father, Ianto Williams, Mrs Palmer. Dad, this is Mrs Palmer who runs this lodging house.' Megan took a deep breath and crossed her fingers behind her back. 'I'd like to apply for the job advertised in the window if it's still open, Mrs Palmer.'

'You want to work for me?' If Joyce was surprised, she concealed it well.

'Yes, please, Mrs Palmer.'

'Then you had better come in.' Joyce opened the door wider. Ianto removed his cap and preceded Megan into a hall that smelled of washing soda and beeswax polish. A gleaming oak staircase led to the upper floors, the wood either side of a narrow strip of jute carpeting, buffed to the same shine as the banister and dado that separated the brown varnished paper on the lower wall from the dark green plaster above it. The black and white floor tiles were spotless, but Megan couldn't help noticing there wasn't a plant, picture or even a coat rack to add a personal touch. Masculine voices echoed from a room on their right.

'The lodgers' sitting room,' Joyce informed them. 'If you'll excuse me a moment, the doctor is examining the officers who have been injured. I must check that he has everything he needs.' She knocked the door, went into the room and emerged a minute later. 'They know where I'll be if I'm needed. We'll talk in my room.'

Megan had never seen a room as crowded with furniture as Joyce Palmer's sitting room. An enormous Welsh dresser filled one wall. Its open shelves displayed a blue and white painted ironware dinner service with tureens large enough to cater for twenty. Ranged in front of the dishes were Joyce's family photographs and an assortment of cheap chalk and glass ornaments, the sort of knick-knacks children won at fairgrounds and gave to their mothers as gifts.

A large square table, covered by a dark green, fringed chenille cloth, dominated the centre of the room. It held a pink pressed-glass bowl filled with wrinkled winter apples. Eight, high-backed oak chairs were pushed tight beneath the table. A rexine-covered sofa and two matching chairs were grouped around a cast-iron, tiled hearth, its fire banked high with small coal. A glossy-leaved aspidistra stood on a small hexagonal table in front of a window hung with crisply laundered white net.

Joyce pulled a pair of green and gold brocade curtains across the nets. 'Sit down.'

Ianto took one of the two easy chairs and Megan perched on the edge of the sofa, facing the fire and revelling in its warmth after the damp, freezing night air.

'What wages are you offering, Mrs Palmer?' Ianto questioned briskly, when Joyce sat in the chair opposite his.

'First things first, Mr Williams. I need to know if your daughter really wants the job and secondly if she's up to it.' Joyce looked intently at Megan. 'It will mean living in and working long hours. I serve a first breakfast for the early shift at six in the morning and a last supper for the afternoon shift at nine at night. And even then, there are sandwiches to be cut for the men on overtime and nights. There'll be some time off during the day, but not much. And things being as they are at the moment, I won't be able to give you more than one afternoon off a week.'

'I'm used to long hours and hard work, Mrs Palmer,' Megan answered resolutely.

'I believe you are. Your uncle is a good man but he had quite a houseful between his brothers and his children. You did your own laundry?'

'My uncle couldn't afford to send it out.' Megan's smile faltered when she thought of the bed linen and towels a lodging house full of policemen would generate, and that was without their clothes. Would Mrs Palmer expect her to wash those too?

36

'Can you cook?'

'Plain cooking, roasts, soups, stews, pastry, simple cakes and biscuits – nothing fancy.' Megan knotted her fingers. She was desperate to stay close to Victor but not enough to lie about her skills. She sensed that Joyce Palmer wouldn't be kind to anyone she had employed under false pretences.

'My daughter has been keeping house for my brother-in-law for five years and he had no complaints,' Ianto said impatiently.

'And you want the job, Megan?' Joyce ignored Ianto's testimonial.

'My uncle is leaving for Canada tomorrow and he can't take me with him.'

'I've heard.'

'I'd like to stay in Tonypandy because I have friends here, and there aren't any other jobs going in the valley.' She and Victor had never seen any point in keeping their relationship secret. The whole town knew they were courting, including Mrs Palmer.

'I own a hill farm in the Swansea Valley, Mrs Palmer. It's back-breaking work trying to scratch a living from rough grazing,' Ianto whined. 'Megan has been sending a little home, not much, just enough to make a difference, but I've had nothing from her since the strike started. That's why I need to know what wages you'll be paying.'

'If I took her on, Mr Williams, I would start her at fifteen shillings a week plus keep.'

'Those hours and that work warrant at least a pound.'

'If Megan proves suitable I will raise her wages to a pound a week after a month's trial. If she is unsuited to the work I will give her a week's wages in lieu of notice.' The tone of Joyce's voice made it clear that her terms were non-negotiable.

'Please, Mrs Palmer, will you give me a trial?' Megan begged.

'One month starting tomorrow,' Joyce affirmed unsmilingly.

'My uncle and his family are leaving on the six o'clock train tomorrow morning. I would like to clean the house after everyone has gone. May I move in afterwards?'

'You may, but the sooner the better.' Joyce left her seat at a tap on her door.

'Just a couple more things, Mrs Palmer.' Ianto remained in his chair and held his hands out to the fire as if he were settling in for the evening. 'I've brought Megan up to be a good Baptist—'

'She will have time off on Sunday to go to chapel.' Joyce went to the door.

'And I don't want her associating with riff-raff. No men and absolutely no Catholics.'

'Your daughter is a respectable young woman, well regarded by everyone in the town, Mr Williams. I have no intention of monitoring her movements during her free time while she lives under my roof. So far as I am concerned she may go wherever she chooses and visit anyone she wishes.'

'Are you a Catholic?' Ianto Williams enquired suspiciously.

'My religion is my own affair, Mr Williams. But as it happens I am not.' Joyce opened the door at a second tap. 'I will be with you in a moment,' she said to someone in the hall. 'If there is nothing else, Mr Williams, I have a lodging house to run.'

Ianto sniffed at the dismissal but finally left the chair.

'You are happy for your daughter to be working here, Mr Williams?' Joyce asked.

'Why shouldn't I be?' Ianto pulled his cap from his pocket in readiness.

'This is a lodging house for police officers. Given that they have been brought in to control the strike, there aren't many men in the Rhondda who would allow their daughters to work here.'

'My family needs Megan's wages and from what I've seen of the miners, it's just as well that she will be living in a houseful of policemen, Mrs Palmer.'

Megan followed her father into the hall. Police Sergeant Martin was standing at the foot of the stairs talking to two constables. One she recognized as Constable Shipton, who had trodden on her dress and knocked down Betty Morgan in the town that afternoon. They all turned and stared at her.

Sergeant Martin was the first to break the silence. 'We meet again, Miss . . .'

'Williams,' Ianto supplied. 'Can I trouble you, sir, to tell me just how you know my daughter?'

Chapter 3

JOYCE PALMER had never been so angry on behalf of another woman. Ianto Williams appeared to be looking to the police officers to confirm his worse suspicions about his daughter. But before the sergeant could enlighten him as to where and when he had met Megan, the door of the lodgers' sitting room opened and the doctor walked out in company with Sergeant Lamb. Both were grim-faced, serious.

'I have arranged for Constable Lamb, the sergeant's brother, to be taken down to Cardiff Infirmary on the next train, Mrs Palmer. I have also sent for a brake to convey him to the station, it should be here any minute. Gentlemen, Megan.' The doctor acknowledged the officers, Megan and her father.

'How serious are Constable Lamb's injuries?' Sergeant Martin asked.

'He has a fractured skull, and his shoulders have been scalded.' The doctor glanced at Sergeant Lamb who remained silent.

'But he will recover?' Sergeant Martin enquired uneasily.

'The doctors in the Infirmary will find out more about his condition when he regains consciousness. I have sent for a second brake to convey Constables Jones and Pritchard to Llwynypia Hospital. Their injuries are comparatively minor. Scalds, bruising and exhaustion. However, I think everyone in Tonypandy is suffering from that last complaint, myself included. With rest and care they should be fit for duty again within ten days.'

'And then the savages in this town can try to kill them all over again,' Sergeant Lamb declared venomously.

'I am extremely sorry to hear about your brother, Sergeant

Lamb,' Joyce Palmer sympathized. 'I hope he will make a full recovery.'

'As do we all. We'll find out who did this, Sergeant Lamb,' Sergeant Martin assured his fellow officer.

'Do you wish to accompany your brother to Cardiff, Sergeant?' The doctor took the overcoat Joyce handed him.

'We can cope without you for one night,' Sergeant Martin assured him.

'You know things are looking ugly in the town and our officers are likely to be out all night again.'

'We will cope,' Sergeant Martin reiterated.

Sergeant Lamb noticed Megan for the first time. 'Good evening, Miss—'

'You all seem to know my daughter?' Ianto interrupted.

'Not in a professional capacity.' Sergeant Martin studied Ianto with a practised eye. 'She was shopping this morning when we were patrolling the town, Mr Williams.'

'Miss Williams will be working here, as my assistant house-keeper from tomorrow,' Joyce supplied.

'I am glad to hear it, Mrs Palmer,' Sergeant Lamb observed caustically. 'Perhaps once she starts we'll have no more cause for complaint about the slow and pathetic service in this house.'

'I hope so, Sergeant Lamb.' Joyce's clipped reply fell just short of being discourteous. She opened the front door. 'Goodnight, Mr Williams. I'll see you tomorrow, Megan. Will you need help to bring your things down?'

'I'll manage, thank you, Mrs Palmer.' The drizzle had become a downpour but Megan was glad to leave the officers. She pulled her hood over her hat again and, ignoring the noise coming from Dunraven Street, turned up the hill.

'You will send fifteen shillings a week home, starting next week,' Ianto Williams stipulated, as they ran through the rain. 'If Mrs Palmer should up your wages next month you may keep the extra five shillings for yourself.'

'Yes, Dad,' Megan answered mechanically, her mind in turmoil. The thought of living in the same house as Sergeant Martin,

40

Sergeant Lamb, Constable Shipton and the other officers terrified her but she couldn't think of any other way she could remain in Tonypandy. And she simply couldn't bear the thought of leaving Victor.

'And you stay away from that Catholic boy.'

'I won't have much time to call my own, Dad.'

'I need you to promise me that you won't see or contact him again.'

'Tonypandy is a small town.' She tried to sound respectful. 'I can't promise you that I won't see him.'

'Think you're so clever, don't you? I warn you now, girl, your carrying on with him will lead nowhere. I was serious when I wrote that I'd rather see you dead than married to a Catholic.'

'In a year and a half I'll be twenty-one—'

'Marry him and you'll never see me, your mother or your brothers and sisters again. Your name will be counted among the dead in the family. It's your choice, girl.'

Megan's heart sank as she opened her uncle's front door. Although she hadn't seen her family in five and a half years, they all wrote to her from time to time and she still felt close to them. It would be a wrench to lose them. But she lifted her chin determinedly. A great deal could change in eighteen months. Possibly even her father's mind.

Sali was turning Welshcakes on a griddle she'd heated on the hob when Megan and her father walked into the kitchen. A lightly sugared, steaming pyramid of cakes was piled high on Megan's largest meat platter. The bowl she'd used to mix the cakes in stood empty on the table.

'I noticed that you had some flour and sugar in your pantry and we had leftover currants and sultanas, so I made a few cakes for your uncle and the children to take with them tomorrow.'

Megan's flour and sugar bins had been empty for over a month, and since the strike had begun there was no such thing as 'leftover' dried fruit. But Megan was touched and grateful that Sali had taken the time and trouble to make the cakes because she suspected that her father wouldn't put his hand in his pocket to buy food for Sam and Daisy on the long journey to the farm. 'Thank you, they'll appreciate it.' She shook the raindrops from her cloak and hung it in the passage.

Ianto folded his cap into his pocket, lifted half a dozen cakes on to a plate and crouched close to the fire to eat them.

'Did you get the job?' Sali eased the last cake on to a spatula and flipped it on to the plate.

'I start work in Joyce Palmer's lodging house tomorrow.' Megan closed the door behind her.

'You're going to work for Joyce Palmer?'

'And what's wrong with that, Mrs Jones?' Ianto demanded. 'I have just been there and from what I saw, Mrs Palmer runs a clean and respectable house.'

'She does,' Sali agreed hastily, responding to the pleading look in Megan's eyes.

'I'll wipe that down and put it away,' Megan offered, as Sali slid the griddle from the hob and closed it.

'Sam and Daisy are asleep and the other three came in an hour ago. I sent them straight to bed.'

'Thank you for staying with them.'

'No trouble.' Sali saw the concerned expression on Megan's face and realized she hadn't taken the job lightly. She picked up her cardigan from the back of a kitchen chair. 'I'll be in first thing tomorrow to help you clean the house before you leave for Mrs Palmer's. Goodbye, Mr Williams, have a safe journey home. It was nice to meet you.'

'Mrs Jones, are you a good friend of Megan's?'

'I like to think so,' Sali replied guardedly. 'Why do you ask?'

'Can she spend her afternoons off with you?'

Realizing that Megan's father hadn't made the connection between her and Victor, Sali had difficulty keeping a straight face. 'She is more than welcome to spend as much time as she likes with me, Mr Williams.'

'Then it's arranged, Megan. You are to spend all of your free afternoons with Mrs Jones here.'

'Yes, Dad.'

Not knowing whether Megan was trying to stop herself from

laughing or crying, Sali gave her a reassuring hug. 'Goodnight. See you in the morning.'

Betty Morgan turned down the wick on the oil lamp that burned on her kitchen table, opened the door and stole along the passage to her front parlour. She waited a moment for her eyes to become accustomed to the gloom before lifting the corner of her curtains and peering outside. The street gaped back at her, empty, quiet and glistening like tarnished pewter in the wet darkness. She dropped the curtain. 'They've gone.'

'You sure?' a muffled voice asked from beneath her parlour table.

'The street's empty and I went out to the ty bach a few minutes ago to check the back and the lane. I can't be certain, but as far as I can see there's no one around.'

Joey lifted the edge of a heavy woollen cloth and scrambled out from under the table. 'Thanks, Mrs Morgan. Did they get any of the others?'

'Not that I or Mrs Rees next door have heard. I've just spoken to her over the wall. But that's not to say the coppers won't recognize you or the others the next time they see you and if they do they'll make your life hell.'

'As opposed to the bed of roses Mr Morgan, my father and Lloyd are lying on.'

'They've learned the hard way to keep a cooler head than you, Joey Evans, and that's why my Ned and your father keep a watchful eye on you youngsters when you man the picket lines. Take care of yourself, boy, and that means no going home through Jane Edwards' house. And don't go giving me that innocent look neither,' she advised tartly. Like everyone in the town, Betty knew Joey's reputation, but she'd watched him grow up and had a soft spot for him. 'I've seen you creeping in and out of her back door a couple of times since her Emlyn was sent down. Your mother would turn in her grave if she could see the way her youngest was behaving. Mark my words; it'll only be a matter of time before someone else notices what you two are up to and when her Emlyn comes out of clink, you'll be for it.'

43

'I don't know what I would do without you, Mrs Morgan,' Joey said smoothly.

'You'd be playing punchbag for the coppers,' she pronounced sternly. 'And it would be a pity to spoil those pretty looks of yours. But I'm telling you now, it's high time you stayed away from women who think nothing of making fools of their husbands and playing games that can only end in tears. Go find yourself a good, clean-living girl. Preferably one who knows how to handle a boy with your wandering ways.'

'I've found one,' he kissed her cheek, 'but you're spoken for, and there's no one else in the town who can hold a candle to you.'

'None of your nonsense now.' She pushed him away.

'I can take a hint. You're expecting Mr Morgan any minute and you want me out of your house.'

Betty stifled her laughter at the thought of Ned showing any signs of jealousy after forty-two years of married life. 'You'd better go the back way, just in case.'

She led the way through the kitchen and opened the door. While she went into the ty bach, Joey vaulted her garden wall. He crouched low on his heels in the lane, studying the shadows. The rain had stopped and there was no sound or movement. He remained stock still for a moment then looked to a house two doors up from Betty's. The curtains were open in the back bedroom and a candle stub burned on the window sill. Moving close to the wall he crept towards the light.

The back door was unlocked, but then so was every door in the Rhondda except those of the shopkeepers and crache. He walked through the basement and up the steps to the kitchen. Feeling his way in the darkness, he went into the passage and climbed the stairs.

'What kept you?' Jane whispered.

'How do you know it's me and not a bogglie?'

'Because I watched you walk in through the back and you haven't said why you're late.' She kept her voice low although there wasn't anyone else in the house.

'There was trouble in Dunraven Street. The police were chasing us and I had to hide until they stopped looking.'

'I would have hidden you,' she reproached.

'Betty Morgan's was nearer. Besides, there's gossip about us as it is.'

'I don't care.' She moved over in the bed to make room for him.

'You don't care if your Emlyn thumps me when he gets out?' Joey was alarmed by the thought. Emlyn might be over fifty but he was also a haulier, and battling pit ponies that balked at dragging heavily loaded trams had helped him develop muscles to rival Victor's.

'Seeing as how he's spent as many nights with Rosie Green, the barmaid in the Pandy as he has with me since we married, he has no cause for complaint. What's sauce for the gander is sauce for the goose.'

'Is that all I am to you, sauce?'

She laughed as he pulled off the last of his clothes and climbed into the bed beside her. 'You're cold.' She shrank away from him.

'No, I'm not. You're too hot.'

'You saying I need cooling down, Joey Evans?'

'Just for a moment.' He dived under the bedclothes and lifted the hem of her nightdress to her waist. 'Get this off and I'll demonstrate a different way to get warm.'

'You will keep coming round after Emlyn gets out, won't you?'

'If you can fit me in between the baker's boy and the milkman.'

'You—'

'We're here now, Jane. Let's make the most of it.' His fingers moved tantalizingly and expertly between her thighs. When he'd succeeded in rousing her, he took her nightdress from her hands, pulled it over her head and dropped it to the floor beside the bed.

'Megan's father is leaving at three in the morning with the two youngest. Her uncle, the boys and his brothers are catching the six o'clock train; I told her I'd call round after they've gone to help her clean the house. She'd welcome another pair of helping hands if you're not due on the picket lines.' Sali set a cup of tea in front of Victor.

'I wish she hadn't agreed to work for Joyce Palmer.' Victor sat hunched over the table.

Sali replaced the teapot on the metal stand and covered it with a knitted cosy. 'You'd rather Megan left Tonypandy?'

'No!'

'Megan's only doing what the rest of us are,' she reminded him mildly. 'Trying to survive until better times. She won't be nineteen for ever, Victor.'

'From where I'm sitting it feels like it,' he complained miserably.

'I'm sorry.' Sali wished she could think of something more comforting to say, but with her own marriage plans in hand, she felt anything else would sound sanctimonious.

He glanced at the clock. 'Dad, Lloyd and Joey are late. As soon as I've drunk this I'll go and look for them.'

'Give them another half hour. The boys next door told me that the police have been blocking Dunraven Street again. If your father and Lloyd did make it to the railway station along with the other union officials, they might not be able to get back.' Sali had become adept at concealing her fears for Lloyd and Mr Evans' safety. As strike leaders they were expected to act as mediators by the police, a position that put them in the firing line of both sides. Every time they left the house, she was terrified that she might never see either of them again.

'And Joey?' Victor asked. 'He went out a good half hour after them.'

Sali didn't answer. From the first week of the strike she had suspected that Joey was actually enjoying the excitement generated by the conflict. It gave him an excuse to disappear for hours at a time, and there were plenty of women in Tonypandy who were prepared to hide Joey Evans under their beds while swearing all shades of innocence to the police. And it took absolutely no imagination on her part to picture what Joey got up to with his saviours after the police moved on their search.

'I'm fine, love.' Lloyd pulled his bloodstained handkerchief away

46

from his cheekbone, and examined his face in the dressing-table mirror.

Ignoring his protestations, Sali left the bed, flung a woollen shawl over her flannel nightgown and poured cold water from the china pitcher into the bowl on the washstand. She tossed in a flannel and wrung it out. 'Sit down.'

'I'm fine.'

'So you keep saying.'

'You don't believe me?'

'Sit down before you fall down.'

'You know something, you've turned out bossy, Sali Jones.' Lloyd finally sat on the bed.

She pressed the flannel against a cut that had sliced his cheek. 'You need someone to keep you in order. Was it a truncheon?' She fingered the wound to check its depth.

He took the flannel from her. 'The police had every right to wade in given what they were facing. Someone started a rumour that management were bringing in blacklegs on the train, so the boys armed themselves with sticks and bucketfuls of stones.'

'And the blacklegs?'

'Never materialized, which makes me think management started the rumour, so everyone would go to the station and leave the side roads clear. It didn't help that some bright officer refused to allow us to see for ourselves when we tried to picket the station. And before you say anything, I wasn't the intended target for this.' He held the flannel over the cut. 'Just the stupid bystander, fool enough to get between two angry people.'

'Why do you always have to see both sides of every argument?' She helped him out of his jacket.

'Because if I didn't, I'd be throwing stones along with the rest of the mob and then we'd not only lose the fight but deserve to. Sometimes I think the blockheads on both sides are more in control than the so-called leaders, and we'll remain, horns locked, in this strike for ever.' He changed the subject. 'Victor said Megan's taken a job in Joyce Palmer's lodging house.'

'He's not happy about it.' Sali sensed that Lloyd had mentioned

47

Victor and Megan because he was tired of talking about a situation that was proving increasingly impossible to resolve.

'So I gather.' Lloyd had left Victor and their father in the kitchen discussing the implications of Megan's new job.

'I could go to Pontypridd tomorrow and ask the trustees of Gwilym James to give Megan a job in the department store.'

Sali's casual conversational tone didn't fool Lloyd. 'When you told me that your great-aunt had left her entire estate and Gwilym James's department store in trust to Harry until his thirtieth birthday and that you and he could draw allowances until then, we agreed you would keep the money for Harry and yourself. You made a solemn promise that not one penny would come my way, or the way of my father and brothers. You assured me you'd give us no expensive presents, no help with the rent or food, or pay for anything other than Harry's education—'

'I'm not talking about money. Just a job for Megan,' she remonstrated.

'Which doesn't exist.'

'Not at the moment, no,' she admitted reluctantly.

'So you'd have to invent one.' He unbuttoned his shirt. 'No charity, Sali. I have my pride, and so do my father and brothers. It's bad enough watching you going cap in hand to the men who control Harry's trust fund for food for the soup kitchen.'

'That's not charity. That's common sense and good business,' she countered indignantly. 'Gwilym James would go bankrupt without the patronage of the colliers. And when this strike is over they'll remember who helped them when they most needed it.'

'And if this strike lasts much longer, Gwilym James might just go bust along with all the other businesses who are giving credit to the colliers.' He winced as he rose from the bed.

'Last time I spoke to Mr Richards,' Sali referred to the solicitor who advised her on business matters, 'he said Gwilym James could hold out for years if it had to. In fact, just before the strike the trustees were looking to use the trust's reserves to invest and expand the business by opening new stores.'

'In Tonypandy?' Lloyd enquired facetiously.

'They were considering it.'

He tossed the flannel back into the bowl and took off his waistcoat and shirt. 'Don't try and tell me it's still an option.'

'Perhaps not at the moment . . .' She saw him smile and lost her temper. 'Be serious, Lloyd!'

'I am, my love. But whatever you and the trustees decide to do with Harry's inheritance is none of my business.'

Hating the thought that her and Lloyd's marriage was dependent on Owen Bull's execution, she said, 'Harry already looks on you as his father.'

'All the more reason for me, my father and brothers,' he added uncompromisingly, 'never to touch his money or ask him for any favours. And as for finding Megan a job, it's not only Victor and me who would think it smacks of charity. Megan would too, and before you say another word, you know it.'

Sali tossed her shawl over the footboard and slipped between the sheets. 'You're a hard man, Lloyd Evans.'

'You complaining?' He pulled his vest over his head, unbuckled his belt, dropped his trousers and drawers, and pulled them off together with his socks. Ignoring the cold, he folded them neatly on to a chair.

'No, Lloyd, but I'd be lying if I said I wasn't worried about the strike and the effect it's having on the valley. Fights between colliers and the police and the army are bad enough, but it's worse when people who should be on the same side fight one another. Federation men and blacklegs – and what are blacklegs anyway? Only men so desperate to feed their families they take whatever paid work management offer. I've seen neighbours who'd do anything to help one another before the strike, brawling in the streets. We can just about manage with four lots of strike pay coming into the house and Victor's allotment and chickens, but there are others who can't. And I can't bear to see children go hungry.'

'You know as well I do that a lot more children will go hungry and for longer if we don't get the owners to agree to pay colliery workers a decent wage. And that means paying miners for bringing slag out of the pits as well as coal.' He climbed into bed and lay beside her. 'But the strike and all its problems will still be there tomorrow and as there's nothing we can do about it until then, I suggest we find something more pleasant to discuss.' He slipped the pearl buttons at the neck of her nightdress and kissed the sensitive skin at the base of her neck.

'You know that I love you, Lloyd . . .'

'And I love you too, sweetheart.'

As she returned his embrace she wished she had the courage to tell him that it wasn't just the problems of the strike she had to contend with. Her monthly meetings with Harry's trustees had never been easy, principally because practically all the men who sat on the board didn't bother to conceal their contempt for Lloyd, his politics, or the lifestyle she had chosen for Harry and herself. But the last meeting had been even more strained than usual. Her brother Geraint had told her beforehand he considered it demeaning and disgraceful that she was allowing the heir to the Gwilym James fortune to live in a collier's house, associate with strikers and eat in a soup kitchen.

She had argued that Harry needed to see what life was like for ordinary people. But Geraint, who strongly disapproved of her association with Lloyd, had been angrier than she had ever seen him before. And she was terrified that he'd compromise her position with the trustees by voicing his opinions at a future meeting.

'You're like a block of ice.' Lloyd wrapped his arms around her but he found it difficult to determine if he was warming or freezing her, or vice versa.

'What are we going to do about Victor and Megan?'

'My father and I will do what we can to make sure that everyone understands she's just a young girl trying to make a living.'

'I hope you succeed.'

'So do I, sweetheart, but not many people are thinking rationally these days. And I'm not just talking about the miners.'

'I wish . . .'

'What?' He blew out the candle.

'A quiet life for all of us,' she said fervently.

'You'd get bored.'

'I could take a boring life right now, Lloyd.'

'I'll remind you of that fifty years from now,' he laughed.

It was on the tip of her tongue to reply that she hoped he would be around to do just that but she was afraid to tempt fate.

The temperature in the kitchen had dropped below freezing because the fire had been raked from the stove after Sali had put Harry to bed, yet Victor and his father still sat, shivering on the easy chairs either side of the hearth.

'If anyone around here dares to say a word to me or Megan about her working in Mrs Palmer's lodging house, I'll tell them to mind their own business,' Victor said decisively.

Billy Evans suppressed a smile. 'Mind your own business' was the strongest reprimand he'd ever heard Victor use to a female neighbour and then only under extreme provocation. 'Given the way most people feel about the police, you're going to be telling a lot of people to do just that.'

Victor's face fell. 'It's not what they'll say to me but to Megan that concerns me. Now that her uncle and his brothers have gone, she has no family left to turn to.'

'Seeing as you want to make her family, she has you, me, your brothers and Sali,' his father reminded. 'But from what I've seen of her, like most women she's too soft-hearted and sensitive for her own good. She'll need to develop a deaf ear and a skin like your blacksmith's apron now she's taken that job with Joyce, and someone,' Billy looked meaningfully at his son, 'should tell her to do just that. The best thing she can do to the gossips who'll have a go at her for taking the job is ignore them.' He pulled his empty pipe from his pocket and studied it thoughtfully.

'You've seen how the police lash out and beat anyone who gets in their way. She'll be living in the same house as them.'

'They'll hardly turn on a young girl who's cleaning up after them and cooking their meals.' Billy watched Victor pale at the thought of Megan skivvying for the men who had been brought in to break the strike. 'There are no bruises on Joyce Palmer that I've seen.'

'Mrs Palmer is a middle-aged women.'

'And Megan is an attractive young girl. Are you afraid that a good-looking young copper will turn her head?' There was an edge to Billy's flippant remark. He knew that Victor was serious about marrying Megan, but he wasn't sure just how serious nineteen-year-old Megan was about Victor. Especially now when she was about to move into a houseful of young men who were earning good wages and could shower her with gifts and regale her with tales of life in the big cities and towns outside Wales.

'No,' Victor said. 'I love her and she loves me. And if it wasn't for her father, we'd have been engaged last Christmas and married last spring. But given the way the police behave, I'm not sure they'll treat her with respect—'

'Because she's a collier's niece.'

'Exactly,' Victor concurred. 'There's no way that Lloyd would let Sali work in that house.'

'There isn't, but then Lloyd will soon be in a position to marry Sali. Do you two intend to get married when Megan is twenty-one?'

'We've talked about it. But given her father's attitude that's all we can do – talk,' Victor divulged miserably.

'You're both very young.'

'Mam was seventeen and you twenty when you married. I'm twenty-five and before the strike I was earning good money.'

'Are you trying to tell me that you've changed the way you feel about the strike?'

'No, it's like you and Lloyd say, we're fighting for a living wage for all the colliery workers. I'd be a fool not to support you.'

'You've never been that interested in the union.'

'Only because you, Lloyd and the other leaders are doing a better job of organizing the workers and negotiating with management than I could ever hope to. You and Lloyd have always been the thinkers in the family, Dad.' Victor shifted uneasily in his chair. He wasn't used to discussing his feelings with anyone, not even his father, only Megan. 'Give me Megan for a wife and in time, God willing, a family, a job that pays a living wage, a couple of good dogs, some chickens, a garden to put them in and grow some vegetables and I'll be a happy man.'

'You know your own mind, I'll say that for you,' Billy smiled.

'The example you and Mam set us, you can't blame me for wanting what you and she had.'

'I was lucky.' Billy's eyes clouded as an image of his wife came to mind.

'We all were.'

'Stay there, I'll be back in a minute.' Billy left his chair and went into the front room. It had been a parlour before his wife had become bedridden with the cancer that had killed her. When she could no longer climb the stairs, he had moved their bed into it, and after her death continued to sleep there, simply because it was the last room they had shared, the place she had drawn her final breath, and where he still felt closest to her.

He opened the cupboard next to the bed and removed Isabella's jewellery box. When he lifted the lid, the faint scent of Attar of Roses wafted into the air along with the tinny music box notes of 'Greensleeves'. Memories he'd tried to suppress because they were too painful to dwell on flooded back.

His mouth went dry, his breath caught in his throat and his heart pounded erratically, exactly as it had done the first time he had caught sight of Isabella Maria Rodriguez. She had been standing behind the counter of the grocer's shop that her uncle had opened in Tonypandy, a small, modest establishment his daughter Connie had since expanded out of all recognition.

He had never seen a woman as beautiful before – or since. Tall, slim, with skin the colour of clotted cream, deep blue-black hair and the almond-shaped, dark eyes she had bequeathed to their eldest and youngest sons. When she had smiled and asked what he wanted, he completely forgot about the tobacco he had intended to buy. His heart was lost.

He left ten minutes later with her permission to ask her father if he could call on her. Six months later they were married, at her insistence in the Catholic Church. But by then, he would have done anything that she had asked of him.

He had carved the jewellery casket for her to mark Lloyd's birth a year later. The musical movement had cost him dear, he'd had to send to a London dealer to get it. He could have bought one in

53

Cardiff but they hadn't stocked 'Greensleeves' and the first time he had set eyes on Isabella she had been wearing a green dress covered by a white overall . . .

'Dad? You all right?'

He looked up. Victor was watching him from the doorway.

'I'm fine. Go back into the kitchen, I'll be with you in a moment.' Billy removed a small red leather ring box that lay on top of the pile of neatly stacked cases in the casket. He pushed it into his pocket, closed the lid and the music died.

'You would want him to have it, wouldn't you, cariad?' he whispered.

A youthful Isabella, elegantly dressed in her summer Sunday best of white lace and wide-brimmed straw hat, smiled back at him from the silver-framed photograph that stood next to his side of the bed.

'Of course you would,' he answered for her.

He returned to the kitchen, walked over to Victor, picked up his hand and dropped the ring box into it. 'You might not be able to marry Megan without her father's permission but given that he's over forty miles away, he doesn't have to find out that you are engaged. And once Megan's seen around town with that on her finger, there'll be no doubt as to whose girl she is. Given your size and our family's reputation for straight talking I doubt too many people will dare say much to her face about working for the police.'

Victor opened the box. 'Mam's engagement ring . . . I couldn't . . .'

'It's not doing any good shut away.' Emotion made Billy brusque. He hadn't seen the gimmel ring, with its two gold hands clasped around a single heart-shaped diamond since the day Isabella had asked him to remove it together with her wedding band from her finger. She had lain back on the pillows and watched him stow them in the casket. He could even recall her wan smile and the light in her eyes when she had said, '*Keep them with the rest of my jewellery for our sons' wives, or, even with God's blessing, our granddaughters.*'

'But Lloyd's the oldest, he should have this,' Victor protested selflessly.

'Sali doesn't want an engagement ring, only a wedding band, and I've already told him that she can have your mother's.'

'There's Joey.'

'If he ever goes out with a girl for longer than a week he can give her your mother's regard ring.'

'Her what?' Victor asked in confusion.

'Regard ring. I gave it to her a month after we started courting. They were all the rage then. Come to think of it, I haven't heard anyone mention them in years. They were called regard rings because they were set with stones in a flower pattern that spelled out the word regard.' He frowned with the effort of remembering. 'A ruby, emerald, garnet, amethyst, another ruby and a diamond. Most of the boys I worked with bought their girls ones set with fake stones. My landlady called me a fool for emptying my bank account to buy your mother the real thing but I knew the first time I saw her that we were meant to be together.'

'Like me and Megan.'

'You loved her the first time you saw her?'

'Yes, but she was thirteen, I was nineteen and she preferred Joey. It took years for me to tell her how I felt. This is beautiful.' Victor lifted the gimmel ring from the box and held it to the light.

'I hope it fits, but if it doesn't you should be able to have it altered. When you can afford it,' Billy added drily. 'And you can tell Megan from me that your mother would have been proud to see her wear it.'

Victor watched his father walk to the door. Was it his imagination, or had he aged? His back was bowed and there was an expression in his face that went beyond simple tiredness. 'If you're sure about giving me this . . .'

'I'm sure.' Billy went into his bedroom, closed the door and checked the curtains were tightly drawn before unbuttoning his jacket and waistcoat. Of his three sons, Lloyd had been the most ambitious. His desire to better himself had won him a place in mining school to study engineering and it irked colliery management to have a man of Lloyd's intelligence and status side with the strikers against them. Victor had always been the fairest; even as a child he wouldn't eat a cake or sweet unless his brothers had been given exactly the same share. And Joey – Joey had always been the wild one. It hadn't escaped his attention that it was after midnight and his youngest son hadn't come home. He only hoped he was with a woman and not in a police cell.

Chapter 4

VICTOR REMAINED in the kitchen long after his father went to bed. Oblivious to the temperature, Joey's absence and the sounds of the house settling around him, he continued to sit, lost in imaginings of what Megan and his life would be like, not 'if' but when they married.

He knew that if he asked him, Lloyd would happily exchange the house he'd rented to Megan's uncle for one of the others their father had bought. It had the double advantage of being furnished and next door to his family. He pictured himself living there with Megan, coming home from the pit after a day's work when the strike was settled, bathing in the cellar, walking up the steps into the kitchen to find her presiding over the stove, the appetizing aroma of roast meats and baking in the air. They would spend quiet evenings sitting by the fire: he would be reading, or carving something from wood, a love spoon or a toy for one of their children; she'd look up from her sewing and . . .

The door opened and Joey strode in. 'What are you doing up?' He made a beeline for the pantry. When Victor didn't answer, he said, 'I've decided to go off to Canada with the others in the morning.' He emerged with just one of Sali's oatmeal biscuits. He was ravenous, but since the strike he had learned to curb his appetite.

'What?' Victor murmured absently, finally focusing on Joey as he sat in their father's chair.

'That got your attention, didn't it?' Joey grinned. 'God, it's bloody freezing in here.'

'Don't swear and don't blaspheme.' Victor glanced at the clock. 'Where have you been?'

'Ask me no questions and I'll tell you no lies.'

'Joey, you're begging for trouble. One day an irate husband or father is going to cripple you.'

'I'm careful,' Joey boasted.

'No, you're not. You're the talk of Pandy.'

'At least I do something about my women, unlike you.'

'And what's that supposed to mean?' Victor demanded touchily.

Unlike the rest of the family, Victor's temper was slow to rise and even slower to fall. Joey dropped his bantering tone.

'Big day tomorrow. If you're going to be up early to wave goodbye to Megan, shouldn't you be in bed?'

'Megan's not leaving in the morning, she's taken a job in Joyce Palmer's.'

'She what?'

'She needs a job and it's the only one going.' Victor closed his fingers around the ring box in his pocket.

'That's not going to go down too well with the people around here.'

'The people around here are going to have to get used to it. One word out of line to me – or Megan – and I'll thump whoever said it.'

'There's no need for you to look at me like that. All I did was point out what's going to happen. You know what people are like, and I can tell you something for nothing now. The women will be the worst, and you can't thump them.'

'I can thump their husbands.'

'You'll end up fighting every collier in this valley.' Joey finished his biscuit and left the chair. 'You can sit up all night if you want to, I'm whacked.'

'Who is she, Joey?'

'Who's who?' Joey lit a candle stub from the oil lamp on the table.

'Your latest woman. She has to be married or you'd be flaunting her around the town.'

'No one you know,' Joey lied.

'When are you going to see sense and learn to leave the married ones alone?'

'They're the best.' Joey arched his eyebrows. 'Ardent, experienced and no expectations beyond a good time, which I am happy to supply.'

'One day someone could be saying that about your wife.'

'Never.' Joey opened the door. 'She'll be too worn out fulfilling my demands. And far too satisfied even to look at another man.'

'I don't envy her trying to keep you in line, whoever she'll be.' Victor rose to his feet. He'd been sitting longer than he'd thought and the cold had seeped into his bones. He turned down the wick on the oil lamp and followed Joey out through the door.

'Whoever she will be, she won't have to do anything for a while. It'll be a long time before I stop dipping into the variety box and settle for just one biscuit.'

'One day you'll fall for a woman and you'll fall hard, Joey. And I can't wait to see it happen,' Victor whispered as he followed him into their bedroom.

Sali dropped the bundle of linen and blankets she'd stripped from Megan's bed next to the piles of laundry in the passage. 'That's the last of the bedding. I'll take it next door and wash it when we next light the fire in the basement.'

'It will have to be a fine day.' Megan gazed at the massive heap. 'I feel guilty about leaving you with it.'

'Don't. Your uncle told Lloyd he could keep whatever was left in the house. It may be easier to rent it furnished. When the strike ends.' Sali tried not to think when that might be.

Victor opened the front door and saw the bundles. 'Want me to carry these next door for you?'

'Please. Stack them in the basement.' Sali glanced from Victor to Megan and rolled down her cardigan sleeves. 'If you don't need me for anything else, Megan, I'll take Harry to school and go from there straight to the soup kitchen.'

'I can finish up what's left. Thank you for your help, I couldn't have managed without it.' Megan watched Victor follow Sali out of the door and returned upstairs to check the empty bedrooms. With the china washed and stacked on the washstands, and the wardrobes, dressing tables and mattresses shrouded in dustsheets, the rooms had a deserted air. As if the occupants had moved out years, not minutes ago.

She went into each room in turn, closing the doors behind her. Leaving her own room until last, she lifted the suitcase she had packed from behind the door, carried it downstairs and left it in the passage. The last of the bundles of linen had gone. She opened the parlour door. The room was freezing, the mantelpiece devoid of ornaments, the square of carpet gone, the furniture covered.

Her father had asked her uncle if he could take a few things back with him for the children. To her amazement, he had slipped the driver of the donkey cart an extra shilling to pick him and the children up outside the house and Megan was certain that even her uncle was shocked when her father's 'few things' included all the linen in the house that wasn't actually on the beds, the everyday as well as the good china, the kitchen clock, saucepans, cutlery and all the rugs and carpets.

She closed the door and looked in on the middle room where her uncle's brothers had slept. The bed was stripped, the frame and mattress shrouded in dustsheets just like upstairs. Sali had done wonders in the hour she had helped her. There was only the kitchen and the basement left and neither needed much clearing.

'Half the town was waiting outside the station to see your uncle's family off.' Victor was watching her from the passage.

'He insisted on saying goodbye to me here.' Her eyes were unnaturally bright when she turned to face him.

'I'm yours until you have to go to Mrs Palmer's. What do you want me to do?'

'There's not much left. Sali did most of the work that needed to be done.' Megan went into the kitchen, took the brass fire tongs from the set of fire irons and started picking out the still warm coals from the fire she had raked out.

'Here, I'll do that for you.' Victor laid his hand over hers and took the tongs from her.

'Thank you. I can get on with the dusting.'

'No, Megan.'

'The place needs dusting—'

'No one is queuing up to rent the place and they won't be until the strike is settled. It can be dusted then.' He dropped the last piece of salvageable coal into a tin bucket.

'I'll clean out the pantry, then. Oh no . . .'

'What's the matter?' He jumped up.

She emerged holding a tiny handkerchief embellished by an embroidered daisy. 'I made this for Daisy's last birthday. She took it everywhere with her. She must have dropped it when I sent her into the pantry to fetch one of the packets of Welshcakes Sali made.'

'It's small enough, you can send it to her in an envelope.' He wrapped his arms around her and handed her his own handkerchief.

She wiped her eyes and blew her nose. 'All I've done since I got out of bed this morning is cry. It's so stupid . . .'

'No, it's not. Your life here is over and you don't know what's coming next.'

'I didn't have a chance to talk over the job with you.' She looked up at him through tear-stained eyes. 'My father wanted me to go home with him, but not to stay. He said he was going to take me to a hiring in Brecon next week. I couldn't bear the thought of being so far away from you. And he and my mother can't manage without the money I send them. Joyce is paying me the same as my uncle to start, so I can give them fifteen shillings a week. If there had been another job I would have—'

'Megan! Megan!' He had to repeat her name twice before she fell silent. 'You did the only thing you could have. I wouldn't have wanted to carry on living in Tonypandy without you.'

'Then you're not angry with me?'

'When Sali told me that you were going to work for Mrs Palmer last night, I talked it over with my father.' He reached into his pocket. 'I would have liked to have given you this somewhere romantic and memorable, like the Old Bridge in Pontypridd or the walk alongside the river, or even on top of the mountain. But I want you to have it before you start in the lodging house.' He opened the small box. The diamond ring glittered in the lamplight on its bed of dark velvet. 'It was my mother's. My father told me to tell you that she would have been proud to see you wear it.'

'But my father—'

'We both heard him yesterday, Megan, and frankly, I'd rather not discuss what he said. Your family are over forty miles away. They don't have to know that we're engaged. And we are, aren't we? You will marry me just as soon as you are twenty-one?'

Megan thought of her father's pronouncement that he'd rather see her dead than married to a Catholic, his threat to count her name among the dead in the family if she did marry Victor when she came of age. But as she looked from the ring into Victor's gentle, grey eyes she felt she had no choice. She loved him and she could never give him up. Not even for her family. 'Yes, I'll marry you,' she breathed headily.

'The day after your twenty-first birthday will be the twenty-fifth of August nineteen twelve.'

'That seems a long way off.'

'It will pass soon enough,' he said, as much to reassure himself as her. 'And in the meantime I'll see you on your days off.'

'Not days, only afternoons, but Mrs Palmer said I might have some time off in between.'

'It won't be as good as having you living next door, but you'll only be around the corner and we'll just have to make the most of whatever free time you do have.' He locked his arms around her waist and hugged her. 'Like now.' Pulling her close, he kissed her, long and lovingly.

'I can't believe we're really engaged,' she said when he released her.

'Now you've said yes, I'll never let you go. You do know that?'

'Yes.' Her smile was tearful, but this time they were tears of happiness.

'Let's see if this fits.' He took the ring from the box and slipped it on to her finger. 'It's a little tight.'

'It's perfect because I won't lose it.' She pushed it firmly down on to her finger.

'I confess I have another reason for giving you this now. I don't want you going off with one of those policemen.'

'As if I would.' She recalled the way the sergeant had looked at her in the shop and in the house last night and shuddered.

'You're cold?'

'No.' She looked up at him and smiled. 'I'll wear it every chance I get, and thread it on the chain you gave me for my birthday and hang it around my neck when I'm working. And every time I look at it, I'll think of you and the twenty-fifth of August nineteen twelve.'

Victor finished cleaning the stove, and carried the sticks, newspapers and the remainder of the coals through the basement into the coalhouse he had filled only the day before. Deciding that he – or Joey, if he could bully him – could ferry the coal into their coalhouse next door, he swept the basement floor, checked the garden and ty bach, closed the doors behind him and returned upstairs.

Megan was sitting, dressed in her cloak and hat. She looked at the spot where the clock had hung until her father had taken it that morning. 'What's the time?'

Victor removed the watch he had been given by parents to mark his twenty-first birthday from his waistcoat pocket and opened it. 'A quarter past seven. Would you like to come next door? The fire is laid. All I have to do is put a match to it and we could have tea.'

'I told Mrs Palmer I would be with her as early as I could and I'd rather find out what I've let myself in for now than sit around worrying about it.'

He picked up her case. I'll carry this for you.'

'I never expected to see this house empty. My uncle's family have seemed like mine for so long, I thought I'd remain with them until I – we – married. And even then I imagined living close by, watching Daisy and Sam grow up.'

'You'll see them again.'

'You really think so?'

'Daisy and Sam certainly,' he said brightly. 'And who knows, if your uncle makes his fortune he could come back here in style some day. Rent the best rooms in the White Hart, and shower you with gold and Indian headdresses.'

'You've been reading too many adventure stories about the Wild West.' She stared at the carver chair at the head of the table,

63

the benches that ran down both sides, and saw her uncle's family sitting, as they done so many times, laughing and talking as they waited for her to serve them a meal. But that would never happen again . . .

Fighting a wave of emotion that threatened to overwhelm her, she turned and saw Victor waiting, her case in his hand. 'Should we lock up the house?'

'Lloyd and I will see to it later.' Victor almost told Megan that he intended to ask Lloyd if they could have the house, but just like her he suddenly felt that 25 August 1912 would never come. 'If you need more time—'

'No,' Megan broke in emphatically. 'After all, it's not as if I'm going to the ends of the earth.'

'I won't go far from the house for the next week unless I'm on picket duty. Even if you only get an hour off, you'll call?'

She nodded and went to the door. Reaching out with his free hand, he gripped her gloved fingers. She returned the pressure and walked out ahead of him.

The yard around Harry's primary school was full of small boys making faces or 'jibs', as they were colloquially known in the Rhondda, and girls performing an elaborate clapping game accompanied by a ditty they had picked up from their parents:

> *Every nice girl loves a collier*
> *In the Rhondda Valley War,*
> *Every nice girl loves a striker*
> *And you know what strikers are.*
> *In Tonypandy they're very handy*
> *With their sticks and stones and boot*
> *Walking down the street with Jane*
> *Breaking every window pane*
> *That's loot!*

The last line was sung with gusto and ended in a double clap as emphatic as small hands could make it.

'Let's hope they won't be teaching that same song to their own children,' Mr Griffiths the headmaster commented to Sali when he saw her at the gate with Harry.

'It's the first time I've heard that one.'

'We had to stop them singing some of the others.' Albert Griffiths and Sali both taught in the evening classes organized by the miners' unions for workers and housewives who had received little or no formal education, and he respected her as a teacher and colleague, although her uncle had forced her to give up her teacher training when her father had died, a few months before she was due to take her final examinations. He looked down at Harry. 'Breakfast in the hall in five minutes, boy.'

'Yes, sir.'

'See you later, Harry.' Sali stooped to receive her son's kiss. Sensing that it was reluctantly given, with a sideways glance at his playmates, she realized it was probably one of the last he'd give her in public for a long time.

'Bye, Mam.' Whooping like an Indian, Harry raced across the yard.

'He's come a long way this term.' Mr Griffiths failed to suppress a grin as Harry pulled down his lower eyelids with his thumbs, stuck his index fingers in his ears and wiggled his tongue at his best friend, Dewi.

'So I see.' Sali knew exactly who had taught Harry to make that face and she resolved to have a word with Joey.

'We'd like to move him out of the babies' and into the first class, if that's all right with you.'

Sali looked doubtful. 'I don't want him growing up too fast.'

'He's bored where he is and you were the one who taught him to read. I'd like to do it today if I have your permission.'

'You have it, Mr Griffiths,' Sali agreed grudgingly, recognizing that the headmaster was better placed to oversee Harry's progress within the school than she was.

'Off to your soup kitchen?'

'Father Kelly's kitchen,' she amended.

'You have enough donations?'

'For the moment. You?' she enquired anxiously.

'For the moment,' he echoed. 'The superintendent of the Neath police force held a collection in his station and sent me a postal order for two pounds fourteen shillings and sixpence yesterday.'

'You cashed it?'

'I did. But if the strikers find out—'

'They'd assume that the Neath police, like all right-thinking individuals, understand their grievances and support them.' Sali repeated a remark Lloyd had made to a member of the strike committee who had argued against accepting donations collected after a football match between the soldiers and the striking miners. 'No one wants to see children starve, Mr Griffiths.'

A teacher walked into the yard and rang a handbell.

'You're right, Mrs Jones. What is important is that the children are fed. Not where the money comes from to do it.'

'As long as you don't stretch the point too far and accept donations from the Collieries' Company or Leonard Llewellyn,' she smiled.

'Those I turned down the first week of the strike. If you'll excuse me, I must go and help serve breakfast.'

'Good morning, Mr Griffiths, and thank you for your interest in Harry.' Sali walked down the road and headed for the centre of town on her way to the Catholic Hall in Trinity Road. When she crossed Tonypandy Square, a woman carrying twins in a shawl, wrapped around herself and both babies, accosted her.

'Mrs Jones, you probably don't remember me . . .' she began hesitatingly.

'Of course I do, Mrs Richards, you were in one of my classes, and these,' Sali admired the twins, 'I take it, are the reason you stopped coming.'

Beryl Richards pointed to the Colliery Cottages across the road. 'I live there.' She leaned closer to Sali and whispered. 'Victor . . . Mr Evans gave us some coal yesterday.'

Expecting Beryl Richards to ask for more, Sali said, 'Victor risked prosecution—'

'I know that, Mrs Jones,' Beryl interrupted. 'Not many colliers are prepared to help the families of the non-union men but Mr Evans is. And people round here say that you and Father Kelly serve anyone who comes to your soup kitchen, so I wondered if you'd do something for Mrs Hardy and her family who live in the huts.'

Sali glanced at the row of dilapidated wooden huts that fringed one side of the square. The entrepreneurs who had sunk the first collieries had erected them as temporary housing for their bachelor workers; half a century later they were still in use, housing the poorest of the poor. The wooden walls were rotting, the glass in most of the windowpanes had been replaced by cardboard, and it wasn't only Mr Evans and Lloyd who called them 'a bloody disgrace'. She'd heard the traders in Dunraven Street describing them as exactly that, too.

'Do you know Mrs Hardy, Mrs Jones? Lucy Hardy?'

Sali recalled a painfully thin, fair-haired woman, who always seemed to have a baby in her arms and several children clinging to her skirts. 'Yes, I believe so.'

'Her youngest boy died last week, her baby not an hour ago. Her husband pawned the last of their furniture when the boy died to buy a coffin. I gave her some coal but they've had no food for days. If you could send a jug of soup down from the Catholic Hall she could feed the other children. Her husband isn't Catholic but Lucy and the children are—'

'It's like you heard, Mrs Richards. We don't ask questions about anyone's religion or politics in the Catholic Hall kitchen,' Sali said firmly.

'The Hardys are too weak to walk up there.'

'Will Mrs Hardy see me?'

'She's in no condition to stop anyone from visiting her, Mrs Jones.' Mrs Richards led the way across the square and opened the door of the first hut she came to. Sali stooped to enter and found herself in a single darkened, bare room. Four children, all pale, emaciated, their stomachs swollen from hunger, lay wrapped in a single blanket on the floorboards in front of a pot-bellied iron stove, which, judging by the temperature in the room, had only just been lit. The walls bore splinter marks and Sali guessed they had held shelves that had ended up in the stove.

A ragged blanket strung on a rope nailed to the walls, curtained off a corner of the room. Beryl Richards pushed it aside and Sali saw Lucy Hardy also lying on the floor curled in a blanket. Next to her lay a grey-white baby, still as a waxwork. Sali froze; there was a pinched look about Lucy's nostrils and a far away, unfocused expression in her eyes that intimated she would soon be in the same state.

A man crouched on the floor beside them holding a cup of water. He glanced up and Sali saw a flicker of hostility in his eyes. The last vestige of a ragged pride that had prevented him from seeking help until it was too late.

Sali looked from Beryl, who was weighed down by her twins, to the man and back to the children. None of them was in a fit state to walk to Connie's shop let alone the soup kitchen. Removing her coat, Sali laid it over Lucy and went outside.

The nearest person was an absurdly young-looking constable with red curls spilling out from beneath his helmet, but moved by the urgency of the situation Sali didn't stop to look for someone she knew. 'Will you help me?' She added, 'Please,' when she saw him hesitate.

He and the officer closest to him walked warily towards her.

'Constable Huw Davies, ma'am, can I help you?'

'Will you go to the Catholic Hall and Rodney's shop for me please. Tell Mrs Rodney that Sali Jones needs a basic parcel of food, especially bread, sent here as soon as possible, and ask Father Kelly to call right away with the doctor and a jug of soup. A baby's just died, the mother is seriously ill and there's four starving children and a man who haven't eaten in days in this house.'

The officer pushed opened the door just as Beryl was leaving the curtained alcove. He saw Lucy lying on the floor with her baby and the children huddled in front of the stove. He shouted to his companion, 'You go to the shop, Wainwright, I'll go to the Catholic Hall.'

Joyce Palmer stood in the doorway of her lodging house, effectively blocking it. 'I will not allow any girl in my employ to have gentlemen visitors.'

'I am not visiting, Mrs Palmer,' Victor explained patiently. 'Megan's suitcase is heavy and I assumed she'd be sleeping in the attic.' He held up the battered trunk, which Megan's uncle had discarded as too large and cumbersome to take to Canada with him.

'I can carry Miss Williams' case upstairs, Mrs Palmer.' Wearing his cape and carrying his helmet, Sergeant Martin joined them.

'There's no need to trouble yourself, Sergeant Martin,' Joyce said stiffly.

'No trouble, Mrs Palmer.' He looked Victor up and down, then stared at him. 'I know you, don't I?'

'We haven't been introduced.' One police officer in uniform was very like another to Victor, but there was something about the way the Sergeant was looking at Megan that set his teeth on edge.

'You're Lloyd Evans' brother.'

'That's right.' Victor met the sergeant's steady gaze.

'Your father and brother are on the strike committee.'

'It's not illegal to be a union man or sit on a strike committee,' Victor replied.

'Yet!' Sergeant Lamb strode up the street and joined them. 'In my experience, wherever there's trouble you'll find the union men. Like last night, when my brother's skull was fractured and several men were scalded.'

'The men on the committee try to stop any fighting before it starts,' Victor countered loyally.

'How is your brother, Sergeant Lamb?' Joyce enquired, anxious to break up the tense confrontation.

'Gravely ill, Mrs Palmer. He hadn't regained consciousness when I left the Infirmary this morning.'

'I am sorry to hear that,' Sergeant Martin said.

'As we've found out to our cost when dealing with the savages in this town, "sorry" doesn't mend broken bodies.' Sergeant Lamb pushed past Victor and Joyce and entered the house.

Joyce moved from the doorway. 'That suitcase does look heavy, Mr Evans, so I will allow you into the house just this once. If you'd follow me.'

Victor removed his cap and waited for Megan to walk in ahead of him. Sergeant Martin placed his helmet on his head, gave Megan and Victor one last look and walked past them.

'I asked Lena, that's the girl I took from the workhouse, to make up the second bed in her room for you. It's next to my own on the attic floor.' Joyce walked up the stairs and Victor and Megan followed.

The first oak staircase was wide and imposing, the second marginally less so. The pine staircase that led from the second to the third floor was so narrow it would have been difficult for two adults to pass. The fourth was scarcely wide enough for a grown man, and Victor was forced to carry Megan's case in front of him.

Joyce passed the first door on the uncarpeted landing. 'That is my room.' She pointed to two doors opposite. 'The linen and storage cupboards. You'll find all the bed linen, spare pillows, blankets and upstairs dusters, and cleaning cloths in them, but I keep both locked, so you'll have to come to me for the key, Megan.' She opened the second door. 'You may leave Megan's suitcase here, Mr Evans.'

Victor dropped it inside the door.

'After you've unpacked you'll find me in the kitchen, Megan. It's at the end of the long corridor to the right of the stairs. Don't be long. I'll see you out, Mr Evans.'

Victor gave Megan a reassuring smile. He saw Joyce watching them and went ahead of her back down the stairs.

Megan walked into the bedroom. It was surprisingly large and clean, but it was also cold and cheerless. The walls were whitewashed plaster, the floorboards unvarnished pine. Two iron bedsteads stood with their heads against the wall opposite the door. Both were made up with white cotton sheets, pillowcases and grey army blankets that served as bedcovers. An iron-framed camping washstand furnished with tin basin, jug, chamber pot and slop bucket stood between them. The curtains were grey cotton. A pine wardrobe and chest of drawers completed the furniture.

'The top drawers in the chest are empty and there's plenty of space in the wardrobe. Your bed is the one nearest the window.'

A scrawny girl, who looked no more than twelve years old, hovered shyly in the doorway. She had close-cropped, curly brown hair and brown eyes, and was dressed in a khaki work overall, thick black woollen stockings and surprisingly good quality leather

70

boots, considering the rest of her clothes. In a decent dress and with longer, fashionably dressed hair she might have been considered attractive.

Megan held out her hand. 'You must be Lena. I'm Megan.'

Lena gave her a limp handshake. 'Mrs Palmer told me last night that you'd be coming today. I hope we can be friends. I haven't had one, not since I left the workhouse.'

'I'm sure we will be,' Megan smiled.

'It's hard work here, but not as hard as the workhouse, and the food's much better. Were you in the workhouse?'

'No, I've been living with my uncle.'

'You have relatives?' Lena said in amazement.

'Yes,' Megan answered briefly.

'You're lucky. My mam and dad died of typhoid when I was six. No one wanted me so I was put in the orphanage. Don't your relatives mind you working here?'

'My family need the money I'll earn.'

'Mrs Palmer pays good wages. I've bought loads of things since I've been here. Like my boots.' Lena held out her foot so Megan could admire them, before backing to the top of the stairs. 'I shouldn't have come up to see you. It's time for me to lay the table for the lodgers' last breakfast sitting.'

'I'll be down as soon as I've unpacked to give you a hand.'

The girl ran down the stairs. Megan lifted her case on to her bed and sprung the locks. The first thing she removed was a framed photograph of her and Victor that had been taken on a day trip to Barry Island in the summer. Encouraged by Joey who had travelled with them, only to disappear half an hour after their arrival, they had posed for the seaside photographer with their arms wrapped around one another.

She only had to glance at it to relive that glorious holiday. Victor had never kissed her so often and shamelessly as during the course of that day – on the beach, later when they had sat in a quiet spot overlooking the sea to picnic on the sandwiches she had made for them, and finally on the railway station while they had waited for a train to take them back to the Rhondda.

Embarrassed, she had tried to remonstrate with him but he'd

insisted that stationmasters were more inclined to turn a blind eye when lovers were saying goodbye. Only they hadn't been saying goodbye – not then.

She ran her fingertips lightly over his image then looked for somewhere to stand the frame. The chest of drawers was on the opposite side of the room to her bed. Setting it on the window sill close to her pillow, she pulled off her gloves. Rummaging in her suitcase, she found the plain wooden box that held her few pieces of jewellery, all of which had been presents from Victor. Removing the silver chain he had given her on her last birthday, she gently slipped the engagement ring from her finger, threaded it on to the chain and fastened it around her neck. Opening the top button on her blouse she tucked both chain and ring beneath her collar and refastened the button. Taking her spare underclothes from the case, she carried them to the chest of drawers.

It didn't take her long to unpack and hang her three dresses in the wardrobe. She stowed her empty suitcase on top until she could take it to the box room.

Wondering how long she was going to have to call this bleak room home, she slipped on her calico apron, tied it around her waist, checked that her hair was tidy and went down the stairs.

Chapter 5

TRAUMATIZED BY the heartbreaking conditions in the hut, beset by feelings of impotency and inadequacy, Sali waited with Father Kelly outside the curtain that screened off the corner. When the doctor joined them after examining Mrs Hardy, he glanced at the children who were sitting around Beryl Richards, drinking soup from cups she had scavenged from the neighbours, before beckoning Sali and Father Kelly outside. It was cold in the square but Sali found the air easier to breathe than the smoke and tragedy laden atmosphere indoors.

'Lucy Hardy's dying and it won't be long. An hour at the most.' Overworked, tired and injured to misery, it didn't occur to the doctor to be tactful.

'Starvation?' Father Kelly couldn't keep the disgust from his voice.

'The death certificate will cite pneumonia, same as the child. The boy who died nine days ago had tuberculosis as cause. But your diagnosis is probably more accurate, Father.'

'That man and those poor children will need all the help they can get.' The priest forced himself to concentrate on practical matters.

'I'll arrange for the children to be admitted to the workhouse.'

'Surely not, Doctor,' Sali protested.

'It's the best place for them, Mrs Jones,' the doctor insisted. 'They're weak, undernourished and they've been in contact with TB. They'll get warm beds in the infirmary, food and rest, and when they're strong enough—'

'That man won't be in a position to take them back. Not until the strike breaks, and,' the priest looked back at the hut, 'even when it does, he'll need to save six months' wages to get his furniture out of hock.'

'I can't do any more here, Father, and there are others who need me.' The doctor snapped his bag shut. 'I'll send the undertaker round. They'll need a coffin – on second thoughts I'll tell him to wait a couple of hours. The mother and child can share one. I'll ask the Distress Committee to pay the bill and arrange a pauper's grave in Trealow cemetery. Goodbye, Father Kelly, Mrs Jones.'

'The Distress Committee's paid out more for coffins than food in the last month.' Father Kelly watched the doctor stop to talk to Captain McCormack of the Salvation Army and Reverend Williams. 'To be sure, we're all flocking round now it's too late.'

'Don't be so hard on yourself, Father. It might not have been too late if Mr Hardy had asked for help sooner,' Sali said quietly.

'It might at that. But that poor baby's corpse and those children!' Father Kelly closed his eyes as though he could blot out the images. 'They're nothing but skin and bone, and that's not enough to keep body and soul together.'

'We came as soon as we heard.' The Reverend and the Captain joined them.

'We can assist Mr Hardy with food, clothes and even furniture. Some of our sponsors have been very generous,' Reverend Williams explained.

'The committee would like to formally ask you to help with the distribution of relief, Mrs Jones,' Captain McCormack added. 'With you being the Evans' housekeeper and two of them being strike leaders we thought you might get to hear of the worst cases before they reach this stage.'

'If colliery workers couldn't afford to pay their union dues, the last people they'll go to for help is the union men.' Father Kelly stamped his feet, ostensibly to keep out the cold, but Sali thought sheer frustration a more likely cause. 'My, but it's bitter today.'

'We need to organize the women,' Sali said thoughtfully. 'Mrs Richards didn't have coal enough for her own family until yesterday, yet she found a neighbour to care for her two older children so she could come here today to light the Hardy's stove.

And I know that if she'd had any food, she would have shared it with the Hardy children.'

'You're right, Mrs Jones.' Father Kelly looked to the Reverend Williams. 'It's the duty of everyone on the Distress Committee to gather as many donations as we can, but I suggest we leave it to the women to decide what's needed most outside of the soup kitchens. Now, if you'll excuse me, I'm off to the pawnbroker to see if I can get that poor woman's bed out of hock so she can at least draw her last breath in comfort.' He lowered his voice to a whisper. 'Damn Mark Hardy's bloody pride.'

'Did I just hear Father Kelly say what I thought I heard him say?' Captain McCormack asked, as the priest stomped off.

'Of course not, Captain,' Reverend Williams answered. 'Everyone knows priests never swear.'

Victor was opening his front door when Ned Morgan, snorting and puffing like a steam engine, hurried towards him.

'Have you seen your father and Lloyd? There's trouble on the corner of Gilfach Road and Primrose Street and your Joey's in the thick of it.'

Victor didn't stop to ask what kind of trouble. 'If they're not in the house, try the Empire Theatre. They were talking about organizing another mass meeting.' He put his head down and ran.

A few minutes later he saw a crowd of colliers blocking the road. Ned had been right. Joey was in the centre of the front line. Abel Adams, an assistant overman who had been promoted on Lloyd's recommendation, stood flanked by two firemen, brothers Sam and Fred Winter. All three looked terrified as they faced a solid line of colliers.

Luke Thomas, one of the most militant strikers who had frequently accused Lloyd of being 'soft' when negotiating with management, was standing next to Joey. 'You can't go any further, Abel,' Luke warned. 'We've received information that you are doing more than maintenance. You're cutting coal.'

'Come on, Luke,' Abel yelled back. 'The only coal we've cut is the load we used to fuel the engines that drive the pumps.'

'If we don't do essential maintenance, the mine will flood and there'll be no point in striking, because none of us will have a pit left to work in,' Sam shouted.

Victor walked up slowly and positioned himself side on, in the narrow space between the colliers and the workers.

'If you are doing work other than your own, you're blacklegs, the lot of you.' Luke pushed his face close to Abel's.

Victor had heard his father and Lloyd complain about the difficulty of keeping Luke in check but there was no denying that if Abel, Sam and Fred were doing anything other than essential maintenance underground, they were, in effect, blacklegs.

'Please, boys, we're only trying to keep the pit open for all of us,' Abel pleaded.

'Go back or you'll get a ducking in the river,' Luke threatened. When Abel stood his ground, he snatched his cap and tossed it to the men behind him. Joey caught it.

'We're not cutting coal for the market,' Sam refuted. 'Just enough to fuel the pump engines.'

'If you're cutting coal you're a blackleg!' Luke decreed.

'Give Abel his cap back, Joey.' Victor spoke softly, but his words cut across the street like a whiplash.

The colliers fell silent. Before Joey could hand Abel his cap, it was seized from his hand.

'I might have known you'd be as yellow as your brother,' Luke jeered at Victor. 'Didn't you hear what they said?' He pointed to Abel, Sam and Fred. 'They've condemned themselves out of their own mouths. They're cutting coal and that's doing other people's work. We've every right to stop them drawing wages and living off the fat of the land while our wives and children starve. We're fighting for a decent wage for everyone and no blackleg is going to prevent us from doing just that. Nothing and no one will.' He raised his voice to an orator's pitch. 'Not police batons, nor cracked skulls. They can beat us – they can starve us – they can break our bones – they can even kill us – but they will find hundreds willing to step up and take the place of every striker they murder. Management, police, soldiers, blacklegs,' Luke spat in the road, 'none of them will succeed in crushing us. It's time we showed these blacklegs what we think of them, boys. We'll stop every man from going to the colliery—'

'Then none of us will have a pit to work in when the strike is over,' Victor interrupted.

'If we don't, it will be down to the likes of soft buggers like you and your brother who wouldn't stand up to management from the very beginning, Victor Evans. You and your "essential maintenance" agreements.' Luke tensed his fists and turned to Sam, Fred and Abel. 'If it wasn't for boot-lickers like you, management would have caved in during the first week of this strike. They'd never have risked the colliery flooding and we would all be in work now with every one of our demands met. A fair and living wage for all and extra for working in dangerous places.'

The colliers shouted noisy approval and moved *en masse* behind Luke.

Victor stepped close to Abel. 'Why don't you three go home, just for now.'

Abel, Sam and Fred needed no second bidding. They backed away before turning round and racing off up Primrose Street.

'Lena's willing enough, but she's used to obeying orders without thinking about what she's doing. She can't be trusted to remember more than one thing at a time or even to do something properly unless you watch her. I've found out to my cost that workhouse standards can't be applied to a lodging house,' Joyce warned Megan, as they washed and dried the dishes from the 'third' and last sitting of breakfast. 'And the worse thing about running a lodging house is that the chores never end. As soon as one lot go to bed the next lot get up.'

'My uncle and his brothers worked different shifts, so I know what that's like.' Megan dried the last breakfast plate and set it on top of the stack on the shelf.

'You know where you are with colliery workers. They're either on the six till two, the two till ten or the night shift and once they're underground they can't nip back, stick their heads around the door and say, "I've a spare ten minutes, Mrs Palmer, any chance of a cup of tea and a scone in the lodgers' sitting room?"

And no matter how busy you are, you dare not refuse,' she said sternly. 'This lot aren't averse to going to the Collieries' Company with their complaints. And that only makes my job all the harder.'

'I understand, Mrs Palmer.'

'Once a policeman goes out through that door you never know when he's coming back. I thought they would start working regular hours once the army were brought in but if anything it's been worse since the troops arrived. There's trouble every single night and sometimes they end up working for ten or twelve hours straight, only to go back out on the streets after a couple of hours' sleep. You've no idea of the number of spoiled meals I've had to throw out in the past month. That's why I've put as many stews and casseroles on the menu as I can get away with. They're easier to keep and heat up.' Joyce set the last of the cutlery on to the tin tray on the wooden draining board and tipped the water out of the enamel bowl down the drain. 'There's a timetable for making the beds and cleaning the bedrooms pinned behind the kitchen door. I used to do it with Lena, but now you're here, you can take over. Knock on the bedroom doors before entering. I've tried to put men on the same shift in the same room but sometimes they swap shifts or work overtime, so they could be in bed when the room is supposed to be empty. And always take Lena with you. I don't want either of you girls working alone in the bedrooms. Do you understand what I am telling you?'

'I'll be careful, Mrs Palmer,' Megan assured her.

'You and Victor Evans have been courting for some time, haven't you?' Joyce fished.

'Two years.'

'Is it serious between you two?'

Megan thought for a moment before answering. Deciding there was no point in concealing the truth from her employer, she pulled out the chain and engagement ring from beneath her collar. 'He asked me to marry him this morning and when I said yes, gave me this.'

'It's very pretty.' Joyce admired the ring. 'I take it you won't be telling your father about your engagement.'

Megan knew Joyce wasn't asking a question. 'My father disapproves of Catholics.'

'I gathered as much last night, but the Evans' have always struck me as a fine family, apart from Joey, that is. That boy is far too wild for his own and any unsuspecting young girl's good. But Victor is very different. You are a lucky girl, even if you will have to wait until you're twenty-one to marry. How old are you now?'

'Nineteen last August.'

Joyce beamed; Megan had given her the answer she'd been looking for. Desperate for help in the house, she was relieved to discover that Megan would be with her for more than a year, because whichever way the strike went, the one thing she could be sure of, was that there would be lodgers in the house. Policemen or miners, it made little difference to her workload apart from the amount of dirt the miners carried in with them after their shift.

'Right, as soon as you've dried that cutlery you can see if Lena's finished laying the table for the next sitting. If she has, you two can start on the bedrooms. Check the rota for changing the sheets and towels. I'd never cope if we waited until Monday to change the lot, so I do two rooms a day Monday to Thursday, one room and our beds on Friday, and another on Saturday.'

'You wash every day?'

Joyce's smile broadened, as Megan's face fell. 'I send the bed linen, towels and the men's socks, shirts and underpants to the Chinese laundry. The tea towels and our personal laundry I'll expect you to do on a Monday morning. You did say that you can wash and iron?'

'I did.' Megan breathed a sigh of relief.

'It's hard enough to cook and clean for forty men without doing their washing as well.' Joyce rinsed out the sink. 'Time I started preparing the beef stew for dinner and you cleaned those bedrooms. Give me a call as soon as you have finished one, so I can inspect it.'

Sali stayed in the hut with the Hardys while Beryl Richards took her twins to the neighbour looking after her older children. She returned with a pillowcase and they wrapped the baby's corpse in it. Father Kelly arrived with Connie's delivery cart containing the Hardy's bed and bedclothes, reclaimed from the Pawnbroker. The delivery boy, Father Kelly and Mark carried the bed behind the curtain and Sali helped Beryl to make it up and lift Lucy into it. When she was as comfortable as they could make her, Mark brought his children behind the curtain to say goodbye to their mother, but Lucy was too far gone to do anything other than smile weakly at them.

Too bewildered by the events of the day even to cry, the children allowed Sali to usher them back in front of the stove, and she told them a story while Beryl cut and handed them slices of bread from one of the loaves Connie had sent.

Father Kelly gave Lucy and the dead baby the last rites then left Lucy with Mark in what passed for privacy, and sat with the children on the floor. They didn't have long to wait. Lucy Hardy stopped breathing at a few minutes before ten in the morning.

Alerted by Mark's sobs, Father Kelly led him out from behind the curtain. Ignoring his children, Mark slumped on the floor and sank his head in his hands. Beryl followed Sali into the screened-off alcove and gazed at the emaciated corpse.

'At least the poor woman passed away with an easy mind, knowing her children had eaten.'

Beryl's words were no consolation to Sali, or Sali suspected, Father Kelly. She sensed the priest was convinced that he had been derelict in his duty, but she was too guilt-ridden herself to remind him that given the demands of the parish and the problems wrought by the strike, he couldn't help everyone.

Sali found it unbearably painful to think that she had passed the Hardy's hut twice a day since the strike had begun on her way to the Catholic Hall and done absolutely nothing for the family. Lloyd would argue that it had been Mark Hardy's place to ask for help, but in a close-knit community like the Rhondda, she couldn't accept that. Everyone should have known about the Hardy's plight weeks ago and Sali decided she would ask Lloyd and his father to make a list of all the non-union men so members of the Distress Committee could visit them, ensuring nothing like this would happen to any other family.

Beryl left to fetch a bowl, soap and flannel from her own house to wash the corpse. Sali listened to Father Kelly trying to reason with Mark on the other side of the makeshift curtain while she waited for her to return.

'The children are weak, Mr Hardy. They'll be needing good food and medical care and they'll get just that in the Infirmary. As soon as they've recovered and you get your home together again, you can take them from the workhouse—'

'No workhouse!' Mark screamed hysterically. 'I promised Lucy, no workhouse! We said we'd stay together no matter what!'

'Now, I'm sure that you promised Mrs Hardy you'd do the best for the little ones. But you heard the doctor the same as me. They need more care than you can give them at present.'

Sali thought rapidly. Lloyd wasn't one to turn his back on anyone in real need and the house next door was practically fully furnished. If she could persuade him to give it to Mr Hardy, she would make sure that the Hardy children received as much attention, food and medicine as they would in the Infirmary . . .

'You can't feed all the hungry children in the valley, no more than you can help every destitute family, Mrs Jones.' Beryl had lifted the blanket and was watching her. 'I could tell from the expression on your face that you're thinking of taking in the children. Don't! Better the parish go broke trying to look after everyone who is living below the breadline. Then management will have to give in to the strikers' demands. That's what my Alun says. And once the pit reopens, Mark Hardy will have a wage coming in so he'll be able to furnish the house and get the children back.' Beryl set the bowl of warm water she had brought on the floor and unbuttoned Lucy's nightdress.

'And who's going to look after the children while he's at work?' Sali took a flannel from the bowl, wrung it out and rubbed soap on to it.

'Why me, of course. The couple of shillings a widower pays out to have his children cared for can come in handy. I looked after Bert Rees's two until he decided that, strike or no strike, he was better off back labouring on his father's farm in Carmarthen.' She removed the nightdress from the corpse, took the flannel from Sali and began washing Lucy.

'He left a family farm to become a miner?' Sali asked in surprise.

'Tenanted farm. If you ask me he's a fool. Tenants have even less rights than colliers.'

When Beryl had finished washing the body, Sali replaced the flannel in the tin bowl. She looked around for somewhere dry to put the soap and balanced it on the window sill.

'Poor thing only has the nightgown she was wearing,' Beryl commented.

Sali straightened her back. 'I'll go up to the house and get a clean one of mine.'

'You don't have to do that.'

'I have too many,' Sali lied.

'And you haven't hocked them?' Beryl asked suspiciously.

'I'll be back in ten minutes.' Sali moved the curtain aside. Mark was still slumped with his back to the wall; his head buried in his hands. Father Kelly shook his head as she approached, but ignoring the priest's warning she crouched down beside him. 'Mr Hardy?' She touched his hand.

He looked at her and she recoiled from the naked pain in his eyes.

'I know someone who owns a house. It's empty and furnished. I could ask if you could have it. You wouldn't have to pay rent until the strike ends—'

'No!' Mark's features contorted in hatred. 'You'd like to see me grovel, wouldn't you, bitch? But I'll take no bloody charity, not from you, nor from anyone.' He grabbed one of his small daughters. Terrified by his outburst, she tried to wriggle free but he held her fast. 'I know who you are. You're Billy Evans' housekeeper. He and his cronies organized this bloody strike and this,' he waved his hand in the direction of the curtain, 'is the result. Women and children starving to death for his damned politics.' Tears poured unchecked down Mark's face but he continued to yell at her. 'You and that damned priest have done enough charitable deeds here today. Does it make you feel good, dishing out crumbs to the poor? Is it enough to buy you a place in heaven? My poor Lucy didn't deserve to starve to death, nor did my two babies.' He broke down and began to sob. 'Get out!' He rose clumsily to his feet and pushed her towards the door. 'I'll look after my own. And I don't need help from no bloody priest or do-gooder.'

Sali opened the door and fled across the square as fast as her legs could carry her.

Dressed in a green canvas overall that Mrs Palmer had given her to do the 'dirty work', her red-gold curls hidden beneath a matching dust cap, Megan waited for Lena to open the door of a bedroom on the first floor of the lodging house. Lena picked up the two empty slop buckets she'd carried upstairs and walked in, Megan tightened her grip on the brush and dustpan she was holding and prepared to follow, but she halted, overcome by the stench that wafted out to greet them.

Even from the doorway, Megan could see that the chamber pots under the double bed and two singles were full to the point of overflowing; the pillowcases were stained with greasy patches of hair pomade, the sheets smudged with bootblack. Piles of soiled shirts, drawers, combinations and socks cascaded from a laundry bag that hung from a hook on the wall next to the wardrobe. Both washstands were filthy, encrusted with dried soap thick with hairs. The washing bowls were brimming with grey, scummy water. The soap in the dishes had melted into pools of jellied fat. Wet towels were draped over the beds and the floor, spreading water stains on the blankets and floorboards. Books, magazines, playing cards, sock suspenders and, to Megan's embarrassment, postcards of girls dressed in feathers and beads and not much else, were scattered over every surface.

'This is disgusting!' After cleaning up after her uncle and his brothers for almost six years, Megan had no illusions about bachelors' habits. But no matter how tired, or drunk, they'd been, her uncle and his brothers had always made their way down to the outside ty bach at night and the only chamber pots she'd had to empty had been Daisy's and Sam's, and not even Sam's since his fifth birthday. Picking her way carefully around the mess, she went to the windows and lifted both casements as high as they would go. Glacial air blasted into the room, along with rain, and smuts from the neighbouring chimneys.

'The worst is when they tip the chamber pots over or throw their clothes into them.' Lena lifted the lid on the slop pail and emptied a wash bowl into it.

Steeling herself, Megan slid a chamber pot out from beneath a bed and emptied it into the second pail. When the chamber pots and toilet china were empty, she replaced the lids on the slop buckets and helped Lena haul them outside the door.

'Mrs Palmer and I usually take those straight downstairs and tip them in the outside ty bach before bringing up clean water for the jugs and cleaning,' Lena said diffidently.

'I can carry them myself. You make a start on stripping the beds.'

'Oh no you don't. Never alone in the bedrooms, Megan, remember.' Mrs Palmer walked up the stairs towards them.

'Sorry, I forgot, Mrs Palmer,' Megan apologized.

'Don't again.' Joyce handed Megan a key. 'To the linen cupboard. I meant to give it to you before you came up. The soiled linen for the laundry goes in the small storeroom next to the scullery. Lena will show you where it is.'

'Yes, Mrs Palmer.' Lena smiled, pleased to be given the responsibility.

'I overheard you complain about the state of the room.'

'It's a disgusting mess, Mrs Palmer,' Megan reiterated.

Joyce peered around the door. 'It's about average. In my experience single men who live in lodging houses fall into three categories: thoughtful, thoughtless and downright filthy. If you stay in the business you'll find all three in every walk of life. Police officers and colliers may be at odds in Tonypandy now, but I've seen men in both jobs who live like pigs and that's probably an insult to pigs. Here, Lena, you take Megan up and show her where the bed linen and towels are kept while I gather this laundry ready to take downstairs.'

Sali knocked on the door of the hut. Father Kelly opened it and she

84

looked cautiously inside. There was no sign of the children or Mark Hardy.

'I've brought a nightdress for Mrs Hardy.' She held out a brown paper bag.

'Come in.' Father Kelly closed the door behind her and they walked to the stove. 'I wasn't sure you'd come back but I'm glad you did. You do know that Mr Hardy didn't mean those dreadful things he said to you?'

'I know how it feels to lose someone you love.' Sali thought of her own father and Harry's father, Mansel, who had been murdered by Owen Bull before he could marry her. 'How you can feel so angry and bitter, you want to lash out at the world.'

'And I'm sure that's all Mark Hardy was doing, God bless him.' Father Kelly crossed himself.

'Have the children gone to the workhouse?' Sali didn't want to discuss Mark Hardy's outburst. She had run from the hut with his shouts ringing in her ears and hadn't stopped shaking until she'd reached her own kitchen. Glad that no one had been at home to see her, it had taken her half an hour to compose herself and another ten minutes to find the nightdress and brace herself to return.

'They left a few minutes after you. The doctor sent the ambulance for them. Mrs Richards' husband, Alun, and a couple of the other men came round and took Mr Hardy off to the Pandy for a wake, although given that none of them have two farthings to rub together it's anyone's guess as to what they'll be drinking. Mrs Richards went to her neighbour's to feed her twins. I offered to stay in case the undertaker arrives with the coffin before she gets back.' He took the bag containing the nightdress from Sali. 'I'll give this to her.'

'I could wait.'

'One of us should be at the soup kitchen.'

'Then I'll go.' Sali took his hint. The priest was telling her to leave as tactfully as he knew how, and she was no more anxious to see Mark Hardy again than, she suspected, he was her.

'You know how the food stocks have a habit of disappearing if one of us isn't around to keep a close eye. Not that anyone ever

85

takes more than a handful of vegetables or a few slices of bread. It's just that the "handfuls" mount up.'

'I'll make sure that the food is eaten in the hall, apart from the jugs of soup and slices of bread that are bought by families or sent out to the sick.'

'I'll be up as soon as Mrs Richards comes back.' Father Kelly patted Sali's arm as he walked her to the door. 'If you're needed here again I'll send for you.'

'I won't be,' she said unequivocally. 'Mr Hardy is best left with people he knows.'

'If I can arrange an emergency meeting of the Distress Committee to make sure nothing like this happens again while the strike is on, you'll come?'

Sali opened the door. 'I'll be there.'

The atmosphere in the foyer of the Empire Theatre was electric with tension. Luke Thomas and the men he'd recruited to stop Abel Adams and the Winter brothers from reaching the pithead, had sought out and confronted Billy Evans with their version of the morning's events. Luke had demanded the strike committee set up an official picket line to stop the men he considered blacklegs from trying to reach the pit again the following morning.

Victor, Lloyd, Ned Morgan and half a dozen members of the committee were standing behind Billy. And although Billy was doing his best to remain calm, Luke wasn't the only man on the brink of losing his temper.

'First it was the pit ponies,' Luke ranted. 'Management moved the lot of them into the colliery most prone to flooding just to get public sympathy. We offered to go in and bring them up and what do the press report? The miners won't allow management in to feed the animals, they'd rather see them starve to death.'

'The ponies are all up now,' Billy interrupted, 'so what's your point, Luke?'

'The point is, you didn't see that we got credit for allowing management to bring them up.' Luke paused for the men standing behind him to nod a noisy agreement. 'You did sod all while the newspapers painted us as drunken, greedy, callous brutes, who were prepared to let dumb beasts starve to death to get ourselves fatter wage packets to spend on beer.'

'I can't control the press, Luke.'

'You can't control any bloody thing, Billy!' Luke exclaimed. 'You and your strike committee allowed management to bring in men to do "essential maintenance" And look what's happened? The bastard blacklegs are doing us out of our jobs by cutting coal.'

'Abel said he was only cutting coal to fuel the engines that drive the pumps.' Following his father's example, Victor lowered his voice in an attempt to defuse Luke's anger.

'Abel's a bloody liar,' bellowed one of Luke's men.

'The more we cave in to management's demands, the more unreasonable they tell the world we are,' Luke raged. 'Leonard Llewellyn goes down to feed the horses and rescue a stray cat and he gets hailed as a hero—'

'We have to keep talking to management and we have to work with them to ensure the pits remain in good condition,' Billy countered firmly. 'And that means allowing men in to do essential maintenance.'

'Why?' Luke demanded. 'The more work management's bloody, blacklegs lackeys do, the less urgency there'll be for the owners to negotiate with us. We want an end to this strike. The men are sick of it.'

'We are all sick of it.' Lloyd's patience was at an end, particularly with Joey after hearing Victor's account of the part he'd played on Luke's unofficial picket line that morning. 'But we have to allow overmen and firemen in to do essential maintenance or the pits will flood.'

'And their idea of essential maintenance is to set the blacklegs to cut coal,' Luke bit back.

'I'll set up another meeting with management—'

'The time for talking is over, Billy,' Luke roared, oblivious to the men around him glancing over their shoulders towards the doorway.

'Joseph James Evans.'

Joey took one look at Sergeant Martin flanked by a dozen constables and didn't attempt to deny his identity. 'Yes.'

'Luke Matthew Thomas?'

'Who wants to know?' Luke retorted belligerently.

'The law,' Sergeant Martin barked.

'I'm Luke Thomas, so go on, arrest me,' Luke challenged. Folding his arms across his chest, he glared defiantly at the sergeant and the officers ranged behind him.

All in good time.' The sergeant turned to Victor. 'Victor Sebastian Evans?'

Victor cringed as he always did whenever he heard his full name. Grateful, nevertheless, that his father had persuaded his mother to relegate Sebastian to his second name, he answered, 'Yes.'

'I am arresting all three of you on the charge of intimidating officials employed by the Glamorgan Colliery with the intent of preventing them from carrying out their lawful employment. If you gentlemen would come with me.'

'The hell we will,' Luke shouted to the cheers of his supporters.

The sergeant moved close to Luke and murmured, 'There are two ways of doing this, *Mr* Thomas. You can come along quietly and calmly of your own free will, or we can make you.'

Billy nodded to Victor and Joey. 'Go. I'll get the Federation solicitor to the police station as soon as I can.'

Lloyd clenched his fists until his finger joints showed white, but he watched impassively while the sergeant and his escort marched Victor, Joey and Luke out through the door.

'Abel's a reasonable man. I'll have a word with him and see if I can get him to drop the charges.' Billy ran his hands through his thick grey hair.

'It won't do any good.' Lloyd went to the door, and watched the police push his brothers and Luke Thomas through a crowd who cheered the prisoners and spat on the officers. 'I doubt that it's Abel and the Winter boys who are bringing the charges. It's management, and they've primed the police to do their dirty work for them. They are going for the easy targets first and loud-mouthed idiots like Luke are a gift.'

'And your brothers? Are you saying that they are out of control?'

'They were in the wrong place at the wrong time.' Lloyd looked his father in the eye. 'You do realize that no matter how hard every member of the strike committee tries to live by the letter of the law, we'll be the next to be arrested. And, if they've made a list, you can bet your last farthing that you and I are at the top.'

Chapter 6

IT TOOK an hour and a half of Lena and Megan's time to clean the bedroom to Megan's satisfaction. When they finished, the china toilet sets and marble surfaces of the washstands gleamed, as did the furniture Megan had asked Lena to polish with beeswax. The beds were made with fresh linen. The toilet jugs held clean water and Lena had laid out the men's shaving apparatus neatly next to the shaving mugs on the washstands. The room was icy but the nauseating stench had dissipated.

Megan picked up the brush, dustpan and cleaning cloths. She left them on the landing while she and Lena lugged the heavy slop pails downstairs and emptied them down the toilet in the yard. They returned upstairs with clean water and Megan consulted the list. But after two months in the lodging house Lena knew the routine by heart.

'Sergeant Martin's room is next. All we have to do then is make the beds and tidy the others in between the officers' shifts.' Lena opened the door next to the room they had cleaned. To Megan's relief it held a single bed and, in comparison with the first room, it was pristine.

The sheets and blankets had been folded back to the foot of the bed to air it, and although the linen was down for changing, it was unstained. The chamber pot was mercifully empty, and even the washstand didn't need more than a quick wipe down to mop up water splashes. A shaving mug, cut-throat razor, nail brush, boxed set of tortoiseshell hair brushes, jar of pomade, toothbrush, glass and toothpowder, soap in a clean dish, manicure set and large bottle of cologne were arranged with regimental precision on the marble surface next to the toilet set.

The slop pail held dirty washing water, the bowl had been wiped out, the linen bag that hung on the door knob outside the wardrobe was full of neatly folded clothes for the laundry. Megan looked around; unlike the other room there wasn't a single photograph, letter or even magazine to be seen.

'The sergeant's a tidy man,' Lena commented superfluously.

'So I see.'

'It usually takes Mrs Palmer and me less than half an hour to do his room.'

'What about the other rooms?' Megan wanted to know exactly what she had let herself in for.

'The rooms with the most beds are the worst. Friday and Saturday we clean the big rooms on the next floor. They each sleep eight in four double beds. It's a lot of work to get them straight.'

'Are there any others like this with just one bed?' Megan asked hopefully.

'Only Sergeant Lamb's. He's not as tidy as Sergeant Martin, but his room isn't as bad as the one we've just cleaned. Apart from the two largest and the sergeants' rooms, there are five that sleep six and one that sleeps two, but those two are real mucky pups.'

'Then it's just as well we don't have to do the laundry as well.' Megan stripped the sheets from the bed and set about remaking it. She couldn't help feeling there was something odd about a man who laid out his possessions in such a precise order. Sergeant Martin clearly liked everything in its allotted place and she wondered about his personal life, or even if he had one. She tried to guess his age – thirty or perhaps thirty-five? And there was no evidence of a wife, family or even girlfriend. Given the way he had looked at her, that made her feel more uneasy about him than ever.

'You've had a long day, Mrs Jones, and from the news we've heard, there's worse waiting for you at home. There's no need for you to come back after you've picked Harry up from school.' Father Kelly took the ladle from Sali, and her place behind the tureen. He carried on filling a row of enamel jugs with soup destined for the families who preferred to eat together at home and bought them from the kitchen for sixpence.

Trying not to think about what was happening to Joey and Victor in the police station, Sali murmured, 'I know I don't, but I will.' She slipped on her coat.

'Go on with you now, you look as tired as I feel.'

'We'll all have a good sleep . . .'

'Don't tell me, after the strike is over. You know, I've heard that phrase so often lately I've set it to music.' He took a deep breath and sang out to the tune of, 'After the Ball is Over' in his booming baritone, 'After the strike is over, after the strife is done, many a head that's broken . . .'

'What comes next?' Sali asked when he stopped.

'I have no idea. I haven't worked it out yet. Take care in the streets now,' he shouted after her.

Sali left the hall. It was three o'clock in the afternoon but twilight had fallen early, greying the streets and casting shadows over the rain-spattered terraces. She looked to the gate and looked again.

'Lloyd, am I glad to see you.' She hadn't realized how exhausted she was until she fell into his strong arms. 'Father Kelly told me that Joey and Victor have been arrested. I thought you'd be at the police station.'

'I knew you'd be worried if the news had reached here. My father didn't want me to wait in the police station with him because he thought it might make the situation worse. He's hoping that one member of the strike committee will be tolerated where more would be seen as a threat.'

'Father Kelly said the union solicitor was going to the police station. Will he be able to clear things up?'

'Frankly, no.' Lloyd tilted his umbrella over her head as a sudden shower driven by a bitter squall of wind gusted down the mountain. 'I was there when they were arrested. The charge is intimidation, and both of them were with Luke Thomas and his cronies when they threatened and turned back men who were trying to get to the pit to man the pumps. They'll have to go to trial.'

'I'm sorry, Lloyd.' She drew closer to him.

'Not as sorry as I am. I can understand Joey getting mixed up in

92

trouble, he always acts before he gets his brain in gear – but Victor?' He shook his head. 'He usually walks away from the likes of Luke Thomas.'

'Perhaps he was trying to protect Joey.'

'That would be just like him.' He folded her hand into the crook of his elbow and caressed her gloved fingers. 'You're not the only one who has heard gossip. I met Beryl Richards in Dunraven Street. She told me what happened this morning.'

'It was horrible. Oh, Lloyd, that poor woman . . .' The moment Sali reached the soup kitchen she had been besieged by volunteers and customers who'd demanded her undivided attention. They hadn't given her a minute to think about the Hardys. Lloyd's reminder conjured the tragedy anew. An image of Mark Hardy's face, contorted with hatred, came to mind and she shuddered from more than cold.

'She also told me what Mark Hardy said to you.'

'He was out of his mind with grief.' Sali was glad it was raining so Lloyd couldn't see her tears.

'He was out of his mind with drink when I last saw him,' Lloyd commented caustically. 'God only knows where the money came from but he could barely stand upright.'

'I can't blame him. Can you imagine what it must be like to lose two children and the person you love most in the world? You've no idea how glad I was to see you waiting at the gate for me just now.'

'After what's happened to Joey and Victor, believe me, I needed to see you more, sweetheart,' he said fervently.

'I wish I could do something for them.'

'My father's doing all that can be done so there's no point in us talking about it. The weather's foul and it's cold so I thought we'd go wild and use some of the coal Victor dug out of the drift to light the stove early and you can make us a mutton stew. Joey and Victor will be glad of it. It's freezing in the police cells.'

'You sound as though you're speaking from experience.'

'Joey's experience. He was blue with cold after he spent the night there for drunk and disorderly when he was sixteen.' He gave a grim smile. 'But my father soon warmed him when he got home.'

'I can make a vegetable stew. We haven't any mutton.'

'We have.'

She was horror struck. 'Lloyd, you didn't—'

'I haven't enticed a sheep from the mountain inside the house and chopped its head off in the basement, if that's what you're thinking.' Neither of them laughed. Since the onset of the strike, sheep stealing had taken over from drunkenness as the most common crime in the valleys. 'The farmer brought a leg of mutton down to the house this afternoon. He said he owed it to Victor for shoeing his horses and fixing his wagon.'

'I have to go back to the kitchen after I've picked up Harry. Our busiest time is between four and six.' Sali had never been so tempted to let Father Kelly down. The thought of making a stew in front of a warm fire with Lloyd, Harry and the rest of the family sitting around the table, reading, talking – but more likely arguing politics – made her long for the calmer days before the strike.

'I could take Harry home and prepare the vegetables. Then when you come back from the kitchen we can have a cosy evening by the fire and discuss our wedding. And don't say that it's the wrong time for a celebration.' He second-guessed what she was about to say. 'We need all the good times we can get, especially at the moment.'

'You know why I don't want to talk about our wedding just yet.'

'Sali—'

'But if you light the stove as soon as you get home with Harry, it will be warm enough to make a cake. I think we've enough flour and a spare egg for a fatless sponge. Joey and Victor will be back from the police station with your father, won't they?'

'That will depend on the success the solicitor has in reasoning with the police. From what I saw of them today, they didn't seem to be in a particularly reasonable mood.'

'Lloyd—'

'As I said, there's no point in discussing things that can't be changed. Here,' he handed her his umbrella, 'you take that with you when you walk back to the Catholic Hall. I'll tuck Harry under my coat. And here's my boy.' Lloyd stepped forward and swung Harry off his feet as he raced across the yard through the rain towards them.

'You beat up any policemen today, Uncle Lloyd?' Harry asked cheerfully.

'Wherever did you get the idea that I beat up policemen?' Lloyd was shocked both by the question and Harry's assumption that it was something that he'd do.

'Bertie Thomas. He said his dad does it all the time and he's a striker like you. His mam doesn't like it but his dad says she has to lump it.'

Lloyd exchanged troubled glances with Sali. Bertie Thomas was Luke's son. 'Well, I'm a striker and like most law-abiding strikers I don't beat up anyone. Come under my coat?'

'No, it doesn't matter if I get wet, I'll soon dry.' Sali recalled that morning and decided not to ask Harry for a kiss. Men lived dangerously; women worried and picked up the pieces. Harry was learning his lessons in life early.

Billy Evans looked up apprehensively as the union solicitor, Geoffrey Francis, walked into the waiting area of Tonypandy police station. Geoffrey dropped his briefcase on to the chair next to Billy, draped his muffler around his neck and shook out his overcoat.

'All three have been remanded in custody to appear at Porth magistrates court in the morning.'

'There's no chance of getting them out tonight?'

'None, Billy. But your boys are both of good character and Father Kelly's offered to speak for them, so I shouldn't have too much trouble getting them bail pending a full trial, which probably won't be held for a couple of months.'

'Will the court want a surety?' Billy thought of his empty bank account. For the hundredth time since the strike had started he wished he hadn't bought that last house. It was hard trying to live on their combined strike pay.

'You have property.'

'For what it's worth,' Billy replied acidly.

'Offer the deeds as security. The court might take it as proof that the boys aren't going anywhere.'

'Can I see them?'

Geoffrey shrugged on his cashmere overcoat. 'I asked. Permission's been refused. But I spoke to them. They're all right.'

'And the case against them?'

'The police say they have witnesses but I doubt they'll produce them before the full trial. I'll see you in court tomorrow. Get there early or you won't have a seat. But whatever else you do, tell your union men to stay away from Abel Adams and the Winter boys. The last thing we need is any more accusations of harassment or intimidation.'

At eight o'clock, Megan was exhausted. Her legs ached from running up and down the four flights of stairs in the lodging house. She had dusted, swept, polished, scrubbed, washed, cleaned and waited at the table until all she could think about was bed. Even the narrow hard bed in the attic next to Lena's seemed like the ultimate luxury, but there was one final sitting of supper to go.

Joyce saw Megan rubbing the calf muscles in her legs. 'As soon as you've served the pie, your time's your own until five o'clock tomorrow morning. Considering it's your first day, you've done well.'

Too weary to talk, Megan nodded.

'Go into the dining room and check that Lena's laid the table properly. I'll be along with the pies in a moment.'

Megan rose from the chair and went into the lodgers' dining room, a large wood-panelled room, with a long table that would seat twenty-five at a push, although with three sittings for every meal there were rarely more than twenty at the table at any one time. There was one person in the room now – Sergeant Martin, who was standing with his back to her, staring down into the fire. He turned as she entered.

'How did your first day go, Miss Williams?'

'Fine, sir.' There was no sign of Lena but the table had been laid incorrectly with all the knives on the left and the forks on the right. Megan set about swapping them over.

'Then it sounds as though you had a better day than your young man. That *was* your young man I saw you with this morning?' he enquired.

'My fiancé,' Megan confirmed, too worried to add the 'sir.' She instinctively reached for the engagement ring around her neck. 'Has he had an accident?'

'Nothing like that.' The sergeant nodded to two constables who joined them. 'He's been arrested.'

'What for?' Megan asked in alarm.

'I can't discuss police matters with people who are not officially involved.' He beamed as Joyce carried in a tray that held two large, steaming beef pies. 'If they taste as good as they smell, Mrs Palmer, we're in for a treat.'

Joyce set the pies on the sideboard. 'Fetch the vegetables please, Megan. As soon as we've served the gentlemen, you can go.'

Realizing she must have heard the sergeant talking to her, Megan flashed her a grateful smile before dashing to the kitchen.

Billy Evans left his chair next to the stove and picked up the cap and muffler he had left on the table. 'I'm off to the County Club to see if I can find out what really went on at the corner of Primrose Street this morning.'

'I'll come down to the court with you tomorrow,' Lloyd offered.

His father nodded. 'But there's no need for you to come, Sali, you have the soup kitchen to run and Harry to take and pick up from school. If the magistrates have a heavy workload there's no saying what time the boys' case will come up.'

'I could ask Mr Richards if he can help Joey and Victor. You know he was my father's solicitor for years before he started advising me about Harry's trust fund.'

'Thank you, Sali, but this is best left to the union solicitor. I may be late so don't wait up for me.' He closed the door quickly behind him to keep in the heat. A few seconds later the front door slammed.

'You think the police are out to get Victor and Joey whatever the facts, don't you?' Sali asked Lloyd.

'They're the sons and brothers of strike leaders, and we all know what management think of those.'

'But the police aren't management and they can't prosecute Victor and Joey unless they have a case against them.'

Lloyd lifted his eyebrows.

'You don't think that they would fabricate evidence . . .'

'There's no point in talking about things we can't do anything about.'

'You're beginning to say that more and more these days,' she complained irritably.

'We could waste an entire evening discussing "what ifs" and be none the wiser at the end of it.' He took the shirt she was mending from her hands, set it on the table, pulled her back towards his chair and on to his lap. 'That's better.' He wrapped his arms around her waist. 'As for my brothers, there's only one thing I want at the moment and that's both of them out of the cells in time for our wedding. Now can we talk about that, please.'

'You know why I don't like talking about it.'

'Owen Bull is going to be executed,' he said flatly, 'and as soon as it happens, we are going to be married, Sali.' Although they both avoided mentioning Owen's impending execution, Lloyd knew Sali scoured the papers for news of the appeal his solicitors had made against his sentence as thoroughly as he did. 'It's time to put Owen, his cruelty to you and Harry, and how he got away with Mansel James's murder for over four years behind you, sweetheart.'

Sali bit her bottom lip until it bled. 'I know but—'

'And as I'll be wearing my best suit to our wedding, I'll expect you to get something new from Gwilym James.'

'I can't buy new clothes when there are people starving in the valley.'

'Yes, you can,' he contradicted. 'And don't say that you can donate the money to the soup kitchen instead, because I happen to know that you can't draw cash from either your own or Harry's store accounts.'

'I'll think about it. But I will get some flowers. It's an extravagance but I'd like to put them on my father's grave afterwards.'

'You can afford extravagances.'

'Not living here in the middle of a strike I can't.'

'I'm not exactly offering you a life with prospects, am I, sweetheart?' he said bleakly. 'Your father would turn in his grave if he knew his daughter was about to marry the man who had once been the assistant manager of his pit, and that's even if I was in work.'

'My father always thought a person's character more important than their status,' she rejoined swiftly.

'That attitude wouldn't have extended to his darling eldest daughter and you know it.'

'My father never said anything unless he meant it.'

'Come on, Sali, everyone knows you're taking a massive step down in the world by marrying me.'

'In my eyes I'm taking a step up. Marrying into a kind, and although they wouldn't thank me for saying it, loving family, who back one another against the world, no matter what.'

'And how many of your family will be at the wedding to see you take this "step up"?'

'I don't know,' she prevaricated.

'Have you invited them?'

'We haven't had formal invitations printed.'

'Don't change the subject, Sali.'

'I've written to Gareth and Llinos at their schools.' She referred to her fifteen-year-old brother and sixteen-year-old sister. 'I know they both intend to spend the Christmas holidays in Pontypridd.'

'In Harry's house.'

'The house Harry will inherit when he's thirty, yes.'

'Have either of them written back?'

'Not yet.'

'And although they are happy to live rent and expense free in your son's house, I doubt they will. Have you invited Geraint?' When Lloyd had worked for Sali's father, he and her eldest brother Geraint had frequently discussed engineering problems, and Lloyd

99

had felt that Sali's brother had, if not exactly liked, at least respected him. But Geraint's attitude towards him had changed on the day that Sali had told him they intended to marry.

'I've mentioned it to him and written to Mother, Mr Richards and Mari – our old housekeeper. You know that Mother is ill—'

'With acute hypochondria that has prevented her from doing anything that requires effort or her leaving her bed in years.' He looked keenly at her. 'Do you realize just how much you are giving up to marry me? At the moment all I can offer you is the trouble that comes from being a union leader, member of the strike committee and having two brothers in jail. Not to mention a life lived at starvation level.'

'You having second thoughts?' she asked seriously.

'I am selfish enough to say absolutely not.'

'In which case, a wise man told me that there's no point in discussing things that can't be altered.' She kissed him. 'This is decadent. With only the two of us in the house we should put that fire out and go to bed.'

'If that's an invitation, I'm accepting.'

'I've saved a candle stub if you want to read,' she teased.

'Since we started sharing a bed I haven't finished a single page outside of this kitchen and you know it.' The front door opened and closed. 'My father must have heard something in the club.'

The kitchen door burst open and Megan rushed in, her cloak open, her clothes and hair soaking wet.

Sali jumped up and helped her off with her cloak. 'A rat in the sewer would be drier.'

'I've just heard about Victor. Is it true? Is he in gaol?' Megan blurted in between gasping for breath.

Lloyd outlined the facts as far as they knew them, while Sali opened the hob, set the kettle on to boil and lifted cups down from the dresser. 'We may as well have a cup of tea while the fire's still hot enough to boil a kettle.'

'Not for me.' Megan retrieved the cloak that Sali had shook out and hung over the back of a chair to dry. 'Mrs Palmer wants me to serve first breakfast tomorrow, and I'm exhausted.'

'How's it going?' Sali asked.

'It's hard work but I'll manage,'

'I'll see you back.' Lloyd left his chair.

'Don't be silly, it's only round the corner.'

'I was thinking of stretching my legs anyway,' he lied. 'Be back in a few minutes, Sali.'

'Here, come closer so I can put the umbrella over both of us,' Lloyd ordered Megan, as they left the house.

She took the arm he offered her. 'Thank you.'

'You look as though you're sleeping on your feet.'

'I am. I can't believe my life has changed so much in one day.' She glanced back at the house that had been her uncle's.

'My father told us that you'd accepted an engagement ring from Victor.'

'Yes.' She clutched it through the folds of her dress. 'I'm afraid of damaging it when I do housework so I wear it around my neck during the day, but I put it on my finger when I served the meals earlier tonight so all the lodgers could see it. I wish Victor and I could marry right away.'

'So does Victor – and Sali and me. You'll make a perfect sister-in-law, Megan.'

'I don't know about perfect but I will be your sister-in-law as soon as I'm old enough to marry without my father's permission,' she said determinedly.

'I see Victor's been giving you Evans lessons in stubbornness.' They rounded the corner and walked down the hill. Sergeant Lamb was standing outside the lodging house in company with two other constables.

'Goodnight, Lloyd.' Megan pulled the hood of her cloak down to conceal her face.

'I'll walk you to the door.' Lloyd had seen her glance at the sergeant and sensed her nervousness.

'It's all right.'

'No trouble.' Lloyd led her to the front door. The street lamp shone down on to his face. 'Goodnight, Megan, I'll let you know what happens with Victor tomorrow.'

'Thank you for walking me home, Lloyd.' She stood on tiptoe and kissed his cheek.

'Mr Lloyd Evans, the famous strike leader?' Sergeant Lamb stepped forward.

'Sergeant.' Lloyd nodded acknowledgement.

'We've saved ourselves a trip, constables. Lloyd William Evans, I am arresting you for the attempted murder of Constable John Lamb. Constables, escort Mr Evans down the station. I'll be along shortly to question him, Miss Williams.' He tipped his helmet to her, as Megan watched the officers handcuff a stony-faced Lloyd and lead him away.

'Mrs Palmer!' Megan dashed into the kitchen where Joyce was making cheese sandwiches for the night shift's break. 'I have to go—'

'Where to, child?' Joyce interrupted. 'You've just this minute walked in through the door.'

'Sergeant Lamb has arrested Lloyd Evans.' The kitchen spun around her and Megan gripped the edge of the door to steady herself.

'Lloyd Evans! Whatever for?' Joyce dropped her knife.

'The sergeant said attempted *murder*.'

'Lloyd Evans! I don't believe it!'

'Sali Jones doesn't know. I have to tell her.'

'I don't doubt someone else has told her by now. If you sneeze in Tonypandy, people at the top end of Clydach Vale ask about your cold five minutes later.'

'I won't be long.' Megan opened the back door.

'You're soaked to the skin, girl. You need to get into some dry clothes before you catch your death—'

'I'll be back in ten minutes.' Megan darted into the alleyway before Joyce could stop her. Lifting her sodden skirts to her knees, she put her head down and ran as fast as she could. The hood of her cloak fell back and water streamed from her hair into her eyes, blinding her. She heaved for breath and her throat dried, but she didn't stop until she reached Victor's front door. She turned the key, opened it and ran through to the kitchen where Sali was talking to Mr Evans and Ned Morgan.

'Megan, whatever's wrong?' Sali led her to the fireplace, relieved her of her wet cloak for a second time and proceeded to dry her hair in the kitchen towel while Megan blurted out the details of Lloyd's arrest. Before she'd finished, Mr Evans was putting on his coat.

'I'll go down to the police station and find out exactly what's going on. I'll walk you back to the lodging house on the way, Megan.'

'Megan should stay and dry out,' Sali protested, trembling uncontrollably as the import of Megan's news sank in.

Megan shook her head, spraying water droplets into the air. 'Mrs Palmer didn't want me to leave the house a second time as it was.'

Billy Evans opened the basement door and picked up the old umbrella Victor used in the garden when it rained. He closed the door, and bolted it from the inside. 'Leave this door as it is until morning, Sali. I'll lock the front door behind me and take the key.'

'We never lock the doors.'

'No one in this family has ever been arrested before, and three in one day is three too many. Some of the boys have had the police in and out of their houses at all hours of the day and night. I don't want them coming in here when you and Harry are alone. And take that worried look off your face,' he ordered. 'You know as well as I do Lloyd's innocent. Attempted murder, my . . . eye!'

'Cells and courts round here are full of innocent men these days, Billy. I think I'll take a walk down to the station with you.' Ned put on his own coat.

'Why stick your head in the lion's den when you don't have to, Ned?'

'I like to hear their growls,' Ned replied.

Sali draped Megan's soggy cloak around her and walked them to the door. She hugged Megan, despite her damp and dripping state. Mr Evans opened the door and removed the key from the lock.

'That will make a hole in your pocket.' Sali eyed the six-inch iron key.

'Can't be helped.' He turned up his collar. 'Try to sleep.'

'You know I won't.'

'If it's not too late, I'll knock on your door when I get back.'

'Will you, no matter what the time?' Sali begged.

He nodded, opened the umbrella and offered Megan his arm. 'Perhaps I should put the umbrella between us to stop you dripping over me,' he joked. 'There really is no need for you to come with me, Ned. The weather's foul, it's late and Betty will be wondering where you are.'

'As I'm older and uglier than your Joey she won't be wondering that much.' Ned thrust his bare hands into his pockets. His leather gloves had been one of the first things to be pawned when their savings had run out. 'Betty knows that at my age the only thing keeping me from my bed at night is union business. And if you have to stay in the station for any reason, you may need an errand boy.'

Sali went inside and listened to Mr Evans locking the door. She watched them walk down the street from Mr Evans' bedroom window – two middle-aged men and a slight young girl between them.

Shivering, she returned to the kitchen and realized that, for the first time since she had moved into the house, she faced the prospect of spending a night behind two locked doors with only her son for company.

Luke Thomas thumped his fist against the stone wall of the holding cell in the police station. 'Another thing about your father and his cronies on the bloody strike committee—'

'Give it a rest,' Joey snarled. 'It's bad enough having to spend the night in this damned dungeon, without having to listen to you go on about how you'd handle the strike if you were in charge.'

'The trouble with you—'

'The trouble with me is you've killed my patience. And I'll kill you if I have to listen to one more of your tirades against the strike committee for the way they're handling the dispute, the colliery owners for working us to death for slave wages or the police for arresting us when all *you*,' Joey jabbed his index finger into Luke's chest, 'were doing was demanding *your* rights.'

'I'm fighting for all of us,' Luke asserted pompously.

'And we believe that, don't we, Victor?' Joey mocked. 'Luke Thomas, the great and noble martyr of Tonypandy, soon to be sainted for the sacrifices he's made for the cause.'

Victor held his fingers to his lips, walked to the steel door and pressed his ear against the grille.

Joey was furious with Victor for silencing him, Luke for his ranting, the police for depriving him of his freedom and incarcerating the three of them in a freezing cell, but most of all with himself, for being stupid enough to join the morning's unofficial picket. He yanked the single grey army issue blanket from the top 'bunk' that was a six by two-foot sheet of steel hinged to the wall and fastened by chains. Shaking it out, he wrapped it around himself.

'You look like one of those Indian squaws in the comic books,' Luke sneered.

'Be careful, Victor. Those beds, if you can call them that, are cold enough to give you an ice burn.' Joey decided the only way he was going to cope with Luke was to ignore him.

'I always said you Evans were soft.'

'What can you hear?' Joey joined his brother at the door.

'Someone shouting. I couldn't swear to it but it sounded like Lloyd.'

'Lloyd has more sense than to get himself arrested,' Joey said tersely.

'If he's here he's probably drunk.'

It took all Joey's will-power to remember that he was ignoring Luke.

Luke sat on the bunk below Joey's and tested it with his weight. 'We'll turn into ice blocks by morning.'

Joey paced to the small barred window and peered outside.

'See anything?' Victor asked from his post at the door.

'Bugger all,' Joey answered. 'The town's quiet.'

'Not surprising if they've arrested every innocent man in the valley on trumped-up charges . . . Did you hear that?' Luke asked, as a thud resounded down the corridor.

Joey vaulted up on to his bunk, tucked most of the blanket under him, wound his scarf twice round his neck, settled his cap on his head, pulled his overcoat sleeves over his gloves and closed his eyes.

'How you can sleep?'

Joey rolled to the edge of his bunk, opened one eye and glared at Luke. 'One more squeak out of you and I'll go from tamping to murdering mad.'

Luke kicked up his feet and fell silent.

Victor frowned from the strain of listening. If only he could be sure it was Lloyd's voice he'd heard – but there were so many sounds. The tiled walls, floors and metal doors had transformed the corridor into an echo chamber, magnifying footsteps and rendering conversation unintelligible. But he hadn't picked up on so much as a whisper outside of their cell in ten minutes.

'Come on, Victor, whatever you heard, you can't do a thing about it locked up in here.' Joey settled back on his bunk and closed his eyes. 'You may as well try to get some sleep.'

'You're right.' Victor pulled the blanket from the bunk across from Luke's, draped it over his shoulders and sat down. But he couldn't forget the voice he'd heard. The years Lloyd had spent working in colliery management had given him a distinctive accent. Not that he'd lost his Welsh intonation, just that he sounded more educated than the average collier. There weren't many men in the Rhondda who spoke like him.

Chapter 7

WE HAVE witnesses who saw you throw the brick that hit Constable Lamb, Evans. Witnesses who are prepared to stand up and testify in court that you took deliberate aim, so there's no point in you trying to deny that you're responsible for his injuries.' Constable Shipton pulled a chair out from under the metal table Lloyd was sitting at, lifted his foot on to the seat and, shifting his weight on to his other leg, glowered down at him.

Lloyd met the officer's gaze without flinching. 'I was outside the railway station yesterday evening, not in Dunraven Street. Several members of the strike committee were with me.'

'The strike committee,' Shipton echoed. 'And, of course, we *always* believe *everything* the members of the strike committee tell us, don't we?'

The constable stationed in front of the door sniggered.

'There were police officers there to prevent us from reaching the station platforms,' Lloyd said calmly. 'They saw me.' He winced as the officer standing behind his chair pulled the handcuffs that secured his arms high behind his back. The strain on his shoulder muscles was agonizing. He felt as though his arms were being torn from their sockets. His wrists burned, skinned raw by the cuffs. But determined to keep his temper, he continued to stare impassively at Constable Shipton.

Shipton tossed a pen down beside a bottle of ink and sheet of paper on the table. 'The court will be more inclined to be lenient with you, if you plead guilty and show remorse, Evans. Agree to sign that confession and we'll unlock your cuffs.'

Lloyd raised his voice in the hope of being heard outside the cell by someone with more integrity than his interrogators. 'How many times do I have to tell you that I will not confess to a crime I did not commit?'

There was a knock at the door. The officer standing in front of it opened it, and Sergeant Lamb walked into the interview room. Shipton kicked the chair he was leaning on back under the table and snapped to attention. When the constable standing behind his chair followed suit, Lloyd tentatively moved his shoulders. Weak and dizzy from relief, he focused on the sergeant.

Sergeant Lamb walked across the small room and glanced at the sheet of paper on the table. 'This confession not signed yet, Shipton?'

'No, sir.'

'Why not?'

'The suspect refuses to confess, sir?'

Lamb circled Lloyd's chair. 'Refuses,' he murmured. Without warning, he lashed out, kicking the chair from under Lloyd. Trussed and unable to save himself with his hands, Lloyd fell awkwardly. He lay sprawled on his back, fighting for breath. Sergeant Lamb returned to the door and stood next to the constable in front of it. Lloyd realized that all four officers were watching him.

He rolled on his side and struggled to his knees. The handcuffs bit into his damaged wrists as he fought to regain his balance. He was poised on the balls of his feet, ready to rise, when the sergeant gave an almost imperceptible nod. The three constables moved. There was no time to tense his muscles before the first kick connected with his stomach.

'You ready to sign now?' Shipton barked.

'I refuse to——' A steel toe-capped boot smashed into Lloyd's ribcage and the remainder of his words dissolved into a scream he barely recognized as his own. He curled instinctively into a foetal position in a futile attempt to protect himself.

Walls and floor blurred into a jagged kaleidoscope of white tiles and grey concrete punctuated by flashes of crimson lightning. Lloyd tried to divorce himself from the pain by concentrating on the light and shadows in the room. The oil lamp was smoking.

There was a smell of grease in the air. The oil had to be contaminated. Why would the police buy contaminated oil?

He was aware of the sergeant leaving the room. Of the door clanging shut behind him.

'Are you ready to sign?'

Too wracked with pain to speak, he lifted his head and shook it. A blow sent him flying into the wall. An ear-splitting crack preceded a tidal wave of agony that flooded from the back of his skull throughout his body, washing all coherent thought from his mind. He felt as though he were dissolving into a sweet grey mist. His last thoughts were of Sali. Then there was oblivion, a nothingness that blotted everything from his consciousness, even pain.

Sali lay tense and rigid, her senses strained to their utmost as she listened intently for the sounds of Mr Evans returning. The bed beside her stretched cold and empty. She caressed the void, aching for Lloyd's presence with a pain that was almost physical. No matter how she struggled to concentrate on other things, she couldn't stop picturing him locked in a police cell, officers with batons closing in . . .

She made a valiant effort to block the scene from her mind. Since the night of the worst riot, the *Rhondda Leader* had been full of articles about police brutality towards innocent people. Church and chapel ministers, solicitors, doctors, teachers, tradesmen – all had written to the paper to complain about incidents they had witnessed. She recalled what had happened to Betty Morgan. If the police didn't balk at knocking down women in the street in broad daylight, what would they do to a strike leader they were holding in the isolation of a police cell?

She felt for the box of matches she kept on her beside cabinet. Sliding it open she removed a match and struck it. The hands on the clock showed two o'clock. Mr Evans had left for the police station before ten – could they have arrested him as well? She lit the candle, pushed her feet into her slippers, slipped on her flannel dressing gown, threw a shawl over her shoulders and walked into the front bedroom that had been Lloyd's before he'd moved into hers.

Leaving the candle on the bookshelf next to the door, she went to the window that overlooked the street, hoping to see Mr Evans returning from the police station.

She jumped back. The street was crowded with shadowy figures in dark capes and helmets. Then, two enormous crashes shook the front of the house, rapidly followed by the tinkling of breaking glass and the harsher sound of splintering wood. Harry screamed. She ran across the landing. He was standing in the doorway of his bedroom, shaking from cold and fear. She gathered him into her arms. Torchlight flickered into the hall below them. The front door swayed drunkenly inwards on its hinges before falling flat into the passage and shattering on the flagstones. Two policemen burst into the hall, both wielding axes. One looked up at her.

'Your name?'

She stared at him, too traumatized to answer.

'This is William Evans' house?'

'Yes.' She finally found her voice but it sounded hoarse, strange. She wrapped her arms around Harry, burying his face in her shoulder, covering the back of his head with her hands.

'Who else is in the house?' Sergeant Lamb picked his way through the wreckage of what had been the front door. Rain blasted in forming puddles around the debris on the flagstones at his feet.

'No one.' Sali forced herself to remain calm for Harry's sake.

'You live here?'

'Yes.'

'A woman lodger?' he queried sceptically.

Sali heard voices raised in anger outside and realized the police had woken the neighbours. Drawing courage from their presence within earshot, she retorted, 'I am Mr Evans' housekeeper.'

'And the child?'

'Is mine.'

'And which of the Evans'?'

It was one question too many for Sali. Fear was replaced by

anger. 'Not that it is any of your business, officer, but I am a widow.'

The sergeant looked to the men behind him. 'Keep everyone back, well away from the house. You, you, you and you.' Two officers joined the two already in the hall. 'You know what to look for. Miscreants in hiding. Letters or papers pertaining to the strike committee or the Federation of Mineworkers. Evidence related to the crimes that have been committed.'

Furious at having strangers smash down the front door, walk in and ransack the house at that time in the morning, Sali snapped, 'Do you have a search warrant, officer?'

'A what?' The sergeant looked up the stairs at her.

'A search warrant,' Sali reiterated loudly, drawing courage from the noise the neighbours were making outside. She lowered Harry to the floor and pushed him gently towards his room. 'You can't take anything from this house unless you have a warrant.'

'I don't need a warrant, madam. Not for the lair of men who have no respect for the law or its officers.' Sergeant Lamb began to walk slowly up the stairs towards her. Sali was terrified, but she stood her ground. She was acutely aware of her own heartbeat, of Harry clinging to her legs, of the commotion outside, of crashes and bangs emanating from the downstairs rooms.

The sergeant reached the landing and stood close to her. 'You're as red as the bastards you live with, aren't you?' he hissed. 'And just like them, you think police officers are fair game. Targets to be maimed and even killed. You Marxist bitch—'

'Harry, into your bedroom, shut the door. Now!' Sali had never spoken roughly to her son before. Frightened, he scuttled into his bedroom.

'Your name?' Sergeant Lamb barked as if he were on a parade ground.

'Mrs Sali Jones.'

Hobnailed boots continued to grate and rasp over the flagstones downstairs. A loud smash accompanied by swearing resounded from the kitchen.

'Have you a warrant?' Sali repeated, shouting in the hope that she could be heard in the street.

'We have men in custody charged with serious crimes. We are looking for evidence.'

'You need a warrant.' Aware of Harry watching through a crack in his open door, she leaned forward and yelled. 'Close your door and turn the key, Harry.' Her foot caught in the hem of her nightdress. The sergeant lifted his hand. Assuming that he was about to hit her, she jumped back and missed her footing. Her knees buckled. She reached out but failed to reach the banister. Stairs, ceiling and walls whirled crazily around her as she tumbled headlong. The last thing she saw was Harry looking down at her and screaming.

Megan was walking with Victor on Barry Island beach. The sky was a clear, cloudless cerulean blue, the sun was shining, but a cold wind blew around her ankles. The screams of gulls, high-pitched, ear-splitting, drowned out all other sounds. She opened her arms to embrace Victor, the wind blew colder . . . the gulls' screeches grew more piercing . . .

Megan woke with a start. The sheets and blankets had pulled free from the bottom of the mattress and her feet were numb with cold. Tucking them back beneath the bedclothes, she sat up to rub them. Although it was darker than a coalhole, she knew she wasn't in the box room she shared with Daisy. In the few seconds it took her to recall the events of the previous day, she became aware that her throat was sore and she had a headache.

The stench of sulphur filled the cold, still air and the gulls stopped screeching. Lena had struck a match, lit a candle and switched off the alarm clock.

'Good morning,' Megan mumbled thickly.

'Time to lay and light the fires.' Lena dived out of bed and poured water from the jug on the washstand into the bowl. She splashed her hands and face, dried them on one of the towels draped over the stand and went to the chair on which she'd folded her clothes the night before. She picked up her drawers and pulled them on beneath the cover of her nightgown. Turning her back to Megan, she shrugged her arms out of the sleeves and pulled on her chemise and petticoats under the tent-like, flannel gown, only removing it when she was ready to put on her dress. She buttoned the bodice and sleeves, sat on the side of her bed and rolled on her black stockings, gartering them below her knees.

Megan peered at the clock. Five o'clock, her normal waking time in her uncle's house, but she had never been so reluctant to leave her bed. Then she thought of Victor, Joey – and Lloyd. If Mr Evans had managed to get them released last night, Victor may have written her a note. She folded back the sheet and blankets, swung her legs to the floor, padded over to the washstand, tipped the water Lena had used into the slop bucket and poured in fresh.

'Mrs Palmer says there's no point in washing properly until all the dirty work's been done for the day.' Lena watched Megan try to lather soap in the icy water.

'She's right,' Megan croaked, taking her flannel from her American oilcloth toilet bag.

'You're talking funny.'

'I got soaked in the rain last night. I must have caught a cold.' Megan fingered the black woollen dress she had worn the day before and hung on the back of the door. It was as wet as when she'd taken it off, which was little wonder given the temperature of the room.

'There's four fires that need seeing to downstairs. I'll do the ones in the kitchen and Mrs Palmer's private room. You do the ones in the lodgers' dining and sitting rooms. Afterwards, all the furniture downstairs has to be dusted and the floors swept while Mrs Palmer makes first breakfast.'

Her throat too sore to speak, Megan nodded. It was only after Lena had left that she realized the girl had taken the private rooms, leaving her to cope with any lodgers who were around, and after yesterday, the last people she wanted to see were Sergeants Lamb and Martin.

Constable Gwyn Jenkins unlocked the door to the corridor that housed the holding cells of the police station. 'Number six, you say?' he called back to the duty officer over his shoulder.

'That's right.'

Gwyn unlocked a door halfway along the corridor. Billy Evans and Ned Morgan were sitting on steel beds opposite one another. Their faces were grey with exhaustion, their chins stubbled with beard, but their eyes glittered, darkly antagonistic, as they glared at him.

'Come to see the monkeys in the zoo, Gwyn?' Billy said bitterly.

'You're free to go,' Gwyn muttered shamefacedly.

'We came down here last night to find out why Lloyd had been arrested. The second we set foot in this place we were charged with affray and thrown into this cell.'

'It was a mistake, Billy.'

'So enquiring about someone you lot have arrested and are holding isn't affray?' Billy questioned coldly.

'Come on, Billy, Ned. You both know me, and the rest of the local boys. If one of us had been around last night you would never have been put in here. But all I can do for you now is let you out and say sorry.'

'Is that an official apology?'

'You know better than to ask that, Billy,' Gwyn replied patiently. 'I can't speak for anyone else on the force, especially now that half the Met is stationed in Pandy.'

'And Lloyd? Was his arrest a mistake too?'

'Lloyd's been charged with attempted murder, grievous bodily harm and malicious wounding with intent,' Gwyn divulged.

'And just who is he supposed to have tried to murder, harm and wound?' Billy tossed aside the blanket he'd draped over his shoulders.

'All I know is what the duty sergeant told me. I haven't seen the charge sheet so I don't know any more. You know the charges against Victor, Joey and Luke?'

'I was there when they were arrested.' Billy retied the laces he'd loosened on his boots.

'All four of them are down to be brought before Porth magistrates court this morning. If you want to be there to support your boys, Billy, you'll need to go home to wash and change into your best suit,' Gwyn hinted.

Billy moved awkwardly towards the door. The cold had seeped into his joints, seizing them.

'The force hasn't heard the last of this, Gwyn Jenkins,' Ned Morgan threatened. 'If your father could see what you've become, he'd be ashamed that he'd ever had a son. He was one of the best colliers ever to wield a pick underground and if he was still with us, I know what side of the picket line he'd be on and it wouldn't be the one with the batons.'

'I'm only trying to earn a living, the same as you, Ned,' Gwyn protested.

'Fine way to do it, arresting your own kind on trumped-up charges.'

'Can I see the boys?' Billy asked.

'Not officially, but . . .' Gwyn glanced around before walking to the end of the corridor and locking the door that connected with the rest of the police station. He flicked through the ring of keys he was carrying and opened the door of the first cell in the row.

Billy and Ned looked over Gwyn's shoulder to see Joey and Luke, boots on, stretched out on their bunks, wrapped in their overcoats, caps, mufflers and gloves. Victor was standing, looking up through the iron grille at the darkened street.

'You boys all right?' Billy said gruffly.

'As all right as anyone can be in a cell,' Victor answered. Joey and Luke opened their eyes.

'Dad, what are you doing here?' Joey mumbled sleepily.

'Same as you, enjoying a night's free hospitality. I'll see you boys in court later on this morning.' Billy turned to Gwyn. 'Can I send down shaving gear and clean shirts for them?'

'Send the clean shirts. I'll arrange for them to have soap, hot water and razors. Someone will be along with breakfast soon, boys.'

'Bread and water,' Joey suggested acidly.

'Oh, I think we can do better than that.' Gwyn motioned to Billy and Ned. They stepped back into the corridor and he closed and locked the cell door.

'Lloyd?' Billy reminded.

115

Gwyn walked to the end of the corridor and unlocked the last cell. As soon as he looked inside his face dropped and he stepped back, crashing into the corridor wall. Billy pushed past him.

Lloyd lay curled on his side on the floor, his face a mass of bruises. His wrists, handcuffed behind his back, dripped blood on to the stone floor. Billy fell to his knees and lifted Lloyd into his arms, cradling him as if he were a child. Lloyd moaned and doubled up, obviously in pain.

'Get a doctor . . .' Billy looked up. Ned was beside him. Gwyn had already charged back down the corridor, keys hanging forgotten in the lock of Lloyd's cell. He was hammering on the door that connected to the rest of the station.

'You wanted to run errands, Ned,' Billy said grimly. 'Get Geoffrey Francis. I want him to see this.'

The main door opened. Gwyn disappeared. Ned collided with Sergeant Martin. The sergeant passed him and made his way down the corridor to the end cell. His knuckles showed white as he gripped the doorpost and gazed at Lloyd.

'Your boys slipped up, sergeant.' Billy's voice was thick, clotted with suppressed emotion. 'My son is still breathing and if I have anything to do with it, he'll carry on breathing long enough to see you lot in court.'

The sergeant continued to stare in silence at Lloyd. If Billy hadn't known better, he might even have said that Martin looked shocked, sickened and – ashamed.

Betty Morgan lifted the kettle from the hob of the stove in the Evanses' kitchen and poured boiling water into the teapot. 'Well, what's the damage?' she asked Nurse Roberts, who was manipulating Sali's ankle.

The nurse had just completed a night shift at Llwynypia hospital, but she had examined Sali as if she had all the time in the world. 'The good news is it's not broken but it's a bad sprain. You'll have to keep off it for a week, Mrs Jones. However, given your other injuries, I'd say you should spend at least that long in bed. You really do need to see a doctor.'

'I'm not that bad,' Sali insisted.

'Say it often enough and you might even believe it.' The nurse rose to her feet and studied Sali. The right side of her face was swollen, her jaw was bruised and the skin on the palms of her hands torn and grazed from where she had tried to protect herself when she had landed on the flagstones at the foot of the stairs. 'I'm worried about your back.'

'You said if I take it easy, it will be fine.'

'Provided there's no damage to the spinal column,' the nurse qualified.

'Sit down and have your tea, Nurse.' Betty pulled a chair out from the table. 'It will be brewed in a minute.'

'I'm sorry there's no sugar.' Sali winced as she took a deep breath. 'But there's milk in the pantry and bread and margarine. I could make you some toast.'

'You won't be making anything for a while, so just sit there and behave yourself.' Betty had appointed herself in charge of the Evans' household. Alerted by the commotion the police had made when they had broken down Billy Evans' door, she had been the first on the scene and the first to break through the cordon of constables when she had seen Sali land at the bottom of the stairs.

Brushing aside Sergeant Lamb's exhortations to 'stay out of matters that don't concern you', she, along with half a dozen other women, had stayed to comfort Harry, and care for Sali. The arrival of an audience had curbed the actions of the police, but the neighbours had been unable to prevent the officers from smashing most of the household china and emptying the contents of the cupboards on to the floor. However, they had been in time to witness the removal of several boxes of papers and letters from Mr Evans' downstairs bedroom.

Betty went into the parlour and brought out three undamaged cups from the set that the late Mrs Evans had kept for 'best'. She poured the tea, handed one cup to the nurse and carried one over to Sali.

'It's almost half past six.' Betty checked the clock. 'As soon as I've drunk this I'll go round to the Jones' house and ask one of the boys to fetch the doctor.'

'There's really no need. I'm all right.' Sali sipped the tea, wishing they had sugar.

'It's no thanks to those damned policemen that you weren't killed outright. Pushing you down the stairs . . .'

'Sergeant Lamb said he'd sue for defamation of character if he heard anyone repeat that allegation. And I can't in all honesty say that he touched me. The last thing I remember is tripping over the hem of my nightgown.' Sali's hand shook and Betty took her teacup from her.

'My Ned swears by the union solicitor, Mr Francis. We need to let him know what's happened here and ask him to find out where my Ned, Billy Evans and the boys are. There's no point in any of us going down the police station to make enquiries. Like everyone else who's gone there in the last twenty-four hours we may disappear, never to be seen again.' Betty glanced at Harry, who was sleeping, tucked up in an eiderdown, on the second easy chair. 'It's a disgrace that a child his age had to see such things.'

'He's calmed down now, Betty.' Sali didn't want to be reminded of Harry's hysterics or how long it had taken her to get him back to sleep after the police had left the house.

'No thanks to the coppers.'

'There's no need to send one of the Jones' boys for a doctor, Mrs Morgan, I'll call in and ask him to visit here on my way home.' Nurse Roberts finished her tea and left the table.

'I still need to send them up to Mr Francis, and you'll need a carpenter, to sort out the front door and the window in the front bedroom, Sali.'

'They smashed the window?'

Betty Morgan didn't have the heart to tell Sali that the police had not only smashed the window in Billy's bedroom but the one in the middle parlour as well.

'I'm off.' The nurse fastened her cape.

'Thank you for coming,' Sali said gratefully.

'I would say it was my pleasure, but I hope I don't see you in this state again, Mrs Jones.'

'I don't know what Mr Evans is going to say when he sees the house,' Sali said after Nurse Roberts had tiptoed around the wreckage in the hall and left.

'He's going to say, what the hell happened here?'

Sali and Betty turned to see Billy and Ned in the doorway.

'Well, you two crept in quiet as cockroaches, I must say. I suppose you'll be wanting tea.' Betty carried her own and the nurse's cups to the sink, so Ned wouldn't see her tears of relief.

'Are Lloyd, Victor and Joey all right?' Sali asked immediately.

'Joey and Victor are fine. Lloyd's another matter.'

'He's hurt?' Sali cried out in pain as she rose to her feet.

'He looks as though he's had some of the same treatment as you, but he was conscious and talking when I left the police station.' Billy helped her back into her chair. 'Bloody police, I'll get a solicitor and throw the book at the bastards. I take it this is their doing.' It said something for his state of mind that he swore in front of Sali, Betty and Harry, albeit that Harry was still sleeping.

'Is Lloyd badly hurt?' Sali's voice wavered tremulously.

'He has a couple of cracked ribs, too many bruises to count and concussion, but the doctor said he'll survive. It appears that he was clumsy enough to fall down the stone steps to the cells, although he doesn't remember it that way. And you?'

'Looks like falling down stairs is catching,' Betty said cynically. 'We'd better put out a warning that the police are spreading the disease.'

'I'm fine, Mr Evans,' Sali protested unconvincingly. 'And I really did fall down the stairs.'

'You're about as fine as Lloyd.' He glanced around the kitchen that looked as though a cyclone had hit it, for all that Betty and two other neighbours had spent most of the night clearing it. 'What the hell did go on here?'

'The police said they were searching for evidence. I asked them if they had a warrant—'

'Did they?' Billy interrupted.

'Not that I saw.'

'Sit down, Billy, you're making the place look untidy.' Betty's poor attempt at a joke fell flat. 'I'll pour you a cup of tea, although brandy might be better.'

'It would if we had any,' Billy agreed laconically.

'You all right?' Betty asked Ned.

'Better than you by the look of it, love.'

'The police took boxes of papers from your room, Mr Evans. I couldn't stop them.' Sali saw Harry move and she flinched in pain as she went to him. Before she reached him he settled back to sleep.

'Sit down and let me see to things for a change.' Billy's face darkened as he looked at Harry. 'Did they go upstairs?'

'They went everywhere,' Betty revealed. 'But they didn't break anything up there that I can see, and we've put everything back into the wardrobes and drawers, although you might have trouble finding some of your clothes for a while.'

'The beds?'

'Have been remade,' Betty informed him.

'No arguments, Sali, I want you and Harry to go up right now so you can catch up on some sleep,' Billy ordered.

It was as much as Sali could do to remain on her feet. 'I want to see Lloyd and there's the soup kitchen—'

'The doctor promised that he would bring Lloyd home in his new car as soon as he's been released from police custody. And when he comes home, like you, he'll only be fit for bed. As for the soup kitchen, it will have to do without you for a while. Father Kelly will understand.' Billy lifted Harry, who was sleepily rubbing his eyes with his fists, out of the chair. 'Come on young man, you're going up to bed with your mam.' Billy looked back at Betty.

'I'll stay as long as I'm needed, Billy.'

'Thanks, Betty.'

'I've a couple of old doors in my shed that I've been drying out since the floods to use as kindling,' Ned said. 'We could use them to board up Lloyd's empty house next door and you could fit the doors and windows from there, into this house until you can afford to buy the materials for Victor to do a proper job.'

'Thanks, Ned,' Billy went to the door. 'Looks like we're finding out who our real friends are.'

'You and the boys have more friends than you realize, Billy,' Betty said warmly. 'Half of Tonypandy came round last night when they heard what was going on here. The only pity is that we couldn't stop the coppers from ransacking the place.'

'I hope you're right, Betty, because we certainly need all the friends we can get at the moment.' Billy carried Harry out of the door and up the stairs.

'A whole . . . flaming night in the police station, a five-hour wait in the court cells and all for two minutes in front of the magistrates. And even then we weren't allowed to say a single word in our defence,' Joey complained indignantly, tempering his language for Mr Francis' sake when he and Victor joined his father and the union solicitor outside the court.

'It's not over yet, Joey. And it won't be until the jury bring in a verdict after a full trial in Pontypridd,' Geoffrey Francis cautioned him.

'When will that be?' Billy asked.

'My guess is not until after Christmas. February perhaps, or maybe March.'

'About Lloyd . . .' Billy had problems restraining his anger every time he thought of his eldest son's injuries.

'They dropped the charges against him. He's been released.'

'Dropped the charges! After what they did to him!'

'Apparently they thought he'd thrown a brick that injured a Constable Lamb in Dunraven Street the night before last. When Gwyn Jenkins and another constable, Huw Davies from Ponty-pridd saw the charge sheet, they went to the duty sergeant and told him they'd seen Lloyd down the railway station at the time of the attack on Constable Lamb. Gwyn told me just now in the court that the doctor took Lloyd home half an hour ago.'

'Unable to stand on his own two feet thanks to the beating—'

Geoffrey signalled to Billy to keep his voice down. He took his arm and led him down a side street away from the courthouse door. Victor and Joey followed. 'You can't talk publicly about Lloyd being beaten because we can't prove that he was.'

'Have you seen Lloyd?' Billy exclaimed in exasperation.

'I saw him at the police station when I interviewed Victor, Joey and Luke. I also had a quiet word in the local sergeant's ear. The police won't be picking up anyone in your family or searching your house again for quite a while, Billy.'

'Let me guess, on condition that I don't make any formal complaint about what they've done to Lloyd, Sali, or the damage they did to my house.'

'If you do, you won't get anywhere,' Geoffrey warned. 'The official version is that Lloyd fell down a flight of stone steps and, as the only witnesses are police officers, it's their combined word against his.'

'So you're saying that the men appointed to uphold the law in this town can beat my son to a pulp, push my future daughter-in-law downstairs, steal my private papers and those of the strike committee and union, smash my belongings and wreck my house—'

'The notebooks of the constables who arrested Lloyd state that he was aggressively drunk when they picked him up and they were forced to restrain him for their own and his safety.'

'Lloyd stayed in last night and we haven't had any drink in the house since the strike started. He was walking Victor's girlfriend, Megan Williams, back to Joyce Palmer's when they arrested him. She'll swear to it—'

'You really want her to do that, Billy, when she is working in the house the police lodge in?' Geoffrey broke in.

Billy looked to Victor, who shook his head.

'We can't put Megan at risk.' Billy sighed in frustration. 'Two people falling down the stairs in one night is bad enough. The last thing I want to see is Megan ending up like Sali and Lloyd.'

'The police don't deny that Lloyd and Mrs Jones have suffered injuries, but they insist those injuries were the result of accidents. Without independent witnesses to either event, you don't need me to tell you which way that will go in court.'

'And the ransacking of my house?'

'Sergeant Lamb's story is that he was acting on information that men responsible for attacking his officers had been seen entering the premises.'

'Information from who?' Billy demanded.

'The police don't have to name their informers.'

'And no doubt these attackers transformed themselves into letters and papers, which is why so many documents were taken from my house. Half the people in the street saw them being removed,' Billy said in disgust.

'I'll see what I can do about getting them back for you, Billy.'

'You do just that.' Billy turned to Victor and Joey. 'It's time to go home.'

Victor thrust his hands into his coat pocket. He hadn't been able to get warm since he had been taken to the police station. 'I'll call in to see Megan, to set her mind at rest.'

'Be sure to use Joyce Palmer's back door and avoid her lodgers.' Billy glanced at Geoffrey Francis. 'They may not all have been told that they're supposed to stop arresting us.'

Chapter 8

VICTOR PAID the conductor on the tram that ran from Porth to Tonypandy with two of the last four pennies he had in his pocket until the next strike pay day. From the outset of the dispute, he, Lloyd and Joey had handed over nine of the ten shillings they received every week to Sali for basic housekeeping expenses, which just about covered the cost of their food. The shilling he was left with made him feel as though he were a twelve-year-old apprentice on 'pocket money' again, with one major difference. The shilling didn't go anywhere near as far as it had done thirteen years before.

As usual since the riots, Dunraven Street was full of police. Pulling his cap low and keeping his head down, he walked quickly until he reached the turn to the lane that ran behind the lodging house. Megan was standing outside the kitchen door, her back turned to him as she scraped leftovers into the pigswill bin. His breath caught in his throat as it did every time he saw her. She was so incredibly beautiful. Even though she'd agreed to marry him he still found it unbelievable to think that she could love him.

He continued to stand, mesmerized by the graceful curve of her neck, the rich red gold of the curls that escaped her calico work hat, the slim lines of her lithe body. She closed the bin, looked back and saw him.

'Victor!' She ran towards him and flung her arms around his neck, grazing his cheek with the edge of the plate and fork she was holding. 'I was so worried. Oh no! Look what I've done! There's gravy all down your overcoat.' She sprang back and set the plate and fork on the window sill.

'It doesn't matter.' He pulled her towards him and kissed her.

'You really are all right?' she asked, when he released her.

124

He caught her hands in his. 'As you see.'

'I was so afraid they'd put you in prison. That I wouldn't see you for months – or even years . . .'

'I can't promise that won't happen, love,' he said soberly. 'Joey and I have to stand trial in Pontypridd. But Mr Francis thinks it won't be until after Christmas.'

'And Lloyd? How is he? I saw Sergeant Martin arrest him last night and the milkman told us they're saying all over town that the police beat him up. Is that true? And Mrs Palmer heard this morning in Rodney's that the police pushed Sali downstairs last night when they raided your house. Was she pushed? Is she badly hurt?' Her questions tumbled out faster than he could answer them.

'I haven't been home yet, so I haven't seen them. But according to my father, battered as they are, they'll both survive.' He gave her the only answer he dared, considering they were standing behind a house full of police officers who might be eavesdropping through open windows.

'Mr Evans?' Joyce Palmer opened the kitchen door.

'I know I shouldn't be here, Mrs Palmer. I only called to tell Megan that I'm free.' When she didn't respond, he added, 'Megan didn't know I was coming and I was just about to leave.'

'Before you do, may I suggest you ask Megan to wipe the gravy from the back of your overcoat before the stain sets,' Joyce advised.

'The gravy!' Megan exclaimed. 'I forgot.'

'Everything by the look of it, Megan, including your manners.' The twinkle in Mrs Palmer's eyes belied her offhand tone. 'Won't you come in, Mr Evans, so Megan can see to your coat?'

Victor went into the kitchen. Megan dumped the plate and fork next to the sink with the rest of the dirty dishes, picked up a clean tea towel, soaked it under the cold tap and sponged the back of his coat. 'It's coming off.'

'Thank you.' He couldn't help but smile at her. Even in her grey work dress, blue butcher's overall and cap she outshone the most beautiful variety stars he'd seen on stage in the Empire.

Joyce intercepted their look and frowned. 'After what happened to your brother when he walked Megan home last night, it might be as well if you leave before any of the lodgers see you, Mr Evans.'

'Have you decided which will be Megan's free afternoon, Mrs Palmer?' Victor asked.

Joyce pursed her lips thoughtfully. 'Saturday afternoon would suit me because I make a cold dinner for the lodgers, which is less work than hot. I'll be able to manage without you, Megan, provided you help Lena give one of the big bedrooms a full clean in the morning as well as lay the fires and cover your normal duties.'

Megan glanced at Victor. When he nodded, she said. 'Saturday afternoon will be fine, Mrs Palmer.'

'Your father was insistent that you should have time to go to chapel. So you will also be free from half past five to half past eight on Sunday evenings. And something tells me that smile isn't in anticipation of the sermons you'll be hearing.' Joyce turned to Victor. 'Mr Evans?'

'I am leaving now, Mrs Palmer.'

'If Megan should happen to spend any of her free time with you, I'll trust you'll keep her – and yourself out of trouble.'

'I've never gone looking for trouble, Mrs Palmer.'

'Your family seems to be attracting it at the moment.'

'Unfortunately. Bye, Megan, Mrs Palmer.' Victor stepped out of the door.

'One more thing, Mr Evans.' Joyce stood on the back doorstep. 'I spoke to Nurse Roberts's mother in Rodney's this morning. Tell your father that if he needs any help while your housekeeper is laid up, I'll be happy to do what I can.'

'I'll do that, and thank you, Mrs Palmer.' Victor gave Megan one last quick conscious look through the window. As he turned to go, he saw to his annoyance, that Luke Thomas and a bunch of his cronies had gathered at the entrance to the lane.

'Victor, just the man I want to see,' Luke said.

'After the events of the last twenty-four hours, you're the last man *I* want to see.' Victor tried to push past.

'Please.' Luke laid his hand on Victor's arm.

Victor shrugged it off and gave Luke a warning look. 'Standing in the dock together doesn't make us friends.'

'But it does give us a common problem. You do realize that if we're found guilty we'll be fined or sent to prison.'

'Given that none of us is in a position to pay a fine, I'd say we'll be sent to prison or sent to prison. And I wonder whose fault that would be?' Victor finally allowed his anger with Luke to surface.

'Come on, Victor, you were there.' Luke raised his voice for the benefit of the men around him. 'We only did what we had to.'

'You prevented essential workers from carrying out maintenance to keep the pit viable,' Victor said coldly.

'I stopped blacklegs from taking our jobs.'

'I have no intention of arguing with you about it. You see things one way, I see them another.' Victor closed the discussion.

'You do support the strike, don't you?' Luke challenged.

'Anyone say any different?' Victor questioned softly.

'No!' Luke backed off. He wasn't a small man but at five feet ten inches he was eight inches shorter than Victor.

'Luke's only trying to say that if this strike lasts much longer, all of us will be queuing outside the workhouse door,' Ben Duckworth, a platelayer, who maintained the underground tracks for the coal trams chipped in.

'The workhouse isn't big enough to house every miner's family in this valley.' Victor recited one of his father's maxims.

'Either way, we could all do with a few bob.' Ben stepped close to Victor and whispered, 'Have you heard that the police and soldiers fancy they've a few boxers in their ranks?'

'I've heard that there've been a couple of matches up the mountain,' Victor replied guardedly. At sixteen he'd been taller and stronger than most grown men. Encouraged by the blacksmith he'd been apprenticed to, he'd started training and fought half a dozen bare-knuckle boxing bouts. His father had been furious when he'd seen his bruises, but spurred on by the guinea he'd made for every match he won – and he'd won half of his bouts – he'd refused to allow his father or Lloyd to talk him out of carrying on. Right up until the Saturday afternoon he'd gone up against a blacksmith from Fernhill Colliery who'd knocked him literally into the middle of the week after next. His winnings had been swallowed up by the loss of fourteen days' pay and he'd never been tempted to repeat the experience.

'Interested?' Luke hazarded.

'In seeing you fight, yes.' Victor chose to deliberately misunderstand Luke, but there was a part of him that would have enjoyed seeing Luke's ebullience knocked out of him.

Ben roared with laughter. 'Luke's talents lie in other directions.'

'So I've seen,' Victor muttered.

'We're recruiting men to go up against the police and soldiers. There'll be a good purse for every winning fighter and a chance for everyone to bet and make a bit on the side.'

'Who's running the book?' Victor enquired suspiciously.

'The soldiers,' Ben admitted. 'The police don't dare do it in case word gets back to the authorities and we haven't the money to set it up.'

'Then the soldiers will be the only ones to make any real money,' Victor declared.

'I've seen you fight. You'll win, and the police and soldiers have seen to it that the victors – your father gave you the right name,' Ben grinned at the unintentional pun, 'aren't paid in guineas but fivers. Crisp, white five-pound notes for an afternoon's work if you're the lucky winner. That's more than most men make grafting for three weeks underground.'

'If you'll excuse me, I didn't get much sleep last night, and I'd like to get home.' Victor touched his cap and eyed the men blocking his path. They moved aside. He walked into Dunraven Street and turned up the hill.

'Mam?' Harry wriggled out from under the bedclothes, leaned over her shoulder and close to her ear. 'Can I get up now?'

Sali turned over and opened her eyes. Harry was sitting on Lloyd's pillow, his nightshirt pulled up around his knees, his eyes sparkling.

'There's no need to ask if you're still tired.'

'I'm hungry.'

The smile on his face turned to a look of fear when the door opened and Victor and Joey helped Lloyd into the room. Lloyd's head was heavily bandaged, the little skin that could be seen between the strips of linen was bruised black, and it was evident that if it hadn't been for the support Victor was giving him, he wouldn't have been able to stand upright. Sali blanched and covered her mouth with her hands.

'I'm all right, sweetheart,' Lloyd mumbled unconvincingly.

Seeing Harry's eyes round in fear, Joey forced a smile. 'No need to look as if you've seen a monster, young man, Uncle Lloyd will soon mend.'

'That's right,' Lloyd added, his speech slowed by concussion.

'We heard you chattering downstairs, Harry. If you get your clothes from your room and go down, I'll boil you an egg,' Victor promised.

Harry looked uncertainly at Sali. She patted his hand. 'Uncle Lloyd and I are both fine, Harry, just tired. You run along.'

Lloyd sank down on the bed beside her after Harry, Joey and Victor left. 'I could swing for whoever put that bruise on your face.'

'I honestly think I did it to myself. I don't recall anyone touching me. But you.' She reached up and stroked his face, and he winced even at her light touch.

'It would appear that a certain Constable John Lamb is in the Royal Infirmary in Cardiff. He was hit with a brick that was thrown in Dunraven Street the night before last. He has a fractured skull and hasn't yet regained consciousness. Someone, I have no idea who, told his brother, Sergeant Lamb, that I threw it. His mates were happy to get their own back by putting the boot in. My face didn't get the worst of the kicking,' he slurred, preparing her for the sight of the bandages that swathed his chest and stomach. 'They were probably congratulating themselves on a job well done until Gwyn Jenkins stepped in and told them I wasn't even in Dunraven Street the night before last. They might have argued with him if he hadn't been backed by a young copper from Pontypridd called Huw Davies.'

'Constable Huw Davies?'

'You know him?'

'I've met him.' She recalled standing at the door of the Hardy's hut looking for someone to help her. 'What's going to happen, Lloyd?'

'To me – nothing. But Joey, Victor and Luke Thomas are going to trial sometime in the New Year. The police had no choice but to drop the case against me but they insist that I wasn't beaten. According to the sergeant who was on duty in the station last night, I tripped and fell down some stone steps. It's my word against that of police officers. And we all know what that means these days.'

'What did the doctor say?'

'That I'll live. Move over. And do me a favour. Help me undress.' He pulled at his jersey.

'You're coming to bed?'

'Yes, and for once, my love, just to sleep.'

Megan laid the fires and served the breakfasts in a trance on Saturday morning. All she could think about were the hours she was about to spend with Victor. But the rooms that slept eight were as bad as Lena had predicted and it took them hours to clear the mess.

Joyce Palmer joined them when Lena was bundling the linen for the laundry and Megan was carrying the brushes on to the landing.

'After you've taken those things downstairs, come into my private sitting room and I'll pay you your wages, Megan, so you can get a postal order off to your father. I've made Cornish pasties for our lunch. You can eat in the kitchen before you go.'

Megan had been about to say that she would eat with Victor and his family, then remembered the strike. Just one week of living in a house where there was no shortage of food had been enough for her to start taking both quality and quantity of meals for granted. 'I will, thank you, Mrs Palmer.'

'Lena, go upstairs, wash, change your overall for your apron and make yourself presentable to wait on the lodgers' table.'

Megan carried the pails and brushes downstairs, washed her

hands in the scullery and ate her pasty standing at the kitchen window.

It was one of those rare winter days in the valley, crisp, clear and sunny, but when she stepped outside she'd felt the effects of a cold wind, even in the comparatively sheltered back yard. Would Victor want to go for a walk in town or over the mountain? She'd be happy just to sit with him in his kitchen but she couldn't expect him to light the fire just for her.

She ran up the stairs to fetch the soft, green wool dress she kept for 'best' and her glacé kid, grey shoes. Taking coals from the kitchen fire with tongs, she dropped them into Joyce's smoothing irons and pressed the dress on a blanket she laid over the scullery table. She polished her shoes and draping her dress carefully over her arm so as not to touch the shoes, raced back up the stairs, debating whether to wear her winter underclothes or her favourite set of summer-weight, Swiss-embroidered Nainsook drawers and petticoat. She would freeze, but it would be worth it to feel beautiful from her skin out.

She washed and changed in the bedroom she shared with Lena using a sixpenny cake of de luxe rose-scented soap that Daisy and Sam had bought her last Christmas. Her powder bowl was almost empty and her scent bottle only held a few drops. Thinking of the five extra shillings a week she would have at the end of the month all being well, she dusted her chest and dabbed scent behind her ears before dressing in her summer-weight underclothes, dress and only pair of real silk stockings. She removed her engagement ring from the chain around her neck and slipped it on to her finger, stopping every few seconds to admire it. She laced on her shoes, combed out her hair and twisted it into a knot that she pinned on the crown of her head. Fastening on her hat with a jet-headed pin that had belonged to her aunt, she fluffed her curls out beneath it, picked up the cape that Mrs Palmer had dried for her in front of the kitchen fire and took one last look at herself in the mirror, before running back down the stairs.

'Miss Williams.' Sergeant Martin met her on the first landing. 'You look very pretty. Going somewhere nice?'

Not daring to ignore him, she uttered a brief, 'Yes, sir.'

131

He continued to stand at the top of the staircase, effectively blocking her path. 'I've been meaning to have a word with you about my room.'

'Sir.' She stared down at her feet as she always did whenever he looked at her.

'The standards in this house have improved so much since you started working here, I wanted to give you a token of my appreciation.' He thrust a box of chocolates at her.

She gazed wide-eyed at the white box with its Heraldic decoration. 'Taylor's Chocolat D'Elite. I couldn't possibly accept this, sir. They are two shillings a box.'

'You've earned them. And you could have more—'

'No!'

'Go on, take them.' He drew closer to her.

'My fiancé wouldn't like it.' She held up her hand to show him her ring in case he hadn't noticed it when she'd waited at the table. 'Mrs Palmer is expecting me. I'm late.' Grabbing the banister to steady herself, she pushed past, fled down the stairs and collided with Constable Shipton. 'Sorry.' She sidestepped, but he moved quicker than her and continued to block her path.

'What's your hurry?' he grinned.

'I have to see Mrs Palmer . . .' She gasped as he pinched her bottom through her dress. Furious with him and Sergeant Martin, she kicked his ankle and ran across the hall.

'There's no need to charge around at top speed, Megan. I am sure that Mr Evans will wait for you,' Joyce said calmly when Megan rushed into her private sitting room. 'Here you are.' She handed her two ten-shilling notes.

'I haven't any money to give you change, Mrs Palmer.'

'You've earned your pound this week.' Joyce gave her a tight smile. 'And I suggest that if Mr Evans walks you home, he brings you to the kitchen door. You're less likely to meet a lodger in the back lane.'

Megan bought notepaper and envelopes in the stationers before joining the queue at the Post Office. She handed over her pound and when she received four shillings and fivepence change she was irritated, as she always was, by the loss of a precious sixpence in purchasing the order and a penny for the stamp.

She carried the order over to the shelf that held pens and inkpots. The nib on the pen was bent, and no matter how carefully she shook it after she dipped it in the ink, it left small blots around her carefully formed letters. She wrote the address of the farm, made the order payable to her father and scribbled:

> Dear Dad and Mam,
> Am very busy in my new job. Everything is going well. Will write a longer letter next week. Give Daisy, Sam and everyone else my love. This is Daisy's handkerchief.
> Lots of love,
> Your Megan

She slipped the note, handkerchief and order into the envelope, sealed it, stuck on the stamp and posted it on her way out. A police officer was standing in front of the door and she stepped into the gutter to avoid him.

'And you could have more . . .'

She wished she could talk to someone about Sergeant Martin and Constable Shipton. But her uncle was on his way to the other side of the world. Mrs Palmer employed her, but she didn't own the lodging house and her own position depended on making her lodgers happy. Victor . . . he was the last person she could confide in. The sergeant had arrested him and Joey. Victor was even more at his mercy . . .

'There's the bitch!'

'Get her!' Beryl Richards broke away from a group of women gossiping on the corner of the street and ran towards Megan.

'Traitor!'

'Turncoat!'

'Coppers' whore!'

'I hope you're comfortable living in the lap of luxury while children starve to death!' Beryl's face was contorted.

'You're not fit to walk the same streets as decent women.'

'Get in the gutter where you belong!' One of the younger women pushed her shoulder.

Megan turned and fled up the hill, clenching her fists and biting her lips in an effort to hold back her tears. She didn't cry. Not until she reached the lane that ran behind the shops. Then she hid between two sheds until she felt she could face Victor with a smile on her face.

'Megan, I hoped you'd come early.' Victor set aside the *Rhondda Leader* he'd been reading when she entered the kitchen. He left the table, kissed her and took her cape.

She set down her handbag and pulled off her kid gloves, before catching sight of the front page: MINERS SENT TO TRIAL FOR INTIMIDATION AND HARASSMENT. 'You've been reading about yourself?'

'It's not the way I'd choose to make headlines.' He flicked the paper over to a page of advertisements for the Roath Furnishing Company.

'You want to be in the paper?' She pulled the pin from her hat.

'Only in a wedding announcement.' He took her hat from her and placed it together with her cape on the rack in the hall.

'Where is everyone?'

'My father's at a committee meeting in the County Club and Joey's working backstage in the Empire. He told my father that he's helping Marsh Phillips with the scenery in return for free tickets to tonight's show, but I think it's more likely he's entertaining the chorus girls. There's a small, dark beauty called Peggy he walked out with a couple of times when she was here in *Driving a Girl to Destruction*. Remember that?'

'It's still the best play I've ever seen.' Megan recalled the evening she had persuaded Joey to look after her uncle's children and she and Victor had gone to the theatre. Looking back now, that magical, carefree time of their early courtship, before the strike had begun, seemed part of another world.

He closed the door when he returned to the kitchen. 'Sali had to go to Pontypridd for a meeting and after hearing that she'd been injured, Mr Richards arranged for a carriage to pick her up here. Lloyd and Harry went along too. I think Sali only agreed they could keep her company on the journey down in the hope that a change of scenery might do Lloyd good. He keeps insisting he's fine but he hasn't been right since he took that beating in the police station.'

'He's seen the doctor?'

'Several times.'

'But you're worried about him?'

'He took a kicking as well as a beating and a boot in the ribs can do a lot of damage. What makes me mad is the police are going to get away with it. Not only what they did to Lloyd, but to Sali and this house. They smashed most of my mother's china and wrecked the place. Every day we discover something else that they broke or damaged.'

'I'm sorry, Victor.'

'I'm sorrier still that you are working for them,' he added feelingly.

'If I had a choice . . .' She thought of the women who had attacked her in the street and tears pricked at the back of her eyes.

'Please, Megs, don't upset yourself. You're only doing what you have to, and there's no point in us spoiling our afternoon by talking about it.' He swept her into his arms and set her on his lap as he sat on one of the easy chairs. 'I lit a fire because we have the house to ourselves. But you look as though you're dressed to go out.'

'I dressed to go visiting – you. And I'm wearing my engagement ring.' She held out her hand to show him.

'So you don't mind staying in?' He locked his arms around her waist and kissed her full on the lips.

'No. Especially if there are going to be more kisses like that one.'

'We won't starve. I killed one of the chickens, and although Sali's not a hundred per cent better, she made soup and a pie. All they need is heating up in the oven.'

She glanced at the fire. 'You haven't been working in the drift mine again, have you?'

'I'm not crazy enough to stand in the dock one day and break the law the next. I used some of the coal your uncle left. Would you like to eat now?'

'I had a Cornish pasty just before I came out.'

'I hoped we could eat dinner together,' he complained.

'Mrs Palmer made the pasties specially for me, Lena and herself. It would have been rude of me not to eat mine.'

'Then we'll eat later.'

'I don't want you to starve on my account. I could heat up the soup for you . . .'

He tightened his grip on her waist to prevent her from escaping his lap. 'I can think of better things to do than eat for a while.'

He kissed her again. Her head swam when she felt the warmth of his fingers cupping her breast through her dress and bodice. In the year that had elapsed since he had first told her he loved her, they had rarely enjoyed the luxury of privacy. Christmas night last year had been memorable because she had managed to send the younger children to bed early and her uncle, his brothers and the older boys had gone out. But it had been one of only four occasions that she could recall being alone with Victor inside a house. And the last time Victor had been filthy with coal and her father had interrupted them, so she felt that didn't count. But even on Christmas night, he hadn't gone any further than he had now, touching her breast through her clothes.

She nestled close to his chest. 'Now we're engaged, you could do more than that.' Her cheeks burned at her own temerity.

'I'm not sure I could trust myself to stop.'

She looked up at him. 'I wouldn't want you to.'

'And if you have a baby?'

'My father would have to let us get married then, wouldn't he?'

'And if he didn't?'

'I hadn't thought of that.'

'Until you are twenty-one your father has the right to do whatever he wants with you. Forbid us to marry, put you and the child in the workhouse or separate you from the child and send you to work miles from here.' He tightened his hold on her. 'I couldn't bear for anything like that to happen to us, Megs.'

She unlocked his hands from her waist, left him and went to the fire. Leaning on the mantelpiece, she looked down into the flames. 'I know my father. He couldn't live with the disgrace of a daughter who'd had a bastard. He would let us marry.'

'I'm not prepared to take that risk.'

'And if I am?'

He fell silent for a moment and when he answered her, she had never seen him looked so grave. 'You know I want to marry you more than anything else in the world. But not that way. Not with your father and the rest of your family thinking the worst of you – and me.'

'I don't care what anyone thinks of me – except you.'

'Yes, you do, Megs.' He rose to his feet and wrapped his arms around her again.

It had taken so much courage to broach the subject of lovemaking with him; she had difficulty believing that he had rejected her. 'Is this something to do with your religion? Don't you Catholics think that . . . that . . . sleeping with someone you're not married to is a sin?'

' "You Catholics?" ' he repeated wonderingly. 'You think we're that different from Protestants.'

'I don't know the first thing about your religion. You've never talked to me about it.'

'Only because I don't want to bore you with it, Megs.'

'Is it important to you?'

'It is, because it was my mother's religion and she set great store by it. I think Joey only goes to church out of habit and loyalty to her. It means more to me, but it's not as important to me, as you – or us.'

'Then you'd give it up for me?'

'If you asked me to,' he answered soberly. 'Lloyd and my father would welcome me to the ranks of the atheists with open arms.'

She looked at him and realized he was serious despite his quip. 'I couldn't ask you to make that sacrifice after you've just admitted it's important to you.'

'It doesn't affect my entire life, Megs.'

'But it does affect your life more than Joey allows it to affect his,' she said wryly.

He threw back his head and laughed. 'If the Church is right and making love outside marriage is a mortal sin, Joey is destined to spend an awful lot of time in hell.'

'Quite!' Although she would never have admitted it, she was smarting from his rejection. 'Everyone knows that Joey has slept with half the women in the Rhondda, never mind Tonypandy, and he's not worried about fathering a child.'

'That's because Joey has no respect for the women he sleeps with and even less for himself.'

'In other words, if they have a baby, Joey can stand in front of the magistrate and say, "Please, sir, it could be me or any of the other men she slept with."'

'I'm not Joey, so I don't know what he thinks.' He fell serious again. 'What I do know is there's only one woman for me and that's you. We have our whole life ahead of us, Megs. Let's not rush into anything. And my parents always taught us that sleeping with a woman comes after marriage.'

'It seems to me only you listened to them.'

'Joey—'

'Never mind Joey, what about Lloyd and Sali?'

'They are getting married. You're bridesmaid, remember, the Saturday before Christmas. I hope you've asked Mrs Palmer for the day off.'

Megan hadn't, but neither was she about to get sidetracked into a discussion about Lloyd and Sali's wedding. 'Mrs Robinson across the road says that she hasn't seen Lloyd close his curtains once at night since you came back from your summer holidays last year.'

Victor's face darkened. 'Mrs Robinson is a poisonous old gossip and Sali and Lloyd had good reason to delay their wedding.'

Feeling that Victor was justifiably angry with her for even listening to a woman like Mrs Robinson, she apologized. 'I'm sorry. I wasn't prying into Lloyd and Sali's business. Just trying to point out that we're engaged and we have the house to ourselves for the afternoon so we should make the most of it.'

'I'm sorry if I've hurt you by loving you too much to use you.' He looked so miserable she couldn't do anything other than forgive him.

'I'll heat some soup for you, and afterwards if you want, we can go out.'

'About all I can afford is a walk up the mountain and a cup of tea in the teashop when we get back.'

Megan almost told him that she had four shillings and sixpence and could pay for both of them to go to the Empire. Then she realized his pride would never allow him to accept money from her. 'A walk and a cup of tea it is, unless you'd like to sit by the fire and forget we had this conversation – for now,' she qualified.

'How about,' he sat down and pulled her back on to his lap, 'we make plans for the twenty-fifth of August nineteen twelve. We could start by talking about where you'd like to live.'

'A coalhouse would do as long as it's with you.'

'Jokes aside, where would you like to live in an ideal world?'

'I know it sounds silly, because you're a colliery blacksmith and your life is here, but whenever I think of us married and living together it's always in a farmhouse.'

'A proper farm?' he asked in surprise.

'With geese, goats and chickens in the yard, ducks on a pond, sheep in the fields, a couple of cows and at least one horse. Oh – and a kitchen garden and orchard. Perhaps it's something to do with growing up on my father's farm, although that's nowhere near as grand as the one I picture us having. It is just a dream,' she said, when Victor grew thoughtful.

'It's funny, whenever I imagine us married, I think of home as something like this house. Next door, for instance.' He had asked Lloyd if he could exchange the house for one his father held in their names and, as he'd expected, Lloyd had happily agreed. But he still held back from telling Megan.

'Next door would be wonderful. Do you think Lloyd would rent it to us?'

'He'd sell it to us outright when the time comes. You know my family owns houses.'

'And your share will be a whole house?'

'At least that.' He didn't want to go into details because there was no point in building even an imaginary future on tenanted houses that weren't bringing in a penny.

'Just think, Victor, no rent or mortgage to pay.'

'Just think, Megan, while this strike lasts, no money.'

'It can't go on for another twenty months.'

'I sincerely hope not.' He started as the front door opened but he refused to allow her to get off his lap.

'Damned chorus girl . . .' Joey barged in. 'Sorry, I didn't mean to interrupt you two. Victor did say it was your afternoon off, Megan, I forgot. But I must say for a newly engaged couple you are behaving very respectably. Victor's collar isn't even undone.'

'That's my fiancée you're talking to,' Victor growled.

'I can see the ring. It looks good on you, Megan. But I do apologize for my brother being a bit slow on the uptake.'

'He is anything but slow.' Megan retorted defensively. She and Victor exchanged glances and they both burst out laughing.

Joey instinctively glanced down at his flies to check that they were buttoned. 'What are you two laughing at?'

'Nothing,' Megan giggled.

'I take it Peggy didn't want to rekindle the memories. Tell me, did she slap your face?' Victor enquired.

'It was all a ploy cooked up by her and Marsh Phillips. I've been doing his job, shifting scenery around for the last two hours while they've been off cavorting at a very private party for two in an upstairs room in the White Hart.'

'And they didn't reward you for your efforts?' Victor didn't even try to keep a straight face.

Joey felt in his jacket pocket and dropped two tickets on the table. 'For tonight's show. As if I'd go and watch Peggy on stage after what she did to me.'

Victor reached over and filched them. 'Stalls no less. Thank you very much, little brother.'

'You're welcome to them. Say, is there any food going? I'm starving after all that heavy lifting.'

'There's soup. I'll heat it up.' Megan pushed Victor's hands back and left his lap. 'As soon you've eaten, Victor, we'll go for that walk. We'll need a few lungfuls of fresh air before we go to the Empire. You know how stuffy it can get in there,' she glanced slyly at Joey, 'especially in the stalls with all those young men breathing heavily at the sight of the chorus girls in their costumes.'

Chapter 9

'YOU'VE LEFT Lloyd and Harry in Ynysangharad House, Mrs Jones?' Mr Richards helped Sali down from the carriage that had pulled up outside Gwilym James's department store in Market Square in Pontypridd.

'I have. Mari's promised to keep an eye on them because Lloyd is still weak. She told me to tell you that she'll have tea on the table at four o'clock.'

'Then I'll try to ensure that we finish our meeting before four. Mrs Williams' teas are something to be reckoned with.' Mari Williams had been Sali's father's housekeeper before his death, and although she was employed in Ynysangharad House only as a nurse and companion to Sali's mother, the elderly housekeeper was somewhat frail and Mari had taken over responsibility for most of her duties.

'Are all the trustees here?' Sali took the arm he offered her and they walked into the store.

'They are. But you are not late. It is a quarter to two and the meeting is not due to start until two o'clock.'

'Mr Horton, how nice to see you.' Sali greeted the manager of the store. His father had occupied the post before him and given fifty years sterling service to Gwilym James before his death. All the reports she'd received indicated that his son was just as dedicated to the business.

'And you, madam. May I enquire after Master Harry's health?' Mr Horton walked them to the lift.

'Master Harry is well thank you. And everyone at the store?'

'The staff have had their usual complement of winter coughs and colds, but we are coping well and the store is running like clockwork. Although the takings have been adversely affected by the strike.'

'Badly?'

'Not as yet, madam. Fortunately we have an excellent customer base among the tradesmen in Pontypridd and the miners in the pits that are still open. I will be upstairs in good time for the meeting but I have one or two things to attend to beforehand.'

'In case I don't have to time to speak to you after the meeting, my compliments to your wife, Mr Horton.' Sali followed Mr Richards into the lift.

'Thank you, madam.' Mr Horton signalled to the liftboy to take the lift to the third floor and the boardroom where the trustees of Harry's estate held their meetings.

'So, how badly has the store been hit?' Sali asked Mr Richards when they alighted and the boy had taken the lift back down to the ground floor. Mr Richards was not an official trustee but two members of his firm of solicitors were, and she knew that he kept a close eye on her late great-aunt's estate.

'The takings are down ten per cent. It's not just the strike. People are afraid that it might spread to other pits. Everyone is cutting back and trying to save against possible future hard times.'

'So we're not really in trouble?'

'Not at all. You know that we were set to expand when the strike broke out. We have enough put aside to see the store and the trust's other business ventures safe, even if the strike lasts two years.'

Sali halted, unable to believe she'd heard him correctly. 'Surely you don't think the strike can go on that long?'

'From what I've heard, Mrs Jones, the colliery companies are out to break the miners. Why do you think that they and the government have gone to the expense of drafting over a thousand extra police into the valleys as well as stationing the Hussars and the Somersets there?'

'Management has to give in, they have to . . .' Her voice tailed. She simply couldn't bear to think of the alternative: Principled men like Lloyd, his father, Victor and even Joey fighting for a cause that was already lost.

*   *   *

142

'It seemed a good idea to go for a walk when we were looking out of the window in your warm kitchen.' Megan snuggled close to Victor, as a keen south-westerly wind picked up speed, whipping their clothes and stinging their faces.

'Is is fresh,' Victor agreed. They climbed the hill, walked past the garden walls of the last terrace and out on to the unfenced mountain.

'Your fresh is other people's Arctic.' She glanced across at him. His eyes were bright, his skin glowing. 'You love being outdoors whatever the weather, don't you?'

'You would too, if you spent eight hours of your working day underground.'

'What's it like down the pit?' she asked curiously.

'Your uncle never told you?'

'We only ever talked about the house, the children, the housekeeping and what he wanted me to cook.'

'Of all the jobs in the colliery, your uncle had the worst, cutting coal at the face and loading it into drams. It's bad enough if the seam is tall enough for a man to stand upright while he pickaxes out the coal and shale, but some of them are barely high enough to crawl into sideways. And the dust at the face – it's difficult to describe to someone who's never seen it. It hangs in the air – thick, filthy – it covers and gets into everything. Your clothes, boots, tools, skin, eyes, ears, nose – it's like trying to breathe in a pea soup of powder. And outside of the light of your lamp, it's blacker than you ever imagined darkness could get. Sometimes it's hotter than a bread oven . . .'

'I thought it would be freezing cold.'

'Not always, and what little breathable air there is around you is clammy and stinking. So now you know why I like the outdoors even in the cold. And the rain isn't so bad either, especially during the day. Because there have been times in the winter when I only see daylight on a Sunday.' He wrapped his arm around her waist.

'But you work with the horses in the stables and aren't they near the cage?'

He laughed. 'You think the horses are near the cage so they can look up and see the light.'

143

'Of course not,' she answered touchily, because that was exactly how she had imagined the stables.

'My job might be head horsekeeper and blacksmith, but shoeing the horses is only part of it. There's a lot of smithy work underground. Maintaining the tracks, the ironwork on the dram wagons and ventilation doors, and that's without seeing to the coal cutters' tools.' They reached the summit of the mountain and he turned and looked back at the valley spread out beneath them like a living map.

On either side of them and across on the opposite mountains, vast interlocking pyramids of glistening black slag and colliery waste spewed down from the hilltops, ending only yards from where the houses began. Directly below was the path they had walked, bordered by yellow-green grass splattered with purple heather and gold-speckled dying bracken. The first four rows of houses, the highest in the valley, were the smallest and poorest. At the end of each terrace was a communal waterspout. And below the tiny two-up two-down cottages were the 'better' streets of larger houses, built behind Dunraven Street.

'I know it's silly, but I can never climb to the top of this hill without looking for our house. My father used to do it every time he brought us up here when we were children. It was almost as if he needed to reassure himself that it was still there, waiting for us to come back.'

'At least you still have a home to look for.' She spoke with more sorrow than bitterness.

'We'll have one of our own one day, Megs, and until then you'll be welcome in ours.' He lifted her chin with the tips of his gloved fingers and kissed her. Her nose was freezing, her lips cold against his. 'I'd better get you back down before you turn blue.'

'Not yet. My favourite place is just over the brow of the hill where you can't see any signs of people.'

'Just slag, mountain and sheep.'

'And the freshest air.' She saw him watching her. 'You know what I mean.'

'I always know what you mean.'

'Race you to that rock?'

'I know better ways to warm up.'

'So do I, but we'd freeze if we tried them here.' Megan ran as fast as she could, but she couldn't catch Victor, who remained a constant two feet ahead of her. It didn't help that she knew he was holding back. Eventually he stopped and grabbed her. Breathless, she fell against him but instead of kissing her as she expected him to, he narrowed his eyes and looked over her shoulder.

She turned and saw a crowd of several hundred men. 'An unofficial strike meeting?'

He frowned. 'It's an unofficial meeting, but I don't think it has anything to do with the strike.'

'Does it mean trouble?' she asked apprehensively.

'Let's take a closer look.' He reached for her hand and started walking.

Sali entered the boardroom of Gwilym James, greeted her fellow trustees and took her place at the head of the table. Mr Richards sat on her right, Mr Jenkins, her late great-aunt's butler on her left. Her Great-Aunt Edyth had stipulated in her will that there were to be twelve trustees. These were to include Sali, Mr Jenkins, the three senior members of staff of Gwilym James, which were at present, the manager Mr Horton, Sali's brother Geraint who held the post of assistant manager, and Mr Horton's son, who, although young at twenty-two, had worked for the store since his fourteenth birthday.

The junior Mr Horton, who had been christened Alfred after his grandfather, always took the minutes of the meetings and arranged for them to be posted to his fellow trustees. Sali also suspected that he had a greater knowledge of the day-to-day running of the store and possessed more business acumen than her brother ever would. But when their uncle had embezzled Geraint's inheritance and he needed a job, she'd arranged for him to take the position that she sensed the store's other employees felt was Alfred Horton's by aptitude, capability and – considering his father and grandfather's devoted service to the James family – birthright.

Every time she saw Alfred Horton, she felt guilty. When Geraint had accepted the position of assistant manager, he had insisted that he would soon move on. Just as he had assured her that he would take responsibility for finding somewhere other than Harry's house for himself, their mother, brother and sister to live in. But as time passed, he ceased to mention 'moving on' or out of Ynysangharad House and she believed he now regarded the post and housing he had taken as a temporary measure, as his by right. Certainly, he behaved more like the master of Ynysangharad House, than she, the mistress, when she visited her mother after the monthly trustee meetings.

The two senior directors of the Market Company that owned Pontypridd indoor market halls and collected the rents for the outdoor stalls, had been co-opted on to the board, and as Gwilym James held fifty-five percent of the Market Company stock, they could always be counted on to vote with Mr Horton. Two partners from Mr Richards' firm of solicitors were also trustees. Mr Richards attended the meetings, but only at Sali's invitation and in his capacity as her adviser. Three directors from the Capital and Counties Bank made up the number.

Sali had read the minutes of the last meeting and Mr Richards had sent her a letter commenting on the business he expected to be covered at the next session. She expected a routine and dull discussion on investments, because the company was too cash rich at that moment for the bankers' liking. But thanks to Mr Richards' tutelage and their weekly correspondence, she was beginning to understand the intricacies of business and high finance.

They sat quietly through the reading of the monthly balance sheets by one of the bank's directors. Gwilym James' overall turnover was down ten per cent just as Mr Horton had warned her it would be. At twelve per cent down, the Market Company had been hit slightly harder, but although profits were smaller the businesses were doing well, especially in comparison to some of the other shops in Pontypridd and the Rhondda. The minutes of the last meeting were read, passed as accurate and, as she'd expected, the bankers, solicitors, Mr Horton and the two directors from the Market Company embarked on an involved debate as to the merits, or otherwise, of various investment opportunities.

Glad to leave the financial decisions to the professionals, Sali gazed out of the window. It was set too high for her to see anything other than an expanse of clear sky and wispy white clouds. Her mind drifted and she mulled over what Mr Richards had said to her about the strike.

During all the years the solicitor had advised her father and her family, she had never known him to be ill-informed. She respected his opinion above everyone else she knew, with the exception of Lloyd and his father. But she couldn't bear the thought that the man she loved and all the other colliers and their families were suffering the deprivations and hardships of the strike for no gain. Yet, she couldn't deny the logic behind Mr Richards' conclusion, and wondered why she hadn't thought the situation through for herself. It had undoubtedly been prohibitively expensive to bring in and house close on a thousand extra police as well as two regiments of soldiers in the Rhondda. And although the colliery owners were prepared to talk, they had made it clear that they weren't about to make any further concessions to the miners' demands other than those that had been already rejected by the union. So why should they suddenly change their minds and offer more?

How much longer could Lloyd and the strike committee hold out? The miners were in no mood to back down, but Christmas was coming, the winter was proving a hard and cold one, and the soup kitchens were struggling to feed the starving population as it was. Connie had told her all the shops that had extended credit to the strikers were teetering on bankruptcy . . .

'Would you like to comment on the point Mr Watkin Jones has just made, Mrs Jones?'

'Pardon?' Sali turned from the window and looked blankly at Mr Jenkins.

'We have reached any other business, Sali,' Geraint explained testily. 'And I have brought the manner in which you are raising Harry to the attention of the committee.'

'The way I bring up my son is my business and no one else's, Geraint.' She was furious with her brother for initiating a discussion with the trustees on the subject.

'And the business of everyone in Pontypridd and the Rhondda

147

who can read and afford to pay a penny for a newspaper.' Geraint lifted a dozen copies of the *Pontypridd Observer* that carried several of the same stories as the *Rhondda Leader* from beneath his chair and set them on the table. He had already turned them to the page that covered the court reports. 'All three of your employer's sons have been arrested and two sent to trial.'

'On what charge?' one of the solicitors asked.

'Take your pick,' Geraint drawled. 'Intimidation, harassment . . . Mr Lloyd Evans, whom I believe my sister is contemplating marrying as soon as she is free to do so, was charged with assault.'

'A charge that was dropped,' Sali broke in heatedly.

'A charge is not a conviction, Mr Watkin Jones,' Mr Richards interposed quietly.

'Two of Mr Evans' sons have been sent to trial,' Geraint countered. 'And Harry calls both of them "uncle".'

'The law in Britain states that a man is deemed innocent until proven guilty.' A steely note crept into Mr Richards's voice.

'That doesn't alter the fact that Sali is bringing up the heir to the Gwilym James estate in the house of a strike leader and a Marxist.'

'It is not illegal to be a Marxist, Geraint,' Sali said firmly.

Ignoring the angry glare Sali was sending in his direction, Geraint crossed his arms, sat back on his chair and looked to his fellow trustees. 'I believe my nephew should be brought up and educated in a manner befitting the gentleman of means and prominence he will become when he takes control of his inheritance. And that, gentlemen, cannot happen while he remains in his present accommodation. It is my contention that we would be negligent in our duty to allow him to remain in Mr William Evans' house.'

'Harry is four years old,' Mr Richards reminded. 'At that age a child needs his mother.'

'And stepfather,' Sali interposed.

'A miner—'

'A qualified engineer,' Sali interrupted.

'Who has joined the ranks of Marxist troublemakers who flout the law and preach the sedition that is crippling the coal industry in Wales. They fight the police and army in the streets—'

'The miners are fighting for a wage that will enable them to live with dignity.'

'You see, gentlemen,' Geraint's lip curled in contempt, 'my sister has, as the result of living in a strike leader's house, joined the ranks of the Marxists.' He turned to Sali, daring her to contradict him.

'If believing that workers should be paid a decent wage for their labour makes me a Marxist, then I am proud to be one,' Sali blazed, losing her temper. 'The first motion I put to the trustees was the raising of staff wages in this store. From which you benefited.'

'The staff here didn't withdraw their labour,' Geraint snapped.

'It is not a crime—'

'That is debatable,' Geraint cut in ruthlessly. 'It is also irrelevant to the point I am making. The family you live with are not fit to raise Harry.'

Mr Richards laid his hand over Sali's and gripped it tightly. 'And who do you suggest should raise your nephew, Mr Watkin Jones?'

'Harry should be brought up in Ynysangharad House. From the terms of her will, Mrs James clearly expected him and Sali to move into the house that he will inherit on his thirtieth birthday. As I am already living there and am his uncle by blood, I believe that I am well suited and placed to act as his guardian.'

'And Mrs Jones?'

'It is ridiculous for the mother of the heir to the Gwilym James fortune to work as a housekeeper for a family of striking miners with criminal tendencies. I dread to think of the example they are setting my nephew.'

'You forget that I am about to marry into the family, Geraint.' Sali followed the lead Mr Richards had set, realizing that she would accomplish more if she managed to restrain herself.

'On the contrary, that is what is at the forefront of my mind.'

'Would you consider moving into Ynysangharad House, Mrs Jones?' Mr Jenkins asked.

'No,' Sali replied honestly.

'Under the terms of Mrs James' will, any member of your

149

family may do so. Perhaps you and your husband, when you marry—'

'Mr Evans would not consider moving into Ynysangharad House,' Sali said uncompromisingly.

'You have discussed it with him?' Mr Jenkins questioned. Sali recalled her father once telling her that the most snobbish and class-conscious people on earth were butlers, and she saw that Geraint wasn't the only trustee who thought it disgraceful that she was raising Harry in a collier's terraced house.

'My future husband is employed by the Cambrian Collieries—'

'When he bothers to work,' Geraint broke in derisively.

'He lived in Pontypridd when he worked in my father's colliery,' Sali ignored Geraint, 'but now both his work and his family are in Tonypandy.'

'There is the matter of Harry's education,' Mr Jenkins mused. 'Surely neither you nor your future husband think Harry should attend a council school in Tonypandy.'

'Harry already attends a council school.'

Geraint's face darkened. 'That is a damned disgrace—'

'Language, Mr Watkin Jones,' Mr Jenkins interposed. 'All the men in your family have been educated at public school, Mrs Jones. Surely you intend to send your son there when he is old enough?'

'I haven't thought about it,' Sali lied. She had thought about little else since she had first been told of the terms of her aunt's will. Her father and brothers had gone to the 'family' school and her younger brother, Gareth still had three more years there before he could move on to university.

There was a murmur of conversation and Mr Jenkins tapped the table.

'All trustees in favour of Master Harry attending public school at the earliest opportunity please raise their hands.'

Sali looked around the table in despair. The only hands that weren't raised were her own and Mr Richards', and he didn't have a vote. 'Surely my son's education is a private matter for myself and my future husband to decide?'

'We are here, not only to manage your son's estate, Mrs Jones, but to also monitor his welfare,' Mr Jenkins informed her pompously.

'May I request a vote on Harry's place of residence,' Geraint proposed. 'I suggest that he should be removed to Ynysangharad House as soon as possible.'

'Let us make this absolutely clear, Mr Watkin Jones. You are asking us to vote that your nephew be taken from your sister's care?' Mr Richards said baldly.

'I am suggesting that both Sali and her son should move into Ynysangharad House.'

'Your sister has already stated that she will not move from her present abode, Mr Watkin Jones.'

'My sister has a choice, Mr Richards. She can either make the welfare of her son her first priority, or continue her liaison with this collier and his family.'

'Mrs Jones,' Mr Jenkins put his hands together, intertwining his fingers as if he was about to pray, 'are you prepared to reconsider your decision not to take up residence in Ynysangharad House?'

'No, Mr Jenkins. I reserve the right to decide where and with whom I live, and where I will bring up my son. Harry is four years old. He loves and trusts his future stepfather and his family and he feels safe and secure living with them.'

'Living with the working – or at present the non-working classes,' Geraint said.

'Although I am here only in an advisory capacity, may I make a suggestion that the subject of Master Harry's education be put into abeyance until he is six years old, when the trustees can discuss the matter again and make a firm decision as to where he should be educated,' Mr Richards interposed.

'And in the meantime?' Geraint queried. 'You think he should be left to live in the squalor of a collier's house, exposed to the most unsuitable political views along with dirt, disease and heaven only knows what else?'

Sali seethed at the injustice of Geraint's description of a home he had never stepped into.

'You would remove a four-year-old boy from his mother's care?' Mr Richards looked Geraint in the eye.

'Yes, I would,' Geraint answered defiantly. 'Placed in new surroundings, and given over to the care of a competent tutor, the boy would soon adapt and forget the errors of his early upbringing.'

'I don't think any of us could countenance taking such a drastic step, Mr Watkin Jones.' Mr Jenkins looked down the table and the other trustees nodded assent. 'To move on, is there any other business?' When no one spoke, he rose from his chair. 'It only remains for me to thank you all for coming. Mr Horton?' He looked to the junior member of the board. 'I trust you will copy the notes of the meeting to all members as usual. Good day to you all. I will see you back at the house, Mrs Jones, Mr Richards, Mr Watkin Jones.'

'Goodbye and thank you, Mr Jenkins.' Sali stared at Geraint as the elderly butler left the room. But her brother turned his back to her and set his face resolutely to the door.

Megan had never seen so many men gathered together outside of a union meeting. A massive crowd circled a small area of raised ground, colloquially known as a 'tump'. Colliers in rags, their good clothes, boots and overcoats long since pawned, stamped their feet and waved their arms in an effort to keep warm as they stood alongside police officers and soldiers dressed for winter in waterproof capes and woollen greatcoats.

'Do you know what's going on?' Megan asked Victor.

'A boxing match.' Victor peered into the distance, but the fighters were too far away for him to recognize either of them. 'Luke Thomas told me they were holding them up here.'

'I've never seen a boxing match.'

'They're not a fit sight for women.'

'You men think we're delicate beings who can't stand excitement and faint at the sight of blood.'

'No, we don't. We know you're all as tough as old boots beneath your pretty faces. What do you think you're doing?' he demanded when she ran off towards the crowd.

'Getting a better look.'

He raced after her, reaching her when she stopped to climb on

152

to a dry stone wall. Holding her arms out like a tightrope walker, she balanced precariously on top and gazed over the heads of the spectators. Two men, stripped to knee-length flannel drawers, circled one another. Blood streamed from one man's head down on to his chest. Every time he tried to wipe the blood from his eyes, his opponent punched him, but although he couldn't possibly see to retaliate, he still lashed out blindly. His adversary had no problem dodging his punches.

'That poor man's getting beaten to death,' she cried out feelingly.

Victor stepped on the wall and held her by the waist to steady her. 'That's Dai Hopkins. The idiot,' he declared, as another punch landed above his right eye. Dai wavered and Victor waited for him to topple like a ninepin, but he remained stubbornly, if unsteadily upright. 'I don't know what he thinks he's doing. He's no boxer.'

'You know him?'

'He's a repairman like Joey. They work together.'

'Why doesn't he give up?'

'Because the referee is a cage hand. Dai's opponent must be either a policeman or a soldier, and the colliers have probably placed money they don't have that he'll win.' A couple of particularly choice instructions to Dai from his butties carried towards them on the wind. 'As a woman and an innocent, I hope you didn't understand a word of that.'

'It's no worse than some of the things my uncle and his brothers used to say to one another when they were arguing.'

Victor eyed Dai's opponent. He was wearing khaki drawers, a soldier then. And he was good. Quick on his feet with a sound punch. Not that he needed much speed or agility to anticipate Dai's moves. Victor was furious with the referee. He should have ended the bout when Dai started bleeding. It was obvious he'd lost the match.

He and Megan continued to watch for another five minutes until, blood-soaked and beaten, Dai finally fell to his knees. The referee blew a whistle and the crowd swarmed over the tump, swallowing up all three figures.

'I hope someone's looking after that poor man.' Megan blew her nose, and Victor wasn't sure whether she was suffering from the cold or a surfeit of emotion.

'He'll be looked after.' Victor jumped from the wall and held out his hands to lift her down.

'Perhaps we should see to him.'

'I'm not taking you into the middle of that crowd. Besides, we've just enough time to go home and have a cup of tea before going to the theatre.'

A small group broke away from the circle and started walking towards them.

'Look, someone is waving to us.' Megan waved back.

'That's Luke Thomas. He may want to see me, but I don't want to see him.' Victor turned his back to the men.

'Why not?'

'Because he's looking for boxers.'

'I remember Joey telling me that you used to box before I came to Tonypandy. He said you would come home covered in cuts and bruises and you were so badly hurt you had to give up.' She snatched at his arm. 'You wouldn't start fighting again, would you, Victor?'

His mouth set into a grim line as he thought of Dai Hopkins. The repairman was no bare-knuckle boxer. He would never have considered fighting if he hadn't been coerced into it. But then Dai had a family, and the men with young children were the most desperate for money.

'Victor?' Megan repeated anxiously.

'You came to see the boxing after all, Victor.' Luke Thomas walked towards them. To Victor's astonishment, one of the men with him was Sergeant Martin.

'You two make unlikely bedfellows.' He looked from the sergeant to Luke.

'There's the law, there's work, there's business and there's entertainment, Mr Evans,' the sergeant said coolly. 'We could all do with some relaxation, which is why I help organize these matches.'

154

'And run the book as well as turn a blind eye?' Victor enquired drily.

'I'm surprised you don't know that it's illegal to run a book. Good afternoon, Miss William.' He tipped his hat to Megan. 'May I ask what you are doing up here?'

'Out walking with my fiancé on my afternoon off.' Megan stole closer to Victor.

Victor laid his arm protectively around Megan's shoulders. 'And, as we have tickets for tonight's show in the Empire, it's time we were on our way. Please, excuse us, gentlemen.'

'You said that Mr Evans was interested in taking up the challenge, Thomas.' Sergeant Martin reached into his uniform pocket and extracted a cigar. Biting off the end, he spat it to the ground. 'I know you colliers are in dire need of champions but I didn't think you'd go so far as to pressgang an unwilling man into fighting for you.'

'Victor is one of our best bare-knuckle boxers,' Luke said with more enthusiasm than accuracy.

'Was,' Victor corrected.

'You've given up fighting, Mr Evans?' The sergeant cupped a penny petrol lighter to shield it from the wind, flicked it and lit his cigar.

Victor hesitated. What Luke had said about being fined worried him. He knew his father had virtually nothing left of their savings and they hadn't received a penny in rent for any of their houses since the strike had started. Sali had her own and Harry's allowances, although he had no idea how much they were, but even if she offered, he wouldn't take money from her. So, just as he'd said to Luke earlier, a fine really would mean prison.

'After seeing what the Somersets' regimental champion did to your colleague, I can understand you being afraid to take up the challenge.' The sergeant blew a plume of smoke in Victor's direction.

Luke was a bombastic idiot who frequently allowed his mouth to outdistance his brain, but even allowing for his flattery, Victor had been a promising boxer before he'd been beaten, albeit very young and inexperienced. If he began training again he knew he could make enough money to keep himself and Joey out of prison – and perhaps even enough to start saving for his and Megan's future. 'I'll think about it.'

'I'll call round your house first thing in the morning. We'll talk,' Luke broke in eagerly.

'I said I'd think about it. If I decide to go ahead, I know where to find you. Good afternoon.' Victor touched his cap, took Megan's arm and led her away.

'You're not really going to start boxing again, are you, Victor?' She had to run to keep up with him.

'I might make a lot of money if I did.' He voiced his thoughts.

'You don't need money.'

'I'll soon have a fine to pay and we'll need money when we marry.'

'You'll be working again long before then, I have ten pounds in savings and four shillings and sixpence a week left over from my wages after I've sent my father his money. You can have it.'

'I don't want your money, Megs.'

'Please, for my sake, don't start boxing again,' she pleaded, blanching as an image of Dai Hopkins, all bloody and battered, came to mind.

He smiled down at her. 'Even if I do and that is an "if", I promise you I won't end up in the same state as Dai Hopkins.'

'Joey said the last time you boxed you were knocked out for days.'

'I was younger then.'

'Victor—'

'Let's not talk about it. Not now. We have the theatre to look forward to. Do you know who's on the bill?'

Megan had never loved Victor more than at that moment. She admired his strength, his principles and his resolution. But she wished with all her heart that she could stop him from doing things she sensed would only lead to more trouble – and in this case hurt and pain.

Chapter 10

LLOYD STRAIGHTENED his back and tried not to lean quite so heavily on the walking stick that he had been forced to use since he'd been beaten. Sali was walking along the riverbank towards him and Harry and he was hoping to impress her with the improvement in his condition in the couple of hours since he'd seen her. 'Hello, sweetheart. Good meeting?'

Sali kissed Lloyd's cheek and stooped to kiss Harry. 'I'll tell you about it later. Mari told me you two had decided to go fishing with her best preserving jar.'

'Look, Mam.' Harry held up the jar, its rim tied with string. It was full of murky and unsavoury looking water.

'Is anything in there?' she asked warily.

'Uncle Lloyd . . . Dad . . . said there might be fish eggs that will hatch in spring when the weather gets warmer.'

'There might at that.' Sali reached for her scented handkerchief and held it over her nose. Even in the cold weather the stench of the river was foul. The water flowed thick with colliery waste, sewage, and hooves and hides from the slaughterhouses. It had been a long time since anything had managed to survive in the murky depths of the Taff, but Lloyd obviously hadn't wanted to disappoint Harry by telling him that.

'But, young man, they will have to be returned to the river or they won't hatch. We don't want to be responsible for killing the baby fish before they've had time to come out of their eggs, now do we?'

'Can I tip them back?' Harry ran off the path.

'Only if you hold my hand when you lean over the bank.' Lloyd gripped Harry's free hand, and Harry upended the jar over the river.

'I'll carry the jar back,' Sali offered. 'Mari has tea ready, and she's made one of her chocolate cakes especially for you. Mr Richards is there too, and he wants to say hello.'

'Mr Richards. Yippee!' Harry yelled using an expression Joey had picked up from one of the comics Sali suspected Joey bought more for his own benefit than Harry's.

'Be sure to wash your hands well as soon as you go in.' Sali watched her son charge down the path, arms and legs flying, cap pushed to the back of his head, coat open to the cold wind. 'I hope it is Mr Richards he wants to see, not the sixpence he always gives him.'

'So, how did the meeting go?' Lloyd lifted his trilby and repositioned it away from the worst of his bruises.

'It was horrible.'

'Let me guess, Mr Jenkins lectured you on etiquette, or the correct way to hand out teacups at a board meeting?'

'It would have been boring but I could have put up with it if he had.' She curled her gloved fingers around his arm, as they headed up the path that ran alongside the river. 'When it came to any other business, Geraint asked the trustees to make him Harry's guardian so he could remove him from the pernicious influences of a strike leader's working-class hovel.'

'Geraint actually used those words?'

'No, but he did say "squalor", "Marxist troublemakers" and "sedition", among others that I'd rather not mention.' Sali preferred to keep the 'choice' Geraint had wanted her to make to herself for the time being.

He wants to bring Harry up in Ynysangharad House?' Lloyd guessed correctly.

'And send him away to boarding school as soon as he's old enough.'

'He will have to go away to school, Sali.'

'No he won't!' she exclaimed, furious with Lloyd for adopting the same stance as the trustees.

'Harry is going to be a rich – and as riches mean power –

important and influential man in Pontypridd and possibly Wales. He is going to need the advantages of the best education money can buy to enable him to cope with the responsibilities of his position.'

'And you think he can only get that education away from me? He's doing well in school—'

'A council school where the teachers have been trained to drain all ambition out of their pupils, because the best they can hope for after they matriculate at eleven is low-paid manual and menial work. And along with basic arithmetic, reading and writing, they learn to bow, scrape and tug their forelocks to their betters,' he added caustically.

'If that's the case, you and your brothers didn't learn your lessons very well.'

'Only because our father taught us to question even our teachers, no, I'll correct that, especially our teachers.' He hit a clump of decaying bracken at the side of the path with his stick. A water rat scurried out, ran down the bank and dived into the filthy river.

'From what I've seen of the colliers in Tonypandy they question everyone, especially those in authority.'

'Harry doesn't need to learn to question anyone in authority because, thanks to his inheritance, one day he will be the authority. There's no saying what he could do, or how far he could go, Sali. He's a bright lad who could become an MP or even prime minister and then he'll be able to change people's lives in ways we poor Marxist revolutionaries can only dream of.'

'I still don't see why he has to go away to school to be educated.'

'Just look at the friends he is making, sweetheart. Boys destined to become colliers – provided there are still jobs for them when this strike ends. Girls who look no further than hooking a man, having babies and running a house.'

'Like me?' she challenged.

'No, not like you.' He stopped, cupped her face in his hands and looked intently into her eyes. 'After your father died, your uncle made all your choices for you, and married you off to a man who turned out to be a murderer. And, although I believe it's

159

wrong to take another man's life, I sincerely hope that Owen Bull isn't pardoned before they hang him on Monday morning.'

She shuddered as she always did whenever anyone said anything that reminded her of the miserable existence she and Harry had led with Owen Bull before they'd escaped to the Evans' house. Everyone in Pontypridd, including all the trustees, knew of her marriage to Owen, and his subsequent conviction and death sentence. But no one ever referred to her as Mrs Bull. She had adopted Jones as a surname because it had been part of her maiden name and in Wales it guaranteed anonymity. But she would be very glad – and relieved – when she could exchange it for Evans. 'I made it easy for my uncle by making love to Mansel and getting pregnant with Harry before he was murdered.'

'Like many of the wonderful things in life, love and lovemaking has been used by priests and religious fanatics down the ages to control the populace. Engendering feelings of guilt where there should only be pleasure. Since you left Owen and started making your own decisions, you've been living your life the way you want to. Haven't you?' he asked, seeking reassurance that they were together as a result of a conscious decision on her part.

'I've never been happier. That's why I'm so angry with Geraint for trying to take control of Harry's life. I want my son to grow up with you and your family in a community of good, honest, hard-working, clean-living, working-class people—'

'Noble sentiments, sweetheart, but you know as well as I do that good, honest, hard-working and clean-living can't be applied to all the working-class people in Tonypandy,' he smiled. 'And don't try telling me that you haven't seen the families I am talking about.'

'All right, I admit there's good and bad in every class. But I don't want Harry to turn out like Geraint and Gareth, a narrow-minded, bigoted snob who can only think about himself.'

'As if Harry would ever turn out like that with you for a mother.' They turned off the path into the lane that led to the back of Ynysangharad House. 'Think of the friends he will make in public school. Rich and important men's sons, the children of people who run this country. If change is going to come, it would be less bloody if it came from within the ruling class rather than imposed from outside. And, look on the bright side, Harry will spend all his holidays with us, so he will still be exposed to your good, honest, hard-working, clean-living working-class people.'

'Laugh at me all you like. I won't give up the guardianship of Harry to Geraint no matter what,' she declared vehemently.

'I'm not laughing at you, sweetheart, and I'll do everything I can to make sure that we keep him.' He stared at the house as if he were seeing it for the first time. 'I don't envy you or Harry. It's easier to be Geraint or me. We have our feet firmly planted in one class. We have our place in the world and know what it is, although I'll be the first to concede that I haven't stayed within the lines, especially when it comes to you. A collier has no right to look at a princes, let alone court her.'

'Hardly a princess. Harry and I were penniless when you and I fell in love.'

'Yet now, because of Harry's inheritance, you are straddling two worlds and that doesn't make for an easy or comfortable life. But if anyone can do it, and do it successfully, it's you. And I have no doubt that, given time, you'll teach Harry to cope.'

'I wish I could believe you.'

He kissed her. 'With me by your side, and Harry for a son, you are going to lead a charmed life.'

Harry, chocolate cake in one hand, plate balanced in the other, waved to them through the drawing-room window.

'School could teach him to despise us as Geraint, Gareth and Llinos do.' Sali hated herself for even considering the possibility.

Lloyd thought of Sali's brothers and sister, recalled their contempt for colliers, open hostility towards him and Sali, and the hypocrisy that didn't prevent their antagonism to interfere with the luxurious lifestyle they enjoyed courtesy of Harry's trust. 'I wish I could promise you that school won't change Harry, sweetheart, but all I can say is that I hope it doesn't.'

'Joey must have gone out again,' Megan said, as they walked into Victor's kitchen. The fire had been banked with small coal, and a cup and saucer stood abandoned on the table.

'He never clears up after himself,' Victor grumbled. He carried the cup to the sink before filling the kettle and setting it on the stove to boil. He glanced at the clock. 'We have an hour. Shall I put the pie in the oven to warm?'

'You're hungry?'

'Yes, and between our combined strike pay, the chickens, the allotments and the pay I receive in kind from the farms for the odd bit of work, we aren't as short of food as some. So you can eat here without feeling as though you are taking the bread out of our mouths.'

'Sorry, I didn't mean to insult you. It's just that—'

'Megs, before all this happened, and I don't just mean the strike, but your uncle leaving and you working for Mrs Palmer, we used to be able to talk about anything and everything. Please, don't let's lose that honesty now. I've never felt as close to anyone before, not even my father and brothers, but in this last week since you moved . . . well, I . . .'

'You what?' She didn't know why she was asking. She knew exactly what he meant.

'I don't know whether it's because I can't call in to see you whenever I want to, or because you're keeping something from me – are you keeping something from me?' He finally summoned the courage to ask the question that had been bothering him.

Megan thought of Sergeant Martin, the chocolates he'd tried to foist on her and his intimation that she could have more, Constable Shipton's leer and his humiliating pinch, Beryl Richards and the other women turning on her in town, and she knew that there were some things that she had to keep from Victor for his own sake. Even at the risk of driving a wedge between them.

'It's like you said, Victor. When I was living next door, you could call in any time you wanted; not only me, but my uncle, his brothers and the children made you welcome. You knew everything there was to know about me. But it's different in the lodging house. I have a life there that you can never be a part of.'

'Is that all it is, Megs?'

'What else could it be?'

The kettle began to boil. He ignored it and took her into his arms. Sensing that her white lies marked the beginning of a rift between them, she held him all the closer as he kissed her.

'Do you have the arrangements for your wedding in hand, Mrs Jones, Mr Evans?' Mr Richards ventured, as he, Sali, Lloyd and Harry sat around the tea table Mari had laid for them in the drawing room that overlooked the formal gardens. Beautiful in summer, the flower and rose beds looked sadly withered and neglected in winter.

'Given the demands the strike committee make on my time and my present financial situation, Mr Richards, we have had few arrangements to make.' Lloyd knew that they were all thinking about the execution that had to take place before he and Sali could marry, and he was grateful to Mr Richards for not mentioning it.

'The register office is booked for half past eleven, the Saturday after next.' Sali sugared her tea. 'Lloyd's father, brothers and Harry will be travelling down from Tonypandy with us, and we're hoping that Lloyd's brother's fiancée will be allowed time off work to act as my bridesmaid.'

'Have you decided what you are going to wear?' Mari asked.

'Yes, but before you get carried away by visions of white lace and orange blossom, remember it will be my second marriage. My outfit will be more practical than bride-like.' Sali filled Harry's cup half full of milk before handing it to Mari to be topped up with tea.

'You haven't arranged a wedding breakfast, as yet?' Mr Richards enquired.

'No, and we won't be. Even if we could afford one, it would be inappropriate to hold a celebration with the strike on,' Sali explained.

'That being the case, may I provide a breakfast as my wedding present to you? And before you object on the grounds of cost, I will donate the same amount of money to one of the soup kitchens.'

'That is an extremely generous offer, Mr Richards, but we couldn't possibly take you up on it,' Lloyd protested.

'As I have already accepted an invitation from Mrs Jones to attend your wedding, Mr Evans, I would regard it as an insult if you refused my gift. Mrs Jones' father was one of my closest friends. I have known her all her life.' He gave Sali a small smile. 'She is a valued friend and I hope that, given time, we will also become friends.'

'I hope so too—' Lloyd began.

'Then it is settled,' Mr Richards interrupted. 'I will arrange for a modest lunch to be served in a private room at the New Inn Hotel.' He held out his plate as Mari cut second slices of the chocolate cake. 'Will you also be going to the wedding, Mrs Williams?'

'I most certainly will,' Mari answered warmly.

'You have invited your family, Mrs Jones?' Mr Richards took two of the chocolate curls from the top of his slice of cake, added them to Harry's and winked at him.

'I have, but I don't expect any of them to come.' Sali hadn't held out much hope before Geraint's unexpected attack on the way she was bringing up Harry. Now, she had none. Where Geraint led, Gareth and Llinos inevitably followed.

'They may surprise you.' From the expression on Mari's face, Sali suspected she was planning to speak to Geraint about it.

'I doubt it. My mother isn't well enough to leave her room and Geraint couldn't have made it clearer that he is opposed to our marriage.' Sali left her chair, took a fresh cup and saucer from the tray Mari had left on the sideboard, poured a cup of tea, added milk and sugar, and cut a slice of chocolate cake. 'I'll take this up to Mother, Mari.'

'She's in one of her moods,' Mari warned.

Sali looked at Harry, who had finished his tea and cake. 'Would you like to come upstairs and say hello to your grandmother with me?'

Harry squirmed on his chair. Sali knew he hated visiting her mother. It wasn't just her stuffy bedroom, which she insisted be kept as dimly lit and shrouded as a tomb, it was also the peevish, whining tone she used to air her endless complaints to anyone courageous enough to venture into her company.

'After you've visited your grandmother you can go into the nursery and play with the toys,' Sali coaxed, reminding Harry of the nursery across the landing that had belonged to Edyth's late nephew, Harry's father Mansel. She picked up the tray.

Lloyd left the table and opened the door for her. He looked questioningly at Harry, who made a face at him. When Lloyd didn't laugh as he usually did, Harry gave a theatrical sigh, slipped off his chair and followed his mother out of the room.

'Did Mrs Jones tell you what her brother said at the trustees' meeting this afternoon, Mr Evans?' Mr Richards asked Lloyd when he returned to the table.

'She did,' Lloyd replied shortly.

'She had every right to be upset.' It was the closest Mr Richards had ever come to criticizing a member of the Watkin Jones family.

'I'm sorry, Mr Evans, this isn't an easy time for either you, or Miss Sali.' Mari poked at the uneaten cake on her plate with her fork. 'Her brothers and sister will never accept your marriage.'

'Never is a long time, Mrs Williams.' Mr Richards attempted to inject some optimism into the conversation. 'Things are difficult at the moment, but circumstances change. And if there is ever anything you think I can do to speed up those changes, Mr Evans, please, let me know.'

'Thank you, Mr Richards. Your friendship means a great to Sali, and to me,' Lloyd added sincerely. He took his teacup and wandered over to the window.

'Won't you even consider moving into this house, Mr Evans?'

'Move in here – into Ynysangharad House?' Lloyd turned and stared at Mr Richards as if he had taken leave of his senses.

'Mrs Jones did say that it was out of the question. But it would make her position with the trustees so much easier if you did.'

Lloyd set his teacup on the sofa table. 'The trustees want Harry to live here and Sali told them I wouldn't move in?'

'You said she told you what happened at the meeting . . .'

'She told me that Geraint asked the trustees to make him Harry's guardian so he could bring Harry up in this house and send him away to school. Not that the trustees wanted the boy to live here.'

'Shame on Mr Geraint,' Mari understood only too well what Geraint Watkin Jones was trying to do. 'Rather than work to

165

regain the family's inheritance that his Uncle Morgan embezzled and lost when he was his guardian, he'd part Master Harry from Miss Sali to make himself more important in the eyes of the world.'

'So you haven't discussed moving in here with Mrs Jones?' Mr Richards asked.

'No, but Sali knows the last thing I want to do is live off Harry's inheritance.'

'Her mother, brothers and sister have no such compunction, Mr Evans.' Mari pursed her lips disapprovingly.

'As they all live here rent and board free, courtesy of the trustees of Harry's estate, do you really think they would welcome Sali, Harry and me with open arms if we did move in?' Lloyd didn't wait for them to answer. 'If you'll excuse me, I'll go upstairs and play with Harry in the nursery while Sali visits her mother. His favourite game at the moment is war and he believes that it takes two sides to make a battle.'

The windows and curtains in Gwyneth Watkin Jones' bedroom closed out both world and light. And, if the musty atmosphere in the room was any indicator, no breeze had been allowed to stir the air for months. The fire was banked high, the temperature unbearably hot. The scents Sali had associated with her mother for the last ten years filled the air. Pungent medicinal odours from the dozens of bottles of patent medicines ranged on her bedside cabinet, a faint fragrance of lavender that failed to mask the stench of the chamber pot and slop bucket, and the stale smell of gravy and meals left to congeal, although there was no evidence of food.

Gwyneth lay in bed on pillows that had been plumped high to support her in a half sitting, half reclining position. The oil lamp was lit and a book lay within her reach but Sali knew she hadn't read to herself in years. She was wearing a robe over her nightgown, and although the doctor had told her that she was well enough to leave her room weeks ago, Sali doubted that she ever would.

The psychological ill-health Gwyneth Watkin Jones had taken refuge in to escape the world after the birth of her youngest son had become more real to her than anything or anyone else. Mari had mentioned that it took half an hour of coaxing, which in Mari's terms Sali suspected meant bullying, to get her mother out of bed just so the maids could change the sheets and even then Gwyneth only went as far as the day bed next to the fireplace.

'It's Sali, Mother, I have brought Harry to see you.'

'Sali?' Gwyneth opened her eyes languidly. 'So, you've finally come. I could die and rot in this room for all that anyone cares.'

'You know that isn't true, Mother.' Sali set the tray she'd carried up on a side table and moved the medicines on the cabinet to make room for the tea and cake.

'You should be living in this house so you can take care of me. I get lonely lying here day after day with no company.'

'You have Mari and Geraint, Mother.' Sali knew better than to mention the servants. Her mother regarded them as beneath her. She looked around. The stale smell was due to her mother's abhorrence of fresh air, but every surface gleamed with polish, the fireplace was clean, the hearth swept, and there was fresh linen on the bed and tables.

Harry pulled at her skirt to remind her of his presence.

'Harry would like to say hello to you, Mother.'

The boy stood behind the footboard of his grandmother's bed, waved and mouthed, 'Hello.'

'Harry.' Gwyneth squinted at the child, who had been named after her late husband. 'You have no idea what agony it is to be in ill-health, Harry.'

Harry frowned, uncertain whether he should answer.

'I live every day in pain, Harry. Have you any idea how that feels?'

'No, Grandmother,' he replied politely.

Sali saw her son hop from foot to foot and knew he couldn't wait to leave the room. 'You can go to the nursery now, Harry.'

'Children are so noisy,' Gwyneth complained irritably, as Harry ran across the landing. 'He needs curbing, Sali.'

'Harry is a well behaved, normal child.' Sali handed her mother the cup of tea.

'He has a sly look about him that I don't like. You need to move

167

in here to see that this house is run properly,' she added, returning to her favourite topic of conversation whenever her eldest daughter visited. 'Mari and your aunt's housekeeper are extremely wasteful.'

'Mr Richards checks the household accounts every week and he has found no evidence of waste, Mother,' Sali contradicted.

'There you go, crossing me again. If your Uncle Morgan had only moved into this house with us . . . or better still, if you had allowed me to stay with him in our house, instead of moving into this great draughty pile of Edyth's . . .'

Sali walked to the grate and pretended to check the fire. Her mother's brother, Morgan, had embezzled and lost Geraint's fortune, including their family home, before killing himself. But, categorically refusing to believe Morgan capable of suicide, Gwyneth constantly referred to him as if he were still alive, and the only person who cared for, or understood her. Sali glanced at the clock on the mantelpiece to check the time. 'Geraint will be home from the store soon.'

'That will make no difference to me. Geraint can never spare five minutes to sit and talk to me. In that respect he takes after your father. He doesn't care how ill I am.'

'Geraint has to work, Mother.'

'I don't see why, when your father left us well provided for. Or perhaps that's only what he told me before he died. Your Uncle Morgan said we were short of money. He had to make economies . . .'

Unable to listen to any more of her mother's ramblings, Sali confronted her. 'You know Uncle Morgan lost all our money in bad investments.'

'That's right, blame my brother. He never comes to see me either.' Gwyneth plucked nervously at the lace bedcover and Sali wondered if her mother actually believed her own stories.

'I am getting married again.'

'Widows shouldn't remarry,' Gwyneth snapped with sudden and astonishing vigour. 'Those whom God has joined together should stay together. Your father may be in heaven, but when the time comes for us to be reunited I couldn't face him, or my maker, if I had married another. It is a sin on a level with adultery.'

'Lloyd Evans and I are very happy, Mother, and he will make a good stepfather for Harry.'

'Selfish to the last. Your place is here, caring for me.'

'You are well looked after, Mother, and I have Harry and my future husband and his family to consider.'

'Mari doesn't even allow me to keep my medicine in the room.' Gwyneth's voice rose to a shriek. 'And she never gives me enough. I am in such pain.' Gwyneth snatched at Sali's arm with a claw-like hand. 'I need more medicine. Now!' she hissed. 'You must know where Mari keeps it. Twelve drops – just twelve drops . . .'

'Mari keeps it under lock and key, Mother, and you know the medicine wasn't doing you any good. The doctor told you that it was making you ill.'

'It was the only thing that was keeping me alive.' Releasing her, Gwyneth buried her head in her pillow and started howling hysterically. Sali felt intensely sorry for her but pitied Mari more. She had heard some of the abuse her mother hurled at Mari for following the doctor's orders. But Mari had stuck determinedly to his advice and had succeeded in halving Gwyneth's consumption of the laudanum Sali's Uncle Morgan had been feeding her.

'I'm sorry, Mother. I will tell Mari that you are upset. Perhaps she can bring you some cocoa.'

Gwyneth lifted her head from her pillow and screamed, 'I want my medicine!'

Sali kissed her on the forehead and left. The pretence of ill-health had become reality and there was nothing that she could do to help her mother, beyond ask Harry's trustees to continue paying her living expenses and medical bills.

'That was wonderful.' Megan's eyes shone, as the audience – who filled every seat in the Empire Theatre, courtesy of the manager, who allowed union men in for half price on production of their cards – rose to their feet and applauded the artistes taking their final bows. The loudest applause and noisiest catcalls were reserved for the star, vocalist Miss Zena Dare, but the ventriloquist Charles Lewis drew the most laughs when his doll bowed and lost his head.

'Do you want to stay to see the bioscope?' Victor asked.

'Not really, we saw it at the beginning. And although Mrs Palmer didn't tell me what time to come in, I don't want to get back too late.' Megan lifted her cloak from her seat behind her and handed it to Victor who draped it around her shoulders.

'I'll have to send Joey round here to help shift the scenery more often while the strike is on.'

Megan followed him to the end of the aisle and they waited for the crowd to disperse ahead of them. When they reached the foyer, Beryl Richards's husband, Alun stepped out in front of Megan.

'I wonder that a coppers' whore has the guts to show her face among decent people!' Before Victor could stop him he spat full in Megan's face.

Megan cried out. Victor tried to hold her, but she slipped past him and ran into the Ladies' cloakroom.

Victor turned to Alun, pulled his fist back and punched him. He hit the wall and slid to the floor.

'Your bloody girlfriend is working for the enemy, Victor Evans,' Alun's companion shouted. But he was careful to remain out of Victor's reach.

'Megan Williams is my fiancée, and like the rest of us, she is only trying to make a living.' Victor glared at the men around him. 'If anyone else speaks out of turn to her, touches her, or does what he just did,' he pointed to Alun who was crawling towards the door on his hands and knees, 'they'd better be prepared to answer to me.'

Intimidated by the determination on Victor's face, the crowd began to drift away.

'What's going on?' Constables Wainwright and Shipton walked in from the street and confronted the manager, who had run out of his office in time to see Victor floor Alun.

'Nothing,' the manager lied slickly. 'If you officers would like to come into my office . . .'

'Nothing?' Constable Wainwright gazed enquiringly at Alun, who was being helped up from the floor.

'Nothing.' Alun didn't dare look Victor in the eye.

'Funny nothing that puts you on the floor and makes your mouth bleed.' Wainwright looked from Alun to Victor and back again. 'If you want to make a complaint, Mr—'

'No complaint.' Alun brushed the blood from his mouth with the back of his hand.

'Mr Evans here is well known to us as a troublemaker,' Shipton added.

'I said I had no complaint.' Alun shook off a helping hand.

Victor went to Megan as she emerged from the Ladies. Her face was bright pink from the scrubbing she had given it. She saw the policemen and Alun's bloody lip.

'I'm sorry,' she whispered. 'I didn't mean to get you into trouble.'

'You didn't.' Victor laid his arm protectively around her shoulders and led her out into the street. 'Has anything like that happened to you before?'

Megan shook her head, but he wasn't convinced.

'I'd rather you told me the truth now, than hear it from someone else later.'

Realizing it was only a matter of time before the gossip reached him, she said, 'A crowd of women called me names when I went to town this morning.'

'I'll—'

'You can't hit everyone who objects to me working for the police, Victor.'

'No, but I can go everywhere with you when you're not working.'

'You already are. The furthest Lena and I go from the house is the backyard.'

'So today isn't the first time you've been assaulted?'

'Yes, it is. But Lena was spat on and knocked down by a crowd of women outside Rodney's shop a couple of weeks ago when she went to place Mrs Palmer's grocery order. Since then Mrs Palmer

171

has sent her order with Mrs Rodney's boy so there's no need for any of us to leave the house.'

'Bloody animals!' It was the first time Victor had sworn in front of Megan but he was so angry he didn't realize what he'd said.

'Lena and I wouldn't be able to go far anyway. We've too much work to do.'

'Promise me that you won't go out without me or Mrs Palmer.'

'Not even up to your house next Saturday?'

'I'll come down and fetch you.' He kept his arm around her shoulders, as they pushed their way through the crowds towards the lodging house. 'Good evening, Ned, Betty,' Victor greeted his neighbours.

'Hello, Mr Morgan, Mrs Morgan.' Betty and Ned pretended that they hadn't seen or heard them. Megan looked down at the pavement. 'I hate this strike.' She spoke through clenched teeth.

'You think we should go back to work?' Victor asked seriously.

'Not without getting the wages and conditions you are fighting for. But it's made everyone in the town hate me and now you feel that you have to fight them. I couldn't bear it if you were hurt because of me, which is why I don't want you boxing. You still haven't promised that you won't.'

He led her into the alley that ran at the back of the lodging house. 'I promise you that I love you,' he whispered huskily before kissing her.

'I love you too.'

He hugged her. 'Come on, I'll walk you to the back door.'

The only light in the alley came from the kitchen window of the lodging house. The blind had been drawn, but Victor and Megan could see a woman's shadow moving behind it.

'Mrs Palmer, washing the supper dishes.' Megan stopped in front of the door, wrapped her arms around his neck and held him close. 'Until next week.'

'What time can I pick you up?'

The door opened and light flooded out. 'Megan will be able to leave at midday next Saturday, Mr Evans, but you're forgetting that she gets time off tomorrow to go to chapel. Why don't you

172

come in for a cup of tea instead of standing out there in the cold?' Joyce invited.

Victor hesitated and Joyce sensed why he hadn't accepted her invitation.

'I have my own private stock of tea, Mr Evans. Bought and paid for out of my wages. So you wouldn't be drinking the enemy's tea. Or do you also object to the way I earn my money?'

'I can hardly do that, Mrs Palmer, when Megan earns her living the same way.' He allowed Megan to walk into the kitchen ahead of him.

'Take your coat off and sit down.' Joyce picked up the kettle, filled it, opened the hob and put it on to boil. She watched Megan hang up her cloak and Victor's coat. 'I'm guessing from that look on both your faces that Megan's day off hasn't gone too well.'

'You're wrong, Mrs Palmer. It was lovely. Victor and I went for a walk up the mountain and to the theatre. I really enjoyed myself.'

'Right up until the time Alun Richards spat in her face and called her a coppers' whore,' Victor said quietly.

'I could tell Sergeant Martin.'

'There's no need for you to do that, Mrs Palmer.' Megan set three cups and saucers on the table.

'Alun won't be doing anything like that again,' Victor said forcefully.

'Not when you're around to protect Megan,' Joyce concurred. 'But you can't fight everyone in Tonypandy, Mr Evans.'

'I've warned everyone that I will sort out the next person to give Megan any trouble.'

Mrs Palmer made the tea and set the pot on the table with the milk jug and sugar bowl. She poured a cup, added milk and carried it to the door.

'I will be in my room reading the paper if anyone wants me, Megan.' She glanced at the clock. 'It is ten o'clock now, Mr Evans, I expect Megan to be upstairs at eleven. We keep the housework to a minimum on Sunday but we still have to give the public rooms a quick once over, prepare and serve the meals, and make the beds. If you intend to escort Megan to chapel, I suggest you pick her up outside the kitchen door at five o'clock. You will have to be back at eight to help with the suppers, Megan.'

'Yes, Mrs Palmer, and thank you,' Megan stammered in surprise.

'Goodnight.' Joyce took her tea and closed the door behind her.

Victor looked at Megan, 'I can't believe she did that.'

'This place will never be home, in the way my uncle's house was, but Mrs Palmer is kinder and a lot more understanding than some of the other people around here.'

'So I'm beginning to discover.' Victor laid his hand over Megan's, as she sat opposite him at the table.

Chapter 11

MEGAN SHOWED Victor out at ten minutes to eleven. She washed and dried their teacups and spoons and put them away. After checking around the kitchen, which Mrs Palmer had already cleaned and tidied, she lit a candle to take upstairs. She knocked on Mrs Palmer's door on her way through the hall and called, 'Goodnight.'

Joyce answered and Megan started climbing the stairs. When she reached the first landing, Sergeant Martin moved out of the doorway of his room. In the week since she had worked in the house she had never seen him other than immaculately dressed in his uniform. But his shirt was collarless, his braces unbuttoned and he was barefoot.

'Good evening, Miss Williams.' She backed towards the staircase that led to the next floor. 'I didn't frighten you, did I?'

She shook her head, not wanting to talk to him.

He moved quickly, clamping his hand over hers, pinning it to the banister. 'You hurt my feelings when you refused the chocolates.'

Megan had seen her uncle and his brothers drunk during the days when they had earned enough to treat themselves to a couple of nights out a week and she recognized the smell of whisky on the sergeant's breath. But there was none of the affable jollity she'd associated with her uncle's infrequent binges. The sergeant's eyes were cold, and from the state of his dress she suspected that he had been drinking alone in his room.

'I can't accept expensive presents, sir. Please,' she asked with as much dignity as she could muster, 'let me go.'

'Was that your young man I saw you with on the mountain?'

175

'I told you that Victor and I are engaged.'

'Then you should know he's a criminal. He'll be up in court soon. He could go to prison.' He knocked her arm aside, closed his free hand around her chin and twisted her face towards him. 'A girl like you deserves a man who earns good money and can look after her.'

'I love Victor.' She grabbed his hand and tried to prise it away, but he was too strong for her.

'Forget him, take my chocolates. I'll buy you more, and silk stockings and dresses. Anything you want. You could have a good time with me. Money no object. We'll go to the best hotels—'

'Please, let me go!' She fought to free her arm.

A door banged downstairs and masculine laughter echoed through the hall.

'Let me go!' she repeated, raising her voice in the hope of attracting someone's attention.

At the sound of a step on the stairs the sergeant retreated to his room, leaving her feeling relieved, light-headed – and angry.

She ran up to her room. Lena was already in bed. Setting the candle down, she turned the key quietly in the lock of the door, undressed, slipped on her nightdress and crawled between the icy sheets. There was something hard beneath her pillow. Her blood ran cold when she slid her hand beneath it and pulled out the box of chocolates.

Victor walked into the kitchen to find Lloyd sitting in one of the easy chairs, staring at the cold ashes in the hearth. He sat opposite him and loosened his collar. His own problems were preying on his mind, but Lloyd looked so preoccupied he tried to set them aside for a moment. 'You look like I feel. Is there anything I can do to help?'

Lloyd glanced up at his brother then at the clock. 'Sorry, I was miles away.'

'I saw.'

'Sali went to bed an hour ago. I meant to follow her up but I started thinking. It really came home to me today just how much she is giving up to stay with us.'

176

'With you, not us,' Victor corrected. 'Your day in Pontypridd didn't go well?'

'That's an understatement.' Lloyd shivered. The temperature had dropped considerably since he had raked out the fire and he hadn't even noticed. 'I looked around Ynysangharad House—'

'You've been there before, and so have I – to the back door,' Victor said without a trace of malice. 'We both know she could live in a mansion with servants at her beck and call instead of here, skivvying for us. But she's made her choice, Lloyd.'

'When I said I looked round, I mean really looked. The size of the rooms, the gardens, the furniture, and like you said, there's so many servants there she'd never have to lift a finger, but instead she works in a soup kitchen and comes back here at the end of the day to do our scrubbing and cleaning.' Lloyd pulled out his empty pipe and stared at it. 'Have you ever thought what Harry is going to think of her and us – me – for bringing him up in this house?'

'Yes,' Victor replied decisively. 'He's going to remember the good times. Being surrounded by people who loved and cared for him. Who were never too busy to talk to him, or read to him. Playing with his friends on the mountain. Going rabbiting with the dogs—'

'Not living in a house without a bathroom, with cheap, old-fashioned furniture?' Lloyd countered. 'Trying to survive during a strike. Eating in a school hall and a soup kitchen, being rousted from bed by police raiding the house and seeing his uncles and stepfather coming home bleeding and bruised after battling with the law?'

'You're the one who's always saying the way a person lives their life is more important than what they own,' Victor reminded.

'I was wrong. Material possessions and wealth bring responsibility – and drawbacks,' Lloyd added. 'Sali's brother, Geraint, asked the trustees today to take Harry away from her so he can be raised like a "gentleman" in Ynysangharad House.'

'As opposed to being raised as a collier here?' Victor shifted in his chair.

'There's no way that I would raise Harry to be a collier. Not with the future he has mapped out for him.'

'Exactly. But it sounds to me as if you're saying that because Sali's brother is trying to take control of Harry's upbringing, you're having second thoughts about marrying her.'

'Only for her and Harry's sake.'

'I'd say they are the last people you're thinking about,' Victor said. 'If Geraint is trying to take control of Harry and his fortune, Sali needs your help and support more than ever. And you're an idiot if you can't see that.'

'You don't think I'm being selfish in marrying her?'

It took a second or two for Victor to realize that Lloyd was serious. 'I've never seen a couple as happy as you. Or a boy who looks up to his father as much as Harry does you.'

'He loves you and Joey more.' Lloyd only realised how petty that sounded after he'd spoken.

'No, he doesn't,' Victor denied. 'He likes us because we're his uncles – his butties the ones he can have fun with because we don't have the responsibility of making serious decisions on his behalf. You're a fool to allow Sali's brother to upset you, Lloyd. You two are made for one another and you're the perfect stepfather for Harry.' He frowned in concern. 'Can Geraint take Harry away from Sali?'

'I don't know.' Lloyd rose from his chair, stretched his cold muscles and gently rubbed his aching ribs. Although days had elapsed since his beating, at times his injuries were almost as painful as when they'd been inflicted. 'The trustees voted him down today.'

'If they've any sense they will continue do that.'

'The trustees may have sense when it comes to making business decisions but they are also snobs and this,' Lloyd looked around the kitchen, 'is not a fit place in which to bring up the heir to a fortune.'

'It's clean, it's comfortable and it's paid for, which is more than can be said for some of the mansions of the crache, or so I've heard. According to Connie, and she should know, the richer the man the less qualms he has about paying his bills.'

'And this coming from a striking miner.'

'We're a better bet than some of the people who drive round in carriages and eat off silver plate.' Victor remembered his own troubles. 'I'd give anything to be in your shoes and in a position to marry.'

'I trust you mean to Megan not Sali.'

'That's not funny.'

'It isn't, but you can't blame me for trying after the day I've had. I saw Joey when we came back from Pontypridd. He told me he gave you and Megan tickets for the Empire. Was it a good show?'

'The show was good, what happened afterwards wasn't.' Not wanting to dwell on his loss of temper, or the insult to Megan, Victor outlined the evening's events in as few words as possible.

'And I thought I had problems. Damn Alun Richards, who the hell does he think he is, attacking a defenceless woman?' Lloyd rubbed his hands together to warm them.

'After what I did to him, he'll think twice before he has a go at Megan again.'

'You can't fight everyone.'

'That's what Mrs Palmer said, but I can have a bloody good try,' Victor snapped.

'I'll have a word with the committee. If they agree, we'll let it be known that the next man to have a go at Mrs Palmer, or any of her staff, will have to answer to us.'

'You'll throw them out of the union?' Victor asked hopefully.

'If it was up to me, yes, but it's the committee's decision, and like all committees we have our idiots. But that's democracy for you. The fool who can talk endless rubbish that sounds good gets elected before the quiet wise man who has a problem expressing his thoughts.'

'Much as I hate Megan working in that lodging house, she'll be safe enough while she's there. No one would dare insult her, Mrs Palmer or that other girl in a houseful of policemen, and she's promised me she won't leave it unless I'm with her.' Victor took a cup from the dresser and filled it with water.

'You have to think ahead to what's going to happen when the police leave,' Lloyd cautioned. 'They won't be stationed in this valley forever.'

'You think Megan could be in for more trouble from the likes of Alun Richards when the strike ends?'

'Most of the boys are decent enough.' Lloyd avoided giving Victor a direct answer. 'Perhaps they just need to be reminded that we're fighting management not defenceless women. When are you and Megan going out again?'

'Mrs Palmer has given her time off to go to chapel tomorrow.' Victor took a sip of water, rinsed out the cup and placed it on the wooden draining board.

'And no doubt she wants to go.'

'Despite your and Dad's best efforts, more people in this valley go to the churches and chapels than Marxist meetings.'

'Only if you count children who are forced to attend by their parents, and men and women who allow the ministers, vicars and priests to do their thinking for them,' Lloyd said.

'Too many people who attend the Baptist Chapel write to relatives in the Swansea Valley. If Megan suddenly stopped going to services, her father might get to hear of it, and she's terrified he'll use the slightest excuse to drag her back home.'

'I doubt he'll do that while she's earning good money and sending most of it to him,' Lloyd commented. 'Surely a good Catholic boy like you can't be thinking of going to chapel with her?'

'After what happened today, I don't see that I have a choice.'

'Aren't you afraid that Father Kelly will excommunicate you?' Lloyd wasn't entirely joking.

'Father Kelly is a pragmatist, he'll give me dispensation.'

Lloyd made a wry face. 'All I can say is thank God I don't have to ask a priest's permission to live my life the way I see fit.'

'I didn't think atheists thanked God,' Victor mocked.

'They don't, and neither do they go to chapel, but I might make an exception tomorrow.' Lloyd knelt down awkwardly, lifted the brush and ash pan from the set of fire irons and swept the hearth.

'You in chapel! You'll set the whole town talking.'

'No more than you did thumping Alun Richards tonight.'

'He had it coming to him.' Victor sat back in his chair. 'If only I could marry Megan, but even if she was of age and moved in with us, I couldn't pay the fifteen shillings a week she sends home to her family . . . unless . . .'

'Unless what?' Lloyd was instantly on the alert. Several moneymaking schemes were being mooted amongst the strikers, all reckless, some dangerous and a few downright illegal. Victor was normally sensible but he was also desperately in love and the fact that he'd lost his temper and floored Alun Richards spoke volumes about his state of mind.

Unwilling to get embroiled in an argument about bare-knuckle boxing, Victor gave Lloyd a self-conscious grin, 'Rob a bank.'

'I can't recommend that as a way to make money in the Rhondda this week. Given the state of the bank accounts of the few who can afford them, the vaults and safes will be empty.'

'You're probably right.' Victor glanced at the clock. 'Dad in bed or the County Club?'

'The club.'

'Joey?'

Lloyd lifted one bruised eyebrow. 'A little bird told me that he's been seen going around the back of Jane Edwards' house.'

'Then the Virgin Mother and all the saints help him if Emlyn gets to hear about it.' Victor was genuinely concerned. 'I'll try to talk some sense into him.'

'What makes you think you'll succeed when everyone else has failed for the last nineteen years?' Lloyd asked. 'But on a brighter note, how are you enjoying life as one half of an engaged couple? Judging by the smile on Megan's face and what she said the last time I spoke to her, she's happy to be wearing Mam's engagement ring.'

'Dad said Sali didn't want it.' Victor was instantly on the defensive.

'Given that she'd been married before, and Dad offered her Mam's wedding ring, she thought it should go to Megan and I agreed with her. I picked you up a small present.' Lloyd delved into his pocket and pulled out a packet wrapped in brown paper and string.

Victor took the parcel and flipped it over suspiciously.

'A French letter,' Lloyd explained. 'At half-a-crown a time

they're pricey but cheaper than a baby. If you're careful it should last a month, or even longer in your case because you don't get as many opportunities . . .'

Victor turned bright red. 'Lloyd!'

Lloyd burst out laughing at his brother's embarrassment. 'For pity's sake, Victor, if you can't talk frankly to your brother about personal matters, who can you talk to? I'm broke, but they're the one thing I dare not economize on, because Sali's family are difficult enough now without her getting pregnant before our wedding day.'

'It's different for you two.'

'Not that different. I know you take your religion and the church almost as seriously as Mam did, and Catholics aren't supposed to control the size of their families but given Megan's father's antagonism towards you, surely you don't want to risk Megan getting pregnant before you marry.'

'I always thought Megan and I should wait until our wedding night before . . . well . . . before . . .'

Lloyd regained his composure before Victor. 'You've been going out with the girl for two years, and you can barely keep your hands off one another when you're in the same room. Don't you think that another two years will put an unbearable strain on your relationship?'

When Victor remained silent, Lloyd said, 'I bought it for you, do what you want with it, but for now, stick it in your pocket. That's the front door opening. And if it's Joey, I'm not risking bankruptcy to keep *him* supplied in French letters.'

'Please, Joey, stay with me, I get so-o-o lonely without you,' Jane Edwards whined. She wrapped her arm around Joey's chest and tried to hold on to him, as he rolled away from her to the edge of the bed.

He wrinkled his nose. It was stiff with cold. Reluctantly he moved his arm out from beneath the bedclothes into the icy atmosphere and shifted the saucer holding the burning candle stub closer to the alarm clock. 'It's after midnight. My father and brothers are getting suspicious.'

'Who cares?' She dug her nails into his arm, as he tried to leave the bed.

'I care. Stop messing, Jane. I'm a mass of bites and scratches as it is and it's difficult to explain them away.'

'To your other women?' She scraped her nails down his arm, shaving off slivers of skin.

'I said stop messing!' He hit her hand away and rummaged through the clothes he'd flung on the floor in search of his drawers.

'I hate sleeping alone,' she pouted.

'You won't have to when Emlyn comes out.'

'Don't remind me. He's old, he smells, he has false teeth that he takes out at night. And he's horrid to me.'

'Then why did you marry him?'

'Because my father threw me out and I had nowhere else to go.' She leaned towards him. He grabbed his clothes and retreated. 'I prefer to have you in my bed,' she purred

'What girl wouldn't?' Joey gave her the full benefit of the smile he practised every night in front of his dressing-table mirror.

'I'm serious, Joey. I've fallen in love with you.'

'No, you haven't.' He pulled on his drawers, heaved his trousers over them and turned to look at her as he buttoned his flies and buckled his belt.

'How do you know what I feel?' she demanded crossly.

'Men talk, Jane, especially after they've had a few pints in the Pandy, and the milkman and the insurance man can still afford to buy beer.'

'They haven't been here in months except to deliver milk and pick up the penny a week Emlyn pays to cover his funeral costs. Well, they wouldn't, would they?' she argued. 'Not when you're here practically every night. But all you ever want to do is go to bed for an hour or two before clearing off to visit some other girl.'

'I swear, Jane,' Joey crossed his fingers behind his back as he hauled his braces over his shoulders, 'I have no other girl.'

'Maybe you haven't visited another one today, Joey Evans. But I hear gossip too.' She knelt on the bed and despite the freezing temperature, allowed the sheet to fall below her knees. 'I never should have married an old man.'

'You told Emlyn he had to marry you because you were pregnant,' Joey reminded her with more honesty than tact.

'It wasn't my fault I lost the baby a week after we married. And afterwards, instead of giving me sympathy, he accused me of lying to him just to get him to marry me.'

'Didn't you?'

'No!' She grabbed the sleeve of Joey's shirt, pulled him towards her and clamped his hands over her naked breasts. 'Your father owns this house. I could stop Emlyn from coming back.'

'Not when his name is on the rent book, you can't.' Joey evaded her clutches, grabbed the candle and lifted it to the floor to look for his boots. 'He's a good tenant. He always paid on the nail until the strike.'

'But I want to live with you,' she repeated petulantly.

'How about as a lodger?' he joked. 'Then you can switch from Emlyn's bed to mine halfway through the night. Better still, you've enough spare rooms; you could ask the milkman and insurance man to move in as well. That would give you a real choice.'

'That's not funny, Joey.'

'Neither is your nagging.' He found his boots and sat on the dressing-table stool to lace them on.

'I've written to Emlyn to tell him that he can't come back here.'

'You've what!'

Even in the dim light of the flickering candle, she saw Joey's eyes round in horror. 'I know you go to the Catholic church and all that, but we wouldn't be the only couple in the Rhondda to live in sin. I don't care what people or the chapel say—'

'Did you really write to Emlyn?' he broke in, hoping she was lying.

'Yes.' She stared at him defiantly.

'And said what?'

'That I love you.'

'Are you insane!'

'You were so peculiar the last time I saw you. I thought you needed a push.'

'What the hell do you mean?'

184

'A push in the right direction. You know you want to settle down with me,' she purred seductively.

'If I was ready to settle down, and I'm not,' he added heatedly, 'I'd sooner settle down with old Mrs Johns. She may never see ninety again but she knows how to cook and her house is clean, which is more than can be said for you and this place.' He loosened the laces on one of his boots and pushed his foot into it only to discover that he'd put his left boot on his right foot.

'That's a horrid thing to say. If I thought for one minute that you meant it—'

'I do! And if you've really written to Emlyn about me, you've done something even more horrid – and stupid.'

She left the bed and walked naked, goose-bumped and shivering towards him. 'If you don't love me why do you visit me every night?'

'For heaven's sake, Jane, I'm nineteen, I want a bit of fun . . .' He wrenched off his boot and thrust it on the other foot.

'And I'm seventeen. That's what makes us so perfect for one another.'

'Have you posted that letter?' he challenged.

'There's no need to shout and, yes, I have posted it.'

'You serious?'

'You obviously aren't,' she said irritably.

'I told you from the beginning that we should enjoy what we had. Jane, it was fun—'

'Fun! Fun! Fun! That's all you can say, Joey Evans. Fun for who, that's what I want to know? You knew I wasn't happy with Emlyn. That I was looking for someone else. And now I could be having your baby—'

'Oh no, you don't pull that one. Not on me.'

'In fact, I know that I am carrying your baby.' She smiled jubilantly.

'It could be anyone's. The milkman and the insurance man are good blokes, they wouldn't stand back and say nothing if you took me to court to claim maintenance for a bastard that wasn't even mine.' Joey froze at the thought of the scandal Jane's accusation would precipitate, the lectures he'd have to suffer from his father –

185

and Lloyd. Quite apart from the five shillings a week the magistrate would order him to pay towards the upkeep of the child until it was at least twelve, what chance would he or she have in life with Jane for a mother? His son or daughter . . . his blood ran cold at the thought.

'You would and all, wouldn't you, Joey Evans? You'd deny any of this happened in court. You, horrible, evil . . . swine.' Realizing from the expression on his face that she'd gone too far to get him back, Jane picked up a pair of pink glass candlesticks from the dressing table and flung them at his head. Joey ducked but not far enough. One of them caught his cheek.

Without stopping to fasten his shirt buttons or tie the laces on his boot, he grabbed his second boot, the rest of his clothes and ran out of the door. And, for the first time since he'd started sneaking into Jane Edwards' house and bedroom, he raced straight down the stairs, through the front door and into the street.

News of Alun Richards' attack on Megan reached the County Club before it closed. Billy Evans stayed only as long as it took him to verify the details before going home. He was discussing the incident with Victor and Lloyd when Joey burst into the house, carrying one boot and half his clothes. He dropped them by the kitchen door and ran to the tap.

'Someone's husband finally catch up with you, little brother?' Lloyd asked.

'Can't you see I'm hurt!' Blood oozed between the fingers Joey had clamped over his face and dripped on to his unbuttoned shirt.

'And how exactly did you get hurt?' Billy wondered just how much more trouble his family could get into in one night.

'Bloody women!' Joey turned on the tap and threw the tea towel under it.

'A woman, not a husband,' Lloyd taunted. 'My, my, could it be that you're losing your Don Juan touch?'

'How bad is it?' Billy Evans went to Joey and prised his fingers from his face.

'Not bad.' Joey pulled away from his father.

'Bad enough,' Billy pronounced. 'Take a look at this, Victor and see if it needs a stitch.'

'I had enough of Victor's horse doctoring after the riot.' Joey dabbed the wet tea towel on his face, pulled it away and studied the bloodstain.

'It's more bruise than cut.' Victor opened the wound and made it bleed even more.

'That hurt,' Joey growled.

'You can't say we didn't warn you that your philandering would lead to trouble,' Lloyd lectured, unable to resist an 'I told you so'.

'Spare me the sermon.' Suddenly faint, Joey pulled his chair from under the table and fell on to it.

Victor filled the tin bowl with cold water, threw in the tea towel and sat next to him. 'Let me take a closer look?'

'No.'

'Joey, be sensible. If that cut gets infected you could end up looking like the monster in that illustrated *Frankenstein* book you keep reading.'

His father's threat was enough. Mindful of his good looks, Joey sat quietly while Victor washed and examined the wound.

'Well, it can't be Emlyn Edwards because he's inside, so was it Jane?' Lloyd knelt on the hearthrug, lifted a pile of sticks and papers from the alcove cupboard, pulled the coalscuttle towards him and began building a fire for the morning.

'Mind your own business.'

'A man would have done more damage, given that you were only half dressed. He also would have kicked you out before you had time to gather your clothes.' Billy took the cloth from Victor and looked Joey in the eye. 'Are you going to tell us what happened? Or do we have to wait for Betty Morgan or one of the other neighbours to enlighten us.'

Joey saw that his father wasn't going to leave him alone until he gave him an explanation. 'If you must know, I was hit by a candlestick.'

'A flying candlestick,' Lloyd whistled. 'Is this a variation on the *Arabian Nights* flying carpet?'

187

Billy held up his hand to silence Lloyd. 'And who threw the candlestick?'

'Someone I thought I knew but didn't,' Joey muttered belligerently.

'Was it an upstairs or a downstairs candlestick?'

'I've said all I'm going to.' Unable to meet his father's eye, Joey took the tea towel from Victor.

'What would you say if I told you that it was an upstairs candlestick and Jane Edwards threw it?' Mr Evans took his place at the head of the table.

Joey's first instinct was to try to bluff it out then he remembered Betty Morgan. Nothing that went on in the street escaped her notice, and the chances were Ned Morgan had already mentioned his wife's suspicions to his father. 'She wanted me to in with her. When I refused she threw the candlestick at me.'

'Did she say whether or not she expected her husband to join the two of you when he is released from prison?' Billy enquired frostily.

'Ow!' Joey glared at Victor who was dabbing iodine on to his cut.

'Your love life is too complicated for me, Joey.' Lloyd left the hearth and washed his hands and face at the sink. 'I'm going to bed. Goodnight.' He dried his hands in the kitchen towel and left the room.

Victor gently touched Joey's cut. 'You may have a slight scar but it will fade. You definitely don't need a stitch.' He tossed the cloth back into the bowl and carried it over to the sink.

'I'll clear that up,' Billy offered. 'Go on up with Lloyd.'

Victor looked from his father to Joey. Sensing that Joey was in for the talking to of his life, he nodded. 'I could do with a good night's sleep. See you in the morning.'

Billy sat back in his easy chair after Lloyd closed the door.

'Before you say anything, I've learned my lesson.' Joey went to the sink and emptied the bowl down the drain.

'Have you?' Billy enquired cynically.

'I have,' Joey reiterated. 'From now on it's only nice girls for me.'

'I hate to disillusion you, Joey, but there isn't a respectable man within a fifty-mile radius of Pandy who'll allow you over his doorstep much less near his daughter. You've earned yourself quite a reputation, boy.'

Joey reached for the soda crystals to disinfect the bowl. 'Jane tonight – it got really nasty.'

'I was sorry when I heard that you'd taken up with her. She's a devious young lady. No one thought she'd get Emlyn to believe her lies enough to take her as his wife, but there's none so foolish or gullible as an old fool.' He rose from his chair. 'Not that you've asked my advice, but if you did, I'd warn you to be wary. You might think after what she did to you tonight, that you've finished with her. But she might not have finished with you.'

Megan discovered that when it came to lodging houses, the designated day of rest wasn't that different from the other days of the week for all that Joyce had said it was the day with the lightest load of housework. Although there were no beds to strip, the fires still had to be laid downstairs before six o'clock, the three sittings of breakfast prepared and served, the vegetables cleaned and the Sunday dinner cooked. And they still had to make the lodgers' beds and tidy their rooms at intervals throughout the day to suit the officers' shifts.

Sergeant Martin came down for the last breakfast at eight o'clock. When Megan saw him walking into the dining room, she went into the kitchen and persuaded Lena to wait on the table while she helped Mrs Palmer with the washing-up. At ten o'clock the sergeant left to patrol the town. Shortly afterwards she and Lena started cleaning the bedrooms, leaving Mrs Palmer to cook the Sunday dinner.

Tidy and scrupulously clean by nature, Megan found it difficult to ignore mess. But following Mrs Palmer's stern advice, after she'd spent too much precious time on the daily bed-making, as opposed to the thorough clean every bedroom received once a week, she'd learned to concentrate on the beds and washstands. So, she and Lena made beds, emptied slop buckets, and did the minimal cleaning of toilet ware. The sergeant's room, as usual,

189

took the least time, and the room next to it, an hour just to clear the beds so they could make them.

Impatient to move on to the next floor, Megan grew irritable with Lena, as the girl seemed even more dreamlike than usual. The more she tried to hurry her, the slower Lena became. Minutes ticked by relentlessly, as Lena tucked in the sheets and blankets on her side of the beds at half Megan's pace. When they finally finished, they hauled the slop buckets downstairs and while Megan emptied them down the ty bach, Lena filled the big jugs they used to carry water.

Mrs Palmer was laying the dinner table for the first sitting when they went up to make the beds on the second floor. Megan waited until Lena was busy cleaning a particularly filthy washstand in an eight-bedded room, before making the excuse that she needed a clean handkerchief. She raced up to the top floor without giving Lena a chance to remind her of Mrs Palmer's rule that they were never to be left alone in any of the lodgers' bedrooms. Exchanging her handkerchief for another, she picked up the chocolates she had hidden in one of her drawers. Creeping down the narrow staircase, she held her breath as she stole past the open door of the bedroom Lena was working in.

She reached the first floor landing and mentally counted off a full sixty seconds. Only when she was certain that no one was watching her, she dived into the sergeant's room, left the chocolates on his bedside table, backed out of the door, closing it as she did so; and stopped dead when she sensed someone standing behind her.

Hands clamped tightly around her waist, and she froze. 'Miss Williams, you've cleaned my room, I presume.'

Colour flooded into her cheeks. She turned her head to see the sergeant standing behind her.

'Why the guilty look, Miss Williams? You were cleaning my room, weren't you?'

'Yes, sir. Please, let me go?'

He released her and opened the door of his room. As he looked inside, she darted up the stairs, running breathlessly towards the room where she'd left Lena working. The door was open but it was empty, the beds still unmade. She heard a noise in the room next door and wondered why Lena had moved on without finishing the room or waiting for her. She turned the knob, opened the door and stood transfixed.

Lena was lying on her back on top of a rumpled bed, her apron, skirt and petticoats pushed to her waist, her bodice unbuttoned, her drawers pulled down to her feet. Constable Wainwright was on top of her, one hand between her legs, the other beneath her bust shaper.

'Megan!' Lena struggled to sit up.

Constable Wainwright gave Megan a look that sent a chill down her spine.

Megan blurted out the first thing that came into her head. 'I shouldn't have left Lena alone.'

Constable Wainwright left the bed, buttoned his flies, straightened his uniform and walked towards her without a backwards glance at Lena who was struggling into her drawers. 'One word to anyone about what you've just seen, and you'll be sorry.'

'Sir.' Megan lowered her eyes and bobbed a curtsy.

'And so will your young man and his family. They could be put away for a long time. So long, the warder will throw away the keys. Now, we don't want that. Or Lena losing her job here, do we?'

Megan shook her head.

'We understand one another.'

'Sir.' She stepped aside so he could walk past her, but as he did so he briefly cupped her breast.

'Sir!' she protested angrily.

'Shipton's right. All you women are the same, begging for a man to give it to you.'

Laughing he left the room and ran down the stairs.

Chapter 12

'I'M SORRY I can't give you any more time off this evening, Megan.' Joyce wrapped the ham sandwiches she'd cut for the officers' supper in scalded cloths and set them on plates in the pantry. 'But with this being Lena's afternoon off, I'll need you back here at eight o'clock sharp to help serve first supper.'

'I'll return as soon as chapel is finished, Mrs Palmer.' Megan's hands trembled as she jabbed her hatpin into her black Sunday winter hat and straightened the lace collar on the brown wool dress she'd had made for church three years before. Despite the pressing with a cloth soaked in vinegar, it was shiny in places. She fingered the material anxiously. If it should go into holes it would be months before she'd be able to replace it, but the chapel elders had given her a warning when she had worn her only other good winter dress to a service because it was a colourful, and in their opinion, highly unsuitable green.

'That'll be your young man.' Joyce opened the door. 'My, oh my, your young man and his brother. Does Father Kelly know that he's lost you both to chapel?' she enquired.

'It's by nature of a family outing, Mrs Palmer.' Joey's experience with Jane didn't prevent him from removing his cap and giving Mrs Palmer an appealing smile. Flirting with women, young, middle-aged or old, had become a habit he could no more relinquish than he could stop breathing.

'All of you are going to chapel? Even your father and older brother?' Joyce's late husband had been a fellow Marxist and friend of Billy Evans and she couldn't visualize either father or son sitting in a chapel pew.

'They're waiting with Sali at the end of the lane. If you're ready, Megan, we should go,' Victor prompted.

'I'm quite ready, Victor. Don't worry, Mrs Palmer, I'll be back on time.'

'Enjoy the service.' Joyce looked after their retreating figures and wished she could leave her lodgers to their own devices for once, and join them. Not because she had any pangs of conscience about missing chapel. But she had a feeling that this was going to be one service the Baptists wouldn't forget for a long time.

'Where's Harry?' Megan saw Sali, Lloyd and Mr Evans waiting at the end of the lane, but there was no sign of Sali's son.

'Connie, Annie and Tonia invited him to high tea.' Victor offered her his arm and she took it.

'A tactical high tea?'

'Harry loves going to Connie and Tonia's for tea; they don't mind him cheating at snap,' Joey said from behind them.

'Is it possible to cheat at snap?' Megan asked Victor doubtfully.

'Joey's done his best to teach him.'

'I heard that,' Joey said.

'You were meant to.'

Megan smiled at Lloyd, Sali and Mr Evans. 'Good evening.'

'I trust it will be for us – and everyone else.' Mr Evans lifted his bowler hat, as Ned and Betty Morgan walked down the hill towards them. 'Ned, Betty, dry evening for once, even if it is a bit cold,' he added, in an attempt to force a reply.

Ignoring the pressure of his wife's fingers digging into his arm, Ned agreed. 'It is that, Billy.'

'We must be going. Billy, Lloyd, Sali, Joey, Victor, good evening.' Betty deliberately omitted Megan's name.

'Have you heard that Victor and Megan are engaged?' Billy stood in front of Betty, preventing her from walking on. 'Would you like to see the ring, Betty? It was Isabella's but she didn't wear it very often.'

Drawing strength from the presence of Victor and his family, Megan dared to speak. 'As my father won't give his permission for me to marry Victor, Mrs Morgan, we'll have to wait until I'm

193

twenty-one. And even then the wedding will be small because it's unlikely he will allow any of my family to attend.' She removed her glove and held her hand in a pool of lamplight.

'We were hoping that when the time comes, you'd help us to arrange the wedding, Betty,' Sali broke in, taking advantage of Betty's surprise at the news.

'Megan's only eighteen so she has three years to go, and in my experience it doesn't take anywhere near that long to arrange a wedding,' Betty replied to Sali while continuing to ignore Megan.

'I'm nineteen, Mrs Morgan, so it's less than two years,' Megan corrected shyly.

'With this strike—'

'Are you suggesting that we have to starve for another two years before management capitulates to our demands, woman!' Ned exclaimed.

'No—'

'We'd better get along to chapel or we'll be late,' Billy broke in. Ned and Betty's arguments could be long and noisy, as he had discovered after years of living in the same street.

Lloyd tipped his hat to Betty and walked ahead with Sali.

'Does the minister have friends in the Swansea Valley who know your father?' Victor asked Megan, as they followed.

'Everyone knows everyone else in the farming community in the Swansea Valley.'

'So your father is likely to find out that you've been to chapel with me and my family.'

'Almost certainly.'

'And what happened in the theatre last night?'

'I hope not.' Megan said, 'Good evening,' to the crowd outside the chapel door but just as she'd expected, they ignored her.

Mr Evans acknowledged the people he knew, adding, 'You all know Megan Williams, my son Victor's fiancée.'

'Victor, engaged? You do surprise me, Mr Evans.' Betty Morgan's sister Alice Hughes joined them, hoping to hear some juicy gossip.

'Megan is engaged to your son, Mr Evans?' The minister stood

194

before the chapel door, dressed in an old-fashioned black frock coat and tall hat.

'Yes. Mr Walker, isn't it?' Billy offered the minister his hand. 'I hope you have no objection to my sons, Mrs Jones and I attending the service this evening?'

'None of you are Baptist.' The minister's disapproval was evident.

'No,' Lloyd agreed equitably. 'But we are all thinking of converting.' He looked Mr Walker in the eye, daring him to call him a liar.

'God's house is open to all, isn't it, Mr Walker?' Ned challenged.

When the minister didn't offer a reply, another voice cut through the crowd. 'That's what it says in the Bible. Isn't that right, minister?'

Everyone turned to see Sergeant Martin in full uniform standing on the steps flanked by half a dozen constables.

'It does, Sergeant Martin,' Mr Walker agreed hastily, overawed by the sight of so many officers heading into his chapel.

'Even police officers, and assistant housekeepers who run their lodging houses?' The sergeant stepped up alongside Megan and she shrank closer to Victor, who guided her towards the chapel door.

The minister hesitated for a split second. 'Of course, sergeant.' He stepped aside and allowed Victor and Megan to enter.

'You'll thank your father, brothers and Sali again for me. I would have never found the courage to go to chapel on my own tonight.' Megan halted outside the kitchen door of the lodging house.

Victor pulled her towards him. 'Yes, you would have.'

'Not without you.'

'Much as I hate to admit it after the man arrested me and Joey, Sergeant Martin helped. You don't like him, do you?'

'How do you know?'

'From the way you avoid looking at him.' He slid his hand beneath her cloak.

'He gives me the creeps. I don't know why,' she added in the hope of allaying any suspicions Victor might have. She was all too

195

aware that Sergeant Martin could make even more trouble for Victor and his family than Constable Wainwright if he chose to. And she didn't dare mention the chocolates.

'He's never said or done anything to you?' Victor questioned after he kissed her.

'You've seen him, he's always polite.'

'Too polite,' Victor qualified. 'Even when he arrested me and Joey he did everything by the book, unlike the sergeant who arrested Lloyd and half killed him. All the same, you'll stay out of his way?'

'I don't need you to tell me to do that.' She wrapped her arms around his waist. 'I felt like part of your family tonight.'

'You are. Pick you up at twelve o'clock next Saturday?'

'Yes, please.' Megan stood on tiptoe and raised her head to receive another kiss, which tasted salty since he had forgone tooth powder for block salt to economize.

Although both of them were aware of his father, brothers and Sali waiting for him at the end of the lane, she clung to him, burying her head in his shoulder, luxuriating in the scents she had come to associate with him. The clean, antiseptic tang of carbolic soap, the oily odour of his woollen overcoat, the smell of his leather gloves, but even more than the scents, she revelled in the sense of security she felt whenever his arms were around her.

'You'll take care of yourself, until next week, Megs.'

She knew that he was as reluctant to leave her as she was to let him go. 'I will, if you promise to keep yourself safe.'

'You don't have to worry about me. I have too much to live for to risk my neck.' He gave her one last smile, turned and walked quickly away.

She watched him join his father, brothers and Sali. When they moved out of sight, she depressed the latch on the kitchen door, walked in, removed her gloves, cloak and hat, hung them on the stand and washed her hands.

The crockery and cutlery for supper were ready, stacked on trays, waiting to be taken into the dining room. She glanced at the clock. Half past seven. The first supper sitting was at eight, the last at nine. She wondered which one Sergeant Martin would opt for.

'Good, you're here nice and early, Megan. Everything all right in chapel?' Joyce walked in, newspaper in hand, her reading glasses perched on the end of her nose.

'Yes, thank you, Mrs Palmer.'

'You look tired, but little wonder the way I work you. As soon as the last sitting of supper is over you can go to bed.'

'Thank you, Mrs Palmer.' Megan attempted a smile but she couldn't help feeling that it was only the beginning of a long and tiring evening.

At half past ten, Megan climbed the stairs to the top floor and went into her bedroom. Feeling slightly foolish she checked the wardrobe and looked under the beds before locking the door. She undressed, washed and changed into her nightdress. A quarter of an hour later Lena still hadn't come up and she could hardly lock her out of their room. Hoping that Lena would turn up soon, she turned the key, checked that the door would open, moved the candle as far away from the curtain on the window sill as possible and dived into bed.

She sat up watching the door, fully intending to wait for Lena so she could ask her to lock the door behind her. But, as the minutes ticked by she rested her head on the pillow and closed her eyes, only for a moment . . .

She woke with a start. The candle had burned low and the flame was guttering in a draught.

'Lena?' Pulling the bedclothes to her chin, she sat up and looked around. There was no one in the room. She picked up the bracelet watch Victor had given her last Christmas. The hands pointed to eleven. Lena had to be in the house. She wouldn't dare come in later than half past ten. Perhaps she had come in the bedroom when she'd been asleep and gone back downstairs for something she'd forgotten. Then she saw the box of chocolates on the chest of drawers. One thing she was certain of. They hadn't been there when she had prepared for bed.

'Sorry I'm late. I didn't wake you, did I?' Lena crept into the bedroom at midnight.

197

'You didn't come up earlier?' Megan asked urgently.

'No. I came in at half past ten and helped Mrs Palmer with the washing-up. It seemed to take for ever.'

Megan picked up her watch and glanced at it again in case she had misread it. She often helped Mrs Palmer with the supper dishes and they always finished them by eleven o'clock. 'Did you have a good time?' she asked suspiciously.

'The best.' Lena sat on her bed and unlaced her black leather boots. They had cost her entire first week's wages, and although she had bought herself two dresses, a skirt, blouse and under-clothes since, they remained her favourite possession.

'You're sure you didn't come up earlier?' Megan pressed, half hoping that Lena had found the chocolates outside the door and brought them in.

'No, why do you ask?'

Megan had put the chocolates out of sight in her drawer and had already decided not to return them to Sergeant Martin again but to throw them away. 'No reason.'

'Fred — Constable Wainwright took me to a hotel,' Lena gushed, high on excitement. 'I've never been in one before. We had a lovely meal, and a maid waited on us. I had brown soup, roast pork, roast potatoes, parsnips, spinach, gravy, apple sauce, a glass of wine and for afters we had iced cabinet pudding. Have you ever had iced cabinet pudding?'

'Yes, once,' Megan replied shortly. 'Which hotel did you go to?'

'The White Hart. Do you know they have private rooms upstairs?'

'Yes, they rent them out to travellers.' Megan also knew from indiscreet hints dropped by her uncle that the landlord wasn't averse to renting out the rooms on an hourly basis. 'You didn't eat in a private room, did you?'

'Yes. It was heavenly, just like a posh house. There was a table, two chairs, two easy chairs, a big huge couch and a bed.' Lena had the grace to blush when she reached under her pillow for her nightdress.

'Lena, ever since I walked in on you the other day I've been meaning to talk to you. You don't really know Constable Wainwright—'

'Oh, but I do. Look.' Lena unpinned a cheap garish brooch from her winceyette blouse and held it out for Megan to admire. Even from three feet away Megan could see it was gilt and glass. 'It's the very first present I've ever had from anyone in my entire life.' Lena sat back on her bed and continued to study it.

'It's lovely, Lena,' Megan said quietly, not wanting to upset the girl. But she couldn't allow the subject to drop, not after 'Fred' had touched her breast and whispered, *'Shipton's right. All you women are the same, begging for a man to give it to you.'* If he talked to her that way, how serious could he possibly be about marrying Lena?

'Does Mrs Palmer know about you and Constable Wainwright?'

'Course not. He was angry when you walked in and saw us together the other day. He only calmed down when I reminded him that you'd promised you wouldn't tell anyone about us because you didn't want me to lose my job.'

Megan realized that Lena either hadn't heard the threat Fred Wainwright had made about Victor and his family, or else had conveniently forgotten it. 'Haven't you ever wondered why he doesn't want anyone else to know that he's courting you, Lena?'

'He's explained all that.' Lena went to the washstand and poured water into the bowl. 'It's because the policemen on duty here aren't supposed to get involved with people who live in the town.'

'But he's not always on duty,' Megan pointed out logically. 'He has free time and surely he can see anyone he wants to and do what he likes then.'

'He said all the officers have been warned not to get involved with the local girls because of the strike. It's like there are two sides. He's on one and because I'm from around here, I'm on the other.'

Given the antagonism between the strikers and the police, Megan could understand the warning, but it didn't make her any the less suspicious of the sincerity of Fred Wainwright's 'courting'.

'Lena, you do know that if you let him . . . do what he wants with you,' she finished tactfully, 'you could have a baby.'

'He says I won't, because he's careful.'

'Then you've been all the way with him!' Despite what she'd seen Fred and Lena doing, Megan was shocked, given the short length of time the police had been in the valley.

'We went to the White Hart because someone always walks in on us when we try to do anything here.'

'Then where were you until now? And don't say doing the dishes.'

'It's Fred's night off and all the men in his room are working, so we were able to sneak in there for a little while. Although I'm surprised he wanted to after the time we had in the White Hart. And I let him do whatever he wants to me because I love him and he loves me. Besides, I like the things he does to me,' Lena added defiantly. She dried her hands and face and undressed and Megan couldn't help but contrast the way Lena stripped naked in front of her with her modest attitude the first night they had shared a room less than a week before.

'Most girls wait until they get married before making love because they are afraid that their boyfriends will take advantage of them,' Megan advised.

'Fred's promised to marry me as soon as the strike is over. And like he says, why should we wait? This month, next month, there's no difference. I'll have a ring on my finger soon enough, and when I do he'll take me back to London with him. He said it's a huge city, even bigger than Cardiff. And there's all sorts of things there, parks with lakes that you can rent boats on and row around, restaurants, hotels, theatres, even a zoo with lions and tigers.' Lena jumped into bed, sat up and wrapped her arms around her knees. 'And he says he'll buy me . . . ' She fell silent at a knock on the door.

'You girls should be sleeping not gossiping.'

'Yes, Mrs Palmer.' Megan slid down in her bed. But even as she blew out the candle she sensed that she wasn't going to get a good night's sleep. Lena was naïve, and Fred Wainwright . . . she hated to think that he was using Lena, but she found it difficult to believe

200

he was doing anything else. She couldn't deny that he was good-looking but she didn't believe for one minute that he intended to marry Lena or take her back to London with him. Quite aside from the threats he'd made about Victor and the Evans and the way he'd treated her, there was something cold and calculating about him. Just as there was about Sergeant Martin. And the thought of the sergeant entering her bedroom and watching her sleep made her afraid – and somehow violated.

For the first time since he had moved into Sali's bedroom, Lloyd knocked on the door instead of simply walking in. 'Victor's just gone down to pick up Megan,' he told Sali through the closed door.

'We don't have to leave for another half hour, do we?'

'No, but he couldn't sit still so my father sent him packing.'

'Lloyd, we've been man and wife in all but name for so long, you don't have to talk to me through the door just because we're getting married today. And considering we'll be travelling down on the same train to Pontypridd, that superstition about the groom not seeing the bride before the ceremony doesn't apply to us anyway.'

Lloyd opened the door and gazed at Sali's reflection in the mirror. She was sitting in front of the dressing table, pinning up her hair. Her suit was plain, just as she'd told him it would be, a deep rich russet that brought out chestnut highlights in her hair. Her blouse was cream silk ornamented with ruffles of lace at the sleeves and throat and she was wearing a cameo brooch he'd given her clipped at the neck. She saw him watching her in the mirror and smiled back at him.

'You look beautiful,' he complimented. 'I can't believe you're actually going to be my wife two hours from now.'

'I couldn't be more of a wife to you two hours from now than I am right this minute, Lloyd.' She turned to face him.

'No second thoughts.'

'None. You?' she questioned anxiously.

'Absolutely not, although I still think this is a very one-sided relationship. You've given me far more than I'll ever be able to give you.'

'That's nonsense and you know it.' She opened her jewellery casket and lifted out the pair of gold earrings he had given her on her last birthday. 'I bless the day I came to this house.' She turned aside and a tear fell from her eye.

He knelt in front of her. 'You shouldn't cry, not today.'

'I wish . . .'

'What, sweetheart?'

'That I'd never met Owen Bull, much less married him. But most of all I wish that we hadn't had to wait for him to be hanged before we could marry. It's as though our marriage will be rooted in tragedy. Blighted before it's even begun.'

'The only tragedy is that you were ever married to him in the first place. Come on, sweetheart, I told you weeks ago that part of your life is over.'

'It's been over for a long time and I still can't believe my luck in finding you.' She turned back to the mirror and wiped the tears from her eyes with an impractical lace-edged handkerchief she had chosen because it looked bridal. She rose to her feet. 'How do I look?'

'Do you need to ask?'

'More fit for a Saturday shopping trip to Cardiff than a wedding?'

'You're all the bride I want.'

'If you two don't hurry up, we're going to hold the wedding without you,' Joey shouted from downstairs.

Lloyd released Sali, straightened his tie and went to the top of the stairs. 'And who's going to be the bridegroom? You?'

'The woman isn't born yet who'll catch me.' Joey whistled appreciatively when Sali joined Lloyd on the stairs. 'On second thoughts . . . '

'Eyes off my wife.'

'She's not your wife yet, and she could change her mind on the way to the register office.'

'There's no chance of that happening.' Sali walked down the stairs and saw Harry watching from the kitchen doorway. She held out her arms. 'You going to give me away, Harry, like we talked about yesterday.'

'Give you to Uncle Lloyd so he will be my daddy.'

'You don't really have to give your mam away.' Lloyd swung the small boy on to his shoulders. 'It's like we said, you get to keep her. It's just a ceremony.'

'That isn't going to take place if we miss the train and your appointment in the register office,' Billy Evans said gruffly, nervous although he would have suffered torments rather than admit it. 'Time we were on our way.'

'You look very smart,' Victor complimented Megan when she opened the kitchen door of the lodging house wearing her green dress and Sunday hat. He handed her a posy of white, hothouse rosebuds and ferns and pointed to his own buttonhole. 'It wouldn't be a proper wedding without flowers.'

'Thank you, Victor, they're gorgeous.' She smelled the roses.

'They're forced, so there is no smell, and don't thank me, they're Lloyd and Sali's only extravagance.'

'As you see, I'm wearing the same old dress.'

'I love your green dress.'

'So do I, but all the same, I wish I'd been able to buy something new.' She fetched her cloak. 'I'm off now, Mrs Palmer, if that's all right.'

Joyce walked into the kitchen carrying a tray of dirty dishes and Victor lifted his cap to her.

'Victor, all dressed up, I see.' Joyce looked Megan over. 'You look pretty, Megan, very bridesmaid-like. Enjoy yourselves. And don't worry about hurrying back tonight, as long as Mr Evans is bringing you home, that is.'

'Don't worry, Mrs Palmer, I'll be walking her home.' Victor took Megan's cloak and draped it over her shoulders. They walked up the lane into Dunraven Street. Alun Richards was standing, hands in pockets, talking to a dozen men in front of the ironmonger's. He saw them and ducked inside.

'Ignoring is better than spitting. Give me another month and I'll have him bowing to you.' Victor closed his hand around Megan's. 'You have any trouble with anyone last week?'

'No, but then I haven't left the house, or wanted to,' she added in reply to his searching look. 'By the time we do the cleaning, cooking, serve the meals and sort out the laundry, we're too tired to do anything except sit in the kitchen with a cup of tea, and sometimes making the tea requires too much effort. I take it we're meeting the others at the station?'

'We are. Have you spoken to Mrs Palmer about Christmas Day?'

'Yes. I'm sorry, Victor, but I won't be able to have Christmas dinner with you and your family. Mrs Palmer has been ordered to lay on a dinner with all the trimmings for the men. They've had their leave cancelled so they'll be spending it here.'

'Then the authorities are expecting more trouble,' he mused.

'You think so?'

'Just talking to myself.' He put his hand into his pocket and pulled out a lace handkerchief. 'A bridesmaid should have something new. Sorry I couldn't run to anything more. But the only one who has bought anything new is Sali, and then only after Lloyd nagged her into it. The rest of us have made do with our best suits.'

'The middle of a strike isn't the greatest time to get married.'

'Middle – I hope it's near the end.'

'Trying out the outfit you intend to wear in court, Victor? I can't see the judge being impressed by a buttonhole,' Luke Thomas shouted from across the road.

Victor waved an acknowledgement but didn't answer him.

'You've had the date for your trial?'

'March.' He gave her a cautionary look. 'It's not something we want to talk about today.'

'No, of course not.'

'There's Sali, Lloyd and the others. Let's go into the station and get the tickets to save time.'

'Victor,' she laid her hand on his arm and held him back, 'if you need money for the tickets – or for anything else today, I have some savings.'

'So do we.' He managed a smile. His father had warned him and Joey that morning that he'd emptied his bank account of what little

204

was left in it, to pay for the train fare and buy a round of drinks after the wedding.

'The bride and groom.' Mr Richards left his chair and raised his glass to Lloyd and Sali. 'May they enjoy many happy years together.'

'The bride and groom.' Mr Evans, Joey, Victor, Megan, Mari and Harry, at Victor's instigation rose to their feet to echo the toast.

Sali gave Lloyd a self-conscious smile. She had told him so often she didn't expect her brothers and sister to attend their wedding that she had almost begun to believe it. It was only when she had walked into the register office to see Mr Richards sitting next to Mari that she realized she hadn't quite extinguished all hope they'd make the effort.

She hadn't known what to expect of a secular marriage ceremony but the registrar had injected a sense of occasion. And by determinedly ignoring her family's absence and concentrating on Lloyd's family and Mari and Mr Richards, the only two friends she had left from what she had begun to regard as her past life, she managed not to miss Geraint, Gareth and Llinos – too much.

'That was a wonderful lunch, Mr Richards, thank you,' Lloyd said when everyone sat down after finishing the champagne Mr Richards had insisted on buying to round off the 'modest' wedding breakfast he had provided.

'Yes, thank you,' Sali echoed.

'Thank you, Mr and Mrs Evans, for allowing me to provide it.' Mr Richards slipped his hand into his pocket. 'I have something else.' He pulled out an envelope. 'Reservations for dinner and a room here tonight. The dinner can be served in your room, if you prefer.'

'We couldn't possibly—'

'Mr Evans, I have no family of my own and I have over the years flattered myself that Mrs Jones . . . Mrs Evans,' he corrected himself with a smile, 'looks on me almost as a relation. Please, make an old man happy.'

'It's not that we don't want to,' Sali broke in, 'it's just that we have Harry—'

'Who would love to spend an evening with his Auntie Megan and me, wouldn't you, Harry?' Victor interrupted. 'We could play Blow Football.'

'And draughts,' Megan suggested, knowing that Daisy and Sam had taught him how to play the game before they had left.

'Yippee!'

'You won't miss us, Harry?' Sali asked.

Harry shook his head and stared at a waitress who was carrying a cake into the room. A large, white-iced cake covered in sugar roses and green icing petals.

'A wedding cake! Mr Richards you shouldn't have.'

'Hardly a wedding cake, Mrs Evans, just one tier.'

'I don't even have my razor.' Lloyd was still reluctant to accept Mr Richards's generous offer.

'Why don't you men stay here and have another drink, while Megan and I walk over to Gwilym James and pick up what we'll need for tonight,' Sali suggested.

'Is that what my life's going to be from now on?' Lloyd joked. 'Abandoned to sit and drink with the men while my wife goes shopping?'

'If that's an example of married life, I'm all for it.' Joey winked at the waitress who was cutting the cake.

'You'll be lucky to find a girl who'll have you,' his father said acidly. 'Right, what's everyone drinking. This round is on me.' He stood in front of Mr Richards, daring him to say otherwise.

Megan followed Sali in bewilderment as she went from department to department in Gwilym James. First the cosmetics, where she bought a cut-throat razor, shaving mug, soap, toothbrushes, tooth powder and soap, then they moved on to household linens where she bought flannels and a pair of towels. Finally they ended up in the ladieswear department where Sali asked to see a selection of lingerie.

'Just look at this silk and lace!' Megan exclaimed. 'It's beautiful.' She picked up a chemise only to drop it when she saw the price tag. 'I don't mean to be rude, Sali,' she whispered, 'but how on earth can you afford to buy anything here?'

'As we're going to be sisters-in-law, I'll tell you, but not here.' Sali picked up the chemise and held it in front of Megan. 'This looks your size, doesn't it?'

'I couldn't possibly—'

'It's traditional for the bride to buy the bridesmaid a present. Gold or silver jewellery usually, but if you'd prefer oyster satin and coffee-coloured lace, it's yours.'

'I'd love it, but—'

'Good, that's settled.' Sali turned to the assistant. 'I'll take the chemise, nightdress, drawers and petticoat please, Miss Rowe. Would you please parcel up the chemise separately, charge everything to my account and arrange for them to be sent downstairs. I'll pick up everything in ten minutes or so.'

Sali led Megan out of the shop and across the road. She stopped in front of the toyshop and looked at a miniature brewery wagon complete with two horses and dozen metal barrels. Pushing open the door, she went inside.

'Mrs Jones,' the manager abandoned the man and woman he was serving and went to Sali, 'how can I help you?'

'It's all right, Mr Thomas, I am sure that your assistant can see to me.' Sali smiled at a young and diffident boy. 'I've come to buy the brewery wagon.'

'The one Master Harry likes so much.'

'And has been in here a dozen times to look at.'

'He's going to have a happy Christmas, Mrs Jones.' The boy pushed aside the wooden door at the back of the window display and lifted it from the window. 'Could I have that wagon as well?' Sali pointed to a smaller, one-horse coal wagon, complete with tiny lumps of coal.

'My pleasure, Mrs Jones.'

A few minutes later, Sali took Megan into the tearooms in the arcade. Handing their coats and parcels to the girl who showed them to their table, they sat down and Sali ordered tea and cakes for two.

'I owe you an explanation,' Sali said in response to the bemused expression on Megan's face.

'You don't have to tell me anything you don't want to.'

'I want to tell you. I was born Sali Watkin Jones. My father owned collieries.'

'You're rich?'

'Was.' Sali picked up the china teapot the waitress set on the table and poured out two cups of tea. 'But not any more.'

'But the clothes, this tea?' Megan asked in surprise

'You must promise me something, Megan, what I tell you now must remain a secret as far as anyone outside the family is concerned. Especially in Tonypandy.'

Megan looked at the serious expression on Sali's face. 'I promise.'

Chapter 13

'WE KNOW that Lloyd and Sali planned a quiet wedding, but the neighbours wanted to do something for them so we organized a surprise party. I hope you don't mind, Uncle Billy.' Connie met her uncle at the kitchen door when he returned from Pontypridd.

Billy glanced into his kitchen. There were so many people crammed into the room; he couldn't have walked across it. 'It's you who's had the surprise. Lloyd and Sali are staying in Pontypridd tonight.' A lump rose in his throat when he saw the table. Connie had covered it with her best tablecloth and, judging by the various patterns on the plates set on it, everyone had contributed something. Food had never been as scarce as it was at that moment in the valley, yet the table was groaning with more than Connie, Annie and Tonia could have possibly carried up from the shop. And everyone in the street was there, as well as some of his friends and Sali's young sister-in-law, Owen Bull's half-sister, Rhian, who had suffered as much from Owen's cruelty as Sali. Rhian had fled from her brother's house the same time as Sali and found herself a job in Tonypandy as a parlourmaid in Llan house.

'I'm sure Lloyd and Sali would have been delighted.' Joey realized that for once his father was lost for words. 'But they've been given a night in the New Inn as a wedding present so you'll have to make do with us. These pasties look delicious.'

'They'll keep until tomorrow, when we have a welcome home party.' Connie's assistant, Annie, knocked Joey's hand aside as he reached for one.

'The sandwiches won't.' Connie picked up a plate and offered it to Megan and Victor, who came in carrying Harry.

'Great idea, Annie.' Joey snaffled two sandwiches before

Connie had a chance to pass the plate on to Betty Morgan. 'Everyone can forget chapel and church for once and we'll have another party tomorrow night.'

'I suppose we could go to morning service only,' Betty said doubtfully.

'You're risking going to hell, Betty,' Billy taunted.

'But only for a visit,' Ned chimed in. 'Billy and I will be there for the duration.'

'You two will choke on your blasphemy one day.' Betty took the sandwiches and joined a group of women who'd appointed themselves tea makers.

'Hello, Mr Evans, Joey, Victor, Megan.' Rhian opened her arms to Harry, who was fighting his way through a forest of adult legs to get to her. 'I'm sorry I couldn't go to the wedding but there was a lunch party up at Llan House and the mistress cancelled my day off.'

'We heard that the officers from the Somersets had been invited to hobnob with the crache,' Ned commented sourly. 'What did you serve them?'

'You don't want to know, Ned.' Billy bit into a sandwich and discovered to his amazement that it was tinned ham. 'Whatever it was, I bet it wasn't a patch on this feast.'

'I brought a small present for Sali and Lloyd.' Rhian opened her bag, removed a box and set it on the mantelpiece.

'As it seems that we're having another party tomorrow in chapel time, you're more than welcome to come back and give it to them then. That way you can see their faces when they open it.'

'Thank you, Mr Evans, I'll do that.' Rhian opened her bag wide when Harry finally reached her. 'If you put your hand in there, you'll find a paper bag and there might be something in it for you.'

'A gingerbread man. Thank you, Auntie Rhian.' Harry climbed on to her lap, kissed her cheek and proceeded to pull the 'eye' currants from the biscuit.

'So, tell me what you've been doing with yourself, besides serving army officers posh lunches?' Joey perched on the arm of the easy chair Rhian was sitting in and beamed at her. Blonde, blue-eyed and extremely pretty, Rhian had just turned sixteen. She was also the kind of 'nice' girl his father couldn't possibly object to him seeing.

'Just work.' Rhian took a sandwich from the plate Megan handed her. 'Thank you.'

'Work as in, sit down and drink cups of tea in between answering the door to visitors and serving them cucumber sandwiches?' Joey suggested.

'Joey obviously thinks that we domestics can get away with doing as little as he does when he works.' Megan countered Joey's mocking remark with one of her own. 'I never get a minute to myself and the lodging house is nowhere near as big as Llan House.'

'There's a lot more of us in Llan House to do the work,' Rhian said.

'I bet you're still up at six and don't go to bed much before eleven.'

'We'll have to start campaigning for the eight-hour day for shopworkers and domestic workers next,' Billy said seriously.

'Hello, Rhian, Joey.' Connie's dark-haired daughter, Antonia, pulled up a kitchen chair and joined them.

'And hello, Cousin Tonia. You two do know one another?' Joey admired Antonia's perfect classical features and dark, Latin looks before glancing back at Rhian. He found it impossible to decide which girl was the prettiest.

'Of course we do.' At her mother's prompting, Antonia took a plate of sardine sandwiches and offered them around.

'So when is your next day off, Rhian?' Joey asked, taking advantage of Antonia's absence.

'Monday.'

'I'm not doing anything. Fancy a walk on the mountain?' His face fell when Antonia turned around and she, Rhian and Megan all burst out laughing. 'Did I say something funny?' he demanded indignantly.

'Go for a walk on the mountain, in broad daylight, with you, Joey Evans?' Rhian chortled.

'And what's wrong with that!'

'Mrs Williams would stop my days off and lock me up in Llan

House for a year if she knew that I was talking to you in a room crowded with respectable people.'

'Old bat!'

'Sensible lady,' Rhian contradicted. 'She includes a warning about you in her "Welcome to Llan House" talk that she gives every new maid. As she says, a girl would have to be eager to lose her reputation to go anywhere alone with you.'

'Or insane,' Tonia added.

'Thank you very much.' Joey picked up another sandwich and walked over to where his father and Victor were talking to Ned Morgan.

'I heard the girls,' Billy smiled.

'You think they're funny,' Joey snapped, not amused by the joke at his expense.

'You can't say I didn't warn you, son.'

Joey ducked behind Ned when Jane Edwards walked in. She looked around, saw him and stared. He turned his back to her, hoping she'd ignore him. 'Perhaps you should have warned me sooner.'

'And perhaps you should have listened to me sooner,' Billy commented, seeing Jane looking in their direction.

Lloyd and Sali were curled together on a sofa set in front of the window of their hotel room. Lloyd had opened the curtains but although their room overlooked Taff Street and the thoroughfare was crowded with late-night shoppers hoping to pick up a bargain before the market closed at half past ten, neither of them were looking down at the street. Instead, they were gazing over the roof of the Park Hotel opposite and up at the clear dark night sky scattered with stars and a sliver of bright new moon.

'Happy?' Lloyd wrapped his arm around Sali's shoulders and pulled her even closer.

'Yes,' she answered. 'You?'

He picked up the bottle of claret that had arrived with the dinner – they had eaten in their room – and refilled both their glasses. 'I have the moon and the stars to look at, and a beautiful wife dressed in a robe that I sincerely hope she'll never wear when there are other men around.'

'You think it's too revealing.'

'Not for me, but that silk is too thin to keep out the cold back home. Anywhere other than our bedroom that is.' He slipped his hand inside her négligé and fondled her naked breast.

She kissed him.

'And now a kiss! What more could a man ask for?'

'I don't know,' she whispered seductively. 'What more could a man ask for?'

He reached into his shirt pocket and pulled out a tobacco tin. Knowing it was where he kept the French letters they used, she closed her fingers over it, took it from him and dropped it into the wastepaper basket beside the sofa.

'I was hoping I was going to need that.'

'You won't, Lloyd. Not now, and not any more.'

'We can't possibly consider having a child. Not in the middle of a strike.'

'Are you suggesting that we should wait until the colliery owners meet every one of your demands?'

'They'd only do that in an ideal world and unfortunately the world we live in is anything but.'

'Precisely,' she said firmly. 'We could wait until the end of our lives and never see an end to the trouble between the miners and the owners.'

'But even so, this is not a good time to bring a child into the world, Sali,' he warned.

'Then when?'

'I don't know, when the strike is settled, when we've won better wages, better conditions, better housing . . .'

'Lloyd, I have a feeling that if we wait for the right time, it will never come. Harry will be five next year and five years is a big gap between brothers—'

'Brother and sister,' he broke in.

'You want a daughter?'

'Most definitely, after having two brothers. I even have a name picked out for her, Isabella Maria Evans after my mother. She never said, but I knew she always wanted a daughter.'

'That's a lovely name. I wish I'd known your mother.'

'So do I.' He swept her into his arms, carried her over to the bed, folded back the bedclothes and dropped her gently on the sheet. Untying the belt on her robe, he opened it. She lay naked, watching him undress.

'Just think,' she said, 'nine months from today there could be four of us.'

'I'm not at all sure about this, Sali.' Peeling off the last of his clothes, he lay beside her.

'Don't you remember what you said the second time we made love. We were in your bedroom.' She took his hand and laid it on her left breast. 'You told me that you wanted my heart, my body, my mind – but most of all you wanted to watch me grow big with your child, because he or she would carry our love into the future.' She moved both his hands to the flat of her stomach and held them there.

'You remember?'

'I remember everything you say to me.'

'Everything?' He caressed her breasts with the back of his fingers.

'The first time you told me that you loved me, you also said that you wanted to live with me day in, year out, until we grew old and grey together.'

'To me, you'll always look the same as you do now.'

'I love you, Lloyd, and I want to have sons just like you. Tall, intelligent, bold men with your vision and spirit.'

'And their mother's kindness.'

When he entered her, he knew she was right. There would never be a more perfect time for them to have a child. Maybe they wouldn't be able to give him or her much in the way of material possessions, or even security, but they would be able to give love. He only hoped it would prove riches enough.

'It's bl—' Ned looked at his wife and realized she was listening in on his conversation, 'blasted disgraceful. Tom and Dai Hayward

214

were up in court yesterday and both of them were fined fifteen pounds. The judge said if they couldn't pay, as if he didn't know that money's rarer than unicorns in this valley, they'd have to go to prison for three months. And that was just for trying to protect women and children when the police charged a crowd with batons.'

'They called it assault,' Victor said evenly. 'And Dai and Tom both admitted that their pockets were full of stones.'

'Assault as opposed to intimidation,' Billy said thoughtfully.

'The sentences they're handing out to strikers are disgraceful,' Ned reiterated. 'You, Joey and Luke could be fined twenty pounds or more and if you can't pay, you could be sent down for as much as three or four months – and with hard labour.'

'We don't know anything for sure yet, Ned, and we won't until the boys' case comes up.' Billy handed his empty cup to Connie who was collecting them. 'Now, how about changing the subject. This is supposed to be a happy occasion.'

Victor looked across the kitchen to where Megan was talking to a group of women, Betty Morgan among them. He caught her eye and raised his eyebrows. Excusing herself she walked over to him.

'I have to go down the garden to feed the dogs and lock up the chickens. Do you and Harry want to come?'

'I'd like to. I'll ask Harry.'

'Get your coats. It's going to be cold down there. I'll wait for you in the basement.' He picked up the candle he'd lit with a newspaper spill, opened the door to the basement and slipped out.

'Harry, Uncle Victor's feeding the dogs. Do you want to come?'

Harry looked up sleepily at Megan from Rhian's arms and shook his head.

'He's fine with me, Megan,' Rhian assured her. 'I don't see much of him so I'm making the most of this cuddle.'

Megan fetched her cloak from the passage and followed Victor out through the door. The steps were shrouded in darkness, but she could see a candle flickering below her. Victor was standing at the old kitchen table surrounded by tins and bowls.

'Harry didn't want to come?'

'He was too comfortable on Rhian's lap. Another five minutes and I think he'll be fast asleep. Do you think anyone noticed us sneaking off?'

'What if they did? We're engaged and as such, allowed to do some courting in peace. Did Mrs Morgan say anything to you?' He opened the tin in which he kept the stale bread Sali baked hard for the dogs.

'Nothing horrible.'

'But nothing nice either,' he guessed.

'She didn't cut me.'

'She wouldn't dare in this house.' Victor pounded the bread with a hammer and broke it into small pieces.

'You must be finding it hard to feed the dogs these days.'

'Like us they're on half rations.' Victor opened a second tin that held boiled slaughterhouse scraps. After mixing them together with the bread in two bowls he opened the back door. You don't have to come, it's cold out here.'

'I'd like some fresh air. It was stuffy upstairs.' She followed him. Most of the chickens were already in the coop. While Victor fed the dogs, she went into their run and coaxed the remaining two inside before latching the door.

'We haven't had any trouble with foxes for a while, but I still like to secure them at night.' Victor wrapped his arm around her waist. 'It's a lovely night.'

'With a new moon and thousands of stars to look down and bless your brother's wedding night.'

'That sounds more pagan than chapel.'

'It probably is.'

He kissed her. 'Do you want to go back upstairs?'

She shook her head. 'No. Today's been marvellous but—'

'We haven't had a minute to ourselves,' he finished for her.

'Is that selfish of me?'

'If it is, it's selfish of me too.'

'It will be even colder up the mountain but we could go for a walk.'

He reached into the pocket of his jacket and fished out a key. 'What's that?'

'The key to our first home, if you want it to be. Lloyd has

agreed to give us next door in exchange for one of the houses our father bought. I realize you know the place inside out, and some windows and the front door are boarded because we used them to repair the damage the police did to our house, but I thought we could look it over. If you want to live in it when we're married I could start doing a few things. I have time to spare at the moment and two years will soon pass—'

'I'd love to look it over with you, Victor,' she said quietly, thinking of all the Saturday afternoons they could work on it together – and the furnished bedrooms where they wouldn't be disturbed.

'Now?' He gave her a searching look.

'Yes, please.'

'I'll go back and fetch the candle.'

'Hello, Joey, how are you keeping?' Jane Edwards asked loudly as she joined him at the sink, where he was stacking plates.

'I'm fine, thank you, Jane. And you?' he answered equally loudly, giving her a warning glance.

'That's a nasty cut you've got under your eye. How did you get it?'

'I had an encounter with a vicious dog, no, come to think of it now, it was a bitch.' His father had carried a pile of coats in from the parlour and Connie, Annie, Antonia and Rhian were dressing to leave. 'If you'll excuse me, Jane, I have to say goodbye to our guests.' He turned away, pretending that he hadn't seen her mouthing, 'I'm sorry, come round later.'

'Joey, as I'm more than twice your age and your cousin, you may give me a goodbye kiss,' Connie offered him her cheek. 'But as Annie, Tonia and Rhian are single and have reputations to think of, you'd best keep your distance.'

'That joke has worn thin. I was about to offer to walk you home.'

'All of us?' Connie asked suspiciously.

'Yes,' he answered in exasperation.

'In that case, we'll walk you back to Llan House first, Rhian, then Joey can walk us home,' Connie said decisively. 'But you take my arm there and back, Joey.'

'I wouldn't have it any other way,' Joey said gloomily. He helped Rhian and Tonia on with their coats, then went to fetch his own.

His father followed him into the hall. 'You really are serious about turning over a new leaf?'

'I said I was last night.'

'In my experience, saying and doing have been two very different things with you in the past.' Billy kissed Connie, Antonia, Annie and Rhian as they passed him in the passage. 'Goodnight, ladies, see you all tomorrow.'

'Don't worry about Joey, Mr Evans,' Annie called back, 'we'll keep him in order.'

'When I left this house, I thought I'd never want to come back because it would spoil my happy memories to see it empty and neglected. It's funny to think that in less than two years we could be living here and making a whole lot of new – and even happier memories.' Megan ran her hand over the dusty surface of the Welsh dresser in the cold, abandoned kitchen.

'Nice funny, I hope,' Victor said. 'If you like, I could build cupboards in the alcoves next to the fireplace as I've done in our house, and we'll need new kitchen chairs. The one your uncle used is fine, but I'd like to replace the benches. They're not very comfortable for visitors.'

'The children used to complain about them.'

'And the garden's not as big as my father's.'

'Would you want to move the dogs and the chickens from your father's house?' she asked.

'I haven't given it much thought, but I suppose I could keep chickens in both gardens. We could certainly use the eggs. And unless Lloyd wants to take over our garden, I could grow vegetables in both. I've no money now, but as soon as the strike is settled we can start thinking about wallpaper and paint. Lloyd, Joey and my father will give me a hand to redecorate the place and there's bound to be other furniture that you want. I could knock a few things together until we've saved enough to buy new. And then there are the bedrooms. Grown-up bedroom suites aren't suitable for children,' he said mischievously.

She bit her lip and turned aside.

'What's the matter?'

'I don't know.' She hated lying to Victor, but she'd had a premonition. And although she couldn't have quantified how she knew, she felt they would never live in the house.

'Why won't you tell me?'

She turned back to him and tried to smile. 'It's silly superstition but I don't want to make too many plans or look too far ahead.'

'Because of your father?'

'Probably.'

'He can't stop us marrying when you are of age.'

'I know.' She wrapped her arms around him. 'Kiss me?'

He sensed that she was afraid. Bending his head to hers, he kissed her, then opened his watch and held it to the candle. 'Half past ten. Time I walked you back to Mrs Palmer's.'

'It's been a lovely day, Victor. Thank you.' She followed him down the basement stairs and out through the door with a heavy heart. She knew she'd hurt him by refusing to discuss the changes he wanted to make to the place. But she had never been so certain of anything as she was that all his plans would come to nothing. There was no point in them even talking about the house. Not when they would never live in it or taste the happiness it promised.

'I'll walk Megan to the lodging house, then I'll come back and put Harry to bed,' Victor said to his father when they returned to the kitchen to find him sitting reading the paper at the table, and Harry curled up, fast asleep on one of the easy chairs.

Billy looked at them over the top of the paper. 'There's no need to rush back. I'll take him up.'

'Don't you want to call in the County Club?' Victor asked.

'There's plenty of time. It never closes before twelve and Joey will be back long before then.'

'Unless he persuades one of the girls to take a detour with him.'

'There's no chance of that happening with Connie in charge, or either of the girls agreeing to go anywhere with him after the way they spoke to him tonight.'

'Goodnight, Mr Evans.' Megan kissed his cheek.

'Goodnight, Megan, don't go working too hard in that lodging house. We'll see you tomorrow evening?'

'Yes.' Megan blew a kiss in Harry's direction and followed Victor into the street. Betty Morgan was on her doorstep shaking her doormat.

'You two sneaked off early.'

'We have to do our courting some time, Mrs Morgan,' Victor answered.

'You cheeky blighter, Victor Evans.'

'At least she's acknowledging us now,' Victor laughed, as they headed up the street.

'I suppose we should be grateful for small mercies.'

He walked Megan down the hill and to the back door. 'Pick you up at five tomorrow.'

'Don't you want to come in for tea?'

He shook his head. 'Despite what my father said, he can't wait to get to the County Club and someone has to stay in the house with Harry.'

'Then I'll see you tomorrow,' she smiled, trying to hide her disappointment.

Instead of walking back up the hill, Victor headed into Pandy Square. He found Luke Thomas and half a dozen of his cronies drinking dark pints of mild beer in the back bar of the Pandy.

'Our man won today, so it's drinks all round.' Luke held up a full glass to show Victor. 'You been thinking about what I said?'

'Yes.'

'Have you heard what happened to Tom and Dai, Victor?' Luke's friend Guto Price joined them.

'I should think everyone in Pandy has by now,' Victor replied.

'Reckon you, and Luke here, could be fined double what they got and if you can't pay, you could go down for three or four months.'

'Proper bloody Job's comforter, aren't you, Guto?' Luke took Victor by the elbow. 'So what's it to be?'

'When's the next bout?'

'Wednesday afternoon. Dai will be glad to hear that you're stepping in.'

'Dai Hopkins?'

'Aye, the Dai you saw lose.'

'Getting beaten half to death more like.' Victor recalled Dai's bloody face and the way he'd fallen to his knees. But then he was taller, stronger and more experienced. And when he thought of the court case coming up, the fines he and Joey would undoubtedly get and all the things he and Megan would need for their new home, he felt he didn't have any other choice. Not while the strike lasted.

Jane Edwards stood behind the lace curtains in her freezing, dark front parlour and watched the street intently. She was so cold her nose was stiff when she tried to twitch it. It had been an hour and a half since Joey had left to walk Rhian Bull and Antonia Rodney home. The two older women might have gone with them, but she knew Joey Evans. Oh, how she knew him! He was after one of the young girls. The question was which one? Not that it would make any difference to her. He'd used her and tossed her aside with no more thought than he gave to a worn-out pair of socks. She seethed in anger every time she recalled what he had said to her.

'I had an encounter with a vicious dog, no, come to think of it now, it was a bitch.'

She had told Joey she loved him, had asked him to move in with her, further humiliated herself by offering to throw her husband out of their home and he had rejected her. All she had left to look forward to was the return of her husband from gaol. An old man who disgusted her . . .

She saw movement in the street. Joey was walking up the road with Victor, both of them talking animatedly. About her? The Evans were polite enough to her face but she was astute enough to realize that Joey's brothers and father didn't like her. She wouldn't make a suitable wife for an Evans. They wanted Joey to settle down with a nice, unmarried girl with an unsullied reputation like that milk-faced maid from Llan House, Rhian, or a rich cousin like Antonia who'd inherit Rodney's stores one day. And there was nothing she could do about it – or was there?

Her hands closed over her stomach and she remembered what Joey had said about the insurance man and the milkman. Had he lied to her or had he really talked to them? She ducked back into the shadows as they drew closer lest they see her at the window.

'You can look out, Joey Evans, you're for it.' Searching for a way to hurt him as he had hurt her, she ran upstairs to her cold bedroom and threw herself headlong on to the bed.

'The pews in the chapels must be empty tonight.' Lloyd pressed his back against the wall to make room for Betty, who was trying to offer food to everyone who'd turned up to congratulate him and Sali.

'The minister will be taking us all to task from the pulpit next week and it will be your and Sali's fault. Piece of cake? I made it special.' Betty pushed a plate of sponge slices sandwiched with her homemade blackberry jam under Lloyd's nose.

'They look delicious, Betty, thank you.' Lloyd felt that he couldn't eat another morsel, but wary of upsetting her, he took the smallest piece.

'Look what Rhian has made for us, Lloyd.' Sali held up a set of embroidered cutwork dressing-table mats.

'They're beautiful,' he complimented. 'And you made them yourself, Rhian?'

'Mrs Williams, the housekeeper up at Llan House, has been giving all us maids embroidery lessons. I hope she doesn't find out that I'm not at chapel tonight.'

'Are you a quick learner at everything?' Joey enquired suggestively, admiring the mats.

'I *always* listen to Mrs Williams and follow her advice,' Rhian replied.

'Except when you sneak off to come here instead of going to chapel.'

'Lloyd and Sali's wedding is a once in a lifetime occasion.'

'What can I do to convince you that I'm a changed boy and serious about wanting to take you out?' Joey whispered in her ear.

'Attract no scandal or gossip for the next ten years.'

'Ten years!'

'Then, if you've been very good, you can come calling on me at Llan House and I may re-consider your offer,' she said seriously. 'But I warn you that is only a "may".'

'I can't help it if people talk about me.'

'They only talk about you because you give them plenty to say,' she informed him tartly.

'So beautiful and so hard-hearted. How about I take you and Tonia to the free concert Father Kelly's organizing in the Catholic Hall next Saturday night?'

'I'm working next Saturday.'

'When are you free?' he pressed refusing to give up.

'Wouldn't you like to know?' She turned her back on him.

Billy Evans opened the door and shouted down the passage at a knock at the front door, 'Come in.'

'I hope whoever's at the door is thin.' Victor looked around. If anything there were even more people in their kitchen than there had been the evening before, as word had spread about the party.

'Mr Evans?'

Recognizing Jane Edwards' voice, Billy reached for a candle. He went into the passage and closed the door behind him. Given the situation between Joey and Jane, he sensed trouble, for all that they had managed to be polite to one another the night before, but he greeted her as her would have any other neighbour. 'Come in, Jane. You know friends are always welcome in this house.'

'I wasn't sure I would be, Mr Evans,' she said in a small voice.

'And why is that, Jane?' Billy enquired warily.

'Because of me and Joey . . .' her voice broke and she began to sob.

That sounds like crocodile tears, Lloyd said quietly to Sali. Keep everyone in here.' He opened the door and he and Victor joined their father in the passage.

'I know you Evans don't like me,' Jane gulped out between sobs.

'Victor?' Billy turned to his middle son.

'I'll get Joey.' Victor returned to the kitchen.

'I'm not sure what's going on, Jane,' Billy said curtly, 'but whatever it is, I think it would be better if we moved out of the passage into the parlour.' He opened the door. Still howling, Jane walked in ahead of him and Lloyd.

'What's the problem?' Megan asked Victor anxiously, as he glanced around the kitchen.

'Joey's,' Victor answered briefly. He looked to the corner where Joey was still trying to flirt with Rhian. Joey saw him, and Victor jerked his head towards the door. 'Jane Edwards is here, and she's crying,' Victor warned when Joey pushed his way through the crowd and reached him.

'Oh God!' Joey exclaimed.

'If that's meant to be a prayer, I'd add to it if I were you. I think you're going need all the help that He and the Virgin Mother can give you.'

'Joey!' Jane left her chair and flung herself at him as soon as he opened the parlour door. He stepped back smartly and crossed his arms across his chest. She stood and stared at him, then fell back weakly.

Although he suspected that Jane was acting, Lloyd caught her and helped her into one of the easy chairs. 'Get Sali, and tell her to bring a glass of water.'

Victor was glad of an excuse to leave.

Jane opened her eyes and looked around, apparently in confusion, before focusing on Joey. 'I am carrying his child and he can't even bear me near him,' she wailed.

Sali brought a glass of water. Briefed by Victor, she closed the door behind her and handed the water to Jane who was suddenly composed enough to sip it. The sound of voices and laughter echoing from the kitchen only served to emphasise the strained silence.

'If you don't need me . . .'

'I'd rather you stayed, Sali. It might be as well to have another woman present after what's Jane's just told us.' Billy looked Jane sternly in the eye. 'Is this the same kind of pregnancy you used to get Emlyn to marry you?'

'No one ever believes a word I say!' Jane set the water on the floor, covered her nose and mouth with her handkerchief and started sobbing again, but Billy wasn't easily deterred.

'Is it?' he demanded.

Jane's shoulders shook as her cries grew louder.

'Could Jane be having your child, Joey?' Billy asked his youngest son.

'She's been with most of the men in Tonypandy,' he retorted defensively.

'That's not what I asked. And if what you say is true, then all I can say is more fool you for joining them. Could she be carrying your child?' Billy reiterated.

'I've slept with her, if that's what you mean,' Joey conceded.

'When is this baby due, Jane?' Billy enquired sceptically.

'In . . . the . . . summer,' Jane blurted. 'And it is Joey's child. No one else has touched me since Emlyn got put away.'

Billy saw Joey blanch, and he realized that for all of Joey's cavalier attitude towards women and lovemaking, this was one eventuality he hadn't prepared himself for. 'Regardless of who the father is, if you really are having a child, you will need help to bring it up. I suggest that you and the new Mrs Evans,' Billy glanced at Sali, 'visit the midwife as soon as possible, so you can make provisions for the birth. And, as no doubt Emlyn will throw you out when he is released from prison and returns to find you pregnant, you'll need somewhere to live.'

'I want to live with Joey—'

'I don't want to live with you,' Joey broke in hastily.

'Just sleep with her occasionally.' His father bit back angrily. 'I've said all I'm prepared to say on the subject for tonight. There's a party going on next door and we have to attend to our guests. I take it you don't want to join us, Jane?'

'Joey wouldn't want me there, Mr Evans.' For someone who'd

been sobbing only a few minutes before, Jane was remarkably coherent.

'I'll not interfere between the two of you,' Billy glared from Joey to Jane.

'I'll leave.' Jane covered her face with her handkerchief again as she left the chair.

'I'll see you out.' Sali opened the door. Jane gave Joey one last look. When he ignored her, she left.

'Jane Edwards,' Lloyd breathed. 'We all warned you, Joey . . .'

'Even if she is having a kid, it's not mine,' Joey said vehemently.

'And how exactly are you going to prove it isn't?' Lloyd enquired.

Joey stepped forward. 'Stay here, Sali, I'll see Jane out.'

'Are you pregnant?' Joey demanded roughly when he caught up with Jane at her front door.

'You think I'd lie about something like that?' she challenged.

'Yes,' Joey replied shortly.

'I'm having your baby.' She opened her door, turned and gave him a triumphant look. 'He'll be calling *you* Daddy, and after what you tried to do to me, I'll see that you'll be footing my bills until it's old enough to start keeping me.' She walked into the house and slammed the door in his face, leaving him standing in the empty street.

Chapter 14

THE FIRST breakfast Lloyd and Sali ate as husband and wife in his father's house was a subdued meal. Although no one mentioned Jane Edwards, Sali only had to look at the men's faces to know that they were all thinking about her. Lloyd, Victor and their father were withdrawn, but Joey looked positively distraught. Clearing her dishes to the sink, she decided that the best way she could help her brother-in-law was to act upon the suggestion his father had made and take Jane to a midwife.

'Will you take Harry to school this morning, Lloyd?' She picked up her handbag and checked she had her purse and hairbrush.

'Of course. Where are you going?'

'I thought I'd call in on Jane before I go to the soup kitchen. If she's free today I'll make that appointment we talked about last night.'

'Good idea.' Billy finished his toast and stacked his cup and saucer on his empty plate.

Sali went into the hall, pinned on her hat and lifted down her coat. Knowing that Harry would tolerate a kiss in the privacy of their home, she returned to the kitchen, kissed his and Lloyd's cheeks and said goodbye to the others before crossing the road to Jane's house. She knocked on the front door and opened it without waiting for Jane to reply.

The kitchen was empty and Sali was taken aback by its filthy and neglected condition. The fireplace was covered in so much rust she suspected it hadn't seen any black lead since Emlyn had been imprisoned. Dust lay half an inch deep on every surface. The pump and sink in the corner were stained with green slime, and the floor was littered with mouse droppings and cockroach carcases.

Trying not to think about the bedrooms, she wondered how an intelligent boy like Joey could have even considered having an affair with a slovenly, married woman like Jane. But then she recalled the way Joey had behaved ever since she had moved in with the Evanses, and realized Jane wasn't the only one without personal pride and morals. Feeling judgemental, she decided that they were as bad as each other and the only person she should feel sorry for was Emlyn. But Joey was family . . .

She called out, 'Jane, it's Sali.'

She heard a thud overheard. A few minutes later Jane meandered down the stairs and into the kitchen wearing a man's knee-length, thick-check flannel dressing gown over a faded winceyette nightdress. She looked sick and pale. Sali's heart sank. She knew Joey was hoping that Jane was lying about the baby, but if appearances were anything to go by, her pregnancy was a forgone conclusion.

'I've been suffering terrible morning sickness.' Jane threw herself down into an easy chair.

'I'm sorry.'

'I bet you are,' Jane retorted nastily. 'What do you want?'

'I came to ask when you'd like to visit the midwife.'

'Not until after Christmas.' Jane didn't offer Sali a seat and she remained standing next to the door.

'But that's over a week away.' All Sali could think of was Joey's feelings of guilt and shame. An examination by a midwife would at least prove the existence of a baby one way or the other. 'The sooner we find out when your baby is going to be born, the sooner we can start planning for the birth and the child's future.'

'I don't see that you Evans have any plans to make. All I want from Joey is his money.'

'The only money Joey has is his ten shillings a week strike pay and that doesn't go far,' Sali reminded her.

'He has a watch and other things he can pawn. I've seen them.'

'You and the baby are going to need more than the few pounds Joey could raise in a pawn shop, Jane.' Sali looked around. Given the conditions Jane was living in, she doubted she was even capable of caring for a child.

228

'I'm going to Trealow today to spend Christmas with my father and the rest of the family. He needs my help and Emlyn's ten bob a week,' Jane added drily. 'I should have moved in with him when my Emlyn got put away. I don't know why I didn't. Ten bob a week doesn't go far but put it with my father's and two brothers' strike pay and it would have gone further.'

Sali would have loved to remind Jane that her father might have objected to her carrying on with Joey under their roof, but she managed to hold her tongue. 'Couldn't you spare an hour sometime today?'

'No, I couldn't,' Jane snarled. 'I promised I'd get there early.'

'You need care—'

'What I don't need is a witch of a nurse poking around my private parts and you Evanses poking your noses into my affairs.'

'If you are carrying Joey's child it's as much our business as it is yours. Especially as you expect Joey to pay for the baby's keep,' Sali contradicted firmly. 'Please, Jane, Trealow's only just down the road. I could make an appointment with the midwife for you and write to let you know when it is.'

'All right,' Jane capitulated. 'But make it for the end of this week. Thursday or Friday might suit me.'

'I'll do that. And the address?' Sali pulled a pencil and notebook from her pocket.

'Cairo Street, but I'll expect you to pay my tram fare when we go to see the midwife,' Jane warned.

Sickened even more by Jane's mercenary attitude than the squalid surroundings, Sali nodded. 'Don't come to the door, I'll see myself out.'

'I know there's no chance of me ever becoming your sister-in-law, but whatever's in here,' Jane patted her stomach, 'will be your nephew or niece. And you Evans won't be able to ignore the fact that there'll be as much of me in this baby as your precious Joey.'

'Sali's gone to the soup kitchen, Victor and Lloyd will go from the school to the picket lines, none of them will be back for hours, so now's as good a time as any to have a go at me,' Joey said to his father.

'What's the point in me saying anything to you now?' Billy left the table and sat in his easy chair.

Joey knelt in front of the fire, raked the coals out on to the tiled hearth, picked them up one by one with the tongs from the fire irons and placed them in a metal bucket. When they were all inside, he set the lid on the bucket to smother them. 'I can take anything except this frosty silence. Hardly anyone's said a word this morning. Not even Harry.'

'If Harry was quiet it was only because he's sensitive enough to realize when something is wrong.' Billy looked at his son. 'What do you expect us to say, Joey? Given what you said to Jane last night, it's obvious you have no intention of marrying her.'

'You think I should marry her?' Joey stared at his father horror-struck.

'That would be difficult given that she's already married.'

'Even if Emlyn could afford to divorce her for adultery, she'd be the last woman I'd marry.'

'Which brings us back to the question of what you thought you were doing with her in the first place,' Billy said evenly. 'I'd be a liar if I said that this was the way I wanted my first grandchild to come into the world.'

'If she's having a child at all,' Joey muttered sullenly.

'If she is, and it is yours, you'll have to pay for its upkeep, you do realize that, don't you?'

Joey lifted the lid on the bucket, checked that the coals were no longer burning, replaced the lid and rose to his feet. He went to the sink and washed his hands.

'Joey—'

'If the child is mine, I won't see it starve. Though God only knows what kind of life it will have with Jane for a mother.'

'You should have thought of that before you slept with her. What are you doing this morning?'

'I may as well go down to the picket line with Victor and Lloyd.'

230

'Stay close to them and keep out of trouble,' his father warned. 'When the meeting is finished in the County Club I'll join you.'

Jane stood back from her front bedroom window and watched Joey and his father leave the house. Ned Morgan hailed them and walked over the patch of rough ground at the end of the street with Billy, leaving Joey to head into town alone. Five minutes later Betty Morgan emerged from her house with a shopping bag. Jane continued to watch the street while she dressed. As soon as she'd laced on her boots she dived into the back bedroom to pick up a battered carpetbag.

She ran down the stairs, opened the front door and glanced up and down the street. It was still dark and no one was around. Running across the road, she opened the Evans' door and slipped inside.

Lloyd left the picket line around half past three when it began to get dark. It was a cold, wet day and he decided to go home and light the fire before Sali and Harry returned from the soup kitchen. He opened the door, felt his way along the passage and entered the kitchen. The first intimation he had that something was wrong was when he struck a match and reached for the oil lamp that was kept on the kitchen table. It was missing. He went to pick up one of the brass candlesticks they kept on the mantelpiece, but the match illuminated a bare shelf. No candlesticks, no clock and no brass spill holder.

Yanking open the sideboard drawer, he lifted out the spare candles, lit one and looked around. Everything else seemed to be in its place. Carrying the candle, he went into the passage and opened the parlour door. The silver vase and clock had gone from the mantelpiece. The photographs of his mother had been stripped from their silver frames and piled on the sideboard.

His blood ran cold as he ran towards his father's room.

'Where's the fire?' Billy asked gruffly as he walked in with Victor and Joey.

'Check Mam's jewellery box in your room,' Lloyd said harshly. 'I think we've been burgled.' He handed his father the candle and returned to the kitchen. Lighting two more candles, he passed one to Victor. 'Look upstairs.'

Joey snatched the candle from Victor's hand and ran up in front of his brother.

'If you'd asked me before today, I would have said that we had nothing worth stealing in this house. Only goes to show how wrong you can be, doesn't it?' Billy crumbled bread on top of the chicken broth Sali had made and spooned it to his mouth.

Joey pushed his untouched bowl aside. 'The bitch!'

'Language, Joey,' Victor reprimanded, 'and we've no proof that it was Jane who took the things.'

'Who else could it be?' Joey demanded, smarting at the loss of his suit, two best shirts, best shoes, waistcoat, silver cufflinks, tiepin and collar studs. 'I still say we should go to the police.'

'Do you want Jane to shout from the dock of the court that you wouldn't support her or the child so she was forced to steal from us to buy food?' Lloyd finished his broth and handed Sali his bowl.

'Most of what was taken can be replaced,' Billy said philosophically. 'I wouldn't have forgiven her if she'd touched any of your mam's things.'

'Jane gave me her mother's address in Trealow. We could go there and see what she has to say for herself.' Sali left the table, stacked the bowls next to the sink and brought back a plate of cheese sandwiches she'd cut.

Lloyd took a sandwich and set it on Harry's plate. 'If she gave you the address I doubt she'll be there, but someone may know where we can find her.'

'She'll have pawned everything by now,' Victor said thoughtfully, 'but given the state of things in the valley no one will be in a hurry to buy them.'

'Including us,' Billy reminded. 'Our savings ran out days ago.'

'It's still worth tracking them down and finding out what it will cost to redeem them.' Victor took a sandwich.

'Why don't you all say it?' Joey shouted angrily.

'What?' Even in the shadowy light of the single flickering

candle, Lloyd thought that he had never seen his brother look quite so guilty – or miserable.

'It's all my fault.'

'You didn't turn Jane Edwards into a thief, Joey, or even a,' Billy glanced at Harry, 'loose woman. I think she was one of those long before she met you. But that doesn't excuse you for taking up with her or the way you behaved towards her afterwards. However, there's no use in mulling over events after they've happened. The only thing we can do now is see if we can salvage anything. I'll take a walk down the pawnbrokers and take a look at the stock he's bought in today.'

'You going with Dad?' Victor asked Joey as he left the table.

'No, I'm going to Trealow.'

'No!' Sali broke in quickly. 'Lloyd and I will go there, if you'll look after Harry, Victor.'

'That sounds an eminently sensible idea to me,' Billy agreed. 'Victor?'

'Harry and I will do the washing-up, then we'll do some sums.' Victor winked at Harry and Harry grinned, knowing that the last thing they'd be doing was schoolwork. Victor was carving him a small fort for his enemy soldiers and it was almost ready for painting.

'If you really don't mind about the washing-up, Victor, I'll get my coat.' Sali was outside the door before Victor had time to answer her.

'Could we speak to Jane Edwards, please?' Sali asked a thin, grey-haired, tired looking woman who opened the door of the house in Cairo Street.

'She doesn't live here.' The woman turned and yelled, 'Shut up!' to a toddler who was standing, crying, on the flagstones behind her. Thin, barefoot and naked apart from a ragged grey shirt, the child looked dirty and neglected.

'Jane said she was coming here to spend Christmas with her family.'

'Is that what she told you?' The woman laughed mirthlessly. 'Well, Jane Jones, as she was before she married Emlyn Edwards, was thrown out this house by her father the day after her sixteenth birthday and he said he wouldn't allow her over his doorstep again even if she was reduced to sleeping in the gutter.'

'You're her mother—'

'Her mother!' The woman laughed again, displaying two rows of broken, yellowed teeth. 'That bitch ran off with an Irishman when Jane was two. No one's seen hide nor hair of her since.'

'Jane told me she was pregnant.'

'She's not trying to pull that one again, is she?'

'What do you mean?'

'That's how she got Emlyn to marry her, and more fool him. At his age he should have known better. Jane had a baby when she was thirteen, had it and lost it, if you take my meaning. The midwife warned her there'd be no more. Not for her. Now, if that's all, I'll go and see to this lot.'

Sali saw that the child in the passage had been joined by two more who were smaller and considerably dirtier. 'We're sorry for bothering you, Mrs Jones.' She glanced up at Lloyd when the woman closed the door.

He pulled her closer to him under the umbrella they were sharing. 'Not that he deserves it after they way he's behaved the last couple of years, but Joey'll be relieved. I can almost hear him saying, "I told you there was no baby."'

'I think we'll all be pleased,' Sali said sombrely.

'I suppose if you think of the things Jane took as a payment to get out of our lives, it's cheap at the price. I wasn't looking forward to having lifelong dealings with her. And we would have had to, if she'd had Joey's baby.'

'You couldn't have walked away from the child, could you?' Sali asked.

'No more than you could have, sweetheart.' He changed the subject. 'We'll go home via the station. Someone may have seen Jane buy a ticket.'

'What's the point?'

'Tracking down the pawnshop. Joey's suit was made to measure and despite what my father said, I know he would like the silver frames back.'

'And if Jane left by tram?' Sali suggested.

'We'll put Betty Morgan on to it. She's the best detective we have in the valley.' He slipped his arm around her shoulders and led her away.

'I hope we never have another Christmas like this one.' Victor pushed up the sash window in the parlour and carefully manoeuvred out the skeletal remains of the Christmas tree he had been given in return for cutting down five dozen others at the farm. Dead needles cascaded around his feet, as he lowered it as far as he could reach and shouted down to his brother, 'You got it, Joey?'

'Let go,' came a muffled reply from the back yard below.

Sali packed the last straw star into the cardboard box of decorations they kept in the loft between Christmases, pushed the lid on and tied it with string. 'This Christmas wasn't so bad.'

'It was perfect,' he said sourly, 'apart from Jane stripping the house of everything we had of any value and disappearing to sell it who knows where, the strike, lack of money, me and Joey waiting for our court case to come up, and the police watching us like hawks whenever we left the house.'

'We had each other, we didn't go hungry and Father Christmas was able to bring Harry his toy cart from us, his coal cart from your father, you and Joey, and some sweets.' Sali brushed the pine needles on the lino into a neat pile, shovelled them into a dustpan and shook them into the ashbin.

'I'm sorry,' he apologized. 'None of that was directed at you. You worked hard to make the holiday perfect for us and, it was – in the house. But no one in the valley could really celebrate, and not just because they didn't have any money. Everywhere you look it's doom, gloom and hope died a death. No one dares plan any further than the next meal, or wants to think about a future for themselves or their families, unless they're emigrating. Most people are even worse off than us, and we're living hand to mouth.' Victor slammed down the window and brushed the needles off his hands and the arms of his sweater over the ashbin. He looked keenly at his sister-in-law. 'You go down to

Pontypridd, Sali. You talk to people, important people, at the trustees' meetings. You must hear things.'

'Like what?' she asked guardedly.

'Are the hardliners like Luke Thomas and his cronies right? Are the owners really prepared to see every man, woman and child starve to death in the valley?'

'I refuse to believe that anyone wants to see children starve, Victor.'

'The colliery companies haven't given an inch over the demands we made five months ago. And,' he confronted her head-on, 'they're not going to, are they?'

Sali recalled the conversation she'd had with Mr Richards. 'The authorities and the colliery companies have spent a lot of money bringing in the troops and police and housing them here.'

'So, they'd lose face if they backed down now? Is that what you're saying?'

'You read the papers the same as the rest of us. The owners say they can't afford to meet your demands because it would push the price of coal higher than the market value and it would no longer be economically viable to run the pits.'

'And the union says that the owners can meet our demands if they cut their profits to a reasonable level.'

'And therein lies the question. What's a reasonable profit?'

'You're even beginning to sound like Lloyd.' He gave her a grim smile. 'They haven't broken us – yet. But they're prepared to let the strike go on until we are starved into submission, aren't they?'

Sali took a posy of dried and shrivelled holly from the bare mantelpiece and dropped it on top of the pine needles in the bin. 'There are people in Pontypridd who believe that they will.'

'People in the know?'

'It's what Mr Richards thinks.'

'I'm sick of the strike,' he burst out angrily. 'Of having no money, of not being able to look forward . . .'

Sali wasn't fooled by his uncharacteristic eruption. He was undoubtedly sick of the strike – they all were – but something else was troubling him more. 'I'm sorry Megan couldn't spend more

236

time with us over the holiday,' she commiserated. The Christmas meals Mrs Palmer had laid on in the lodging house had generated extra work and the longest Megan had been able to get away had been an hour and a half on Christmas afternoon.

Victor watched Sali empty the last of the pine needles into the bin, picked it up and carried it to the basement door in the kitchen. He glanced at the clock. 'Are Lloyd and Harry going straight from the children's free show in the Empire to the soup kitchen?'

'I said I'd meet them there.' Sali had cleaned the kitchen while Victor had swept the hearth and laid the fire they'd light that evening. She'd prepared a vegetable soup, made the beds and sorted the laundry. There was nothing else she could do until the fire was lit.

'Joey and I'll walk you to the Catholic Hall.'

'There's no need. I want to call in on a couple of families on the way.'

'Distributing distress relief funds?'

'While the donations are still coming in.' She went into the passage to fetch her coat.

'Charity!' he exploded resentfully. 'When all we're asking for is a living wage and the chance to earn it.'

'I'm sorry, Victor.'

'So am I.' He gave her a sheepish smile. 'None of us can be easy to live with at the moment.'

'You're not.' She pinned on her hat. 'But there's no other family I'd rather be with. Are you and Joey going rabbiting?'

'We'll try, but I don't think there's a rabbit or hare left alive between here and the coast.' He helped her on with her coat.

'Do me a favour?'

'If I can.'

'Don't forget to take the dogs with you this time, and be extra careful with those bunnies. They've become particularly vicious lately.'

He gazed at her. 'You know, don't you?'

'That you've taken up bare-knuckle boxing? We all do, Victor.

You're not fooling anyone. If it's just a question of money,' she began diffidently, 'I could ask the trustees for a loan . . .'

'To pay court fines?' he said sceptically.

'For emergency expenses,' she amended.

'We have our pride, Sali.'

'So Lloyd keeps telling me. Just remember it's not only Megan who loves you. We all do, even if your father and brothers don't say it.' She kissed his cheek.

He walked her to the front door and watched her leave, then returned to the kitchen, picked up the ashbin and carried it down to the basement. Joey had chopped the tree into kindling and they heaped the pieces on top of the needles.

'That'll keep us going for a day or two. I'll go up the farm tomorrow afternoon when you're with Megan and see if I can pick up some more wood there.' Joey left the bin at the foot of the steps ready to be carried back up to the kitchen. He watched Victor flex his hands. 'You don't have to keep doing this, you know.'

'Another two afternoons will bring in another ten pounds.'

'Only if you win.'

'You don't think I will.'

'I can pay my own fine.' Joey ignored Victor's question.

'With what?'

'All right, I have no money, but I can do time as well as the next man.' Joey lifted his coat and cap from the peg.

'And what will that prove other than you're prepared to let them cage you like an animal? If you've time to spare, you'd be better off trying to find out where Jane sold our things.'

'And what do you suggest I do if I find them?' Joey enquired acidly. 'Say, "Could you hang on to them, sir, until the strike ends and I can make enough to buy them back?"'

'We might be able to swap our watches for Mam's silver photograph frames. They are the only things Dad regrets losing. You haven't heard anything?'

'Like what?'

'Where Jane's gone.'

'If anyone around here knows, they're not talking.'

'You've asked around?'

'Only Betty Morgan, but she knows everything there is to know about everyone in this valley. Rumour has it she spends her nights flying around outside bedroom windows on a broomstick.'

'Just don't let her catch you saying it,' Victor warned. 'Got the rags, goose grease, blanket and water bottles?'

Joey held up the haversack he used to carry his snap tin and water bottles underground. 'I had a few words with Connie yesterday.' He followed his brother into the yard. 'Her delivery boy has joined the army. He's off next week and she said I could take over until the strike ends.'

'Will you?'

'She's only paying him seven bob a week, but since Dad emptied the bank account when Lloyd and Sali married, we can do with every penny. I know there's no way that I'll earn enough to buy back everything Jane took, even if we track it down. And the fine will be even more impossible to meet, but money's money and if I do my stint on the picket lines at night the boys won't be able to complain.'

'As it's the least popular time, they'll love you for it.'

'God, but it's cold up here. Better watch out that bits of you don't drop off when you strip off.' Joey turned up his collar and wound his muffler around his mouth as they headed up the mountain. He glanced across at his brother.

Lost in thought, Victor was striding directly into the raw, cutting wind. He had fought three double bouts in the last month and, although the police and army champions were good, he had won all six fights and remained comparatively and outwardly unscathed. The blows he had taken had landed on his chest, shoulders and arms. The resultant bruises had been large and colourful, but they had remained hidden by his clothes except when he undressed for bed. And because he and Joey shared a room and a bed, invisible to everyone except his younger brother.

'Know who you're up against?' Joey asked, more to make conversation than curiosity.

'The police have put up a man called Fred Wainwright, the Somersets a private, Reg Wilde.'

'Are they good?'

'Reg Wilde is the one who beat Dai Price to a pulp, but then, Dai's no boxer.'

'And Wainwright?'

'I know him by sight. He looks fit.'

Victor halted when they reached the summit. He turned and looked back down the mountain towards their house.

'It's still there.'

'Let's hope it always will be.'

'You worried?' Joey asked, concerned by Victor's taciturnity.

'No more than I am before any fight.'

'It's not too late to back out.'

'With all the strike pay the boys have riding on me?' Victor turned his face back into the wind. 'Come on, if we don't get moving I'll be forfeiting the match as a no show.'

'You can punch harder than that, Evans!' Luke Thomas yelled so loudly that Joey picked up his brother's clothes and his haversack and moved away. He continued to stare intently at the two figures circling one another on the tump. The police champion wasn't as quick on his feet as Victor, but for all of that, when his punches hit home they connected solidly.

Victor dodged a left hook aimed at his jaw, only to have a right land below his ribs, winding him. Before he could recover, another left split the soft skin below his eye.

'I've a week's strike pay riding on your brother. There'll be hell to pay from my missus if he loses,' Alun Richards complained.

'You've a bloody nerve backing him after what you did to Megan Williams,' Joey said angrily.

'Victor clobbered me afterwards so I'd say that makes us quits. I was even thinking of charging him for using me as a punchbag.'

'I wouldn't try it if I were you,' Joey advised.

'Get him, Evans! Don't go soft on us!' Luke screamed.

Wainwright drew his fist back. Victor feinted and floored him with a single punch to the jaw that split his lip. Wainwright stood for a moment before crumpling slowly, first to his knees, then sideways on to his right arm. As his eyes closed, his seconds ran up and dragged him to the edge of the tump.

Joey went to his brother and draped the blanket over his shoulders. Blood had seeped from the cut below his eye down the left side of his face.

'You OK?' Joey asked, as Victor gulped in air.

'I will be in a minute.'

Joey pulled out the water bottle, tipped it over a rag and used it to staunch the cut. 'I don't know what Dad and Lloyd are going to say when they see the mess Wainwright's made of your face.'

'Stop boxing,' Victor suggested succinctly. He tightened the cord on his drawers and wrapped the blanket around his bare chest.

'You've done enough for one day. Someone else can face the army champion.'

'You know the rules, winner of the first bout fights the next champion.' Victor took the rag from his brother and pressed it on his eye, leaving Joey free to rummage in his haversack for the tin of goose grease. 'Besides, I've money riding on this one.'

'How much?' Joey asked.

'My winnings from the last double bout.'

'Five quid!' Joey paled as he slapped a layer of grease over the cut in an attempt to stop the bleeding. 'You crazy?'

'If I win I stand to double it.'

'And if you lose you will have fought the last bout for nothing.'

'You fit for the next match, Evans?' Sergeant Martin studied Victor's injuries.

'Fair's fair,' Joey answered defensively. 'Give him chance to get his breath back.'

Victor looked at the sergeant. 'Ten minutes?'

'You got it.' The sergeant walked away.

'I can't stand that man, but you have to admit he's straight,' Victor said quietly.

Joey unscrewed the top from the second water bottle. Victor rinsed his mouth and spat before drinking deeply.

'Your own money on the sergeant major or my brother?' Joey

turned to the non-commissioned officer who had reopened the book to take fresh bets on the last fight of the day.

'Think I'm dull enough to answer that?'

'If we had money to finance a book we could make enough to keep two soup kitchens going on the profits.' As Joey watched, Sergeant Lamb walked up to the corporal and handed him two white fivers. Joey didn't know why, he just hoped that the money was going on his brother.

'You sure Sali told Victor that we know he's boxing again?' Billy Evans questioned Lloyd, as they walked towards the crowd of men gathered around the tump.

'Yes.' Lloyd noted the dark blue and khaki uniforms in the crowd. 'Given the number of policemen and soldiers up here, now would be a good time to stage a demonstration against the garrisoning of the town.'

'Given that most of the miners are also up here, who do you suggest stages it? Bloody hell, that must have hurt!' Billy exclaimed as a crack, louder than the shouts of the men, rent the air.

'Give it him back with interest, Victor!' Ned Morgan turned around as Billy tapped him on the shoulder. 'Your boy's good, Billy.'

'He may be good, but so is his opponent.' Lloyd cringed as Reg Wilde landed a punch on Victor's damaged eye.

'Victor didn't pick up that cut in this fight. They both started with injuries,' Ned informed them.

'I always thought bare-knuckle boxing was inhuman. I was wrong, it's barbaric.' Billy flinched as yet another of Reg Wilde's blows landed on Victor's face.

'Victor's giving as good as he gets,' Ned shouted excitedly.

'Is he?' Billy couldn't see any further than the damage being inflicted on his son.

'There's Joey.' Lloyd forged a path through the crowd towards his younger brother, who was stationed in the first line around the fighters. Before he reached him, Victor reeled from the impact of a punch that landed in his stomach. Blinded by pain, his sight obscured by blood, Victor retaliated without taking the time or trouble to aim. Reg was crouched, preparing to follow his blow. Victor's punch caught him on the temple. He toppled to the ground like an axed pit prop.

Victor sat on the ground swathed in the blanket, his knees drawn up in front of him to minimize the pain in his chest and stomach, his head thrown back so Joey could tend to the cuts on his face.

'You did great, butty,' Luke congratulated. 'Thanks to you, there'll be a few families putting jam on their bread next week.'

'You showed the bastards what we're made of, Victor. Good on you,' Ben Duckworth congratulated.

Besieged by miners anxious to pat his brother on the back, Joey had to fight to retain his position.

'How's Wilde?' Victor asked.

'Who cares about a bloody soldier?' Luke swore.

'I do.' Victor raised his head and glared at Luke, as much as someone could glare with both eyes swollen and half closed. 'I'll find out for you.'

'Lloyd?' Victor turned his head. 'You came to see me box?'

'We both did, son.' Billy crouched on his haunches beside Victor. 'When are you going to give this up?'

Victor continued to sit patiently while Joey tended to his cuts.

'When?' Billy repeated.

'When the strike ends and life returns to normal.'

'Not long then,' Luke jeered.

'Reg Wilde's out cold but his friends reckon he's been worse,' Lloyd informed Victor.

'He's going to recover?' Victor asked in concern. 'I didn't do any permanent damage?'

'By the look of you both, I'd say you inflicted no more damage on him than he did on you,' Lloyd replied.

'You came up trumps, Evans,' Luke gushed as he returned from the corporal with a fistful of winnings.

'I threw a lucky punch.' Brushing Joey's hand aside, Victor rose to his feet, picked up his clothes and pulled on his trousers. Discarding the blanket, he yanked on his vest, felt in the pocket of his shirt and handed Lloyd a ticket. 'There should be ten pounds on that.'

'I hope it was worth it, son.' Billy handed Victor his cap, as Lloyd joined the queue of men waiting to be paid out.

'If it covers my own and Joey's fines, and enables me to put enough aside to pay Megan's father off and keep her from working in that lodging house until she's old enough for us to marry, it will be worth it,' Victor said flatly.

'Same time Wednesday, Mr Evans?' Sergeant Martin asked.

'I'll be here.' Victor buttoned on his shirt.

Chapter 15

'IF YOU'RE trying to conceal those cuts, you won't do it with goose grease, Victor.' Sali watched him as he stood in front of the shaving mirror in the kitchen and smoothed a film over his battered face. 'It's fine for stopping the bleeding and helping wounds heal, but by putting a shine on the bruises it highlights them.'

'I don't want Megan to worry.'

'My face powder might cover the worst, but Megan isn't stupid. One look at you, and she'll know exactly what you've been up to.'

'Now that is something I would like to see,' Joey laughed. 'Victor wearing women's face powder.'

'Isn't it your turn to man their picket line outside Ely pit today, Joey?' Billy asked abruptly.

'Yes.'

'Then finish your meal and get going.'

Victor had set aside a pound of his winnings to buy coal from the men who were working the illegal drifts on the mountain. He hadn't dared work in them himself since he'd been arrested, but he had no qualms about supporting the colliers who were prepared to risk fines and imprisonment to keep the people in the valley in fuel. And since it was Megan's afternoon off and snowing, he'd decided to build a fire and keep it in all day. Sali had taken full advantage of the luxury. Rising early, she had baked bread, made a chicken stew from an aged broiler chicken he had slaughtered and vegetables from the allotments, as well as two tarts from wrinkled apples he had stored in the attic.

Lloyd poured his father, himself and Harry second cups of tea. 'I'll never take the kitchen being warm, cosy and full of good cooking smells for granted again.'

'I'll see to it that it's still warm and cosy for you when you come back from Pontypridd.' Victor looked from the mirror to the window. The valley and surrounding mountains were covered in a compassionate layer of snow that had transformed the slag heaps into glistening Alps and obliterated the scars inflicted by the mines. 'Switzerland couldn't look better at the moment.'

'The Swiss might think so. Wrap up warm,' Billy cautioned Joey, as he pushed the last piece of eggy bread from his plate into his mouth. 'Keep your temper and stay out of trouble.'

'Do you need to ask?' Joey flashed a smile and left the table.

'Yes,' Billy growled. 'Seems to me you've forgotten what happened a couple of weeks ago a bit too quickly.'

'I'm a changed man. No more loose women for me.' Joey checked his hair in the mirror and went to fetch his coat.

'What's a loose woman, Dad?' Harry asked.

'One who doesn't tie her shoelaces properly,' Joey answered, earning himself a scowl from Sali.

'If you wait, we'll walk down the hill with you,' Lloyd called after Joey.

'You going down to Pontypridd with Sali?' Billy asked Lloyd.

'I thought I would, as it's the first trustees' meeting since our wedding. Who knows, Sali's brothers and sister may even condescend to have tea with us. Geraint and Llinos haven't gone back to school, have they, Sali?'

'Not as far as I know.' Sali wiped egg yolk from Harry's mouth with her handkerchief. 'But as we've only had a Christmas card from them with their names scribbled at the bottom I'm not sure. Although Mari wrote to say that she's looking forward to seeing us.'

'Harry and I thought we'd look at the books in the nursery and see if there are any that we want to bring back here,' Lloyd saw Harry make a face as he sipped his tea. He picked up the milk jug and poured in an extra helping.

'Mam says I can borrow them, and Dad says the horse and carriage will be waiting at the station to meet us.' Harry finished his tea, slid off his chair and carried his plate and cup to Sali at the sink.

'If you come downstairs with me, Harry, I'll give your boots a quick once over,' Joey offered. 'You can't go to Ponty with them scuffed like that.'

'When are you two going to tell Harry that Ynysangharad House and Gwilym James are his?' Billy asked, after Joey and Harry left for the basement.

'When he's old enough to understand the responsibility that comes with his inheritance,' Sali replied.

'And when will that be?' Billy pressed.

'Sooner rather than later if my brother continues to make trouble at the trustees' meetings. I'm dreading today.'

Lloyd saw that Sali wanted to change the subject. 'Going to the County Club?'

'Where else? We can't do much for Victor and Megan besides give them the house to themselves one afternoon a week.' Billy left his chair. 'Ned and I have arranged to draft a new proposal with the strike committee that we intend to present to the owners when they condescend to meet us again. If we don't start talking to them again soon, we'll be facing a hungry spring and summer. And I'm not sure how much more of this hardship our members can take.'

Victor saw his father, brothers, Sali and Harry out of the house before slipping on his coat and cap. He opened the front door and glanced out. It had stopped snowing, but the sky was heavy with cotton-wool clouds the colour of a dove's breast, and the temperature had risen slightly. A sure sign that snow was about to fall again. He took the old umbrella from behind the basement door, turned up the collar on his coat and glanced in the mirror on the hallstand. There were no windows in the hall but the damage to his face was apparent even in the light that filtered through from the open front door. Checking the kitchen door was firmly closed to keep the warmth in, he walked outside and down the street.

Betty Morgan was sweeping snow from the pavement in front of her house. When she saw him she propped her brush against the wall and waved. 'I need to have a word with you, Victor.' Treading carefully on the icy pavement, she joined him.

'Mrs Morgan.' He tipped his cap.

'I heard that Mr Walker, the minister of the chapel, has written to Megan's father about your engagement.'

'Has he?' Victor said non-committally.

'Aren't you worried?'

'Megan and I knew that her father would find out about our engagement sooner or later when I gave her my mother's ring, Mrs Morgan.'

'The minister thinks he'll come hot foot to get her and drag her back to the Swansea Valley.'

'I see.'

'Is that all you can say, Victor Evans?' she snapped irritably.

'There doesn't seem to be much else that I can say until Mr Williams gets here, does there, Mrs Morgan?' Victor tipped his cap again and went on his way.

Sergeant Lamb was standing in the doorway of the lodging house talking to Constable Wainwright, who was sporting even more bruises than himself. Ducking into the alleyway, before they saw him, Victor went to the back door and tapped it. Megan opened it, already dressed in her cape and hat.

She gave him a broad smile before turning back to someone in the room and shouting, 'I'm off now.' She stepped out, hooked her arm into his, glanced up and her smile became a look of horror.

'It's not as bad as it looks,' he lied. 'The Post Office first?'

'The police?' she asked.

'In a way, but self-inflicted.'

'You're boxing,' she reproached.

'I have been for a few weeks and you haven't noticed.'

'Presumably because you've been lucky enough not to get hammered before now.'

'The Post Office?' he repeated.

Not wanting to spoil their one afternoon a week, she reined in her temper. 'Yes.'

'The quicker we get there, the quicker we'll be back home. I've lit a fire and Sali's been baking. I've been looking forward to a nice, quiet afternoon.'

'You probably can do with the rest. Why did you do it, Victor?' she asked sadly.

'Because I need money to pay my own and Joey's fines – and something else that I want to talk to you about. Come on, Megs, before we turn into snowmen.' He opened his umbrella as flakes fluttered down, coating her cloak and hat.

'Perhaps we should ask Mari to look after Harry so that you can go to the trustees' meeting with me?' Sali suggested. She, Lloyd and Harry watched the falling snow transform the bleak Rhondda valley into something resembling a pantomime fairyscape.

'Why?' Lloyd moved closer to Harry, who was standing at the window of their carriage, tracing the build-up of snow on the pane with his mittened hands.

'Because I should formally introduce you to them now we're married. Especially as I want to make you Harry's guardian in case anything should happen to me.'

'You think you need to do that officially?'

'Considering what Geraint said at the last trustees' meeting, most definitely. The only real home Harry has ever known has been with you and your family. Do you mind legally adopting him?'

Lloyd turned to Harry, who was still ostensibly engrossed by the snow, although he suspected that the boy was also listening intently to every word. 'What do you think, Harry? Do we need a piece of paper that says I'm your dad?'

'You are my dad,' Harry answered with childish logic.

'That says it all,' Lloyd smiled.

'Not if I'm out of the picture and Geraint has his way.'

'You'll never be out of my picture.' Lloyd grasped Sali's gloved fingers. 'But if it will set your mind at rest to make Harry's and my relationship legally binding, go ahead. But the trustees' meetings are something else. You know my views on keeping Harry's affairs separate from me and my family.'

'I'll ask Mr Richards to draw up the necessary papers, and whether or not he thinks it's a good idea for you to attend the meetings,' Sali said decisively.

'I'll go on to Ynysangharad House with Harry. If you need me, you can send for me.' Lloyd lifted Harry on to his knee so he could look out of the window.

'Are we having tea with Mr Richards and Mari?' Harry asked.

'Yes. You like Mrs Richards and Mari, don't you, darling?' Sali asked.

'Yes. Do I have to see Grandmother?'

'Not if you don't want to.' Lloyd looked at Sali over the top of Harry's head. 'You said yourself your mother barely knows where she is, or what she's doing.'

Sali nodded agreement. But she was more preoccupied with thoughts of Geraint than her mother. He lived in Ynysangharad House and worked alongside other members of the committee. She couldn't help wondering just how much damage he had done to Lloyd's reputation – and hers – since the last meeting.

'Here, let me take your cloak and hat and hang them on the drying rack.' Victor lowered the rack Sali used to dry clothes on in winter, and arranged Megan's damp cloak and hat on it before hoisting it back up to the ceiling in front of the range. 'Have you had dinner?'

'Mrs Palmer made a shepherd's pie for us today.' Megan sat in the chair and held her hands out to the fire.

'But you'll have some tea and a slice of Sali's apple pie?'

'I'll have some tea, please, but I'll save the pie for later, if I may. Victor, there's no need for you to box,' she said eagerly. 'I offered you my savings—'

'We'll need your savings when we get married. Next door might be furnished but there's room for improvement and there's linen, crockery and cutlery. They all cost money.'

'How much have you made boxing?'

'Including what I made betting on myself yesterday, twenty pounds give or take.'

'Twenty pounds! That's a fortune. More than enough to pay any fines you and Joey get. You'll stop now?' she begged.

'I wish I could be as sure as you that twenty pounds will be enough to pay our fines and costs.' He set the kettle on to boil and took his mother's best cups from the dresser, which they had been forced to use for every day ever since the police had smashed most of the china.

'Then how much do you think you'll need?' she asked seriously.

'I'll only be able to answer that after the case has been heard, Megs. If we're lucky they'll find us innocent, but we'll still have to pay our costs.'

'How often do you box?'

'Double bout once a week.'

'Victor, there'll be nothing left of you.' She left the chair, reached up and ran her fingers lightly over his damaged face.

'I fought two double bouts without you even knowing. It was just bad luck that I was up against a champion yesterday. But I'm learning and getting better. I promise you, I won't be in this state next week.'

'You can't possibly know what state you'll be in after your next match,' she countered, allowing her irritation to show.

He circled her tiny waist with his hands and kissed her forehead. 'When I win, I make five pounds, plus the profit from any bets I put on myself.'

'And if you lose?'

'First rule of boxing, winner takes all.' The kettle began to steam. He released her and picked up the teapot.

'You said that you and your family were just about managing on your strike pay. I can see that you need extra money for your fines. But there's no point in your boxing after that.'

'If I made enough to pay your father fifteen shillings a week until your twenty-first birthday, would you leave the lodging house and come here and live with us?'

'Victor I—'

'Would you?'

'As your common-law wife?'

'As my fiancée and our guest,' he contradicted emphatically. 'Everything would be above board. Sali's in the house and there's a spare bedroom upstairs.'

'If my father got to hear of it, he'd kill me.'

251

'Because he thinks so little of you he'd assume you were living in sin,' he said in disgust.

'For disobeying him and living in the house of a Catholic.'

'My father's an atheist.' He made the tea, put the cosy over the pot and set it on the stove.

'My father thinks they are even worse than Catholics.'

'Is there anyone your father doesn't hate?' When she didn't answer, he said, 'So you won't leave the lodging house?'

'I don't see how I can – for the moment, Victor,' she qualified.

'Because I may need all the money I have and more for the fines?' he said bitterly.

'The strike won't last for ever.'

'I'm beginning to think it just might.'

She held out her hand. He took it, sat down and pulled her on to his lap.

'I love you far too much to see you get hurt this way. Especially for me.' She kissed the scar below his eye. He winced as she slipped her fingers beneath his sweater. 'It's not just your face, is it?'

'I promise you one thing, Megs.'

'What?'

'Once I have enough money to pay the fines and your father, I'll never box again. But there is a condition: you have to leave the lodging house and live under this roof.'

'Victor—'

'Please, let's not argue about it. Just enjoy what time we have.' He kissed her again, and soon the only sound in the room was the ticking of the clock.

'I always think that change, especially change that might be seen as even slightly controversial, is best taken slowly, Mrs Evans. But I agree with you, the sooner Mr Evans legally adopts Harry the better.' Mr Richards moved his chair slightly so the waitress could set a plate of cheese and plain scones on their table, the only dainties Sali would allow Harry to have, although he had been bestowing longing glances on the chocolate and iced fancies under the glass case on the counter.

Robert, the coachman from Ynysangharad House, had met them at the station with the carriage and, to Sali and Lloyd's surprise, Mr Richards had been inside. After driving to Gwilym James and arriving there half an hour early for the trustees' meeting, Mr Richards had asked Robert to wait for Harry and Lloyd, and taken them all across the road into the tearoom in the arcade.

'You can arrange the adoption, Mr Richards?' Sali asked.

'I'll speak to my clerk and set everything in motion first thing on Monday morning. In the meantime, much as I hate bringing up the subject with young people of your and Mr Evans' age,' he gave Lloyd a small smile, 'as you are Harry's official guardian, Mrs Evans, it might be as well if you both make wills in favour of one another.'

'I have already made a will leaving everything I own to Sali and on her death, Harry and any future children we may have.'

'Have you appointed an executor?'

'My father and brothers.' Lloyd took the tea Sali had poured for him.

'Very wise, Mr Evans. Mrs Evans?'

'I have nothing much besides Harry to leave.' Sali placed a cheese scone on a plate, cut it in half and set it together with the butter dish in front of Harry. 'But if you could draw up a will and leave everything I own to Lloyd, and also make him Harry's guardian until Harry comes of age, I would be grateful.'

'And the executors?'

Sali didn't hesitate. 'Lloyd's father, brothers and, in case they need help to carry out my wishes, your firm.'

Mr Richards looked thoughtfully at Harry, who was engrossed in spreading butter. 'I would be derelict in my professional duty if I didn't advise you to cover all eventualities. Have either of you thought what would happen to Harry if there should be an accident that affects both of you?'

'Lloyd's father and brothers should become Harry's guardians. They are the only adults he knows and trusts apart from Lloyd and myself.' Sali looked to Lloyd, who nodded confirmation.

'And your brothers and sister, Mrs Evans?'

'May visit Harry, but only if he wants to see them.'

'Mr Watkin Jones could challenge your decision, Mrs Evans.'

'I don't doubt he will after the way he behaved at the last trustees' meeting.' She poured milk into her tea.

'Perhaps he should be given a copy of your will as soon as it is signed so any objections he wishes to make can be,' Mr Richards hesitated, choosing his words carefully, 'dealt with.'

'That sounds like a good idea.' Sali glanced at her bracelet watch. There was still ten minutes to go before the meeting was due to start. 'I read the agenda Mr Horton junior sent me. It appears straightforward apart from any other business. Have you any idea what Geraint is going to bring up?'

'Mr Watkin Jones told me there is nothing he wishes to discuss outside of the agenda today.'

'You spoke to him after the last meeting?' Sali probed.

Mr Richards blotted his lips with his linen napkin. 'Would you be kind enough to pour me another cup of tea if there is sufficient in the pot, Mrs Evans? And I believe we have time for another scone before the meeting. You and Harry can stay here in the dry if you like, Mr Evans. I'll ask Robert to bring the cab across the road for you.'

'You can scarcely breathe.' Megan saw Victor's eyes crease in pain and she tried to leave his lap, but he locked his arms around her waist, imprisoning her in his grasp.

'I'm a bit bruised, that's all.' He smiled wickedly at her. 'A few more kisses might make me feel better.'

'Oh yes?'

He kissed her tenderly, but when she parted her lips, his kiss grew fiercer, more intense. She lifted her hand, intending to stroke his cheek and he cried out. She leaped to her feet and that time he didn't even attempt to stop her.

'You are in agony, aren't you?'

'No.' He grimaced. 'You stuck your elbow into a bruise, that's all. Please, come back down here.'

She knelt in front of the chair, lifted his sweater and unfastened the buttons on his shirt.

'There's a vest under that and this isn't the way I imagined you undressing me.' He gripped both of her hands in his but not before she'd pulled his vest free from his trousers and pushed his braces aside. She cried out in horror. 'Victor, you're all shades of black and blue . . .'

'And purple and yellow,' he added in a resigned tone. 'Joey's already told me I look like a rainbow.' He rose to his feet and tucked his vest and shirt back into his trousers. 'Forget about them and come back down here.'

'I couldn't. I'd be terrified of hurting you again.'

'A little thing like you.'

'There's no way that chair is big enough for the two of us,' she argued, 'and I'm not sitting on your lap again.'

'Please?'

'No, Victor, I couldn't relax.'

'Then there's only one thing for it.' Rubbing his chest where she'd accidentally hurt him, he left the room. She heard him walking up the stairs. A few moments later he returned with the eiderdown from his and Joey's bed, and two pillows. He covered the hearthrug with the eiderdown and arranged the pillows on it.

'What are you doing?'

'What does it look like?' He sat on the chair and unlaced his boots.

'Making a bed.'

He grinned at her again. 'You clever girl. You can go to the top of the class.'

'And what class would that be?'

He lay on the eiderdown, slipped a pillow beneath his head and held out his arm. 'Mine. Now will you please give me a cuddle?'

She held back. 'Won't it look peculiar if someone walks in?'

'My father and Ned Morgan have a proposal to write for the Federation. The last time they put one of those together, they were in the library of the County Club until two in the morning. Lloyd and Sali won't be back until after they've had tea in Ynysangharad House and caught the train up from Pontypridd. That will be seven o'clock at the earliest. And, as my father won't allow Joey to forget he's in disgrace, he won't dare move from the picket lines around Ely Colliery until he's relieved at eight o'clock for fear that someone will carry tales. So, we've the house to ourselves for the afternoon.'

'And if Mrs Morgan or one of the other neighbours decides to come round to borrow something?'

'We'll give them an eyeful and enough to talk about for a month.'

'Victor!'

'As one half of an engaged couple you should expect to attract gossip.' He raised his eyebrows and gave her a pleading look. 'Please. I promise to dismantle the bed before anyone comes home.'

She unlaced her boots and set them under the chair next to his. Kneeling beside him, she lowered herself on to the eiderdown, careful not to touch him.

'I'm bruised, not made of glass.' He reached up to one of the easy chairs and pulled down a blanket Sali had knitted from odd balls of wool and used to cover Harry if he fell asleep during the day. Shaking it over both of them, he crept close to her. 'This is more like it.' He slid his arm beneath her shoulders and eased her head on to his chest.

'It's surprisingly comfortable.'

'And warmer than the bedroom.'

Slowly, tentatively, she rested her hand lightly on his chest. 'Am I hurting you?'

'You could never do that, Megs.'

'I just did.'

'You only reminded me how much someone else had hurt me.' He pulled a pin from her hair with his free hand. 'I love to see your hair loose.'

Here, let me.' She sat up, removed the remaining pins from her hair and dropped them together with the one Victor had already taken into her shoe.

'Do you think our children will have red curly hair, like you?'

'I hope not,' She lay back beside him. 'I was teased horribly about my hair when I was little.'

'I can't see why. It's beautiful.'

256

'It's not.' She kissed him and wrapped her arm around his neck. 'But thank you for saying so.'

He slid his hand beneath her sweater. 'Are you warm enough to take this off?'

A lump rose in her throat, but she pulled her sweater over her head and pushed it below her pillow. He kissed her again and unbuttoned her blouse, pulling it free from the waistband of her skirt. His hand moved, warm, sensuous, inside her chemise and bust shaper, and over her breasts as he teased her nipples with the tips of his fingers. She felt the colour mounting into her cheeks when he folded back the blanket, opened her bust shaper and gazed at her naked breasts before kissing each in turn.

'Women wear so many clothes,' he complained when he tried and failed to unfasten her skirt.

Fighting embarrassment, she looked deep into his grey eyes. 'Would you like me to undress for you?'

He sat up and looked away for what seemed like an eternity, and she wondered if he were going to reject her a second time. 'Just in case someone does try to come in, I'll lock the door.' He left the makeshift bed, went to the door that led to the basement steps and slid the bolt home before going to the door that connected with the passage. He turned the key and looked back at her. She was standing with her foot on the chair.

Knowing he was watching her, Megan unfastened her garters and unrolled the stockings from her legs. Laying them on a chair, she stepped out of her skirt, folded it and set it next to her stockings. Her petticoats, blouse and bust shaper followed. She heard the breath catch in his throat as she pulled down her drawers. He continued to stand, mesmerized, as she lifted her final garment, the beautiful chemise Sali had bought her, over her head.

Whether it was the warmth of the room, the peculiarly clear white light that filtered through the window from the snow-filled atmosphere, or simply his love for her, she appeared to glow – pale and translucent, like a nude in a Renaissance painting. Too overawed to do anything other than stare, Victor finally regained his senses when she held out her hand to him. He walked slowly towards her, took her reverentially in his arms and embraced the length of her body with his own.

'Aren't you going to undress?' Megan felt that she should have been ill at ease, but somehow she sensed that her nudity made him more vulnerable than her.

'I couldn't trust myself to hold back,' he whispered thickly.

'And perhaps I wouldn't want you to.' She continued to gaze into his eyes.

'Megs . . .'

'It's time, Victor.' She lifted his sweater and unbuckled his belt.

'We have made all the investments suggested and ratified by the board at our last meeting, however,' George Owens, the managing director of the Capital and Counties Bank, looked over his half-spectacles at the trustees assembled around the table, in my own and my colleagues' opinions, Gwilym James' account is still cash rich.'

'You are suggesting that we need to make more investments, sir?' Mr Horton asked the obvious question.

'I most certainly am, and given Master Harry's age, I would recommend they be long-term.'

'My father believed property to be the best long-term investment, Mr Owens.' Sali looked up from the notepad on the table in front of her.

'I wouldn't disagree with that pronouncement, Mrs Evans.'

Sali wondered if the director ever used one word when he could use six. 'Mr Jenkins,' she turned to her late great aunt's butler, who was, as usual, chairing the meeting, you mentioned that before the strike there was some discussion as to whether or not Gwilym James should open a branch in Tonypandy.'

'A decision that was quite rightly put into abeyance at the outset of the strike,' Geraint stated strongly. 'Only an idiot would invest in the Rhondda Valleys at the moment.'

Sali looked at her brother for the first time since she had entered the room. 'The strike won't go on for ever, Geraint.' Her heart was beating erratically but she managed to speak calmly.

'You are absolutely correct on that point, Mrs Evans. And now, when property prices are on a downwards spiral both in Tonypandy itself and the surrounding area, it might be a good time to reappraise the situation.'

Sali thought she saw her brother flinch, when Mr Owens addressed her by her married name for the second time.

'Although I am only here as Mrs Evans' adviser, I would like to support Mr Owens' assertion. Property prices in the Rhondda are never likely to be as low again as they are the moment, with so many businesses going into bankruptcy.' Mr Richards moved his chair closer to Sali's.

'And we wouldn't actually be committing ourselves to anything if we looked around for a suitable property that we could turn into a branch of Gwilym James.' Mr Jenkins appeared thoughtful as he considered the idea. 'Tonypandy is a sizeable town, not as large as Pontypridd, of course, but then, a store there wouldn't need to be as commodious as this one. Or even necessarily stock the same extensive range of goods.'

'Then may I put forward the proposal that we brief the solicitors among our members to begin searching for properties suitable to be converted into a department store in Tonypandy?' Mr Owens tapped his pen on the table.

'I will second the proposal.' Mr Richards' deputy in his solicitors' firm, raised his hand.

'All in favour?' Mr Jenkins looked round the table. Sali noticed that the last hand to be raised was her brother's.

'As Harry's mother and legal guardian, may I make another more general suggestion?' Sali ignored Geraint and leaned forward on her elbows, looking to Mr Horton senior at the opposite end of the table. 'I believe that the largest investments made on my son's behalf should be in the immediate locality. Gwilym James' and the Market Company's prosperity was founded and built on the custom and goodwill of the people of Pontypridd and the Rhondda. It was my late Great-Aunt Edyth's policy to invest her money in the area and, until Harry is old enough to make his own decisions and control his own interests, I think we should continue as I believe my aunt would wish. Perhaps we could hold a vote on the suggestion?' She looked around the table. Mr Jenkins was the first to raise his hand, but the others were quick to follow suit. However, she couldn't fail to notice that yet again, Geraint was the last to concur.

'Master Harry.' Mari caught and hugged Harry as he charged through the door and ran up to her. 'I've made your favourite chocolate cake for tea, but you can't have a slice until you've eaten at least two egg and cress sandwiches. And there's a fire lit in the nursery, so you can go straight up to play.'

'Dad said we could look at the books and if I see any I like, we might be able to borrow them.' Harry wriggled out of his coat and handed it to her.

'Would you like something to eat or drink?' she shouted after him, as he ran up the stairs.

'We had tea and scones with Mr Richards in the tea shop in the arcade.' Lloyd handed her his own coat and trilby. He looked around the spacious wood-panelled hall with its magnificent red-carpeted sweeping staircase and couldn't help but contrast it with the poky passage and narrow staircase in his father's house.

'Miss Llinos and Master Gareth are out, Mr Evans.'

'You don't have to make excuses to me for Sali's brother and sister, Mari. I didn't expect them to wait for our arrival.'

'It's the least they could have done, seeing as they didn't go to your wedding.' Mari opened the door to the drawing room. 'Shall I ring for tea?'

'No, thank you.' Lloyd walked to the fire and stood in front of it, warming himself. 'I'll give Harry a few minutes to look through the books before joining him. He prefers books to toys and as we've worked our way through most of the ones we have at home, Sali thought we could borrow some from the nursery.'

'As if Master Harry can borrow what's his!'

'You do know we haven't told Harry that he owns this house,' Lloyd warned.

'Yes, and although I've no right to put my oar in, I think you and Miss Sali should tell him before someone else does, Mr Evans.'

'The someone else being Geraint?' Lloyd enquired drily.

'If Mr Harry, my old master that is, could hear some of the

things his son has been saying lately, he'd be out of his grave and giving him the hiding he never gave him when he was alive. You and Miss Sali should be very careful around Mr Geraint, Mr Evans.'

'Couldn't you call me Lloyd, Mari?'

'It wouldn't be proper,' Mari replied briskly. 'It's bad enough that Miss Sali insists I sit down and have tea with you and Mr Richards without getting any more familiar. I'm a servant and you're a—'

'Collier?' Lloyd interrupted.

'Miss Sali's husband.'

Lloyd sat in a chair beside the fire. 'What has Sali's brother been saying that's upset you?'

Mari walked to the window and straightened a perfectly hung curtain.

'You can wait until Sali gets here, if you'd rather speak to her.'

'No, I wouldn't. But I'm not sure what to do for the best, Mr Evans. I heard Mr Geraint talking to Mr Jenkins.'

'The butler?'

'The butler who is chairman of the trustees,' she reminded him. 'Mr Geraint was trying to persuade him to sign a statement saying that Miss Edyth didn't know what she was doing when she made out her will in Master Harry's favour.'

'And what did Mr Jenkins say?'

'Nothing.'

'Nothing,' Lloyd repeated.

'Nothing at all. He just sat there listening to Mr Geraint, then someone rang the front doorbell and he went to answer it. If Mr Geraint has spoken to him about it since, I haven't heard them.'

'Heard or overheard?' Lloyd enquired astutely.

'I happened to be cleaning the pantry when they were talking in the kitchen. It's not my fault they didn't see me.'

'Do me a favour, Mari?'

'Anything I can, Mr Evans.'

'Don't mention this to Sali until I have had a chance to talk it over with Mr Richards.'

'Of course, Mr Evans.' Mari looked relieved. 'If anyone will

261

know how to deal with Master Geraint's scheming and conniving, it will be Mr Richards.'

Chapter 16

VICTOR CLASPED Megan's slender waist and lifted her up and off him. 'I didn't hurt you, did I?' He set her down on the eiderdown beside him.

'Only a little.' It was the truth. She hadn't known what to expect from lovemaking, especially when Victor had refused to rest his weight on her, but the sharp pain had been brief and quickly supplanted by the most intense feeling of intimacy and passion she had ever experienced.

'I'm sorry.'

'I'm not. I'm glad it happened. But I was terrified of hurting you.' She checked that the old towel they'd laid over the eiderdown was still beneath them before snuggling down next to him.

'If that's pain, give me more,' he whispered. He gripped her fingers when she ran her fingertips lightly over his bruised chest. 'Sorry, love, I have to leave you, but don't move an inch, I'll be back as soon as I can.' He unlocked the door that led to the passage and padded up the stairs. She heard the clink of china and realised he was washing himself and the French letter he had used. When he returned he was wearing a woollen dressing gown.

'I should wash too.'

'Not for a moment.' He tossed his dressing gown aside and lay back beside her.

'You're cold,' she complained.

'Then warm me.' He pulled her close to him. 'I never realized how wonderful your bare skin would feel next to mine.'

'I'm glad we've had this first time together. No matter what happens to us in the future, no one can take it away from us.'

'You're talking as though we aren't going to be married, Megs. This is just the beginning—'

'I know it is, Victor,' she broke in quickly. 'It's just that my twenty-first birthday seems so far away.' She tried to sound positive, although the premonition she'd had in her uncle's old house returned, frightening her yet again.

'Not that far,' he said forcefully. 'And then, just think what it will be like. Going to bed and sleeping together every single night . . .'

'Making love every chance we get . . .'

'Waking up beside one another every morning.'

'But for now, I really must wash.' She rolled away from him and picked up the old towel they had used.

'Leave that, I'll burn it. Take my dressing gown and use my bedroom. It's the first left at the top of the stairs. My towel is the green one. Don't dress,' he pleaded, as she picked up her clothes.

'I can't stay naked.'

He glanced at the clock. 'There's hours to go before Lloyd and Sali get home, and they'll be the first. Let's lie here and hold one another for a little longer.'

'Perhaps just for half an hour,' she capitulated.

'Then I'll be the one to warm you. Don't be long. I'm missing you already,' he called after her, as she ran lightly up the stairs.

The gas lamps hissed and glowed in the darkness. It had stopped snowing during the late afternoon, but the temperature had dropped sharply and it was bitterly cold when Lloyd and Sali left Tonypandy Station and made their way to Dunraven Street. They wound their mufflers around as much of their faces as they could and pulled their hats down to protect their heads, but their noses and the skin around their eyes remained exposed and raw. Snow crunched beneath their boots, freezing their feet even through their thick soles. Only Harry, who had fallen asleep on the train and was tucked, still sleeping, inside Lloyd's coat, was warm.

'You didn't really expect Geraint, Gareth and Llinos to sit down and have tea with us in Ynysangharad House, did you, sweetheart?' Lloyd asked.

'Yes, I did,' Sali said crossly. 'They could have made the effort and just for once recognized that you are my husband and, as such, accorded you some respect.'

'Apart from hurting you, I couldn't care less what they think of me, my family, or colliers in general.'

Sali looked at Harry's face peeking out between the lapels of Lloyd's coat. 'I care because we each have a family, yet mine won't have anything to do with us.'

'Except to take Harry's money.' Lloyd shifted Harry higher in his arms. 'Have you considered that they might be too embarrassed to have tea with us because they feel guilty about living off Harry's estate?'

'I know you're only trying to make me feel better about them, but I think snobbishness not guilt is keeping them away.'

Lloyd recalled the hurried words he'd exchanged with Mr Richards after the old man had seen Sali and Harry into the carriage that had taken them to the station. Mr Richards had promised to speak to Mr Jenkins about his conversation with Geraint, but the solicitor's assurance hadn't made him feel any easier. And knowing Sali would only worry about Geraint's plotting if she knew about it, he decided not to mention it to her until he had to. 'Now that we're almost home, you can forget about your brothers and sister.'

'For another month.' Sali looked across at his face, shrouded in shadows as they left the pool of light generated by one gas lamp and entered another. 'I'm not concerned about myself, Lloyd. They can ignore me, and for that matter you, all they like. But there's Harry.'

'He has enough people to love him, don't you, Tiger?' Lloyd smiled, as Harry moved his head and looked around the street in wide-eyed amazement. 'We're home, sleepyhead.'

Sali opened the door. 'Hello, anyone in?' She unwound her muffler from her face and neck and hung it together with her coat in the hall.

Lloyd stepped in behind her and took off his coat.

'Leave Harry's,' Sali said, when she saw her son shiver. 'I'll take him down to the ty bach and it's cold out there.'

Lloyd walked down the passage and opened the kitchen door. A gust of welcoming warmth blasted out to meet him. He stepped inside and burst out laughing. Sali looked over his shoulder.

'You've woken them,' she reproached. Megan sat up rubbing her eyes, Victor moved next to her, the knitted blanket falling from his shoulders, and Sali stepped back in embarrassment when she realized both of them were naked.

Lloyd closed the door. 'Are your clothes in there with you?' he shouted through the keyhole.

'Yes,' Victor yelled back.

'Let us know when you're dressed. But hurry up. It's colder than the inside of Bracchi's ice cream cart out here.'

'I could die of shame,' Megan declared, as she and Victor scrambled into their clothes. 'You and your "only another half hour."'

'The last time I looked at the clock it was four o'clock.'

'It's a quarter past eight now.'

'You decent?' He tucked in his shirt and buttoned his braces.

'Almost.' She rolled on her second stocking and fastened it with her supporter. Shaking her hairpins into her hand, she slipped her feet into her boots.

Victor opened the door.

'Good evening, Victor, Megan.' Lloyd strolled in, set Harry down on a chair and beamed at both of them. 'Did you have a good day?'

'Not one word out of place, Lloyd,' Sali warned, seeing Megan blush crimson as she gathered the cushions and eiderdown from the floor.

'Don't feel you have to move those on our account, Megan,' Lloyd said lightly.

'Stop teasing!' Sali spoke more sharply than she intended because she was finding it difficult to keep from laughing herself. Victor took the cushions and eiderdown from Megan and stumbled awkwardly up the stairs.

'I'll just go up with Victor, wash my hands and face and do my hair.' Megan ran after him.

Sali set the kettle on to boil and opened a second hob to heat up the stew. By the time Victor and Megan returned, both kettle and saucepan were gently steaming.

'Supper's almost ready.' She gave Megan a smile.

'I don't know what you must think of me,' Megan blurted uneasily.

'That Victor's a lucky man.' Lloyd lifted his eyebrows suggestively.

'That's enough, Lloyd,' Sali reprimanded. 'We think the same of you we always did, Megan. Not another word. Let's just enjoy what's left of the evening, shall we?'

'Please don't tell Joey, he'd never let me live it down,' Victor muttered to Lloyd, when Megan went to help Sali lay the table.

'My lips are sealed,' Lloyd agreed solemnly, but his eyes sparkled with mischief.

'Can I say the absolute last word on the subject?' Sali asked, overhearing them when she set cutlery and soup bowls on the table. 'It says something for the state of Victor and Megan that they fell asleep on Megan's only afternoon off. Both of them are exhausted.'

'Megan has an excuse the hours she works.' Victor lifted Harry, who was still sleepy, on to his lap.

'I'd say you have an excuse too, the battering you've been taking lately. Have you seen his bruises?' Lloyd asked Megan thoughtlessly.

'Lloyd!' Sali admonished.

'I meant on his face.'

'She could hardly miss them.' Sali gave Megan a sympathetic glance as she checked the stew. 'Another few minutes and I'll pour this out.'

Lloyd looked down at Harry, then winked at Sali. 'I don't think Harry's the only one who should have an early night, sweetheart. After the day we've both had we should go up with him.'

'I feel dreadful . . .'

'Please, Megan, stop thinking about it.' Victor started laughing.

'It's not in the least funny,' she hissed, as Betty Morgan's door opened.

'Evening, Mrs Morgan,' Victor said to his neighbour.

'Evening, Victor, Megan. Something funny?' Betty enquired suspiciously.

'Life, Mrs Morgan,' Victor answered.

Betty looked up and down the street before closing her door on them. It had started snowing again and large flakes drifted lazily downwards into the hushed street. Everything seemed suddenly and unnaturally silent.

'If nothing else, it will teach Lloyd to knock on the kitchen door before he walks in on us again.' Victor wrapped his arm around her shoulders.

'I'll never be able to do . . . what we did in the kitchen again.'

'Then we'll have to use my bedroom.'

'I couldn't possibly . . .'

'Yes, you could,' he contradicted. 'I'll issue my family a warning to stay well away in future.'

'Then they'd all know that we . . . we . . .'

'They've assumed we've been making love for years. Why else do you think they rearrange their entire Saturdays around your days off?'

'They do?' she questioned in amazement.

'Of course.'

'I hate the thought of them putting themselves out for us. And,' she closed her eyes, 'what happened . . .'

'I told you to forget it. And it could have been much worse. Because you forgot to lock the door when you came back downstairs, Joey or even Betty Morgan could have walked in on us. Now *that* we would have had difficulty living down. And remember, when Sali and Lloyd saw us, all we were doing was sleeping.' He hugged her when they reached the back door of the lodging house. 'We could have been doing a whole lot more, Megs.'

'But we were both naked,' she whispered.

'A memory I'll cherish until my dying day,' he smiled. 'See you tomorrow?'

'Yes.'

'You don't really want to go to chapel, do you?'

'I didn't go last week, or the week before,' she reminded him.

'All right, chapel it is. And our house next Saturday afternoon.' He lowered his voice. 'The bedroom this time. And don't worry, there is a lock on the door.'

'You're not coming in for tea?'

'It's almost eleven. Time you were in bed.' He glanced at the darkened kitchen window. 'It appears Mrs Palmer already is.'

'I doubt I'll sleep after this afternoon.'

'You'll sleep and I order you to have sweet dreams about us. Very sweet dreams.' He gave her one last kiss and walked away.

She put her hand on the doorknob but before she could turn it a man stepped out of the shadows between the coalhouse and wood shed. The knob slipped between her fingers and she cried out.

'Miss Williams. I didn't mean to startle you.'

'Sergeant Martin, what are you doing there?'

'Waiting for you. I never have a chance to speak to you in private inside the house.'

'It's late, I have to go to bed.' She fought to get a grip on the doorknob.

'What I have to say to you will only take a minute, Miss Williams. I would be honoured if you would accompany me to the Empire Theatre in Cardiff next Saturday. I know a local girl wouldn't want to be seen with a police officer in Tonypandy . . .'

'I keep telling you that I am engaged, Sergeant Martin . . .' Megan faltered when she recalled her conversation with Victor. What if the sergeant had eavesdropped, heard her say that they had both been naked?

'You must realize that your liaison with Mr Evans is totally unsuitable, Miss Williams. He is a common criminal. My intentions towards you are honourable.'

'Sergeant, I am engaged to Victor Evans,' she repeated forcefully.

'Engagements can be broken, Miss Williams.' He advanced towards her.

Megan pulled off her glove in the hope that she'd be able to turn the slippery doorknob. The metal burned, ice cold in her hand.

'I have heard that your father will not give you permission to marry Mr Evans.'

'Sergeant, please go away!' The door finally opened inwards and Megan fell forward on to the floor of the dark kitchen. The sergeant stepped into the doorway behind her. She tried to scream but failed to make a sound. He leaned over her. She could smell the tobacco and whisky on his breath, the heavy, sickly scent of his pomade. Finally finding her voice, she hooted, 'Mrs Palmer.'

A door opened in the hall and the nauseating scents faded as the sergeant melted into the shadows that shrouded the yard.

'Megan, is that you?' Mrs Palmer lifted the lamp she was carrying and saw her sprawled on the floor. 'Whatever are you doing down there?'

'I fell when I opened the door, Mrs Palmer.'

'I fell? How?'

'It's snowing, my boots were slippery.' Megan rose, dusted the snow from her cape and hung it on the stand. Taking off her hat, she pushed it gently back into shape.

'Would you like a cup of tea?' Mrs Palmer reached for the kettle.

'No thank you, Mrs Palmer. I am very tired. I think I'll go to my room.' All Megan wanted to do was crawl into bed, pull the covers over her head and think of the time when she and Victor would be able to live together, if not as husband and wife, then at least in the same house. She only wished that there were some way other than his boxing, to realize their dream.

Sali stared at the two small suitcases standing next to the kitchen door and mentally ran through the list of items she had packed into them. 'I've put in extra sets of warm underwear for both of you. And your thick sweaters. I know you want to wear your suits because they look smarter, but don't risk catching cold, especially when you change trains. It can be draughty on the platforms.'

'We're going to Cardiff and London, sweetheart, not the North Pole.' Lloyd pushed his chair back from the breakfast table, went into the passage and lifted his own and his father's overcoats from the pegs.

Sali wasn't fooled by his easy manner. She knew the Cardiff and London meetings of the Federation of Mineworkers Executive Councils, which he and his father were attending as South Wales delegates, were crucial. She opened the pantry door and emerged with a brown paper and string carrier bag. 'I've made you cheese sandwiches and packed a couple of bottles of water.'

'After the breakfast you've given us, we won't be able to eat a thing until dinner time, and the union have arranged for that to be laid on in the hotel in Cardiff, so the sandwiches are best left here for the boys.' Mr Evans took the jacket of his three-piece suit from the back of his chair and slipped it on over his waistcoat.

'If you're sure,' she said doubtfully.

'I'm sure, Sali. Lloyd and I will be eating like kings for the next couple of days, which is more than can be said for the rest of you.'

'Your stud isn't in properly.' Sali straightened her father-in-law's collar and adjusted the knot on his tie.

'Thank you. I like having a daughter-in-law to fuss over me.'

'What's London like, Uncle Billy?' Harry spooned the last of the porridge from his bowl into his mouth.

'It's an enormous city,' Billy tried to recall all Harry's favourite things, 'full of horses, carts, toy shops and sweet shops.'

'Our teacher says it's where the king lives in a palace bigger than the whole of Tonypandy put together.'

Lloyd gave Sali a quizzical look.

'Harry's learning about kings and queens down the ages,' she explained, hoping to stop her husband from launching into one of his anti-royalist tirades in front of Harry, who was apt to repeat everything that was said in the house to his teacher.

'Alfred who burned the cakes and William the conker.' Harry climbed down from his chair.

'Conqueror, Harry.' Lloyd went to the sink and dipped his toothbrush into a saucer of salt. 'He was given the title because he had a huge army of heavily armed, vicious soldiers, who fought everyone who tried to stop him from taking whatever he wanted, whether he owned it or not.'

'Just like the colliery owners.' Joey spread margarine on the last piece of toast on his plate.

'Harry hears enough of that kind of comment from Luke Thomas's son,' Sali reprimanded.

'London is also full of museums, libraries and art galleries, Harry. Mam and I will take you there one day when you're older.' Lloyd finished cleaning his teeth and rinsed his mouth. He put on his overcoat.

'What's this? A party in the passage,' Billy Evans complained, when Joey and Victor followed him and Lloyd out of the kitchen door.

'We have to wave you off, don't we?' Joey pushed his toast into his mouth, scooped Harry up and sat him on his shoulders.

'And wish you luck,' Victor added. 'A lot of hopes are riding on this afternoon's meeting.'

'Cardiff's meeting isn't as important as the one in London tomorrow.' Lloyd set his trilby on his head and checked the angle in the mirror.

'Neither will count for much if the owners keep refusing to reopen negotiations,' Billy warned.

Joey glanced from Lloyd to Sali and saw she was close to tears. 'I'll take you to school this morning, Harry. Do you want to play cowboys and Indians on the way?'

'He most certainly doesn't if it involves throwing dirty snowballs.' Fighting emotion, Sali lifted Harry from Joey's shoulders and dressed him in his overcoat and cap.

'I'll walk with them to keep Joey on the straight and narrow. We may as well go straight to the picket line from the school, so don't expect us back until late this afternoon, Sali.' Victor shook Lloyd's hand then his father's. 'Good luck.'

Sali wrapped a scarf around Harry's neck and pushed the mittens she'd knitted him on to his hands. 'Have a good day in school and be good.'

'Just like your Uncle Joey,' Joey added.

'Not at all like your Uncle Joey, who always speaks before he thinks. If you don't get going, Harry will be late.' Sali walked Joey, Victor and Harry to the door and waved them off.

'I'll see if Ned's ready. Bye, Sali.' Billy kissed her cheek, picked up his case and walked out of the front door ahead of Lloyd.

'Take care of yourself and don't let Father Kelly work you too hard.' Lloyd drew Sali back into the passage, wrapped his arms around her and kissed her. 'Why the tears, sweetheart? I'll only be gone a couple of nights.'

'I know, I'm just being silly.' She went to the door with him. 'Take care of yourselves, both of you,' she called after them, as they walked down the street with Ned Morgan.

All the neighbours had come out of their houses to see them off and shouts of 'Good Luck' and 'Show the owners what Welsh miners are made of' echoed after them.

Betty Morgan sniffed back a tear. 'I won't be able to settle to anything for a good half hour. I never can whenever Ned goes off on one of his union jaunts. Want a cup of tea while the fire's still in?' she asked Sali.

'Yes, please, Betty.' Sali watched the three men approach the corner that led down the hill. Lloyd turned, waved to her and blew a kiss. She blew one back, then followed Betty into her house.

'Look what Fred gave me yesterday.' Lena held out her wrist and showed off a rolled gold bangle to Megan.

'Very pretty, but you could catch it on something if you try to do your work wearing it.'

'No, I won't, because I keep it pulled high on my arm.'

'Haven't you girls finished clearing the dining room yet?' Mrs Palmer walked in with a clean cloth folded over her arm, ready to lay the table for the next meal.

'Sergeant Lamb's only just finished eating, Mrs Palmer. He came in late from the night shift.' Lena hoped that Mrs Palmer hadn't heard her talking about her bangle. Fred was cross enough that Megan knew about them and he was constantly warning her not to talk to him in the house when anyone else was around, or say a word to a soul about their meetings.

The front door opened, banging loudly as it was thrown back on its hinges.

'What on earth . . .' Mrs Palmer ran into the hall.

Red-faced, breathless, Huw Davies leaned against the newel

post, his helmet abandoned on the stairs, shouting at the top of his voice, 'Everyone up now!'

'What's happened?' Mrs Palmer asked.

Huw set his hands on his knees and gulped in great mouthfuls of air. 'Train crash . . . Hopkinstown . . .'

'Constable, what's all this noise?' Sergeant Lamb appeared at the top of the stairs, barefoot, his trouser flies open over his combination underwear.

'Sergeant Martin sent me, sir.' Huw gasped for breath again. 'All officers . . . not on duty in the town are wanted urgently at Hopkinstown . . . There's been a train crash. Men and officers from the West Riding Regiment are on their way, but the request is for all the assistance we can give.'

'Dead and injured?' the sergeant barked.

'Initial reports say both, sir . . . but we've no numbers. There's a train waiting at the station to take rescue personnel to the crash site, sir.'

'Go to the other lodging houses. Get as many officers as you can. I'll wake everyone here.'

Huw Davies ran out without picking up his helmet or closing the door behind him. Joyce shut it quietly, as the sergeant started banging on the bedroom doors on the first landing.

'Victor's father and brother were going with the other miners' leaders to Cardiff by train this morning for a conference.' Megan whispered. A cold chill ran down her spine.

'Scores of trains go up and down the valley lines every day,' Joyce snapped to conceal her own fears. 'They're probably perfectly safe in Cardiff right now.'

'Do you think so?' Megan looked to her employer for reassurance.

'Constable Davies, do you know what train crashed?' Joyce asked, as he dived back in and retrieved his helmet.

'All I know is the train left Treherbert at a quarter past nine . . . it was due in Pontypridd before ten but it hit a coal train.' Jamming his helmet on his head, he charged back out of the house.

'Do you know what time train the Mr Evans were catching?'

Megan shook her head. 'But Victor would. Can I run up and see

274

him?' She was already untying her apron. 'I'll be as quick as I can . . .'

'The Evans may not even know about the crash yet, and if they don't, you'll only alarm them to no purpose. If they do,' Joyce sighed, 'they won't be able to do anything about it. The troops and the police are trained to deal with disasters.'

'But—'

'All that can be done for the moment is being done, Megan,' Mrs Palmer said firmly. She stepped aside as men ran down the stairs and out through the door. 'We have a house to run and as all the bedrooms will be empty, now is a good time to clean them. When you and Lena have finished you may go up to see your young man. Not before. He may have heard something by then.'

'Tell your father to organize the next strike in summer,' Alun Richards grumbled to Joey as he warmed his hands over the rusting dustbin, more hole than metal, which the men on picket duty were using to burn rubbish.

'If he had a choice, he wouldn't be organizing a strike at all. He'd prefer to settle for peaceful negotiations,' Victor said. 'And he certainly didn't pick the time. The owners did that when they cut our wages and tried to impose new conditions of employment.'

'Let's hope this is the last time we need to strike.' Joey glanced across at Luke Thomas, who was whispering with his cronies. They were too animated for his liking and he hoped that Luke wasn't coming up with any more bright ideas about tackling blacklegs.

'Ben.' Victor nodded to Ben Duckworth and his son who joined them. 'I thought you weren't due here until this afternoon.'

'I'm not.' Ben drew Victor aside. 'There's been a train crash in Hopkinstown. I've heard it's the one the union leaders were on.'

'Anyone hurt?' Victor paled.

'All I can tell you is that our leaders were on it. I thought that maybe you and Joey would want to go down there and see if you could find out . . .'

Ben was talking to himself. Victor had grabbed Joey and both were running as fast as they could towards the town.

'One of us should go back to the house.' Joey jumped on a tram heading down the valley ahead of Victor, after they had called in Rodney's and asked Connie if she'd go up the house to stay with Sali.

'You want me to press the bell so you can get off?' Victor asked.

'I couldn't do anything that Connie can't. This not knowing whether Dad and Lloyd are safe is killing me.' Joey dug in his pocket for pennies as the conductor approached. 'Two to Hopkinstown please.'

'Train crash?' The conductor took the money and rolled out two tickets.

'You know anything about it?' Victor asked urgently.

'I got there too late to see the crash, but I saw the result from the embankment when I took my break. It's a right mess. Wreckage strewn over the tracks the length of Hopkinstown. The guard's van and a couple of carriages have been turned into matchwood. The passengers couldn't have known what hit them.'

'Do you know how many were killed?' Joey demanded.

'I've heard dozens but no one can really know, not yet. I saw them laying out bodies in the railway sheds. They were covering them with blankets. Two of them were so small they couldn't have been more than young kids. I did hear that three important men – union leaders or councillors or the like – have been killed.'

'Did they say who they were?' Joey rasped, and his hands shook.

'No. They won't let you near the tracks either. Troops and police are swarming all over and keeping people back.' He moved on up the aisle leaving Joey and Victor looking at one another.

'That doesn't mean that Dad or Lloyd—'

'I know,' Joey broke in abruptly, unable to bear any platitudes.

'Another half hour and we'll be there.' Victor turned away from his brother and stared blindly out of the window. He couldn't imagine a world without Lloyd and his father.

'Victor promised that he and Joey would be back the minute they find out anything.' Connie set a kettle on to boil in Sali's kitchen to make tea for her and Betty Morgan.

'They could be hours. I can't just sit here and do nothing until

276

they come back.' Sali paced uneasily to the door to the passage and opened it.

'Where are you going?' Connie followed her, and watched her put her coat on.

'Just out in the street, down to town – I don't know. Somewhere, anywhere that someone knows what's happening in Hopkinstown. That's it,' she said eagerly. 'I could go down to Hopkinstown . . .'

'And if Lloyd and Uncle Billy are already on their way back here?' Connie asked.

Sali opened the front door to find the neighbours congregated in the street. Two police officers were pushing their way through the crowd.

'Constable Davies,' Sali shouted, recognizing Huw Davies from the time she had needed help in the Hardy's house and the numerous occasions he had slipped her money for the soup kitchen since. And, unlike most people, he insisted on his donations remaining anonymous. 'Do you know anything about the train crash in Hopkinstown?'

'Do you?' Mrs Hopkins from the end of the street buttonholed him, preventing him from reaching Sali.

'Please, ladies, let us get through to Mrs Evans,' Huw pleaded, as the women swarmed around him and his colleague.

'Two coppers, that means someone's dead for sure.' Mrs Robinson folded her arms and rocked back on her heels. 'They always send out two to tell a woman she's a widow. One to do the talking and one to catch her when she falls. When our John was knocked down and trampled to death by the brewery cart's shire horses outside the White Hart, two coppers came to the house five minutes later. They hadn't finished scraping him up off the road before they told my sister . . .'

'Please, ladies, this isn't helping,' Huw pleaded strongly.

The one word that stuck in Sali's head was 'Dead'. It reverberated repeatedly through her mind like a mantra. *Dead. Dead. Dead.*

'Mrs Evans.' Constable Davies was holding her arm but he was looking over her head at Connie who was still standing in the passage. 'Someone told me Mrs Morgan is here.'

'That's right. Please, won't you come in, Constable?' Remembering her manners, Connie stepped back and opened the kitchen door.

Somehow, Sali found herself sitting across the hearth from Betty in an easy chair. Betty was leaning back, white-faced, dry-eyed, staring at Huw Davies. Connie held her hand.

'Your husband's head injuries were severe, Mrs Morgan. The message we received at the station said his death was instantaneous. I know it is no consolation, but you have our very deepest sympathy.' Huw Davies turned to Sali. 'Your husband and father-in-law were recognized by a reporter from the *Pontypridd Observer*, Mrs Evans. He was absolutely certain it was them. They were both injured and sent on by train to Cardiff Royal Infirmary.'

'How badly injured?' Sali's felt strange, disembodied, as if she were watching a scene on stage at the Empire Theatre.

'I'm afraid I don't have any further information, Mrs Evans.'

'I have to go to them.' Sali left her chair.

'I'll go with you,' Connie offered.

'No, Connie, you stay with Betty,' Sali said quickly. 'But will you do me a favour? Pick Harry up from school, or if you can't go yourself, send someone he knows like Annie or Tonia to fetch him.'

'Of course I will, but you can't go to Cardiff by yourself,' Connie protested, as Sali buttoned her coat and straightened her hat.

'The trains aren't running between here and Pontypridd because of the crash, Mrs Evans,' Constable Davies warned.

'But the trams are?'

'Yes.'

'Then I'll get a tram to Pontypridd and a train from there to Cardiff.'

'Sali, please, let me send for Annie,' Connie begged. 'She can stay with Mrs Morgan. You can't go on to Cardiff alone.'

'She won't be going alone, Connie.' Father Kelly appeared in the doorway. 'I'll be travelling with her.'

Chapter 17

SALI LOOKED at her watch when the cab Father Kelly had hired at Cardiff station drew up outside the Infirmary. She read the time but it didn't register. If anyone had told her that a century had passed since they had left Tonypandy, she would have believed them. Minutes had crawled by like hours, especially on the tram that had taken for ever to reach the market town at the head of the valleys, and afterwards, when they had been forced to wait for half an hour on Pontypridd station for a train.

'Let me pay the driver.' Father Kelly slipped his hand into his cassock pocket.

Sali didn't argue. She opened the door, jumped down from the carriage without waiting for the cabman to lower the steps and ran as fast as she could to the main entrance. The entrance hall was crowded with people, most apparently milling about aimlessly.

A doctor was talking to a group of men scribbling on notepads. Two porters wheeled a trolley out of a side corridor towards them. Sali stepped forward and studied the occupant. A red blanket was pulled to the chin . . . Was it true hospital blankets were red because they didn't show the blood?

She took a deep breath to steady herself then she saw that the person lying on the trolley had long hair. A woman, it was a woman, not Lloyd. She looked frantically around.

'Can I help you?' A nurse approached her.

Father Kelly joined her. 'A Mr Lloyd Evans and a Mr William Evans were brought here after the train crash in Hopkinstown. Where can we find them?' He laid his arm around Sali's waist to support her.

'If you go to the desk and give your details to the gentleman there, he may be able to help you.' The nurse disappeared through a set of double doors.

Father Kelly led Sali to the desk and repeated his question. As the receptionist thumbed through a leather-bound ledger, Sali heard someone call her name. She turned. Her hand flew to her mouth. Lifting her skirts, she raced blindly down the corridor.

'You're hurt, your head – you're bandaged, you're . . .'

'Alive, sweetheart. Just cut and bruised and only slightly at that.' Lloyd held her close and buried his face in her hair. 'I'm alive,' he repeated as if he couldn't quite believe it himself.

'Your father?' She looked up at him but tears blurred her vision.

'Dad's in surgery.' Victor stood behind Lloyd. Joey joined them and she could see from the stricken look on both their faces that something was seriously wrong.

'He's broken both his legs, sweetheart,' Lloyd said softly. 'One of them badly. They're operating on him now. The doctor told us he has no choice but to amputate it to save Dad's life.'

Mrs Palmer met Megan at the kitchen door as she carried in the last tray of dirty dishes from the final sitting of supper. She took the tray from her.

'Your young man is in my sitting room. You can join him.'

'Is he—'

'I'll see that you're not disturbed, Megan.'

Megan instinctively ran her hands over her hair and smoothed her apron and skirt as she crossed the hall.

'Miss Williams, I would like to speak to you about last night.' Sergeant Martin appeared in front of her.

'Excuse me, Sergeant Martin, but I can't talk to you now. I have a visitor.' Megan opened the door, stepped inside, closed it behind her and leaned against it. Victor was sitting in an easy chair beside the fire, an untouched tray of tea and biscuits set on the sofa table at his elbow. He saw her and left the chair.

'I'm sorry I couldn't come any earlier,' he apologized.

'I've been so worried about you and your father and Lloyd.'

'Connie said you'd been up to the house.' He hugged her.

She wrapped her arms around his neck and returned his embrace. 'Is there any news?'

'They were both taken to Cardiff Infirmary. But Lloyd's home now. He cut his head and face but his injuries aren't serious. My father broke both his legs, the right one so badly they had to amputate it.'

'I'm sorry, Victor.' She led him to the sofa and sank down beside him.

'They're lucky to be alive. I don't know what you've heard, but eleven people were killed. Ned Morgan, three councillors and two children among them. Betty Morgan's in a terrible state. Sali asked her to stay with us tonight, but she insisted on having Ned's body brought back to her house so she could sit up with him. Her sons, daughter and their families have come down from Ferndale to be with her.'

'And you, Joey, Lloyd and Sali?' she asked solicitously. 'How are you?'

'We waited in the Royal Infirmary until they finished operating on my father. The doctor said it was successful, a clean amputation below the knee, so when the wound heals, they should be able to fit Dad with an artificial leg. But we weren't allowed to see him afterwards. And we won't be able to visit until Sunday. He's a strong man, but . . .' Victor faltered.

'You're not sure how he's going to cope.'

'No.'

She gripped his hand tightly. 'I wish there was something I could do for all of you.'

'You've done enough in promising to marry me. And my father has good friends. The union men have rallied round. There's even been talk of offering him a full-time union position. It's flattering, but as Lloyd said, he's worked underground all his life. I doubt that management will want to employ a one-legged repairman. Anyone with a disability is a liability in a colliery.'

'Perhaps they'll find him a job on the surface.' She desperately tried to find something positive to say.

'Perhaps,' he echoed despondently.

'Lloyd really is all right?'

'He seems to be.' He rose to his feet. 'I'd better be getting back.'

'You don't want any tea.' She went to the tray.

'Lloyd, Joey and I drank more tea than there's water in the Rhondda in the Infirmary today. And most of it was about as appetizing,' he added. 'See you next Saturday?'

'Of course. But I'm not sure about the week after. I was going to ask Mrs Palmer if I could work some of my afternoons off to build up enough time to take a day off when your court case comes up next month.'

'Please don't, Megs.'

'I want to be there with you, Victor.'

'And I don't want you to see me standing in the dock.'

'It's not as if you've done anything wrong,' she argued. 'The only thing you're guilty of is fighting for your rights.'

'But there's no telling what lies they'll say about me in court,' he said wearily. 'And I don't want you there to hear them. I promise you, as soon as it's over, I'll come back here and tell you how it went. Mrs Palmer has never refused to let me see you.'

She summoned enough courage to voice her thoughts. 'And if you can't call in because they've sent you to prison?'

'I'll send Lloyd in my place.'

The weeks after the train crash passed in a blur of mixed emotions for Sali and the Evans. Their normal routine was disrupted to the point where none of them could think further than what had to be done in the next few hours: Harry's trips to school; buying the groceries; and for Sali, doing the necessary cleaning, cooking and washing to keep the household functioning.

Victor and Joey completed their shifts on the picket lines, but Lloyd stayed home, ostensibly to recuperate from his injuries, but they all knew that he was half expecting a message from the Royal Infirmary to say their father's condition had worsened. Despite the doctors' assurances that Mr William Evans was making a good physical recovery from his injuries, they were all concerned about the acute depression he had sunk into since he had been told of the loss of his leg. Visiting times were torture, because he rarely said more than 'yes' or 'no' in answer to any question, and evinced little interest in the family, the progress of the strike or union affairs.

Victor took to calling into the lodging house late at night, when he knew Megan would be washing the supper dishes, and despite Joyce's initial attitude to 'gentleman callers', far from disapproving, she began to put the kettle on around that time to make tea for him.

Betty Morgan insisted on making Ned's funeral in Trealow cemetery as grand affair as possible given the financial restraints imposed by the strike. Victor, Joey, Lloyd and three of Ned's closest friends carried the union official out of his home for the last time and into the horse-drawn hearse the undertaker had donated free of charge.

It was a freezing, wet and windy day, but practically the entire mining community turned out to walk behind the hearse and the two carriages containing the chief mourners. Deaf to her sons' and daughter's entreaties, Betty spent every penny of Ned's insurance money on a plot and headstone, and the funeral tea she and the Federation organized was augmented by the contents of most of the precious hoarded tins in the town.

Sali felt the entire event was surreal, like a celebration gone mad, because so many people turned up with food and flowers they couldn't possibly afford. Betty remained obdurately brisk and practical throughout the days of planning and condolence visits, only to collapse when it was over. But she refused to leave her house, even when her sons begged her to move in with their families.

Sali and the other neighbours set up an informal rota, which meant the widow was never left alone for more than an hour, and if Betty noticed that the frequency of her neighbours' visits had increased, she was too sunk in the indifference that had set in after Ned's death to comment on it.

Sundays continued to be swallowed up by their journeys to Cardiff where Billy lay, white-faced and dark-eyed, fighting pain in an overcrowded ward in the Infirmary. And although the doctors and nurses continued to remain optimistic, Lloyd, Victor, Joey and

Sali weren't so easily reassured. And all the while, Joey and Victor's impending court cases loomed closer. Sali and Megan weren't certain whether they wanted the day to arrive swiftly or not.

'Constable Davies, isn't it?' Megan was carrying a pile of freshly delivered laundry through the hall of the lodging house the week before Victor and Joey's cases were due to be heard by Porth magistrates, when Huw Davies walked through the door with a suitcase in his hand.

'Yes, Miss Williams.' He removed his helmet, revealing the mop of bright ginger curls that, to his eternal embarrassment, no amount of pomade could tame. 'I'm moving into Constable Wainwright's bed. He's been sent back to London for personal reasons. His wife is ill.' He stepped back to allow Megan to walk up the stairs ahead of him.

'I thought you were a local man, Constable Davies.' Megan said the first thing that came into her head, in an attempt to conceal her shock. She hadn't trusted Fred Wainwright's courtship of Lena, but it hadn't occurred to her that he might be married.

'I'm from Pontypridd, but,' he gave her a shy smile, 'they offered me extra split shift money and my board and lodge if I moved in here so I could be available for duty at five minutes' notice.'

'Are they expecting more trouble when the miners' trials come up?'

'I wouldn't know,' he answered evasively. 'Constable Wainwright told me his bed was in one of the rooms on the second floor.'

'It's in one of the eight-bedded rooms. I hope you're tidier than your room mates.'

'My sister trained me and she's a hard taskmaster. She's had to be; I've six brothers at home as well as my father.' He parried her questioning look. 'My mother died some years back.'

'I'm sorry.' She stopped outside a door on the second floor. 'This is yours, Constable Davies. You're sharing the double bed beneath the window with Constable Shipton.'

'Thank you, Miss Williams. Miss . . .' He acknowledged Lena, who was taking the stairs two at a time as she ran down from the top floor.

'Constable Huw Davies, Miss Lena Jones.' As Megan effected the introduction she intercepted the look of admiration Huw Davies was giving Lena. Although Huw looked absurdly young to be a policeman and Lena more like a schoolgirl than maid, the thought occurred to her that they would make a handsome couple. But Lena had to be told about Fred Wainwright's betrayal and she suspected that would hit her hard and make her highly suspicious of any man who tried to pay her attention for quite a while. 'If you'll excuse me, I must put this laundry away. Have you left the key in the cupboard door, Lena?'

'Yes,' Lena answered. 'I heard you on the stairs and I thought you'd need help to carry up the rest.'

'As I don't have to be on duty for an hour, I could help you carry the laundry to the cupboard, Miss Jones,' Huw offered.

'The lodgers aren't allowed on the top floor.'

'But there's no reason why Constable Davies couldn't help you to carry the things to this floor, Lena,' Megan said. 'I'll make a start on putting these sheets away. See you in a few minutes.'

'I know we've only just been introduced, Miss Jones,' Huw began shyly as he climbed the stairs behind Lena with his arms full of laundry. 'but would you like to go out with me one evening? To the theatre perhaps, or a chapel social?'

'Out with a policeman?' Lena questioned in astonishment. 'But you aren't allowed to mix with the locals.'

'That would be a bit difficult for me, seeing as my family live in Trallwn in Pontypridd and I am local to Glamorgan if not Tonypandy. My father and brothers are policemen not miners, but this job hasn't exactly been easy for me. Police or not, we all sympathize with the colliers.'

'I can't go out with you, Constable Davies,' Lena said finally.

'You have a gentleman friend?' Huw's disappointment was evident in his voice.

'Our Lena here is footloose and fancy free, Huw. But as you've probably guessed, shy.' Constable Shipton walked out of their communal bedroom. 'Constable Davies is replacing Constable Wainwright, Miss Jones.'

Lena stared at Shipton in disbelief.

'How about it, Miss Jones? Shall we visit the Empire Theatre on your next afternoon off?' Huw repeated.

'Go on, Miss Jones, let your hair down for once,' Tom Shipton encouraged. 'Oh and by the way, we need fresh water in our room.'

'As soon as Megan and I have finished putting away this laundry we'll do your room,' Lena said numbly.

'The girls aren't allowed into our bedrooms except in pairs, Huw,' Shipton explained. 'See you in our sitting room? There's probably a cup of tea going.'

'I'll be down as soon as I've dropped this off.' Huw looked around for somewhere to put the bale of laundry.

'Put it at the foot of the stairs, Constable Davies.' Lena turned her head so he wouldn't see her tears. 'I'll carry it up from there.'

'I'll get that.' Joey left the breakfast table on the morning of his and Victor's trial and answered the front door. 'Since when do you make me get up from the breakfast table by knocking?' he complained to Megan, who was standing on the pavement.

'Since I'm not sure what Victor will say when he sees me here,' she explained, unfazed by his show of temper. 'He told me he doesn't want me at the trial but Mrs Palmer said I could have time off if I wanted to go. And I want to,' she added defiantly.

Joey stuck his head out of the door and looked up and down the street. 'Well, we've a fine dry day if it does come to a hanging. You coming in?'

Megan hesitated. 'How is Victor?'

'Eating the condemned man's last breakfast.' She paled and he added, 'Just joking.' He led the way down the passage and into the kitchen. 'Victor, look what the wind's blown up the street.'

'I told you I didn't want you at the court, Megan.' Victor's greeting was all the more cutting for being spoken in a monotone.

'Sali, is my clean collar upstairs?' Joey deftly pocketed the collar Sali had hung on the back of his father's empty chair.

'There's a spot on my waistcoat that needs seeing to, sweetheart.' Lloyd held up his entirely blameless waistcoat.

Sali was already out of her chair. 'If you two come upstairs with me, I'll see what I can do.'

'Where's Harry?' Megan asked Victor when they were alone.

'Sali took him down Connie's after an early breakfast. Tonia is walking him to school.' Victor stacked his cup and saucer on his plate and carried them to the sink.

'Can I go with you today?'

'I have no idea how long we'll be in the court, and you have to work.'

'No, I don't. Mrs Palmer called on Mrs Morgan yesterday and offered her a job. Mornings and relief work so Lena and I can take a full day off every week. She's taken over from me today.'

'Betty Morgan has taken a job in a lodging house full of policemen! Ned Morgan will spin in his grave.' Busying himself so he wouldn't have to look at her, Victor buttoned his waistcoat, picked up his watch from the table, clipped the chain to the bottom buttonhole and dropped it into the specially made pocket.

'Ned Morgan's been in his grave for nearly a month and that's a full month without even strike money,' she reminded him. 'What's Mrs Morgan supposed to live on? Fresh air?'

'The train company will have to pay her compensation.'

'So Mrs Morgan hopes, but there's no sign of it coming. And in the meantime, the ten shillings a week Mrs Palmer has offered her to come in five mornings a week will pay her bills. So,' she steeled herself, 'as I'm not needed in the lodging house today, can I please come to the court with you?'

'To see me in the dock?' He finally looked at her.

'To support you. I know Sali's going, because she told me she is. She may need me to go to the school and fetch Harry if your case runs into late afternoon.'

'You're determined to go no matter what I say, aren't you?' He shrugged on his suit jacket.

Megan opened the cupboard where Sali kept the clothes brush

and brushed the back and shoulders of his dark brown woollen suit. 'There's a public gallery.'

'So I can't stop you from going. Is that what you're saying?'

She gave him a slightly sheepish smile. 'Exactly.'

'I've taught you too many lessons in how to be an Evans.' He took the clothes brush from her. 'I suppose you may as well walk down the hill with us.'

She locked her arms around his neck and kissed him.

'As long as you know that's a common criminal you're kissing.'

'My common criminal, Not any old one.' She opened the door and shouted up the stairs, 'Sali, Lloyd, Joey, I'm coming to court with you.'

'Good.' Joey ran down the stairs. 'I wish Dad was here,' he muttered to no one in particular as he took his overcoat from the hall rack.

'Don't we all,' Lloyd agreed feelingly as he joined him.

Porth magistrates' courtroom smelled schoolroom musty, a mixture of dust, beeswax polish and chalk, although Victor couldn't see any evidence of the chalk. An uneasy silence had settled over the packed public benches, as all three magistrates on the bench focused intently on the witness box, where Abel Adams, dressed in his frayed and only suit, was giving evidence.

Unnerved at being the centre of attention, Abel pulled nervously on his jacket lapel. 'Luke Thomas called me a blackleg, which I never was nor will be. I—'

'Then, as we have been given to understand the term used by Mr Luke Thomas, you would not describe yourself as a blackleg, Mr Adams?' the leading magistrate interrupted.

'In no way, sir,' Abel protested stoutly. He looked from the magistrates to Luke, who was standing stiffly to attention alongside Joey and Victor in the dock. 'I support the strike and my fellow workers in the struggle for better wages and conditions, but if some things aren't done to keep the pits in good condition, none of us will have a colliery to go back to when the dispute is settled. And the only people who have the know-how to do those things are the experienced workers like myself, Sam and Fred.'

'That would be Mr Samuel Winter and Mr Frederick Winter?' the magistrate clarified with irritating precision.

'Yes, sir.' It took Abel a moment to recover from the magistrate's second interruption. 'All three of us were – are – employed by management to carry out essential maintenance in the pit. Water has to be pumped out of the shafts on a regular basis, otherwise the workings are liable to flood and then the mine would be no use to anyone, management or collier.'

'And on the day in question you were ordered by management to pump water out of the pit?' The leading magistrate scribbled a note on the sheet of paper in front of him and showed it to his colleagues.

'Yes, sir.'

'And the defendants stopped you from going about your lawful business?'

'Luke Thomas did, sir.' Abel glowered at Luke. 'He said we were digging coal for market.'

'And were you?'

'We were only digging coal to fuel the engines that work the pumps. I tried to explain that to him but he wouldn't listen.'

'Thank you, Mr Adams.' The magistrate folded his arms across his chest and sat back in his seat.

'But Victor Evans—'

'I said thank you, Mr Adams. You may return to your seat,' the magistrate repeated curtly.

'But, sir—'

At a nod from the magistrate, two policemen moved either side of Abel and forcibly escorted him from the witness box, while he was still murmuring Victor's name. The leading magistrate turned his attention to the police officers sitting on the front benches.

'Sergeant Lamb?'

'Sir.' The officer rose to his feet.

'We are in receipt of the sworn witness statements submitted by the police. Is there anything you wish to add?'

'We would like it to be placed on record that we have submitted written evidence to the court, in order to prevent the harassment and,' the sergeant gave the three men in the dock a significant look, 'further intimidation of the honest citizens of this town. It is our experience, sir, that people are too afraid to make any complaints against members of the Federation of the Union of Mineworkers for fear of repercussions against them and their families. That is why it was necessary for us to submit our evidence in this anonymous and secretive form to protect the identities of our informants.'

Lloyd, along with every other man sitting in the public gallery, leaped to his feet to protest the injustice of a system that allowed evidence to be presented to the court in such a way that the witness, and the veracity of his or her statement, couldn't even be questioned.

The leading magistrate shouted for the restoration of order, the police sitting on the front benches left their seats and turned to the public gallery, but it took them several minutes to quiet the protesters.

'My father's right,' Lloyd muttered tersely to Sali, pitching his voice below the din. 'It's too much to expect justice in this country for the working man. Especially when he dares challenge the establishment.'

Victor, Luke and Joey rose to their feet and stood shoulder to shoulder, facing the magistrates on the bench. Despite the air of solemnity, Victor felt faintly ridiculous. All three of them standing to attention in their best clothes as if they were going to a wedding, waiting for the magistrate to begin his summing up after listening to the police relate a version of events at which no officer, or, given the quality of the evidence, any of the supposed 'witnesses' could have possibly been present.

The stipendiary magistrate finally ceased whispering to his colleagues, clasped his hands together and leaned towards the dock. 'This case is the result of a long period of high feeling, which came to a climax on the morning in question. In particular Thomas's conduct was not commendable. In fact, it was reprehensible.' He fixed his attention on Luke. 'Luke Thomas, you are a troublemaker who has no hesitation in flouting the law, or showing contempt for the officers employed to keep the peace in

Tonypandy. Therefore, after giving careful consideration to all the evidence, we impose a fine of fifteen pounds or six weeks imprisonment.'

A gasp rippled through the public gallery. The magistrate held up his hand and shouted for silence. Two policemen again turned to the public benches in preparation to enforce his order.

'As to your accomplices,' the magistrate looked at Joey, 'in the case of Joseph James Evans, a fine of ten pounds or one month's imprisonment will be imposed. In the case of Victor Sebastian Evans, a fine of ten pounds or one month's imprisonment will be imposed. Costs of sixty pounds to be born equally by all defendants, fines and costs to be paid within one week, or all three defendants will be incarcerated in prison.'

Angry shouts and catcalls echoed around the courtroom.

The magistrate rose to his feet. 'There will be a short adjournment before the next case.' He and his two colleagues stepped down from the bench and walked out through a door behind them.

Abel Adams glanced up and down Porth Square. Joey, Victor and Lloyd were waiting at the tram stop with Megan and Sali. He crossed the road and walked towards them.

'Victor, I'm sorry,' he began hesitantly, unsure how Victor would take his apology. 'I tried to tell the police and the magistrate that you stopped Luke and the others from having a real go at us but they wouldn't listen.'

'It's not your fault, Abel,' Victor said flatly. 'They were out to get Joey and me and they did.'

'But still—'

'Just do us all a favour, Abel,' Lloyd said grimly, 'keep manning the pumps so we have a colliery to go back to when the strike is over.'

'I'll do that, Lloyd.' Abel shook his head. 'Thirty pounds, or a month inside, just for stopping Luke and his butties from beating the Winter boys and me to a pulp. It's wrong, and worse than wrong, it's savage.'

'Tell you what, Abel,' Joey said, 'if you feel that badly about our sentence, you can do mine for me.'

'I . . . I . . .' Abel stammered his way to silence.

'Joey was joking, Abel. But thank you for trying to make them listen,' Victor said. Abel nodded and moved away.

'It was decent of Abel to apologize for something he had no control over,' Lloyd commented.

'We have a week to get the money and I'm only ten pounds short to cover both our fines, so I should do it,' Victor lifted his cap as a crowd of women approached.

'You've made fifty pounds boxing?' Lloyd asked Victor in surprise.

'Thirty boxing, twenty by betting on myself over the last few weeks.'

'Neither of you is going to gaol,' Sali said decisively.

'No, they're not,' Megan broke in earnestly. 'Because I have more than ten pounds saved. I want you and Joey to have it, Victor . . .'

'I wouldn't hear of it.' Victor bristled in indignation.

'Why not take the loan Megan is offering?' Sali looked for a middle ground that would allow Victor and Joey to keep their Evans pride, and also permit Megan to help. 'You could pay her back as soon as the strike is over.'

'Then there would be no more need for you to box,' Megan said eagerly.

'The loan would only be for a short while.' Sali was hoping for support from Lloyd, but he remained stubbornly silent, refusing to be drawn into the argument. Angry with him for what she felt was misplaced pride, she nudged his ankle gently with the toe of her shoe.

'We're getting married, aren't we?' Megan removed her glove and laid her left hand with its glittering engagement ring over Victor's.

'You know we are, the minute you're twenty-one.'

'And then everything I own will become yours.'

'And vice versa,' Victor agreed grumpily, sensing the way the argument was headed.

'Then what possible difference will it make if I lend you some money a little earlier. My motives are purely selfish.'

'Selfish!' he exclaimed.

'Absolutely. What would I do on my afternoons off if you weren't around?' Megan said tartly.

Sali suppressed a smile but Lloyd burst out laughing. 'Answer that one if you can, Victor.'

'What I'd like to know is who made those anonymous statements about us that Sergeant Lamb submitted to the magistrates,' Joey said darkly.

'The troubles caused by the strike are being used to settle a lot of scores.' Lloyd turned away from the sight of Luke Thomas being marched to the police station in handcuffs. Knowing he had no chance of paying his fine, Luke had opted to go to gaol at once. 'Much as I hate to say it, little brother, given your behaviour over the last couple of years, there are a lot of husbands, fathers and brothers who've good reason to get back at you. We all warned—'

'You're not Dad, so spare me the bloody lecture!' Joey thrust his hands deep into the pockets of his overcoat and stormed off.

'Where are you going?' Victor shouted after him.

'For a walk!'

'Not into more trouble, I hope,' Lloyd said.

'I'd have a job to get into any more than I am now,' Joey bit back before turning the corner and walking out of sight.

'Happy days,' Lloyd muttered. 'Joey's never been easy to handle, but I swear he's been ten times worse since Mam died.'

'Dad being in hospital hasn't helped.' The tram arrived and Victor helped Megan on to it.

Sali and Lloyd sat in the double seat behind them. 'We'll leave you in Dunraven Street, Megan,' Sali said. 'Lloyd and I have to go to Connie's to pick up Harry and from there we're going on to Pontypridd.'

'And we won't be back until eight o'clock at the earliest.' Lloyd said meaningfully. He took a shilling from his pocket and handed it to the conductor. 'Four, please.'

'I can pay my own fare.' Megan opened her purse.

'Give the penny to Victor. Since the strike started we have so little money we've made it communal, not that it goes any further.' Lloyd pocketed the tickets and the eight pence change.

'You have a meeting, Sali?' Victor asked.

'With Mr Richards in Ynysangharad House,' she answered.

'While Sali talks business, Harry and I intend to investigate the books and toys in the nursery again. We've already read all the ones we brought back last time we were there. If you're not in a hurry to return to Mrs Palmer's, Megan, we'll see you when we get back.' Lloyd pulled his handkerchief from his pocket and sneezed.

'As I don't have to do anything in the lodging house until tomorrow morning, Mrs Palmer's not expecting me until late this evening.' Megan glanced self-consciously at Victor. He removed his watch from his waistcoat, opened it and showed it to her. It was only four o'clock.

The tram stopped and Sali and Lloyd stepped off it first.

'If we see Joey on our way down to the railway station we'll warn him to keep away,' Lloyd said before Megan and Victor turned up the hill.

'There's no need,' Megan blushed.

'See you later.' Victor gave Lloyd a stern look of disapproval.

'When are you going to stop teasing those two?' Sali asked. 'And don't say what's the point in having a brother if you can't rag him.'

'All right, if you ask me nicely, I'll stop.'

'I'm asking nicely.' Sali took Lloyd's arm and they headed for Rodney's. 'Can I have a word with you before we pick up Harry?'

'That sounds ominous.'

'I don't just want to see Mr Richards to sign my will and sort out the adoption papers for Harry.' She braced herself for an outburst. 'I'm going to ask him to sell the ring Mansel gave me.'

'I won't hear of it,' Lloyd said flatly.

'Mansel gave it to me as an engagement ring. I'm hardly going to wear it now I'm married to you. It is worth two thousand pounds . . .'

'If you really want to sell it, and I don't think you should, any

294

money you make is yours and Harry's. I point blank refuse to touch it, and so will my family.'

'Harry will have more than enough money. When Mr Goldman, the pawnbroker, valued it for me, he said that I shouldn't take less than eighteen hundred pounds for it.'

'Money you want to use to keep my family until the pits reopen?' he enquired angrily.

'No.' She gripped his arm hard, forcing him to slow his pace. 'I want to buy property as an investment for Harry's brother or sister.'

He stopped, turned and stared at her. 'You're—'

'Yes, I am. And, as you've so often said, the family shouldn't be dependent on Harry and that goes for future as well as present members. Mr Richards and the trustees told me that the price of property has never been as low in the Rhondda as it is now so I thought I'd ask Mr Richards to take a look around and see if he can find a sound investment. You're not going to argue with me about that, I hope?'

He shook his head dumbly.

They moved closer to Connie's window, away from the crowds who weren't shopping so much as escaping their bleak, unheated houses.

'I'm sorry. Now is hardly the time or place to break the news to you, but we've never had any secrets between us and I thought you should know that I intend to sell the ring before I finalize the arrangements with Mr Richards.'

'When – when will the baby be born?' His voice was rough with emotion.

'About the middle of October.'

'You've seen the doctor?'

'No, but I had a chat with Nurse Roberts when I bumped into her on my way to the soup kitchen the other day. You are pleased?' She looked at him through anxious eyes.

He continued to stare at her for a moment then hugged her, much to the amusement of the passers-by.

'Can we keep it to ourselves – just for the moment?' she

pleaded when she released him. 'Joey and Victor have enough to worry about between their fines, the strike and your father.'

'We can keep it from everyone for now, sweetheart, except my father,' he said decisively. 'A granddaughter might be just what he needs to spur on his recovery.'

Chapter 18

'LLOYD DIDN'T mean anything when he said he'd tell Joey to stay away from the house, Megs. He's only trying to get back at me for the way Joey and I teased him when we first realized that he was carrying on with Sali.' Victor closed the front door and followed Megan into the kitchen. He glanced at the stove. Lloyd had laid the fire before they'd left for the court. He picked up a box of matches from the mantelpiece. 'We could put a match to that and sit down here, or . . .' Turning round, he swept her off her feet.

'Don't!' she protested, as he pulled her hat from her head and the pins from her hair. 'Mrs Hopkins was standing at her window when we walked up the street. You know what she's like. She could call in just to check what we're doing.'

'She wouldn't dare.'

Megan tried to wriggle free but it was hopeless. The more she struggled the more Victor tightened his grip. 'Victor . . .' She dissolved into laughter when he tickled her.

'Shall I make another bed down here?'

'Absolutely not.'

'Then it will have to be my bedroom, that is, unless you don't want to?'

Blood flowed, hot, burning, into her cheeks, but she forced herself to look into his grey eyes. They were tender and so very loving. 'I . . . I want to,' she said softly. 'Does that make me shameless?'

'Definitely.' He shifted her weight in his arms so he could open the door. 'But then, I've discovered that I love my woman shameless.'

Joey wandered aimlessly along Dunraven Street. The light was fading and as the cold spring sun sank over the hills it took what little warmth it had brought to the valley with it. The temperature dropped, but he was scarcely aware of it as he lingered in front of shop windows that had been reduced to displaying the absolute essentials. He stared at a barrel of lamp oil, incensed at the choice he had to make. Either he took Victor's money or went to prison. Much as he hated the thought of being beholden to Victor, he balked at the prospect of prison more.

'Joey?'

He glanced across the road and saw Rhian with two other maids from Llan House, Meriel and Bronwen. They were standing, obviously waiting for him to join them. Keeping his hands in his pocket, he sauntered towards them.

'I heard about what happened in court today, Joey, I'm sorry,' Rhian sympathized, when he was within earshot.

'I'm surprised you're prepared to be seen in public with me, after what you said the last time I asked you out,' he growled, irritated by what he took to be her pity.

'Rhian, Bronwen and I are more than a match for you, Joey Evans,' Meriel simpered. Joey wondered why attractive girls often had incredibly plain best friends. Meriel was so overweight her fat rippled when she moved, her mousy hair was greasy and her face was covered with angry red spots.

Sensitive to the moods of those around her, Rhian realized Joey was depressed. 'Meriel, Bronwen and I were just going to the teashop. Why don't you join us?'

'You're not afraid to be seen with me?' He knew he sounded bitter, but he couldn't help himself.

'You're outnumbered three to one, it is still daylight and we're going into a teashop. I think our reputations will survive.' Rhian's blue eyes sparkled and her whole face lit up when she smiled. Joey recalled something Betty Morgan had said to him last November, only five months ago yet it seemed a lifetime.

'Go find yourself a good, clean-living girl. Preferably one who knows how to handle a boy with your wandering ways.'

For the first time, he realized what the old woman had meant.

To have a girl like Rhian smile exclusively at him made him feel special. He felt in his pocket. He had the shilling he kept back from his strike pay, and a cup of tea was only a penny. Given that he'd never get together enough money to pay his fine in a week, he may as well treat them and it might go some small way to rehabilitating his reputation. He'd heard the gossips were speculating that Jane Edwards' sudden departure from Tonypandy had something to do with her visit to his house the night before.

Either way, it certainly wouldn't do any harm for him to be seen in a teashop with three respectable housemaids who were in the care of the formidable Mrs Williams, renowned throughout the Rhondda for keeping her girls 'decent'.

'If you're going to the teashop anyway, can I buy you girls a cup of tea?'

'Only if you let us buy you a penny bun.' Meriel linked her arm into his. 'No girl can afford to be indebted to Joey Evans and that's if only half of the rumours flying around town about you are true.'

'Probably all of them are – and more we don't know about.' Despite her condemnation, Rhian took Joey's free arm. 'A cup of tea it is, and if you're very good and don't make a single suggestive remark, we'll even allow you to walk the three of us home.'

'Mr Evans, could I have a word with you in the library about your investments?' Mr Richards drew Lloyd aside after Mari and Sali went into the drawing room.

Lloyd had long since sold all the investments Mr Richards had been handling for him to buy property, but he recalled the hurried conversation they'd had about Geraint and Mr Jenkins a few weeks earlier. 'You run on ahead,' he said to Harry, who was hanging back waiting for him. 'I'll join you and Mam in a moment.'

The fire that fire blazed in the library hearth was as cheerful as the one in the hall. Lloyd knew there'd be others in the dining and drawing rooms as well as the nursery, bedrooms and servants' quarters.

'The coal that's burned in this house in a day would keep our entire street supplied for a week,' he commented.

'This fire isn't lit until late afternoon. Mr Geraint prefers to sit here in the evening than in the drawing room,' Mr Richards explained.

'While his sister freezes in the house of strikers,' Lloyd said disparagingly. 'I take it you want to speak to me about Sali's brother and Mr Jenkins?'

'Yes, but first please allow me to extend my sincere sympathy to you and your father. The accident was dreadful. And I was so sorry to hear of your father's injuries. I trust he is making a recovery.'

'A slow one, Mr Richards, but the doctors have told us that he will be able to leave hospital next month.'

'I am glad to hear it. If there is anything that I can do . . .'

'As my father was on Union business, the miners' welfare fund is paying his doctors' and hospital bills, temporarily, until compensation can be sorted out with the railway company.'

'You will convey my good wishes to him for a speedy recovery.'

'I will, Mr Richards. About Geraint,' Lloyd continued impatiently, 'you've spoken to him?'

'No, but Mr Jenkins made an appointment to see me. He was concerned about some of the things Mr Geraint had been saying to him and he wanted to know if Mr Geraint had grounds to challenge Mrs James's will.'

'Has he?'

'None whatsoever. The will was properly drawn up by myself, and signed and witnessed by Mrs James' doctor and Doctor Green, the headmaster of Cardiff Grammar School. He was a close friend of the late Mr James as well as Mrs James and happened to call to enquire after her health on the day the will was ready for signing.'

'So what happens now?'

'That rather depends on you and Mrs Evans, Mr Evans. I have not spoken to Mr Geraint about the matter and apart from refusing to sign the document Mr Geraint wished him to, neither has Mr Jenkins. As Mr Geraint appears to have dropped the matter, I thought it might be prudent if we did the same.'

'If he knows we are aware that he tried to challenge Mrs James' will, and had no grounds for doing so, he might make life easier for Sali. Particularly at the trustees' meetings.'

'He might,' Mr Richards agreed. 'But if I might caution you, he might not, so don't be too hasty in anything you say or do. Mr Geraint's place on the board of trustees is assured while he remains one of the three senior members of the staff of Gwilym James. And while he sits on the board, he can make life extremely awkward for Mrs Evans.'

'Not for much longer if I can help it,' Lloyd muttered as he opened the door to the hall.

'Mr Evans?'

'Just talking to myself, Mr Richards. Shall we join the others?'

Victor settled his head comfortably on his pillow, lifted his arm and folded it around Megan's shoulders. 'I knew it would be good between us but I never thought it would be this good.' He ran his fingers through her long red curls, winding them around his fingers before laying them over his chest. 'Couldn't you write to your father again to try to persuade him to let us marry?'

'It wouldn't do any good, Victor,' she said sadly. 'As it is I can't understand why he hasn't come back to drag me home, or as he threatened, to Brecon to work on a farm.'

'I know why he hasn't, and so do you.'

'You think it's just the money?' Her green eyes glittered up at him in the shadowy light of the candle.

He realized she was looking for an assurance that her father loved her for more than the weekly postal orders she sent, but he'd never lied to her before and he wasn't about to start. 'In a word, yes.'

'My parents must really need the money to leave me here after the minister wrote and told them that you came to the chapel with me.' It wasn't much of an excuse for her family's attitude, but it was the only one Megan could think of.

'Which is why I think that if I keep paying your father fifteen shillings a week until your twenty-first birthday, he would let us marry.'

'My father will never give us his permission.'

'Why does he hate Catholics so much?' Victor asked.

'I don't know. Perhaps the chapel has something to do with it. The minister back home was always preaching against the popish

301

doctrine but he never explained why. I remember that when I was small I used to wonder what "popish" meant.'

'Does your father know any Catholics?'

'I don't think so. But I'm glad I do.' She curled up close to him and kissed his chest. 'This is wonderful, Victor, and I'd like to stay here for ever, but it's getting late. I know Lloyd and Sali won't be back for hours, but we should get up and dress in case Joey comes back.'

'Joey's in one of his moods. He's so angry with himself, all of us and the world in general, he'll be out late.'

'You don't know that.'

'What I do know is that I locked the bedroom door, so he can't walk in.' He lifted his head from the pillow, looked down and gave her a crooked smile. 'Just another five minutes.'

'That's what got us into trouble last time.'

He glanced at the clock. 'It's half past five now. Supposing I set the alarm for six in case we go to sleep?'

'I'd be a lot happier if I got up and dressed right now.'

'Really?' He ran his fingers lightly, teasingly down her naked body beneath the blankets.

'Victor . . .' Her protest turned to a sigh when he slipped his hand between her thighs. 'You know what that does to me.'

'Yes.'

'I . . .' He silenced her with a kiss that became another and another, and moments later, nothing existed for either of them, outside of the passion that consumed them both.

Lloyd heard the sound of a carriage pulling up outside Ynysangharad House when he crossed the hall on his way from the drawing room to join Harry upstairs in the nursery. A key turned in the lock, the front and porch doors opened and Geraint walked in. He stared at Lloyd. Knowing it was useless to wait for his brother-in-law to acknowledge him, Lloyd went up to him and extended his hand.

'Good evening, Geraint.'

Geraint hesitated and looked at Lloyd's hand before briefly touching his fingers. 'Lloyd.'

302

Lloyd debated whether to offer an explanation for his presence and decided against it. He had made the first move; it was up to Geraint to make the second.

Geraint rang the bell and a footman appeared. 'Mr Jenkins not on duty, Aled?'

'It's his day off, sir,' the footman replied.

'I forgot.' Geraint handed the boy his hat and coat. 'I've heard about your brothers' convictions and sentences,' he said to Lloyd after the servant had left.

'I didn't realize that news travelled so fast between Porth magistrates' court and Gwilym James's in Pontypridd.'

'I made enquiries. I thought it my place to do so for my nephew's sake.'

'You nephew is upstairs in the nursery, if you would like to see him.' Lloyd tensed his fists and spoke softly. Sali would have known that he was struggling to control his temper. But Geraint remained oblivious to his mounting anger.

'I may look in on the boy later.'

'You're a hypocrite, Geraint.'

'I beg your pardon?'

'Why won't you admit that you couldn't give a damn about Harry or your sister?' Lloyd said flatly. 'All you care about is yourself, and that you continue to live in this house, rent and expense free.'

'That is just the sort of vicious lie I'd expect to hear from a man who deliberately seduced a vulnerable woman out of his class. But then,' Geraint's lip curled, 'Sali and Harry's allowances must be useful in a houseful of men who'd rather strike than work.'

The taunt was one too many. Forgetting Mr Richards's advice, Lloyd said, 'No one in my family, including myself, has touched a penny of Harry's money. Unlike you, your mother, brother and sister, who are happy to live at his expense. But you're not even satisfied with that, are you, Geraint? You want the lot, which is why you tried to persuade Mr Jenkins to sign a document stating that Mrs James wasn't *compos mentis* when she made her will.'

'How do you . . .' Realizing he'd confirmed his guilt, Geraint fell silent.

'Know?' Lloyd finished for him. 'Does it matter?'

'You may have fooled my sister with your working-class hero act, but you haven't impressed me. Unlike you, Harry will be a gentleman, and I intend to see that he is brought up in this house, not a miner's slum. And if I have to go to the courts to ensure that he has the upbringing he deserves, I will.'

'You don't even know Harry. You haven't seen him more than a couple of times in his life and even then you ignored him.' Lloyd was so angry he was unaware that he'd raised his voice.

'There's little point in my seeing the boy when he's living with a bunch of criminals. You and your family would negate any influence I try to bring to bear. As it is, your brothers are on their way to gaol and you and your father will follow when this strike is broken . . .'

'What do you mean?'

'This strike is criminal. Everyone realizes that except you monumentally stupid miners. You have broken the law by withdrawing your labour. You and your strike committee have crippled the mining industry and caused an economic disaster that has affected the whole of South Wales. And you can't see any further than your inflated wages claim and demands for feather-bedded working conditions that will cost a fortune to implement—'

'All we want is a living wage and safe working conditions.'

'Expensive conditions,' Geraint mocked.

'This coming from a man whose father was killed in a colliery explosion.' Lloyd didn't even bother to conceal his contempt.

'You leave my father out of this.'

'He was the best employer I've had the privilege to work for and one of the best men I've ever met. It's a pity his sons aren't more like him. And that's why I intend to see that his grandson and namesake will be brought up the way he would have wanted'.

'You dare to assume to know what my father would have wanted?'

'What I do know is that your father would never have threatened to take Harry away from his mother at the tender age of four in an attempt to get his hands on his inheritance.'

304

'He certainly wouldn't have left him to live in a collier's house surrounded by criminals. I will get the boy under this roof and away from you and my sister—'

'And how do you propose to do that, Geraint?'

They both turned to see Sali and Mr Richards standing in front of the library door.

'By making the trustees see common sense,' Geraint shouted at Sali. 'Harry will be brought up in this house, by people qualified to care for him.'

'Are you saying that Lloyd and I aren't qualified to bring up our own child?'

'Dad!' Harry hurtled down the stairs towards Lloyd.

'He's calling you Dad now?' Geraint's face contorted in disgust.

'How long have you been there, Harry?' Lloyd stepped on the bottom stair and held out his arms. Catching Harry he lifted him up.

Harry didn't answer, but he clung so tightly to Lloyd that Lloyd guessed he'd heard most of the argument.

'Wouldn't you like to live in this nice big house, Harry, and play in the nursery every day? You will have to live here when you're older—'

'Geraint!' Sali said.

'Your mother hasn't told you that you will inherit this house, Harry? Or that you will be a very rich man?'

'Come on, Harry,' Lloyd set him down on the bottom stair and turned his back on Sali's brother, 'we're going up to the nursery, so you, Mam and I can talk.'

Mrs Williams heard the crunch of footsteps on gravel, as the maids walked around Llan House to the kitchen entrance. She opened the door and looked out. 'I thought I heard you girls . . . Joey Evans! I warned you that you're not welcome around here.' She held up the lamp and peered at him.

'It's all right, Mrs Williams, we made him behave,' Rhian said.

'There were three of us, Mrs Williams, and one of him,' Bronwen added. 'So if anyone's lost their reputation it's him. He may even be considered fit for decent company after we sat him at a table in the teashop next to the vicar's wife, and made him drink four cups of tea and eat a bun. He's promised to sign the temperance pledge next week, haven't you, Joey?'

Having promised no such thing, Joey gave Mrs Williams a weak smile and lifted his cap. 'Good evening.'

'Go inside, girls, supper's on the table in the servants' hall. Joey,' Mrs Williams stepped out and called after him as he walked away.

'Mrs Williams?' He turned back.

'I was sorry to hear about your father's accident. You will give him my best wishes for a speedy recovery when you next visit him in the Infirmary?'

'Yes, Mrs Williams.'

'And I was also sorry to hear about the sentences that you and your brother received today. Everyone in Tonypandy knows that your brother's wasn't warranted.'

'And mine was?'

Mrs Williams ignored his question. 'I gather Jane Edwards has left Tonypandy.'

'Apparently so,' he answered evasively.

'Not that you'd know anything about her reasons for leaving her house and her husband.'

'I can't help you there, Mrs Williams.'

'How you can stand there, looking as if butter wouldn't melt in your mouth . . .' She shook her head. 'Well, I suppose there's no harm in you walking my girls home again, Joey Evans, if they let you. But I warn you now; I'll get the carpet beater out if I ever see you alone with one of them. Understand?'

'Perfectly, Mrs Williams.'

'Now get off with you. And if you've any sense, you'll go straight home without stopping off to visit some married woman who's no better than she should be.'

This house is mine?' Harry looked at Lloyd in wonder.

'Yes.'

'And everything in it?'

'And everything in it,' Lloyd reiterated seriously. 'But other people have to look after it for you until you are grown up.'

'Is that man downstairs one of the people who are looking after it for me?'

'You know that man is your Uncle Geraint, Harry.' Sali picked up the soldiers Harry had scattered over the floor and returned them to their box.

'I don't like him.'

Sali was about to make a protest, but Lloyd shook his head, warning her off.

'I'm not leaving you and Mam – ever.' Harry crossed his arms and set his lips together.

'I promise you now, Harry, that you won't have to leave us, until you want to.' Lloyd lifted Harry on to his lap and hugged him.

'I won't ever want to.'

'You will have to leave us to go to school, but that won't be for ages yet and we'll talk about it some more when the time comes.' Lloyd looked at Sali, who nodded agreement.

'I take it you don't want to stay for dinner, Lloyd?' Sali set the box of soldiers on the shelf.

Harry's hair was damp from perspiration, his face unnaturally warm. Lloyd suspected it was as much from a surfeit of emotion as the heat of the fire.

'Harry has school in the morning. The sooner we get home the sooner he can go to bed. How about it, young man?' Lloyd refrained from mentioning Geraint, although he doubted that after the scene downstairs he and Sali's eldest brother would ever be able to sit at the same table and make even semi-polite conversation again.

Harry climbed off Lloyd's lap, went to the shelf and picked up the box of soldiers. 'If this is my house and everything in it is mine, can I take these home?'

Sali thought for a moment before answering him. 'Just this once, darling, but our house isn't big enough to take all the toys and books that are here, you know that.'

'I only want these. They have a different uniform to the ones at home and I can have better battles.'

Sali held out her hand. 'Bring them with you and we'll go downstairs and get your coat.'

The brake the Federation had paid to bring Billy Evans on the last leg of his journey home from the Royal Infirmary in Cardiff, met him, Lloyd and Victor at Tonypandy Station on a wet and windy Saturday morning. Billy acknowledged the men who had come to wish him well, but he insisted on getting straight into the cab to prevent them from making any speeches. Victor and Lloyd helped him and they set off.

Harry was sitting just inside the open front door watching and waiting for the first sign of them, and the moment he spotted the brake turning the corner, he ran down the passage into the kitchen.

'Uncle's Billy's here.'

Sali set down the jug of mint sauce she had been mixing to go with the shoulder of mutton Victor had earned up at the farm. She exchanged anxious glances with Joey, who was polishing the brass fire irons as part of his drive to prove to the family that he had turned into an altogether more helpful, considerate and responsible being after the fiasco of his relationship with Jane Edwards.

'Remember what Lloyd said,' Sali warned.

'I will.'

They were all worried. Mr Evans had continued to remain withdrawn and almost detached from life during the months he'd spent in the hospital, never showing the slightest emotion – anger or pleasure – on their Sunday visits, although the doctor had warned them that rage and irritability in a patient were common after an amputation. The 'two visitors to a bed' rule the ward sister rigidly administered meant they hadn't been together as a family since the morning he and Lloyd had set off for Cardiff. But whenever they exchanged notes after their visits, they all agreed that he appeared to be indifferent to the happenings within the Union, had never once asked about the strike, or the family. Even the news of his forthcoming first grandchild had only resulted in a faint smile.

'Uncle Billy!'

Sali held Harry back, as the cab drew to a halt outside the door. Lloyd opened the door, jumped out and unfolded the steps. Victor followed and they leaned back inside.

Pale-faced, watery-eyed, Billy grabbed the sides of the open door of the cab and levered himself out of his seat. Victor reached for his father's crutches. Billy leaned forward as if he were about to protest, but seeing there was no way that he could step down from the cab holding them, he allowed Victor to keep them. Lloyd gripped his father's arms, and lifted him to the pavement. Balancing on his remaining leg, Billy retrieved his crutches and shook off Lloyd's hands.

'I can manage,' he said gruffly.

'We're all ready for you, Uncle Billy.' Harry ran out to meet him. 'Mam has cooked us a dinner, Dad has bought you tobacco and I put the newspaper on your chair—'

'Later, Harry.' Billy tucked his crutches under his arms, leaning heavily as he swung forward. 'I'm tired. I'm going to my room.'

'We have to light a fire in Dad's bedroom. It's freezing in there, but he insists he doesn't want to join us, even for dinner.' Victor returned, grim-faced, to the kitchen from the front room.

'Even if we had enough coals, he'll see it as fussing and won't stand for it,' Joey warned.

'Perhaps Harry—'

Lloyd shook his head. 'No, Sali, it's not fair to use Harry; you saw how abrupt he was. Did he say anything, Victor?'

'Only that he wanted peace and quiet. When I told him we'd be quiet in the kitchen, he said he hadn't had a minute to himself since the accident five months ago.'

'That's true enough.' Joey grasped at the idea. 'How would you like to lie on a bed in an open ward for almost five months, surrounded by twenty nosy sick people who have nothing better to do than watch you being washed and humiliated day and night by bossy nurses?'

'Dad was in a side ward,' Victor reminded.

'Only for the first month,' Joey countered.

'You sound as if you were there, Joey.' To Sali's annoyance, Lloyd lifted the plates down from the dresser. Since the day she'd told him she was pregnant he'd begun treating her as if she were at death's door.

'When Victor and I swapped over halfway through visiting a couple of Sundays ago, I talked to one of the patients who was allowed out of bed to use the bathroom. He was miserable as sin and he'd only been in there for three weeks. He said he couldn't wait to be discharged.'

'Let's hope it is just the adjustment of coming home after months in hospital.' Lloyd suspected his father regretted the loss of his independence more than his leg; it was a loss any man would find hard to live with, and a collier, whose job depended on his physical strength and agility, more than most. The doctor's assurances that his father would be able to live a full life once his wound healed and he was fitted with an artificial leg hadn't elicited the slightest response from the patient. Lloyd had even begun to doubt the doctor's prognosis and wonder if anything would ever lift the depression his father had sunk into.

'Shall I take him in a tray?' Sali inserted a skewer into the meat to check it was cooked. When the juices ran clear she lifted it out of the oven.

'I will,' Lloyd said.

'Can I come with you, Dad? I can give him this.' Harry held up a picture he'd spent all morning drawing of himself with the entire family on the mountain. Lloyd smiled when he saw that Harry had pictured his father standing behind the dogs so you couldn't see his legs.

'Yes, Tiger.' Lloyd ruffled his hair. 'As long as you realize that Uncle Billy is tired and that might make him a bit grumpy.'

'It's taken me longer than I thought it would to make it, but this is the last of the ten pounds that I borrowed from Megan to pay Joey's and my fine. If you put it in the tin, Sali, I'll give it to her next Saturday.' Victor set five pounds on the kitchen table.

'It's cost you dear in pain to earn it.' She set a chair in front of the sink. 'Sit down and I'll clean up your face.'

Victor didn't argue with her. The champion the police had found to replace Wainwright was even quicker on his feet. He also packed a harder punch and his ribs felt as though one of the pit ponies had trampled on them.

'You will give up now, won't you?' Sali smeared grease on the smaller cuts after she'd cleaned them.

'I'd like to save enough to pay Megan's father fifteen shillings a week so she can leave the lodging house.'

'The strike can't go on much longer and then you can start earning your money a sensible way.'

'Until the pits reopen, I'll make my money the only way I can.'

Sali grimaced as she filled a bowl with clean water. A cold spring had given way to a warm June and July, but nine months in there was still no sign of the strike breaking, and the soup kitchens were stretched to their utmost, supplying the most basic of rations to the miners' families. Nearly all the children she saw in Harry's school and on the streets were as thin-faced, pale and listless as their parents. It was becoming increasingly obvious that the miners couldn't hold out much longer, but despite the best efforts of the strike leaders, management categorically refused to make a single concession to their demands.

The kitchen door opened, and Mr Evans swung in on his crutches. 'I thought I heard someone come in. You been fighting again, Victor?'

'I earned another five pounds boxing. It's enough to pay Megan back what Joey and I owe her.'

'Looks like it cost you that much in blood to get it,' Billy said caustically. 'Make sure that your brother pays you back as soon as he can.'

'How did the fitting for the artificial leg go?' Victor knew that he risked incurring his father's wrath for even asking.

'All right.'

'Lloyd said you'll have it next week.'

Mr Evans didn't answer Sali and she didn't press him. The men who visited him told him he looked well and congratulated him on making a remarkable recovery but she and his sons knew better. He spent most of his days – and they suspected nights – sitting alone in his room, looking through the photograph albums his wife had compiled.

'Who's after you now, boy?' Mr Evans asked Joey, as he dashed into the room, cap in hand, gasping for breath.

'Lloyd sent me up to get Victor. There's serious trouble down at Ely pit in Penygraig. Hundreds of police are there, the boys are throwing stones at them and the engine house. It's turning really ugly . . .' Joey fell silent, as a strange expression crossed his father's face.

'What does Lloyd think that Victor can do?'

'The men have a great deal of respect for Victor and his opinions, even more so since the trial.' Sali knew that Victor would never say anything about the authority he commanded with the strikers, so she said it for him. 'They know Victor was innocent and that he stopped Luke Thomas from beating up Mr Adams.'

'Are there blacklegs down there?' Billy looked to Joey.

'So rumour has it, although Lloyd couldn't find anyone who'd actually seen them.'

'I'll go with you.'

'You—'

'If Lloyd sent for Victor it has to be serious. Joey, run down to Connie's and ask her to send her delivery cart up here for me.'

'Are you . . .' Sali fell silent, as Victor frowned at her. There would undoubtedly be trouble and most probably fighting down at Penygraig, but it was also the first time that Billy Evans had shown any signs of animation since he'd left the hospital.

Chapter 19

SALI SANK down on her chair after the men left. She looked up at the clock. Another hour and it would be time to fetch Harry from school and go on to the soup kitchen. Since Lloyd's father had come home from the hospital, she had cut down on the number of hours she worked there, although the only one he would allow to help him wash, change and shave was Lloyd.

She stared at the fire. There was little point in lighting it as she usually did before she fetched Harry, because there was no way of knowing how long the men would be.

'Hello, anyone in?' Megan walked into the kitchen.

'You managed to get an hour off.'

'Two. I overheard the police officers talking. They said that the strike was about to end . . .'

'That was premature: The strike committee agreed to hold another meeting with management next week, but as the owners are refusing to put anything new on the table I doubt that the men will decide to go back to work. Please sit down,' Sali invited. 'I'm sorry, I haven't lit the fire. With the men on the picket lines, there's no point in doing it for a while, so I can't offer you tea, but I made some vinegar biscuits yesterday and as Joey says, there's plenty of water in the tap.'

'I'm fine, I had a cup of tea and a slice of apple pie before I left Mrs Palmer's.' Megan saw the bowl of water and jar of goose grease on the table next to the sink. 'Victor's been boxing again.'

'I'm afraid so.' Sali tipped the water down the sink.

'I wish he wouldn't.'

'That makes two of us.'

'Is he badly hurt?' Megan bit her lip anxiously.

'He's been worse. Just a few small cuts on his face.'

'One of the officers also said there's trouble at Ely Colliery,' Megan said warily. 'I hope Victor hasn't gone down there.'

'He left ten minutes ago. Lloyd was already there. He sent Joey up to get Victor to see if he could calm the men before trouble breaks out again. As usual, there are rumours of blacklegs. Mr Evans went with them.'

'Is he well enough?'

'No.' Sali didn't say any more. The picket lines were no place for an able-bodied man, let alone one in her father-in-law's condition, but she knew from past experience that voicing her concerns would only make her worry all the more. All she could do was concentrate on other things until the crisis was over.

'Will it ever be over?'

'I don't see how we can hold out much longer. The union's paid out so much in strike money it's virtually bankrupt, and without the ten shillings a week it pays every striker, no one would eat. Lloyd and his father are talking to management, that's all management ever do – talk. But,' Sali smiled determinedly as she took the chair opposite Megan's, 'as we can't do a thing about it, let's forget the strike. It's a lovely day, the sun is shining and I'm only sorry that Victor isn't here to enjoy it with you. I wish I could tell you when he'll be back, but your guess is as good as mine.'

'You walking over to get Harry from school?'

'Much to his annoyance. He insists he's old enough to walk there and back by himself, but I don't agree. He can do it next term when he's five and not before.'

'If you don't mind, I'll go with you. I could do with some fresh air. How are you keeping?' Megan nodded to Sali's thickening waistline.

'Fine. I'd be happier if Lloyd, his brothers and his father wouldn't fuss over me quite so much. They won't let me lift a coal bucket or carry a tray, although I keep telling them I'm having a baby, not dying on my feet.'

'Think about it, Sali, the last baby to be born in this house was Joey. They're probably scared witless in case the midwife doesn't arrive in time and they have to do something.'

314

'I wish you were still living next door,' Sali said sincerely. 'It would be good to have another woman to talk to whenever I feel like a chat. But then, when you're twenty-one—'

'Please, don't say anything,' Megan interrupted uneasily, her blood running cold. 'I don't want to tempt fate.'

'I can understand that after waiting so long to marry Lloyd. Sometimes, even now, I find it difficult to believe that we really are married.'

'And happy despite the strike?' Megan asked a little wistfully.

'Most definitely. I'll comb my hair and then we'll have a wander in Dunraven Street. We can window shop before we go to the school.'

'Sounds good to me.' Megan knew Sali was as worried as her about what was happening in Penygraig. Window shopping wasn't the best way to pass the time, but it was cheap, and there was a chance that they might meet someone who could take their minds off whatever was happening outside the Ely Colliery for a few minutes.

'The Evans know how to pick their women,' Luke Thomas commented enviously to Alun Richards, as they leaned again the wall of Alun's house in Pandy Square in the company of half a dozen other strikers who had nothing better to do than watch the world go by.

'They certainly do.' Alun stared at the inch or so of leg Megan was showing above her ankle. 'Good-looking, the pair of them.'

Megan and Sali continued to stroll arm in arm across the square, oblivious to the glances they were attracting from admiring men and other women. Dressed in a two-year-old, green sprigged cotton summer dress, which looked new because she'd had so few chances to wear it, her mass of red curls loosely wound on top of her head, Megan glowed, a picture of health in comparison to the pale-faced, haggard women around her. The lightweight, beige linen maternity suit Sali had bought in Gwilym James, because none of her ordinary clothes fitted her, was elegant and looked expensive. Its box jacket hid her burgeoning figure, and like Megan she positively shone with health and happiness. They stopped, still

315

arm in arm, to speak to Betty Morgan, who was leaving the lodging house.

'Those women ought to be shot. All three of them,' Mark Hardy growled from the doorway of his hut where he wasted most of his days, sitting staring into space. 'Standing there fat, healthy and dressed to the nines, flaunting themselves while others starve.'

'I'm the last person to put in a good word for Megan Williams or Betty Morgan. Any woman who earns her bread by working for the enemy gets nothing but contempt from me.' Alun spat on the pavement to emphasize his disgust. 'But whatever else you want to say about Sali Evans, the Evans are living off strike pay, same as the rest of us.'

'Not the same as the rest of us at all,' Mark Hardy snarled viciously. 'They get four lots of pay and they've a garden big enough to keep chickens and grow vegetables in. They're not much worse off than when they were in work.'

'Fair's fair. Victor Evans gives away what he can to the soup kitchen. And before he was dragged into court and the police started watching him too closely for him to risk working in the drifts, he often used to slip the missus the odd bucket of coal.' Alun spoke up in Victor's defence.

'Maybe a couple of buckets of nicked coal and a handful of vegetables to the soup kitchen makes him all right in your book but not mine.' Mark scowled. 'Just look at those three.' He focused on Sali, Megan and Betty again. 'They may as well stand there and shout, "We're all right and to hell with the rest of the world."'

'Like us, Mark, they're just trying to survive,' one of the other miners pointed out mildly.

'Survive! Victor Evans' girl has a job where she can eat herself silly skivvying for bloody coppers and it shows. Tell me truthfully, have you seen any other women in this town lately with curves like her and Lloyd Evans' wife? And Betty Morgan's been looking healthier since she started working in Palmer's lodging house. Bloody Ned Morgan . . .'

'No speaking ill of the dead,' Alun warned. He looked closely at Mark. If he hadn't known any better he would have said he was drunk. But Mark only got a couple of shillings a week from the distress fund and the half a jug of soup and few slices of bread a day that Father Kelly sent over from the soup kitchen because Mark was too proud to eat in the hall.

'Ned, Billy and Lloyd Evans started this strike—'

'With our backing,' Luke reminded. 'We had a free and democratic vote, remember?'

'No, I bloody well don't.'

'You were told about it. Everyone in the pit was.' Arguments had become Luke's lifeblood since the strike had started, the one occupation open to him that actually taxed his brain.

'I never voted to strike.'

'That's democracy for you, Mark,' Alun said calmly. 'The majority not the minority get their way.'

'And did the men who voted for the strike know that it was going to mean women and children starving to death?' Mark trembled with suppressed emotion.

One or two of the men exchanged embarrassed glances and drifted away from the group. Everyone felt intensely sorry for Mark and what had happened to his wife and children, but that hadn't stopped them from apportioning some of the blame for their deaths on his pride and stubborn refusal to ask for help before it was too late.

'Deserve to be shot, the bloody lot of them,' Mark muttered. 'All the Evans, and their women and Betty Morgan, deserve to be shot and if there was a God that's what he'd do, shoot the lot of them. But then perhaps shooting's too quick . . .'

'Mark, man, you're upset, you don't know what you're saying.' Luke walked towards him.

'You stay away from me, Luke Thomas. You're as bad as the rest of them. Deserve to be shot . . .' Mark went into his hut and banged the door so hard the remaining men standing around Alun's house thought it would fall off its hinges.

'Silly sod's gone off his rocker,' Luke declared.

'Can you blame him?' Alun asked. 'Wife and two kids dead from starvation, all his other kids in the workhouse and, as he hasn't the means to keep them, there's no prospect of him getting them out. When he went up there yesterday to try to see them he

317

discovered the oldest girl had been sent into service. They wouldn't even tell him where. Said she had a better chance of a new life if she made a clean break from her old one.'

'That's hard,' Luke commiserated.

'It is. She's only eleven.' Alun glanced at Megan again. She lifted her skirt as she stepped around a steaming pile of horse manure behind the brewery cart. Her shapely ankle and slim leg brought his wife's sagging body and thinning hair to mind.

'You looking at what I'm looking at?' Luke asked.

'Just can't take your eyes off them, can you?' Alun said.

'Some men are born lucky, and I'd say none are luckier than Lloyd and Victor Evans. Just the sight of those two women is enough to make me want to follow them home and forget my missus.'

'Careful I don't tell her that,' Alun laughed.

'Tell who what?' Beryl demanded, leaving the house.

'Just men's talk, my darling,' Alun answered flippantly.

'You can go in there,' Beryl pointed into the house, 'and look after the twins while I go down to Rodney's to see how much food ten bob can buy this week.'

Sali and Megan picked up Harry from school, and walked towards the town centre and Mrs Palmer's lodging house. After leaving Megan at the back door, Sali carried on to the soup kitchen where Father Kelly was telling bad jokes and being more determinedly cheerful than usual, in an ineffectual attempt to make everyone forget what was going on outside the Ely Colliery in Penygraig. She was glad when their first customers came in and she, Father Kelly and their helpers were kept too busy serving food to make any extraneous conversation.

After Father Kelly saw the last people out of the hall at seven o'clock, he closed the doors, drew Sali aside and handed her the keys.

'You want me to lock up for you?'

'If you'd be so kind.' He picked up his hat.

'You're going to Penygraig?'

'Someone has to mediate between the hotheads. From what I've seen, there are men on both sides determined to get stupider and more pig-headed with every passing day. Now don't you go trying to clear everything up here, in your condition, it can wait until morning.'

'Looks like Mrs Gallivan and Mrs O'Casey have everything in hand.' Sali drew his attention to their two hardest working volunteers.

'They're both fine charitable women and God loves them for it. I'll see you here tomorrow afternoon, Sali, but only if it's convenient for you.'

Sali blanched at his inference that it might not be convenient. Every time there was fighting at a pithead, Lloyd, or one of his family, seemed to get injured. She looked at a picture of the Virgin Mary in the corner of the hall and uttered a wish, which became a prayer, that this time, all four men would escape without a scratch.

She and Harry returned to an empty house at half past seven. Hoping that at least one of the men would return home in time to eat supper, she put a match to the fire, set the vegetable stew she had prepared earlier on to boil, and heated water to wash Harry. At half past eight Harry fell asleep on her lap, unable to stay awake even to hear her read him his favourite chapter of *Treasure Island*. She carried him up to bed, slipped him between the sheets, drew the curtains in his tiny bedroom, returned downstairs – and waited.

She banked up the fire with small coal that smouldered more than burned, but it was enough to keep the stew warm. Setting *Treasure Island* aside, she went into the parlour and looked along the bookshelves for something to read. Knowing she would find it almost impossible to concentrate, she picked out one of her favourites, Dickens's *A Tale of Two Cities*. Curling up on an easy chair, she opened it at the first page, but it was hopeless.

She sat staring at the clock, watching the hands crawl round from nine to ten to eleven o'clock. Unable to sit still a moment longer, she went to the front door and opened it. Betty Morgan was sitting on a kitchen chair she'd set in her open doorway. She was knitting but Sali noticed that her attention was focused on the street, not the fine white wool in her hands.

'You worried?' Betty asked.

'Have you heard anything?'

'Not since I met you on my way home from the lodging house this afternoon. But as I said to you then, they were sending as many police as they could to Penygraig. I tried telling the sergeants that a glimpse of a uniform is all that's needed to drive a collier crazy these days, but neither of them would listen to me, no more than either side is prepared to listen to common sense. If you ask me, I think the whole world has gone mad.'

Not wanting to think about what might be happening on the picket lines, Sali asked, 'Would you like a cup of tea?'

'I wouldn't mind.' Betty knew she was more likely to hear any news if she remained in her doorway, but she sensed that Sali was in need of company. Sticking her needles into the ball of wool, she left her chair, picked it up and carried it back down her passage. Closing her front door, she walked across the road into Sali's kitchen.

'The kettle will take another five minutes or so to boil, Betty,' Sali apologized, 'we haven't the coal for a big fire.'

'Daft, isn't it?' the older woman said. 'Here we are, sitting on one of the biggest coalfields in the world and hardly anyone can afford to keep a fire in for more than an hour or two a day. And, when the men dig the outcrops on the mountains that are there for the taking, they get fines they can't pay and are put into prison where they are given three meals a day while their families carry on starving and freezing.'

'When you put it like that, I have to agree with you. The world is mad.'

Betty saw the frown on Sali's face. 'Worrying about them isn't going to do that baby you're carrying any good. I've known Billy Evans for close on thirty years and those three boys of his since they had the first nappies put on them. They know how to watch out for themselves and each other.'

'They haven't been doing so well lately. Mr Evans hasn't recovered from the train crash. Victor has a couple of cracked ribs from boxing, the last time the police arrested Lloyd they beat him, and Joey's temper flares . . .'

'Lloyd and Victor will keep him out of trouble. Who's there at this hour?' Betty shouted at a knock on the front door.

Quicker on her feet than Betty, Sali ran and opened it. 'Constable Davies, is Lloyd or—'

'No one is hurt, Mrs Evans.' He removed his helmet and his ginger curls shone in the fading light. 'Can I come in?'

Sali opened the kitchen door wide, but although Huw Davies closed the front door behind him, he remained in the passage.

'I can't stay. The sergeant doesn't know I'm here, and things still might turn ugly in town. There was trouble down the Ely colliery this afternoon. I'm sorry to have to tell you that your husband, father-in-law and brother-in-law have been arrested. The union solicitor has seen them and is doing all he can for them, but they'll be kept in the cells in the station overnight. They should make bail after their cases have had a preliminary hearing in Porth magistrates' court in the morning.'

'This is becoming a regular occurrence,' Sali said bitterly. 'What's the charge this time?'

'Your husband and father-in-law have been charged with riotous assembling to disturb the public peace, your brother-in-law with assaulting a police officer,' Huw divulged uneasily.

'Which brother-in-law?'

'Victor. Joey followed us to the station with a crowd of strikers after the arrests and he's been there ever since so I guessed he hadn't been home to tell you what's been going on.'

'It was good of you to call,' Sali said contritely, realizing that Huw had risked a reprimand or worse from his sergeant to give her the news.

'There's over a hundred angry men outside the police station. I only hope we succeed in calming them down and moving them on before we have to arrest anyone else. The men on the picket line in Penygraig threw stones and injured a couple of constables from the Worcester force. There's a lot of anger on both sides. I'd better be getting back before I'm missed.' He opened the door.

'Thank you, Constable Davies.' Sali offered him her hand and he shook it.

'I wish I'd brought better news, Mrs Evans.'

'It was good of you to come.'

Huw put on his helmet, straightened it and ran off down the street.

Betty Morgan joined Sali on the doorstep. 'Have you noticed the Welsh coppers are the only ones in Pandy who dare walk alone around the town. The English coppers don't even go round in pairs any more, it's threes and fours.'

'I haven't noticed, Betty, but now I come to think of it, you're right.' Sali looked at the old woman. 'The kettle should have boiled. Do you still want that tea.'

'Please.' Betty laid her gnarled, calloused hand over Sali's. 'I can stay the night if you want me to.'

'I won't sleep,' Sali warned.

'My Ned might have gone but that doesn't mean I've stopped caring about the strike and the men. We'll sit up together.'

'As it looks like we won't be seeing our beds until morning, it's good to have a warm night for it.' Luke threw his head back and stared up at the night sky. A full moon and a million pinpricks of starlight shone down on him. The vastness made his head swim and he reached out and grabbed the nearest shoulder.

'Watch who you're mauling, Thomas.' Joey brushed Luke's arm aside.

'Touchy tonight, aren't we?' Luke jibed.

'Lay off him, Luke.' Alun Richards leaned against the wall behind him. The lower end of Dunraven Street was outlined in ghostly blue-black shadows and the men around him, standing strained and silent, seemed to merge into the scene, casting a peculiar and dreamlike atmosphere.

'It feels like we've been waiting here for bloody years not hours. Anyone got the time?' Luke looked around. 'Sorry, dull question. The only honest men in Pandy who can answer that are the pawnbrokers, seeing as they've got all our watches.'

'It was gone midnight when I called in my house and that was hours ago,' a muffled voice answered.

Joey paced impatiently to the edge of the pavement. 'If they've beaten my father or brothers the way they beat Lloyd last time . . .'

The door of the police station across the road opened. Bright yellow lamplight flooded out and a dozen constables marched out of the building. They stood on the steps for a moment before two figures broke away and crossed the road. Ignoring the officers walking towards them, Joey continued to watch the constables standing outside the station. They were holding batons and he suspected there were others inside preparing for a charge.

'Get ready, boys,' he muttered out of the side of his mouth.

Sergeant Lamb was the last to leave the station. He stood, hands behind his back in the doorway, staring directly at Joey who remained in the front line of the colliers.

'Joey?' Gwyn Jenkins approached him, Huw Davies walking closely behind. 'I'm sorry, son—'

'I'm not your son,' Joey snapped belligerently. He squared up to Gwyn.

'I've just spoken to your father and brother—'

'You beaten them up yet?' Joey's question prompted an angry murmur from the men behind him.

'No one is going to touch a hair on their heads.'

'It's not their hair I'm worried about.'

'They won't be harmed,' Gwyn assured him. 'The local sergeant is on duty tonight and he's looking after them. Look,' Gwyn parried the angry glares of the men standing around Joey, 'the last thing, Billy, Lloyd, Victor or any of us want is more trouble, or for any more colliers to get arrested.'

'You can't arrest the whole bloody lot of us.'

'Isn't one fine enough for you, Luke?' Gwyn asked. 'If any officer other than Huw or me hears you using language like that, you'll find yourself back in court for swearing.'

'Please, have a bit of common sense,' Huw pleaded, when he saw a collier pull a stick from his sleeve. 'One glimpse of a weapon and the sergeant will roust a couple of hundred officers from their beds and order a baton charge.'

'You have my word that Billy, Lloyd and Victor Evans are being well looked after,' Gwyn reiterated. When the men facing him remained hostile and silent, he added, 'You saw Geoffrey Francis leave the building. Didn't he tell you they were fine?'

'That was hours ago,' Luke shouted. 'Anything could have happened to them since then.'

'The only thing that's happened to them is they've been given a fish and chip supper,' Gwyn retorted.

'After you charged them and put them in a cell,' Joey reminded.

Gwyn and Huw waited for the chorus of catcalls, derogatory whistles and groans to subside.

'What I'd like to know is why you're not charging the whole damned lot of us,' Alun Richards demanded.

'We'd clog up the courts if we did that,' Gwyn said patiently.

'So, it's easier to pick on our leaders than all of us?' Luke taunted.

'Victor isn't a strike leader,' Joey argued.

'Victor has admitted that he tried to prevent a police officer from arresting your father, Joey,' Gwyn said.

'My father's just come out of hospital, he's a sick man—'

The sergeant barked an order and the constables standing on the steps marched forward. Another dozen moved out of the station behind them, and another dozen and another dozen after that.

'For Christ's sake, go home, boys,' Gwyn pleaded.

'And the minute we've gone you'll beat my father and brothers just like you beat Lloyd the last time he was in here.'

'You have my word, Joey. They'll be fine. Please, go,' Gwyn begged.

Gwyn and Huw stood impotently watching the strikers produce more sticks they'd hidden in their clothes. Some of the men raised their hands and the officers saw the dull gleam of stones. Missiles were thrown at the advancing line of constables across the street.

'When are you going to see sense?' Gwyn shouted in desperation.

'Haven't you heard?' Joey yelled back. 'Sense was the first casualty of this bloody strike.'

'Were any of the officers badly hurt last night?' Victor asked Megan and Mrs Palmer the next morning when he sat in the kitchen of the lodging house drinking the tea Mrs Palmer had poured for him. He'd called in on his way home from the magistrates' court and every time he looked at Megan, clean and pristine in her freshly laundered cotton dress and white apron, he was all the more conscious of his unwashed and crumpled state.

'Cuts, bruises, nothing serious,' Joyce revealed. 'Which, from what I've heard, is about the same as most of the strikers got for their trouble.'

'Seems to be, or so I heard someone say in the court today. Our Joey has a new lump on his head, as well as a black eye. But he'll live.'

'You going to get another fine?' Megan asked Victor anxiously, wondering if he would ever be able to give up boxing.

'Probably.' Victor decided there was no point in worrying Megan by telling her that half the constables down at the colliery had seen him push a police officer to the ground. His only defence was his concern for his father. An officer had grabbed him, causing him to lose a crutch. He sensed the excuse wouldn't sway any court in his favour.

'The whole town is sick of this strike, police as well as colliers.' Joyce Palmer pushed the sugar bowl towards him.

'I agree with you there, Mrs Palmer. The end can't come soon enough. No thank you.' He left the sugar bowl in the middle of the table. 'We've done without sugar for so long now, I'm used to the taste of tea without it.'

'So, what happens now?' Megan rose to her feet as he left his chair.

Victor finished his tea and set his cup back on its saucer. 'We wait for the case to come to court and I try to fit in as many boxing matches as I can in the meantime to pay our fines.'

'There has to be another way . . .'

'Tell me what it is and I'll do it. Thank you for the tea, Mrs Palmer.'

'You're welcome, Victor.' She cleared his cup and saucer.

'Pick you up on Saturday, Megs?' he asked, as she opened the door for him.

'Can I walk Victor out, Mrs Palmer?'

'Be my guest, Megan. Take care, Victor. And tell your father and Lloyd to be careful. The men need their strike leaders. That's why your family is being targeted. Everyone knows they are the brains of the union and the strike committee, and the authorities aren't stupid. They realize that if you cut off the head the rest of the body is useless.'

'They're aware of it, Mrs Palmer, but thank you for your concern. Good morning.'

'And a good morning to you, Victor.' Mrs Palmer watched him step through the doorway that seemed far too small for a man of his size. Megan went after him and closed the door behind her.

'I worry about you.' She wrapped her arms around Victor's waist.

'There's no need, Megs, I can take care of myself. And now,' he gently disengaged her arms and kissed the top of her head, 'I am going to go home and have a bath, in cold water if there's no warm. I always feel filthy after a night in the cells.'

'The way you're talking anyone would think that you spend every night in the police station.'

'Believe me, love, two nights in one lifetime are two too many.' He kissed her again and walked down the lane.

'Victor?' Huw Davies ran after him as he emerged into the street. 'I'm sorry about yesterday . . .'

'Joey told us this morning what you and Gwyn did to try to calm the situation outside the police station last night. I'm only sorry you didn't succeed,' Victor said earnestly. 'Our Joey has a hot temper, particularly when he feels our father is being threatened, but if it's any consolation to your injured colleagues, he's suffering for losing it this morning.'

'At least Joey hasn't been charged with an offence, unlike you, your father and brother. Look, I have four tickets for a chapel concert on Sunday and I know Megan gets time off. I thought that we could take Megan and Lena . . .'

'Don't you think it would be odd for a miner and constable to be seen together?'

'It's in Pontypridd.'

'It would still be odd. And to be honest, if I can persuade Megan to give chapel a miss, I'd like to spend a quiet couple of hours with her. Given the charges I'm facing I might not be able to have too many of those in the foreseeable future.'

Huw nodded.

'I am right, aren't I?' Victor pressed. 'I'm going to get a prison sentence?'

'You may be lucky,' Huw hedged.

'How long?'

'I don't know that,' Huw protested.

'Your guess would be better than mine.'

'A couple of months, but you might get a lenient jury or a judge who'll settle for a fine.' Anxious to change the subject, Huw pulled a box from his pocket and retreated to the comparative shelter of the lane. 'Do you mind giving me an opinion on this?' He opened the box.

Victor looked down. 'Very nice,' he complimented, admiring the gold engagement ring set with three small diamonds.

'Do you think Lena will like it?'

'I'm not an expert on engagement rings, Huw.'

'You gave Megan a nice one.'

'It was my mother's, so I had no hand in choosing it. Have you asked Lena's opinion?'

'She doesn't even know I'm going to ask her to marry me. I thought I'd surprise her.'

'Knowing women, she's already guessed what you're going to say.' Victor smiled. 'When are you going to ask her?'

'Tonight. I've booked a table for dinner in the dining room of the White Hart.'

'You taken her there before?' Victor probed.

'At the prices they charge!'

'And you think she doesn't know what's coming?' Victor's smile broadened.

'You're right, she probably does have an inkling,' Huw conceded. 'I took her down to Pontypridd to meet my father, sister and brothers on her last day off.'

'They got on?'

'Like a house on fire.' Huw punched Victor playfully on the

shoulder. 'You're not the only lucky man in the Rhondda when it comes to women, you know.'

'Just the luckiest,' Victor joked. 'Good luck tonight.'

'Thank you. You know, I'm more nervous about this dinner than I was facing you lot down Penygraig yesterday.'

Chapter 20

THE QUIETEST time of day in Joyce Palmer's lodging house was between the last serving of tea and the first of supper. The housework was finished for the day, and once the fires had been replenished and the vegetables prepared for the evening meal, Joyce retired to her sitting room. Since the weather had turned warmer, Lena and Megan had taken to climbing the stairs to their attic room to read, gossip and mend their stockings. Knowing Lena was excited about the evening off she had cadged from Mrs Palmer because it was the only one Huw was free that week, Megan had offered to see to the fires so her fellow maid could go upstairs and prepare for her big night out.

'Someone's bought a new dress.' Megan walked into the bedroom and found Lena unpacking a large white box.

'It cost thirty-five shillings. I've never given so much money for a dress in my life. But it has real lace and silk panels.' Lena held the pale blue frock up in front of her.

'It is beautiful, and it will look gorgeous on you.' Megan wished, and not for the first time, that she could keep more than four shillings and five pence of the pound she earned a week for herself. She had bought herself a cotton dress length the week before, and the ten shillings the material had set her back and the five shillings the dressmaker would charge her to make it up, had taken up most of what was left of her month's wages after she'd sent her father his money.

'You don't think it's too much for the dining room of the White Hart?' Lena asked.

'You're the one who's already been there.'

'To an upstairs room.' Lena blushed and turned aside. 'You were right and I was wrong . . .'

'Huw isn't like Fred Wainwright,' Megan said quietly.

'I know. Huw treats me like a real lady. He didn't even kiss me until we'd been stepping out together for two months and he's never tried to take advantage of me. Not the way Fred did.'

'He took you to meet his family, so he has to be serious about you.'

Lena burst into tears.

'Whatever is the matter?' Megan led her to the bed, and gently pushed her down on to it.

'You know what I did with Fred,' Lena sobbed. 'It was wrong. I never should have let him touch me. Huw thinks I'm a nice girl, and I'm not. I let Fred do things to me that a girl should only do after she's married. I'll never be the same again . . .'

Megan slipped her arm around Lena's shoulders and handed her a handkerchief. 'That's nonsense. Of course you are a nice girl. You just made one mistake with a man who took advantage of you. But anyone with eyes in their head can see that Huw Davies loves you. He won't mind . . .'

'Yes, he will. No man wants damaged goods. What I did was dirty and unforgivable. I'm no better than one of those women who stand in the lane at the back of the Empire Theatre after the show and let men do whatever they want for a few shillings. I've been stupid . . .'

'You were taken in by the wrong man, that's all,' Megan consoled. 'It can happen to anyone.'

'It didn't happen to you.'

'Only because I was lucky enough to fall in love with the right man straight off.'

'And if you hadn't, do you think that your Victor would have forgiven you?'

Megan hesitated, then realized Lena wasn't looking for truth but reassurance. 'Of course he would have.' But she couldn't help wondering whether he would or not.

'Huw will hate me when he finds out,' Lena blew her nose, 'and he will find out if I marry him. Men can tell. And that will be just too awful.'

'You could try talking to him about it.'

'I couldn't,' Lena gasped. 'I'd die of embarrassment.'

'Has he told you that he loves you?'

'Yes.'

'And you've told him that you love him?'

'Yes.'

'Then everything will be fine between you, because loving someone means taking them as they are and wanting the best for them,' Megan said seriously. 'Take my advice, pick your moment, tell him the truth and . . . that's Mrs Palmer calling me. It's probably time to lay the table for supper.' She left the bed and looked back at Lena. 'You'll be all right?'

Lena nodded.

'You sure? I could come back up later if you need any help with dressing or anything.'

'No,' Lena said softly. 'I'll be fine.'

'Everything will be all right, Lena. All you have to remember is that Huw is a good man and he loves you. Have a good time tonight. I do envy you having dinner in the White Hart – twice. But then,' Megan smiled, 'perhaps Victor and I will have dinner there one day.' She refrained from adding, 'After the strike.'

Sali returned to the kitchen after putting Harry to bed to discover that Mr Evans and Lloyd had returned from a strike committee meeting in the County Club. She'd expected it to go on until the early hours. All four men were sitting around the table, bleak-faced and silent.

'What's wrong?' She looked from her father-in-law to Lloyd.

'The committee has voted to put the recommendations of our leaders, Mabon and D. Watts Morgan, that we accept the employers' terms to a mass meeting; word is the men want to call off the strike.' Lloyd clasped his hands on the table in front of him.

Sali sank down on her chair next to him. 'Has management agreed to any of your conditions?'

'None,' Joey said angrily. 'Not even a minimum wage of five

shillings a day for underground workers over eighteen. We'd be going back for less than we earned before the strike started.'

'The men could vote to continue the strike,' Victor said quietly.

'Most of us have been beaten black and blue by the police, one miner's been killed, two have committed suicide, dozens of others are in prison on trumped-up charges, women and children have starved and died, Ned Morgan and the others were killed in a railway accident that according to the experts shouldn't have happened, and for what?' Billy Evans looked at his sons in despair. 'Nothing! As Joey said, we'll be going back to work for less than we were getting when we walked out almost a year ago.'

'As Victor said, the men could vote to continue the strike,' Sali suggested hollowly.

'All this! We've gone though all this,' Joey shouted angrily, 'only to go crawl back to management like whipped dogs to work and die underground for pence that will barely put food on the table. But never mind, the colliery companies can put more profit in to their shareholder's pockets, they'll be able to buy bigger mansions and employ more servants and—'

'Joey, you're not helping,' Lloyd remonstrated.

'I'm going down the Pandy.' Joey walked out.

'I'll keep him out of trouble.' Victor followed.

'I am so very sorry.' Sali laid her hands over her husband's and father-in-law's.

'We tried.' Billy Evans's eyes were diffused with anguish. 'At the end of the day that's all we can say, we tried. But there'll be trouble at the meeting tomorrow. Joey's not the only one who's going to be outraged at the thought that we've put our families and ourselves through this for no gain.'

'You're quiet, Lena.' Huw looked up at her from the ring box he'd set on the table after they'd finished their dessert of summer pudding and cream. 'Don't you like the ring?'

'It's beautiful, Huw.'

'I wouldn't be upset if you didn't like it.'

'I love it, Huw.' She looked at the ring but she didn't dare to touch it. Megan's voice echoed in her head.

'*Everything will be fine between you, because loving someone means taking them as they are and wanting the best for them . . . Pick your moment, tell him the truth and . . .*'

She simply couldn't tell Huw the truth. Not now, and she knew with absolute certainty, not ever. She couldn't bear to destroy that warm, loving look on Huw's face by telling him that she wasn't the girl he thought she was. That she'd allowed another man to . . .

'Lena, what's wrong?' Huw asked. 'I know something is.'

'It's nothing.' She forced a smile. 'I'm just overwhelmed, all this wonderful food and now this ring.'

'Aren't you going to try it on?' He took the ring from the box, lifted her left hand from the table and slipped it on to her finger. 'It's a little big, but the jeweller said he could make it smaller with clips, or if you prefer another ring altogether he'll exchange it.'

'It's lovely, Huw.' A tear fell from her eye.

'Lena . . .'

'I'm sorry, Huw. I've never loved anyone as much as I love you. When Mam and Dad died and I had to go into the orphanage, I thought I'd never have a family again and you've been so kind . . .' She blew her nose and looked across the table at him. 'I'm fine, I really am,' she added unconvincingly.

'I have so many plans for us. As soon as this strike is over I'll be sent back to Pontypridd and you'll come with me. We'll get married here or there, it makes no difference, it can't come soon enough for me. I get decent pay and I'll find a house we can rent not too far from my father, sister and brothers, and . . .'

While Lena listened to Huw describe the life they would live together in Pontypridd, she recalled the lies Fred Wainwright had told her. She not only heard but felt the sincerity in Huw's voice, the excitement as he planned out the life that both of them would share and she wondered why she had never been able to see through Fred from the moment she'd met him as Megan had.

'Well?' Megan asked, when Lena walked into their bedroom at eleven o'clock.

'Huw gave me a ring and asked me to marry him.' She held out her hand and showed Megan the ring.

'It's very pretty,' Megan complimented, sensing that something was wrong. Lena was far too composed for a girl who had just become engaged. 'You do love Huw, don't you?'

'More than anyone else in the world.'

'And you told him about Fred?'

'I will, tomorrow. Tonight wasn't the right time. Do you mind if I burn the candle for a little while longer? I have a letter to write.'

'Not at all.' Megan thought of the letter she would write to her family, if her father would only change his mind and approve of Victor. 'Congratulations.'

'Thank you.'

Lena put the sheet of paper, envelope, pen and ink she had borrowed from Mrs Palmer on top of the chest of drawers. Pulling up the chair, she sat down, opened the inkbottle and began to write.

Megan was almost asleep when Lena blew out the candle. She turned over, snuggled down into her pillow and tried to conjure an image of Victor, but before she had time to picture him, his face and eyes glowing as he walked up the mountain, sleep overtook her.

The alarm woke her at six. She glanced across at Lena's bed in the soft summer light that filtered through the grey cotton curtains. It looked as though it hadn't been slept in. Had Lena woken early and gone downstairs to begin work? Or . . . she recalled the times Lena had disappeared when she had been courting Fred Wainwright and wondered if she had made an early morning tryst with Huw.

Smiling at the thought of what she and Victor would be doing on her next day off, she left the bed, washed, dressed, made her bed, opened the curtains and pushed up the casement window.

Leaving the room, she ran down the steep narrow staircase. A young constable was standing on the second landing holding a glacé kid, low-cut evening shoe.

'This yours, Miss Williams?' He held it out to her.

'No,' she took it from him. 'It's Miss Jones'.' She glanced up and cried out in horror.

Lena hung above them, suspended by a rope that had been tied around her neck and secured to the topmost newel post. Her head was tilted at an unnatural angle, her face black.

Megan sat on the sofa in Joyce Palmer's sitting room; a glass of brandy was on the sofa table beside her but like everything else around her, it seemed unreal. She had the oddest feeling that if she tried to touch anything it would dissolve beneath her fingertips. It was as though she'd stumbled into a nightmare. Any moment the alarm clock would ring, Lena would switch it off and shout, 'Good morning,' before leaping out of bed to take first turn at the washstand.

She glanced at Mrs Palmer who was sitting beside her, then at the clock set precisely in the centre of the mantelpiece. It was a quarter past seven in the morning and because it was high summer there was only the kitchen fire to see to, but nothing had been done. None of the rooms had been tidied or dusted and the cloth hadn't been laid on the breakfast table. Yet no one, not even Sergeant Lamb, was complaining.

Joyce patted her hand and Megan looked at her employer as though she were seeing her for the first time – a middle-aged woman, who was struggling to remain brisk, efficient and in complete control of herself and the household, even in the face of Lena's suicide.

'We haven't done any work,' Megan muttered numbly.

'I sent one of the constables up to Mrs Morgan's house. She would have been in at eight anyway. I'm sure it won't make much difference to her if she comes in an hour earlier.' What Joyce didn't say was that she had also asked the constable to knock on the Evans' door and fetch Victor and Sali. Megan was clearly in shock and someone had to take care of the girl, preferably away from the lodging house. She had yet to shed a tear for Lena, and in Joyce's experience, the longer the grieving process took to begin, the more crushing it was when it finally took hold.

'It's my fault, Mrs Palmer. I should have realized what Lena meant when she said she would tell Huw in the morning. I saw her writing the letter and I did nothing . . .'

'You have to put that idea right out of your mind, Megan,' Joyce said sternly. She had listened carefully to Megan's account of not only what Lena had said to her the day before, but also the sordid story of Fred Wainwright's seduction and betrayal. She had seen but not read the letter Lena had written to Huw Davies and left together with the ring on her bed.

If anyone was to blame for Lena's death, Joyce believed it was her. She had taken Lena out of the workhouse and assumed responsibility for her welfare. But instead of protecting the young girl, she had allowed a married man to take advantage of her naïvety and innocence.

If only Lena had come to her with her problems, if only she had been in a position of knowledge, so she could have talked sense to the girl and told her that one mistake didn't mean your whole life was ruined . . . if only . . .

Joyce grasped Megan's hand. She had long thought 'if only' to be the saddest words in the English language. But whatever else, she was determined Megan wouldn't be blighted by them.

'You did all you could for Lena and more. You were her first true friend. I heard you two laughing and gossiping in your room night after night. Her work improved beyond all measure from the day you came to this house.' She looked Megan in the eye. 'Now listen to me and believe me,' she said solemnly. 'The only person responsible for Lena's death is Lena. No one else tied that rope around her neck and no one pushed her off that banister, she jumped.'

'And Fred Wainwright?' Megan hated even mentioning his name.

'It was Lena's choice to do what she did with the man. Fred didn't force her in any way, did he?' She looked earnestly at Megan.

Megan recalled the time she had walked into the bedroom Fred Wainwright shared with seven other men and found him and Lena in a compromising position, and the threats Fred had made about arresting Victor and the Evans' if she told anyone what she had seen, which Lena didn't even remember afterwards.

'He didn't force her.'

Joyce continued to hold Megan's hand, keeping the guilt that was eating at her conscience to herself. The least she could have done was warn Lena. She should have realized that there were men prepared to use an innocent young girl, men without integrity or morals, who put themselves and their own pleasure before everything else.

'Joyce.' Betty Morgan rapped the door and opened it.

When Joyce saw Betty standing next to Sali in the hall, she had to fight the urge to rush over and hug them. Leaving the sofa, she held herself as stiffly upright and straight-backed as ever. 'Would you please lay the table and make a start on the men's breakfasts, Betty? As you see, we're at sixes and sevens this morning.'

'I'll do that right away, Joyce.'

'Sali, if you have time, perhaps you'd sit with Megan while I help Betty?'

'Of course.' Sali went to the sofa and took Joyce's place.

Megan rose to her feet, her movements slow and jerky. 'I have to work . . .'

'You have to sit down and rest.' Joyce pushed her back on to the sofa.

'Victor came down with me, Megan,' Sali said quietly. 'He went into the lodgers' sitting room to offer Constable Davies his condolences.' She looked at Joyce. 'Victor said Constable Davies showed him an engagement ring yesterday that he had bought for Lena.'

Joyce nodded, unable to face any more discussion of the events that had led to Lena's suicide. 'If you'll excuse me, Sali, I must see if the undertaker has finished. I wanted to lay Lena out myself, but because it was an unnatural death, the doctor had to be called. He brought a nurse with him, and she offered to help the undertaker lay Lena out in her coffin while I saw to other things. If you would like to see Lena, she is in the empty storeroom off the back porch.'

'If you come back up to the house with me, Megan, we could pick flowers for Lena from the garden before we see her,' Sali suggested. 'One of Victor's rose bushes is particularly lovely at the moment. It's a mass of creamy white blooms.'

'I'd like that,' Megan whispered in a strained voice.

'Mrs Palmer, if there's anything that I or any of my family can do to help with the funeral . . .' Sali remembered that Lena was from the workhouse, and she shuddered at the thought of the small, vivacious girl being buried in the common paupers' grave in Trealow cemetery.

'When Lena started working here I advised her to take out a penny a week burial insurance. My mother gave me that same advice when I married and when all my family were killed, I was grateful. It meant that they could be buried with dignity. As Lena can now.'

'Outside the cemetery walls.' Sali spoke her thoughts aloud.

'Of course – that's where they put suicides.' Joyce struggled to contain her emotion.

'Have you sent for the minister?'

'I should have sent for him when I sent for you, Mrs Morgan, the doctor and the undertaker. It was stupid of me. The minister is the first person most people send for when there's a death.'

'Did Lena go to chapel?' Sali asked.

'I gave her Sunday evenings off, like Megan, but she never mentioned going to chapel to me and I didn't ask her where she spent her free time. A person's religion is their own affair,' she said decisively. 'I haven't set foot in a chapel since my husband and sons died and that's my choice. I know people talk about me behind my back for not going and I didn't want to stoop to their level with Lena. The poor girl had been ordered about every minute of every day when she was in the workhouse. I thought she should have a little independence . . .' Joyce realized she was talking too fast. 'Did Lena ever say anything to you about going to chapel, Megan?'

'No, Mrs Palmer.'

'She had Baptist down as her religion on the form the workhouse gave me, but if she never attended a chapel it could be a problem finding someone to bury her.' Joyce fiddled nervously with her collar.

'I could ask the ministers on the Distress Committee if they'd be prepared to officiate at the funeral,' Sali offered.

'I'd be grateful. Now,' Joyce looked around the room, 'I have a lodging house to run and you,' she turned to Megan, 'are taking the day off, and that's an order.'

'No, Mrs Palmer.' Megan rose to her feet again.

'I am not arguing with you, Megan. I am telling you. You're no good to me, or the lodgers, in the state you are in. And you won't be any use until you get a good rest. Now go to your young man's house with Sali and let them look after you. Come back and sleep here tonight if you want to, but frankly, I think you'd be better off staying there. I'll ask Mrs Morgan to stay over for a night or two until you're – feeling better,' Joyce finished lamely, in a desperate attempt to push the traumatic events of the morning from her mind.

'We'd love to have you, Megan. There's a spare bedroom next to mine,' Sali broke in.

'You'll never manage just with Mrs Morgan, Mrs Palmer, and to be honest I'd rather be kept busy. If I sat around I wouldn't stop thinking about . . .' As the finality of Lena's death hit her, Megan began to cry. Her quiet sobs soon escalated into raw howls that tore at Joyce and Sali's heartstrings. Gathering Megan into her arms, Sali sat back on the sofa with her.

'I will stay with her, Mrs Palmer. You see to the house.'

Joyce fled. Her own emotions were in too fragile a state to risk remaining in the same room as Megan.

Sergeant Martin opened the door of the lodgers' sitting room at Victor's knock. He showed him in and left. Victor looked around and, at first glance, assumed the room was empty. Then he saw Huw Davies slumped in a chair in the furthest corner from both the window and the fireplace. A brass and glass screen framing an embroidered spray of sunflowers blanked off the bare hearth, but although there was no fire, the room was oppressively warm. He noticed the signs of neglect that meant it hadn't been cleaned that morning. A thin layer of dust on the mantelpiece, waste-paper baskets overflowing with yesterday's newspapers and toffee wrappers, ashtrays spilling cigarette butts and grimy pipe cleaners over the surrounding surfaces. Dirty cups encrusted with dried tea leaves . . .

He imagined Lena and Megan, dusters in hand, emptying the mess into buckets, restoring the room to order. And now Lena . . . he swallowed hard. If it was painful for him, it had to be a hundred times more agonizing for the man who had loved the girl enough to buy her an engagement ring.

Victor moved towards Huw, who remained motionless in the chair, like a carefully balanced waxwork figure. His head was hidden in his hands, his fingers buried in his ginger hair. He was so still that if it hadn't been for his peculiarly uncomfortable position, Victor could have believed he was sleeping.

He debated whether to disturb him. Perhaps it would be kinder to tiptoe away. Then he thought, kinder for whom? He and his family owed Huw Davies a great deal. The officer had badgered his fellow policemen into making substantial and generous donations to Father Kelly's soup kitchen after he had seen the deprivation in the Hardy's hut. He had risked, if not his career, certainly a severe reprimand two nights ago when he had slipped away from the police station to tell Sali that he, his father and Lloyd were safe in the cells. He recalled the tickets to the concert Huw had offered him and Megan.

Taking a chair from beneath the table, he set it beside Huw's.

'I am so desperately sorry, Huw.' Victor would have liked to been more eloquent, but he couldn't think of any other words to express his feelings.

Huw dropped his hands and revealed his face. His eyes were red-rimmed, raw, but not from tears, and Victor sensed that Huw's grief went beyond weeping.

'You saw the ring I bought her. You said she'd like it.'

'Any girl would have, it was beautiful, Huw.'

'She said she liked it. I loved her and she said that she loved me.' Huw opened his hand to reveal a single sheet of crumpled paper covered in spidery writing. 'But not enough to trust me. She thought that I wouldn't forgive her. That I'd be angry with her. You knew about her and Fred Wainwright?'

'No,' Victor replied honestly.

'Megan did. She told me this morning that she knew about them, and that she'd advised Lena to tell me about Fred.'

'If Lena told Megan anything in confidence, Huw, Megan wouldn't have talked to me about it.'

'As if I would have cared about anything Lena had done before she met me. It was none of my business. All that was important was what we had together. Forgive her! I had nothing to forgive her for. And now . . . now I've lost her . . .'

Lloyd and his father were always telling Victor that he was too sensitive. That he suffered the pain of others as if it were his own. It was true. He only had to look at another being, human or animal, in torment, to feel their hurt. And it was all too easy for him to place himself in Huw's position. He knew that he wouldn't – no, couldn't – go on, if Megan weren't a part of his life. He would rather be dead than exist with the knowledge that he would never ever see her again.

Aware that Sali would stay with Megan as long as she was needed, he ventured, 'If you need company . . .'

'Sergeant Martin's given me four days' leave.'

'Are you going home to Pontypridd? Because if you are, I could travel down there with you.'

'No! Legally I can't claim Lena's body, but Mrs Palmer already has, and I'm hoping that she'll let me see her again and help arrange her funeral. It's all I can do for her now.' Although Huw's eyes remained focused on the room around them, Victor sensed that his mind was drifting back into a world where Lena still lived.

Victor continued to sit quietly with Huw, waiting for him to make the next move. Time lost all meaning and he couldn't have said with any certainty if it was minutes or even an hour later when Mrs Palmer knocked on the door and joined them.

'Constable Davies, the undertaker has finished. Lena is laid out in her coffin in the room off the back porch if you would like to see her.'

Huw left his chair.

'You don't have to see her, it's only if you want to.' Mrs

Palmer knew from painful experience that sometimes it was better to remember loved ones as they'd been when they'd lived.

'I'd like to spend as much time with her as I can before the funeral. If that's all right with you, Mrs Palmer.'

'You have more right to be with her than anyone else in this house, Constable Davies,' Joyce said shortly.

'Huw,' Victor laid his hand on his arm as the policeman went to the door, 'afterwards – if you can bear to be around people – you would be more than welcome in our house.'

'A policeman in a house of strikers?' Huw shook his head. 'But thank you for asking, Victor.' He left the room.

'Megan's with your sister-in-law in my sitting room, Mr Evans. Sali and I have tried to get her to agree to spend the day with you, but she insists she'd prefer to work.'

'May I talk to her, Mrs Palmer?'

'I'll take you to her.'

'I need to keep busy, Victor.' Megan sniffed back her tears and dried her eyes with her handkerchief. She felt oddly calm and completely numb after her outburst. 'Nothing will seem right, whatever I do, but it would be even worse if I went home with you and sat around with your family. We'd only end up talking about Lena, you know we would, and that's the last thing I need. I can't stop thinking about her as it is. There's a lot of work that needs doing here. Two of the bedrooms need a thorough clean and their beds changed, and all the others need a quick once over. There's the downstairs room to see to and the lunch and dinner to prepare, cook, serve and clear up after . . .' She realized she was talking for the sake of it. 'Please.' She looked into his eyes. They had never appeared so tender or full of love. 'I need time to accept that Lena's gone before I face even you, Victor.'

Victor nodded a resigned agreement. He understood what she meant, and he was also thinking about the meeting that his father and the strike committee had called that afternoon in the Empire. Megan would be safer in the lodging house than he and his family would be in the theatre.

'Perhaps I'll come up this evening,' she conceded.

342

'I'll be in town this afternoon. I'll call in around six o'clock, not to stay, or for tea, but just to see how you are. And,' Victor considered the trouble his father and Lloyd were expecting, 'if you change your mind and decide to walk up to the house beforehand, don't come up by yourself, ask Betty or Joyce to walk with you.'

She kissed his cheek. 'Thank you for understanding, Victor. Either way I'll see you tonight.'

'There's going to be serious trouble at the meeting in the Empire this afternoon, isn't there?' Sali asked Victor, as they walked up the hill.

'Yes,' he answered briefly.

'You will be careful, won't you? And watch out for your father, Lloyd and Joey.'

'If by that you mean ducking Joey's punches, because he's as likely as any of the other hotheads to throw them if the vote goes against continuing the strike, I'll try. And as Dad isn't used to his new leg yet, I'll make sure that his chair is placed well out of the firing line. I only hope that he and Lloyd have managed to pressgang enough of the cooler-headed members of the committee to police the meeting. We're going to need all the help we can get to keep some of the younger colliers under control.'

'And not just the younger members.' Sali tried to ignore Luke Thomas and his friends, standing, surly-faced, hands in pockets, on the corner of the street.

After a scrap meal of bread, homemade apple jelly and margarine, eaten in strained silence, Billy and his sons left for the Empire. Sali watched them walk down the street, went back into the kitchen and stacked the dishes ready for when the fire would be lit. She glanced at the clock. It was half past one and the meeting wasn't due to start until two o'clock, another half an hour. Her thoughts turned to Megan and Mrs Palmer – and Lena, lying cold and stiff in her coffin. She washed her hands and face, brushed her hair and pinned it into a chignon on the back of her head. Taking a pair of scissors from the drawer and a basket from the pantry, she went into the garden and spent ten minutes cutting a dozen of the finest rosebuds she could find.

She arranged them in the basket, left the scissors in the basement, made her way to the lodging house and knocked at the back door. Mrs Palmer opened it.

'I brought flowers for Lena.' She lifted the basket.

'They're beautiful, Sali, and the first we've had.' Joyce refrained from adding. 'And the only ones we're likely to have from the neighbours.' In every other experience she'd had of sudden and unexpected death in the valleys, friends and neighbours had rallied around offering help. She was discovering just how different was the death of a suicide who'd worked in a houseful of policemen. 'Would you like to take them through? Constable Davies is sitting with her. He hasn't left her all morning.'

'And Megan?' After Megan's shattering display of grief, Sali was almost too afraid to ask.

'Megan's seen Lena and paid her respects, but she insisted on working afterwards. I felt that I had no choice but to let her carry on. If you want to see her, I could call her.'

'I'd rather not disturb her.' Sali followed Mrs Palmer through the back porch. Joyce opened the door, then stood back and closed it as Sali stepped inside.

Lena was lying in an open coffin supported on trestles. Her dark curls were brushed away from her face and she was covered to the chin by a white shroud. Sali forced herself to look at her face. Her eyes were closed and apart from the deathly white, bloodless colour of her skin she could have been asleep.

'She looks peaceful, doesn't she?' Huw Davies rose from the wooden kitchen chair that had been placed next to the coffin.

'Yes, she does. Please, don't disturb yourself, Constable Davies. I only came to bring these.' Sali looked around for somewhere to put the basket of flowers but the room was bare apart from the coffin, its stone walls whitewashed, the floor unadorned grey concrete.

'Thank you, they are beautiful.' Huw took the basket from her.

'From Victor's garden. I am so sorry, Constable Davies. I know how inadequate that sounds. If there is there anything that I can do, I would consider it an honour to be asked.'

'Find someone to bury her if you can, please, Mrs Evans. I know you offered to ask the ministers on the Distress Committee if they would. The Baptist minister heard what happened and called in, but only to tell Mrs Palmer that he wouldn't bury Lena even if she'd been a regular worshipper at his chapel, and she wasn't. I tried arguing with him, but he insisted that he has firm guidelines on dealing with suicides and he is not allowed to read the service over self-murderers.'

Sali laid her hand lightly on Huw's shoulder. 'I am so sorry.'

'I don't care what kind of a priest you get. As long as it is someone who will talk about Lena, and how wonderful she was, and not about the way she died.'

He turned back to Lena. There was a broken yet loving look in his eyes. Sali felt like an intruder as she stole quietly from the room.

Chapter 21

SALI RETURNED home but, unable to settle and knowing she wouldn't until the men returned from their meeting, she left the house again and went to the soup kitchen. Father Kelly wasn't expecting her but she hoped to find work there that would keep her from brooding over what was happening in the Empire.

'Sali, it's wonderful to see your beautiful face on this tragic day,' Father Kelly greeted her. He set a chair for her in front of the table where he was chopping leeks, carrots and onions to put in the soup. 'I called on Mrs Palmer before I came here to offer her and Constable Davies my condolences. I only just missed you but I did see the beautiful flowers you'd left.' He lowered his voice lest any of his more conservative helpers overhear what he was about to say. 'Constable Davies told me the Baptist minister's opinion on self-murderers, so I said a few prayers over the poor girl's coffin.'

Sali didn't know much about the Catholic Church, but she did know that suicide was considered a mortal sin and Father Kelly, like the chapel ministers and church vicars, should have taken a hard line and refused to pray over Lena's corpse. 'Do you think there's a chapel minister in Tonypandy who'll conduct Lena's funeral?'

'In short, no. The deacons, the elders and the chapel councils are firm when it comes to matters of policy. They know right, they know wrong, and somewhere between the two they lose all humanity.' He picked up a cloth and wiped his eyes, which Sali suspected were watering from more than just the onions. 'Such a pretty young girl and such a tragic end. And to think she had her whole life ahead of her with Constable Davies. The poor girl must have been in absolute torment to do such a thing. If only she had reached out to someone who could have helped her. But as I said to Mrs Palmer and Megan Williams, they're not to go blaming themselves. God alone knows what went through that tragic girl's mind last night. And He acts in mysterious ways, but it's not for us to question the Almighty. Mrs Palmer told me that the undertaker's arranged for the funeral to take place outside the walls of Trealow cemetery on Monday next. You and all your family will be attending?'

'We will,' Sali said decisively.

'Good for you.' He glanced at the sink where Mrs Gallivan and Mrs O'Casey were peeling potatoes. 'I will be attending – but only as a friend you understand. I won't be wearing my cassock, but you can tell Mrs Palmer and Constable Davies that I've prayed for guidance and if they want a friend – not a priest, you must make that point absolutely clear to both of them – just a friend to say a few words over Lena Jones' coffin, they have one. There isn't a parishioner, or a bishop, who can object to me doing that much. And if there is anyone else who wants to say a few words as well, then so much the better.'

'Father Kelly . . .'

'And why would you be scuttling in here at that speed, young Sam Richards?' Alun Richards's eldest son had charged into the hall and skidded to a halt in front of the table. 'Here.' The priest handed him a slice of raw carrot. 'But don't go eating that straight away, or you'll be choking.'

Sam grabbed the carrot and held it in his hand. 'The men have voted to go back to work.'

A saucepan and a colander crashed down on to the wooden floor behind Sali and Father Kelly. Mrs Gallivan burst into tears.

'You're sure about this, boy?' Father Kelly said solemnly.

'The colliers started fighting each other in the theatre. The manager called in the police to throw them out and now they're fighting all over Dunraven Street. It's bedlam down there,' Sam said cheerfully, relishing the importance of his position as harbinger of bad news. 'The shopkeepers have pulled down the shutters they had fitted after the riots and closed up all their shops.'

'Dear God, it's over.' Annie O'Leary took a chair and sat next to Sali. 'It's finally over.' Only the night before Connie had confided that they only had two weeks credit left with their suppliers before the shop would have to be declared bankrupt.

'You're an educated man, Father, tell me what was it all for?' Mrs Gallivan cried. 'Everyone going hungry, women and children dying of starvation, men of broken heads. All this trouble and all this fighting. Men being gaoled and for what? Only for the miners to turn back now and take the crumbs they turned down ten months ago. We look like fools and not one collier's family will be a penny better off.'

'The men felt that they had to fight for better conditions and a wage to support their families with dignity, Mrs Gallivan,' Father Kelly observed sadly.

'They didn't succeed,' Mrs O'Casey said.

'They didn't know they were going to fail when they started out, and even if they had, I've a feeling that the best of them still would have tried. God willing, it will give them the experience and the courage to attempt to better their lot again some time in the future.'

'So we can starve again?' Mrs Gallivan returned.

'There's greater shame in accepting the injustices in life without protesting, Mrs Gallivan, than there is in trying – and failing – to alter them.' Father Kelly untied the apron he was wearing. 'Take over here for me please, Mrs Evans. It looks like I might be needed in Dunraven Street.'

'Victor, I heard about the way the vote went and the trouble up at the Empire. Are you all right?' Megan asked, when he called, as he had promised, at six o'clock.

'As all right as most of the others.' He stepped out of the shadows and she saw that he was sporting a fresh bruise on his cheek and his fists were raw and bloody. 'No one's badly hurt and the committee's already contacting management to call off the strike. It's my guess that they'll need a couple of weeks' grace to get the pits ready and then we'll all be back to where we were a year ago,' he added despondently.

'Sit down. Can I get you tea?'

'No, thank you, Megs. Mrs Palmer not around?' He looked around the kitchen as he sat at the table.

'She went up to help Mrs Morgan pack and bring her things down. Mrs Morgan is moving in, just for a few days, until . . . until Lena's funeral,' she added, making a heroic effort to control herself.

'As soon as I'm back in work, Megs, I want you out of here and living with us. I'll be able to send your father his fifteen shillings a week.'

'And pay the fine you're likely to get for assaulting a police officer as well?'

'If I can't do the two, I'd rather go to prison than have you carry on living and working here.'

'Mrs Palmer said now that the strike's settled, it'll only be a matter of time before they start moving the police out and the colliers back in here. And we've barely another year to go before my birthday.' She fished the chain holding her engagement ring out of the bodice of her dress and held it out to remind him.

'I wish it were tomorrow.' He pulled her on to his lap and buried his face in her red curls. After the stench of sweat and blood in the Empire, she smelled fresh and clean of the garden scents he loved, lavender, rosemary and rose petals. Closing his eyes, he held her close.

'Now that the strike is finally over, promise me you won't box again?' she pleaded.

'Not after we go back to work, Megs.'

'That's not good enough, I want you to promise that you won't, ever again.' She pushed him back and tried to look at him.

'I've a fight arranged next week.'

'Victor . . .'

'I've got to go.' He couldn't meet her eye. 'Some of the boys have cuts that need stitching. I'll see you on Saturday.'

'Jenkins and . . .'

'Johns, sir.' Gwyn Jenkins and another local constable crossed Pandy Square and stood to attention in front of Sergeant Martin.

'Do you know this person?' The sergeant indicated a man

snoring loudly in the gutter. Even from three feet away they could smell the stench of beer and vomit on his unwashed clothes.

'Mark Hardy, sir,' Gwyn revealed.

'The man whose wife and children died, and whose other children were put in the workhouse?'

'You know about that, sir?' Gwyn asked.

'Don't look so surprised, constable, you'd be amazed at some of the things I know about the people in this town,' the sergeant replied. 'Does he live around here?'

'The huts, sir.'

'Do you know which one?'

'Yes, sir.'

'Then take him home.'

'You don't want him arrested, sir?'

'I think the man's suffered enough, don't you, Constable Jenkins?'

Gwyn looked to his companion. 'You heard the sergeant,' he said, after Sergeant Martin walked away.

'I heard him, but I don't see him getting his hands dirty,' Johns complained. 'I'd as sooner touch a dead rat.'

'There's no use in whining.' Gwyn bent down. 'I'll take his feet, you take his head.'

'How come you get the end that's not likely to leak or spurt? Look, he's crawling with lice and fleas. God only knows when he last cut his hair and it's alive . . .'

'Moan, moan, moan, that's all you ever do, Johns,' Gwyn interrupted.

They lifted Mark Hardy gingerly, and stepping sideways, carried him to his front door. Kicking it open with his foot, Gwyn dropped Mark none too gently inside.

'The Lord only knows where he's getting the money to buy his drink, because he's nothing left to sell.' Gwyn looked round the bare hut, then down at Mark. 'Sweet dreams, sunshine, because as sure as hell, your life is anything but.'

Megan was almost too tired to think by the time she carried the last of the supper trays into the kitchen from the dining room. Mrs

Palmer and Mrs Morgan were upstairs in her bedroom, clearing out Lena's things. She had been sincere when she told them she preferred to work than face all the pretty clothes, shoes and small luxuries that Lena had bought herself with the first money she'd ever earned – and been so proud of.

She went into the back porch and pushed open the storeroom door. Huw Davies was still holding vigil over Lena's coffin. She had to call his name three times before he answered, and even then he refused her offer of tea and sandwiches, just as he had refused all of Mrs Palmer's offers of food and drink throughout the day.

She returned to the kitchen, scraped and stacked the dishes, and filled the enamel bowl in the sink with hot water from the kettle on the stove. Yawning, she reached for the box of soda crystals on the window sill and sprinkled a handful into the washing-up water. She found it difficult to keep her eyes open, and realized that in spite of her grief and misery, she was so exhausted she would sleep. And that meant she wouldn't be able to think about Lena – Victor's boxing – or anything else for that matter.

She kept moving, afraid that if she stopped, she'd fall asleep where she stood. She hadn't stopped working all day except for brief snatched meals, when she, Mrs Palmer and Betty Morgan had sat around the kitchen table, poking at the food Mrs Palmer had put on their plates, unable to eat for thinking about Lena, lying in her coffin in the room behind them.

Scraping all the leftover food on to one plate, she opened the back door, stepped outside and lifted the lid on the pigswill bin. As she leaned over the bin she thought she saw a shadow move alongside the wall of the ty bach behind her. She whirled around, and a sharp blow to her temple caught her off guard.

Crimson fireworks burst into the darkness. She opened her mouth intending to scream, but a hand clamped over it. She fought with every ounce of her strength, but a heavy weight on her back pushed her slowly, relentlessly to her knees. Hands closed around her neck, squeezing the air from her windpipe.

The fireworks faded, she had to fight for every breath, a grey mist clouded her eyes yet she was aware of a hand moving over the back of her legs, lifting her skirts and petticoats. She kicked wildly, hoping to topple the bin, to make a noise. But her feet hit thin air.

She heard the sound of her clothes tearing. A cold draught blew over her naked flesh. Hands plundered the secret places of her body. She dug her nails into the arm around her neck. Bit down on the hand in her mouth . . .

There was a moment's respite as her attacker moved. Her head hurt unbearably, but she forced herself to turn – just in time to see the lid of the bin hurtling down towards her in the light that pierced the darkness from the open doorway. It was thrust over her face, and she was sent reeling and twirling into a black void.

Huw Davies stroked Lena's face tenderly with his fingertips, willing her deep brown eyes to open and gaze back into his. But they remained closed, and it was then, when she continued to lie, cold and unresponsive, that the realization finally came to him that he hadn't spent the day sitting with Lena, but the shell she had occupied. Bone weary, he sat back on his chair. When he moved, the candle Mrs Palmer had brought in when it had begun to get dark, flickered, and the white walls of the storeroom swayed alarmingly inwards.

Light-headed and suddenly, desperately thirsty, he left the chair, and because his legs had gone numb, stumbled towards the door. Fighting the peculiarly disabling sensation of pins and needles, he wrenched it open and lurched into the back porch. The back door was wedged open, by something lying half in, and half out of the open doorway.

He stooped down. A naked woman was spread on her back, her skin startlingly white in contrast to the red scratches that marred her skin and dark pools of blood congealed around her breasts and thighs. Her clothes had been torn from her and shreds of cloth, spattered with blood, littered the porch and backyard. Her face and neck were hidden beneath the circular lid of a metal bin.

Heart thundering, nauseous, he murmured,' Please God, not again,' as he cautiously lifted the lid. Her face was a swollen mess, her lips bloody, her eyes closed, and there was a deep cut across her neck that looked as though a cord had been tightened around it, but there was no mistaking the rich, red-gold curls. Her lips parted and she moaned.

Uttering a fervent, 'Thank you, God,' he stripped off his tunic, covered as much of her as he could, scrambled to his feet and ran through the kitchen, shouting for Mrs Palmer.

Betty Morgan carried a tray of tea into Joyce Palmer's sitting room. Huw Davies was sitting on the sofa besides Lloyd Evans, both staring down at their boots, each sunk deep in their own thoughts. Sergeant Martin stood in front of the empty fireplace looking at Victor, who was leaning against the wall beside the curtained window. His back was turned to them, and he didn't turn his head when Betty entered.

'Sergeant Lamb would like to talk to you, Sergeant Martin, Constable Davies. He's in the lodgers' sitting room.' Betty poured a cup of tea, put five sugars and a dash of milk into it and handed it to the sergeant before pouring the same for Huw.

'Is the doctor still with Megan?' Lloyd asked.

'Yes.'

'Has he said how she is, Mrs Morgan?' Sergeant Martin questioned.

'Mrs Palmer came into the kitchen when I was making the tea. She said Megan's injuries are bad.'

'You only had to look at her to see that much.' Huw took his tea and walked unsteadily out of the door. The sergeant followed him.

Betty poured two more cups of tea, handed one to Lloyd and carried the other over to Victor. She nudged his elbow as she set it on the table in front of him. If he saw her, he didn't acknowledge her.

'Did Mrs Palmer say anything else, Betty?' Lloyd abandoned his tea on a side table.

'No, but I'm sure the doctor will be in to see you as soon as he's finished, as you're the nearest thing to a family Megan has in Tonypandy.' She opened the door and almost walked into Sergeant Martin, who entered and resumed his place in front of the cold hearth.

'I wanted to tell you that we are doing everything we can to catch whoever did this to Miss Williams, Mr Evans,' he said solemnly. 'We have every available man out in the streets. And it can only be a matter of time before we arrest her attacker – he is bound to be heavily bloodstained.'

Lloyd glanced at Victor, but his brother continued to lean, silent and unresponsive, against the wall. 'I hope you catch him before he does what he did to Megan to some other poor girl.'

There was no way of knowing whether Victor had heard him or not, as he kept his back turned to them. The sergeant went to the door. He opened it and the doctor appeared in the hall. Much to Lloyd's irritation they held a hurried and whispered conversation before the doctor joined him and Victor.

'How is she?' Lloyd rose from the sofa.

Victor finally turned around. 'Will she live?'

'I understand that you and Miss Williams were engaged, Mr Evans,' the doctor answered.

'Are engaged,' Victor insisted vehemently.

'I'll not lie to you; she's been the victim of the most vicious assault I've seen perpetrated on a young girl. She's sustained several blows to the head; one to her temple was particularly severe and probably caused her to lose consciousness. I don't think any bones are broken, but until she comes round, it's impossible for me to hazard a guess as to the extent of the damage to her brain.'

'Was she raped?'

The doctor was taken aback, not by the question, but by Victor's self-control. He might have been enquiring about the weather. 'She's been violated. Raped, torn and damaged. I've had to stitch wounds over her entire body and I've given her a strong sedative. She should sleep for at least twenty-four hours, but she'll be in considerable pain when she wakes. Mrs Palmer and Mrs Evans are washing and dressing her now. I'll call back in the morning.'

'No,' Victor broke in harshly. 'I've begged and pleaded with her to leave this house and she wouldn't. But I'll not leave her here one minute longer. I'm taking her home.'

'Mr Evans, I'd advise most strongly against moving her.'

'Victor only has to carry her up the hill,' Lloyd reminded him.

'The distance is immaterial. She needs rest, care and quiet.'

'Which she'll get in our house,' Victor affirmed. 'I'll wrap her in an eiderdown and keep her very still when I carry her.'

'If you're determined to move her, I suppose I could take her up to your house in my car. And she is sedated,' the doctor added, as if he were trying to convince himself that it was safe to move Megan.

'I'll run up to the house and ask Joey and Dad to make up the bed in the spare room. I'll be back to give you a hand to carry her up.' Lloyd gripped Victor's shoulder.

'There's no need, Mr Evans. I'm sure that your brother, wife and I can manage between us.'

Victor knocked on the door of the dining room, which Mrs Palmer had transformed into a makeshift surgery. Megan lay stretched out on a sheet that covered the table. Joyce and Sali had dressed her in one of Mrs Palmer's nightdresses because Joyce couldn't bear to rummage through Megan's things to look for a clean gown. They'd also wrapped her in a blanket. All that could be seen of her was her bandaged head, and Victor blanched when he saw the extent of the injuries to her face.

He slid his hands gently beneath the blanket and lifted her tenderly into his arms. Megan's head lolled towards his chest but otherwise she didn't move. Holding her close not to jar her, he carried her into the hall, past Sergeant Martin and outside to the doctor's car.

Sali walked up the stairs behind Victor. She could hear Lloyd, Mr Evans and Joey walking around the spare bedroom, and when she entered, Lloyd and Joey were straightening a tapestry blanket over the double bed they'd made up with clean sheets and blankets. Mr Evans was behind the door filling the jug on the washstand with water and Sali was touched to see that the men had forgotten nothing. They'd cut a piece of soap for the soap dish, set out a saucer of salt and a new toothbrush – the last one in the cupboard – and hung a clean flannel and towels on the stand.

Lloyd folded back the bedclothes and Victor lowered Megan into the centre of the bed. Sali helped him to settle her, still wrapped in Joyce Palmer's blanket, on the mattress and pillows.

'Leave the blanket around her,' Victor stopped Sali from folding it back. 'The doctor said we shouldn't move her more than necessary. And I'm sure Mrs Palmer won't mind if we keep it for a day or two.'

'It's a warm night,' Sali warned, as he covered Megan with the sheet, blanket and bedcover. 'We'd better fold some of the bedclothes back.'

'I was surprised the doctor allowed you to bring her back here.' Joey was holding on to the doorpost as if he couldn't trust himself to remain upright without its support.

'I certainly wasn't going to leave her where she was.' Victor touched Megan's hair, which was stiff with dried blood, and smoothed it back over the bandages.

'Look after her, boy.' Billy Evans laid his arm around Joey's shoulders and they went downstairs.

'Will you sleep with her tonight, Sali?' Victor asked.

Sali unbuttoned the top buttons at the neck of Megan's nightgown, folded back the blanket and thick bedspread to the foot of the bed and pulled the sheet to Megan's chin. 'It makes more sense for you to stay with her, Victor.'

'We're not married—'

'Only because her father won't give you permission. She's your girl. If you don't stay with her tonight, none of us will get any sleep for your pacing.' Lloyd took a box of matches from his pocket and set it beside the extra candle he'd laid next to the candlestick on the bedside cabinet.

'If you need me for anything in the night, Victor, just call out.' Sali straightened her aching back and rubbed it. 'I think I'll go to bed.'

'I'll join you in a few minutes, sweetheart.' Lloyd pushed the door closed after she left and looked from Megan to Victor. 'A word of advice.'

'What?' Victor asked grimly.

'If you want to keep your sanity, forget about whoever did this to Megan. Concentrate on her, on getting her well again, and leave it to the police to track the monster down.'

'The police!' Victor dismissed scornfully. 'She was living in a houseful of policemen. The chances are it was one of them who did this to her.'

'You can't go round making wild accusations, and there'll be hell to pay if one of the officers hears you saying that. If there's any justice in the world, Megan will be able to tell us who did this to her when she wakes.'

'And if she can't?'

'You have to leave it to the police,' Lloyd reiterated.

'I can't leave it, Lloyd. You have no idea how I fee . . .'

But there was a strange expression in Lloyd's eyes and Victor recalled the bruises Sali had sported when she had first come to live with them, her reluctance to disagree with anything that was said, or speak unless she was spoken to and above all, her pathetic eagerness to please everyone around her. It had taken months of coaxing just to get her to laugh at Joey's bad jokes.

'I know exactly how you feel, Victor,' Lloyd said. 'And, believe me, for both your sakes, the only thing you should be concerning yourself with now is getting Megan well again.'

Victor looked at his brother. 'I can't promise anything beyond that I'll try.'

'Just keep thinking about Megan, and how she'll feel when she wakes.' Lloyd left the room.

Victor stared down at Megan. Whatever the doctor had given her to make her sleep was working. She hadn't stirred since he had lifted her from the table in Joyce Palmer's dining room. He went to the window and opened the curtains. A full moon shone down from a clear night sky. He returned to the bed and shielded the candle with his hand. The moonlight was sufficient. He blew out the candle, stood still, stopped breathing and listened hard. Megan's chest rose and fell slightly as she took light, shallow breaths. Moving slowly and cautiously, he lay fully clothed on top of the sheet next to her. Turning on his side, he stared at her, and began to pray to the Virgin Mary and all the saints he could think of that she'd open her eyes and recognise him in the morning.

The shrill screech of a police whistle shattered the dawn calm of Pandy Square. The milkman's horse whinnied, backed in the shafts of the cart and reversed it as Constable Shipton charged out of Mark Hardy's hut. He blew his whistle again and beckoned to the police officers running into the square. Jenkins and Johns were the first to reach him, but Sergeant Martin was close on their heels.

'In here.' Constable Shipton pushed open the door. Johns retched when he saw Mark Hardy lying on his back in the middle of the empty hut, a cut-throat razor in one severed hand, his other hand connected to his arm only by a flap of skin. Blood had pumped out of his wrists, forming thick puddles on the floor and there were splashes on the walls around him.

'Look.' Shipton prised open the hand that was barely attached to Mark's arm and unwound a silver chain from his fingers. Entwined in the broken links was an engagement ring. 'It's Miss Williams', isn't it?' He looked to the officers around him for confirmation.

'I wouldn't know. I've never seen it before.' Gwyn Jenkins watched a louse walk along the razor held loosely by the severed hand. It stopped at a clot of blood.

'She used to wear it round her neck. Under her blouse,' Shipton reminded them.

'If it was under her blouse, how come you saw it, Shipton?' Sergeant Martin asked.

'I can't remember.' Shipton shifted his weight from one foot to the other. 'Probably when she was cleaning our bedroom, it must have fallen out of her collar.'

'Jenkins, you stay here.' Sergeant Martin looked up at the officers who'd been alerted by Shipton's whistle and were crowding around the door. 'The rest of you, back to the lodging house. Johns, get the undertaker, and close the door behind you. We don't want any more people tramping in here. It's not a bloody peep show.'

Johns nodded and did as the sergeant asked.

'Everyone knew this bloke was a lunatic,' Shipton gabbled. 'He went mad when his wife and kids died and the rest of his kids were taken to the workhouse. He was always sitting in his doorway, drunk as a lord, yelling about the Evans and blaming them for the strike and killing his wife. That's probably why he picked on Victor Evans' girl.'

'How come you decided to search this hut, Shipton?' Sergeant Martin asked quietly.

'I saw blood on the doorstep. You said that Miss Williams' attacker would be bloodstained. I put two and two together.'

'There are stains on your uniform, and scratches on your face,' the sergeant observed.

'I got caught up in the ruckus in the Empire. More blood flowed there this afternoon than in the slaughterhouse last week.' Shipton backed towards the door. 'Here, you don't think that I had anything to do with this—'

'This what?' Sergeant Martin looked him coolly in the eye.

'This suicide, and Miss Williams' attack. It's obvious, isn't it? Mark Hardy attacked her, stole her ring, came back here and slit his wrists.'

'Virtually cutting one hand off and then the other.'

'Yes,' Shipton agreed quickly.

'Bit difficult to cut one hand off when the other's severed from the arm, wouldn't you say?' The sergeant switched his attention from Shipton to Gwyn Jenkins. 'Jenkins, did you see this razor here when you dropped Hardy off yesterday evening?'

'No, sir, the hut was empty.'

'Completely empty? You're prepared to swear to that?'

'Yes, sir.'

'Those scratches on your face? How did you get them again, Shipton?'

'I told you, at the Empire—'

'I've never seen a collier with long fingernails, not even in the strike.' The sergeant picked up the razor with two fingers. He held it, still dripping blood over the floor. 'Yours, Shipton?' He eyed the constable. 'You attacked her, didn't you?'

'No!' Shipton blustered.

'You attacked her,' Sergeant Martin repeated.

Shipton wrenched the door open so hard the hinges tore out from the rotting wood.

'Why did you do it, Shipton?'

'She was just like that other one, begging for it. Wainwright agreed. He had the knickers off the other slut. All I wanted was my share.' He turned and started running.

'After him!'

Sergeant Martin and Gwyn Jenkins raced out of the hut. Shipton dived down a back street that led to the river. By the time they reached the bank, he had gone.

Even the doctor began to worry when Megan didn't wake the next day, or the day after that. On the third morning after Victor had carried her into the house, he opened his eyes to see that it was broad daylight. He'd slept for longer than he'd intended, but that was hardly surprising after two sleepless days and nights. Rain spattered against the window pane, signalling an end to the fine, warm spell of weather they had been enjoying. The light was grey, portending a damp, overcast day. He turned his head. Megan's eyes were open and she was looking at him.

'Good morning.' The blank expression in her eyes terrified him and he could barely hear himself speak for the beating of his own heart. The doctor had given him so many warnings of potential brain injuries . . . he held his breath, willing her to recognize him.

She looked from him to the room. Her bruised, swollen face creased in pain and from the desolate expression that filled her eyes, he saw that she remembered.

'You're safe in our spare bedroom.'

She looked at her arm and saw that she was wearing one of her own nightdresses. 'The yard . . . my clothes . . .'

'Betty Morgan packed your things and brought them up. Sali and I have been looking after you.' He took a deep breath. 'Did you see who attacked you?'

Tears fell from her eyes. 'I . . . tried to fight . . . I tried . . .' She fumbled at her neck. 'My ring . . .'

'We'll find it.'

'And if we don't?' she cried.

'Then I'll get you another.' He laid his hand lightly, tenderly around hers. 'I love you, Megs, I didn't realize just how much until I thought I'd lost you.'

'Victor, was I—'

'It doesn't matter, Megs. You're alive and we have each other, that's all I care about. We have one another and you're alive,' he repeated. He realized Lloyd was right. The only important thing was Megan.

'Victor—'

'Just get well, my love.' He brushed her forehead with his lips. 'I can't bear to see you like this. Please, get well.'

Chapter 22

TWO DAYS after Megan woke, the doctor pronounced her weak but out of danger and told her that she could sit up in a chair in the bedroom if she felt strong enough. Before the relief had time to sink in, Sergeant Martin arrived to question her. The only times Victor had left the bedroom was when the doctor had examined Megan, and Sali had helped her to wash and change her nightgown, and he categorically refused to allow Sergeant Martin to talk to Megan in private.

Victor set a chair at the furthest point from the bed as possible given the confines of the room and, leaving the dressing-table stool for Sali, sat next to Megan on the bed throughout the sergeant's interview. He was quickly irritated by the sergeant's manner and his repeated assertions that Megan had to recall something about her attacker.

'Megan has told you all she can remember, sergeant,' he broke in, when he could feel his temper rising. 'It's time you went so she can get some rest.'

But even as the sergeant closed his notebook and returned his pencil to his pocket, he persisted in his interrogation. 'You are absolutely certain that you never saw the man's face or anything else that could help us to identify him, Miss Williams?'

'I am sure, sergeant.' Megan was holding Victor's hand with both of hers. 'As I said, what little I can remember is confused and mostly pain, but I know that he hit me from behind and I never saw his face.'

Victor studied the sergeant. If he hadn't heard him declare that he would do all he could to track down and arrest Megan's

362

assailant, he could have sworn that Sergeant Martin looked positively relieved at Megan's failure to provide any clues.

'Miss Williams has had enough for one day,' Sali said firmly. 'She needs to rest.'

The sergeant finally left the chair. 'Thank you, Miss Williams, I know it couldn't have been easy for you to talk to me. Mr Evans,' he gave Victor a hostile glance.

Sali opened the door and stood rather pointedly holding it.

The sergeant stepped out on to the landing. 'It's a pity, Mrs Evans. Miss Williams was a sweet young girl. I'm not ashamed to admit that I admired her myself. And now,' he shrugged, 'she's absolutely ruined. Unfit for decent company.' He hadn't bothered to lower his voice and Sali fought the urge to push him down the stairs when he descended them, oblivious to Megan's sobbing in the bedroom behind them.

'You understand why I had to visit you as soon as I heard Miss Williams was making a recovery, Mrs Evans.' The Baptist minister, Mr Walker, took the cup of tea Sali handed him and looked around as if he were hoping for food. Obviously conversant with the routine of strike-affected houses, he had turned up on the doorstep just after she had lit the fire for the afternoon and Joey, Lloyd and Mr Evans, who had taken to walking as much as possible since he had been fitted with his artificial leg, had left to pick up Harry from school.

'I assume you came here to enquire after Megan's health, Mr Walker.'

'Of course,' he agreed, a little too heartily for sincerity. 'She is a member of our chapel and as her spiritual adviser it is imperative that I see her in her time of trouble.'

'The doctor has forbidden her to receive visitors for the time being so she can rest.' Sali was aware that the doctor's decision had been based more on Megan's devastation at the sergeant's remark and the gossip circulating around Tonypandy than any medical necessity.

'I have to caution her about staying in this house, Mrs Evans.'

'You don't think I'm qualified to take care of Miss Williams, Mr Walker?' Sali challenged.

'Your father-in-law is an atheist, his sons practising Catholics.'

'Only his younger sons. My husband holds the same views as his father,' Sali interrupted, incensed that the minister considered religious conventions more important than Megan's health.

'This really is a most unsuitable house for a Baptist to reside in.'

'You think it would have been preferable for Megan to remain in the lodging house where she was brutally attacked and raped, Mr Walker?'

'There is no need to use that word, Mrs Evans,' he rebuked.

'It is the unpalatable truth, Mr Walker. Megan was beaten and raped. She has not yet recovered from her injuries and she will remain here, under my care, until she does.'

'I must warn you, Mrs Evans, her father will not be pleased at your attitude or the thought of his daughter residing in this Godless house.'

'You have written to him?' Sali was already regretting that she had stretched the household rations to give the minister a cup of tea.

'I have no doubt that he knows of the misfortune that has befallen his daughter.'

'Misfortune is hardly the right word,' Sali said hotly.

'I advise you, most strongly, to return Miss Williams to Mrs Palmer's lodging house as soon as possible.'

'That is out of the question.'

The minister finished his tea and handed her his cup. 'If you will excuse me, I have others in my flock to attend to.'

'I know Mrs Palmer would appreciate a visit, Mr Walker. She, Mrs Morgan, Megan and Constable Davies have found it very hard to come to terms with Lena Jones' death. Her funeral is to be held tomorrow.'

'A self-murderer can command no Christian mercy, Mrs Evans. They have broken one of God's most important commandments: *Thou shalt not kill.* And the Bible informs us that they are condemned to burn in the fires of hell for all eternity.'

'Mr Walker,' Lloyd walked into the kitchen with Harry, 'You have come to enquire after Megan?'

'I came to give sound advice, Mr Evans, which your wife has seen fit to ignore.' The minister picked up his hat and went to the door.

Lloyd saw the minister out and returned to find Sali pouring tea for him and Harry. 'I've taught you well, sweetheart. You've finally learned how to upset chapel ministers.'

'Mr Walker doesn't think that a den of atheists and Catholics is a suitable place for a Baptist to convalesce.'

'Let me guess, he threatened to write to Megan's father?'

'He told me that Mr Williams is already aware of what's happened to her.'

'So aware that he hasn't written to enquire after her. How is Megan today?' he asked.

'Quiet. Victor went back up after the doctor's visit and hasn't left her since. Apart from helping Megan to wash and change and taking sandwiches, and after I lit the fire, tea up there, I've left them alone.'

'I wish there was more we could give them than privacy, but if there is I can't think of it.' He looked at Harry, who was sitting cross-legged on the hearthrug. He had set out his toy soldiers around Joey's old homemade fort and the new, small one Victor had made him and was engrossed in a pretend battle. 'Have you tried talking to her?'

'No.'

'Why not?'

'Because I know how she feels. She needs time to come to terms with what's happened, and Victor's the best person to help her.'

'There's gossip in the town,' Lloyd divulged.

'I know. Connie called. She told me some of the things that people are saying.'

'Don't listen to them, sweetheart. Tomorrow they'll have Lena's funeral to talk about and next week they'll move on and crucify someone else's reputation.'

'I know you're right.' She went to the sink and lifted a pan of potatoes that she had peeled on to the stove. 'I only hope that while they are still talking about Megan, no one says anything in front of Victor.'

'Can I get you anything else, Megan?' Sali emptied the bowl of water she'd used to wash Megan into the slop bucket beneath the washstand.

'No, thank you, Sali. You're so kind . . .'

'Kind nothing,' Sali patted her 'bump'. I'm looking for you to return the favour when this one decides to put in an appearance.'

'If I'm still here.' Megan fought back tears.

'And where else would you be, Megs?' Victor walked in, smelling of soap, his hair brushed and his dressing gown over his arm.

'If you need anything in the night, shout,' Sali kissed Megan's forehead before leaving the room.

'Victor, do you really want to carry on sleeping with me?' Megan asked, as he hung his dressing gown on the hook on the back of the door.

'You don't want me to?' He was clearly upset at the thought that she didn't.

'I'm better than I was. I don't need anyone to sit up with me.'

'Megs, I haven't been sitting up with you. We both slept reasonably well last night, or at least I did. Didn't you?' he asked anxiously.

'There's your father, brothers and Sali – they must think it strange. We're not married . . .'

'They're not hypocrites, Megs. We're engaged, they know what we got up to, and although there doesn't seem to be any permanent damage, you're still very weak and it makes sense for one of us to sleep with you. And,' he smiled, 'as Lloyd and Sali are used to sleeping together now, and my father has been suffering from insomnia since his accident, that only leaves Joey and me. Now which one of us would you prefer as a bedmate?'

Megan winced as she turned on to her side. She watched him unbutton his shirt. 'Victor, you do know that it can't ever be the same between us. Not after what's happened. That man—'

'Ssh!' He held his finger over her lips. 'I don't want you saying another word to me about what happened. I told you, it doesn't matter.' He sat on the bed, gathered her into his arms and stroked her hair. 'You did all you could to fight back, Megs. You have to keep remembering that it wasn't your fault. You – we – have to forget it.'

'And if I have a baby?' Her eyes rounded in fear as she looked up at him. 'I asked the doctor if I could have a baby. He said he didn't know . . . that I wouldn't know until . . .' She burst into tears. 'How can you bear to be near me? I'm not fit to be with decent people. I look at Sali and Lloyd, so happy about their baby, and I wonder how I'd feel if I had to carry the baby of someone who did that to me . . .'

'First, we don't know that you are having a baby and if you are, *you* won't be having it.' He swallowed hard, desperately trying not to think of the father. '*We* will be having it.'

'You'd bring up the baby of a man—'

'Like the doctor said, love, let's wait and see. If it comes, it won't be easy to cope with, and I won't pretend that it will. But first we have to get you well again, and once you are, we'll take the rest one day at a time.'

'You deserve someone better.'

'I want you, Megs. And no more talk like this. I love you, I need you and we are both going to get a good night's sleep. And, apart from the funeral tomorrow, I am not going to leave your side until I have to go back to work.'

'And then?' She looked up at him apprehensively.

'We'll live our life one day at a time until we can marry. It's the only thing we can do, and I promise you now, they'll be happy days. Very happy,' he reiterated forcefully in an attempt to make her believe every word he'd said.

Annie O'Leary walked into the Evans' kitchen the following morning, to find Joey, Lloyd, Mr Evans and Victor milling about in their best suits, getting under one another's feet as they took turns to comb their hair in the shaving mirror.

'I'll be glad when you all get back to work and start shaving and bathing in the cellar again,' Sali grumbled good-naturedly.

'Anything special you want me to do?' Annie asked Sali, who was pinning a jet mourning brooch into the neck of her black silk blouse.

'Nothing apart from keep an eye on Megan and Harry. He's enjoying his summer holidays from school, aren't you, poppet?' Sali stroked her son's cheek as he knelt in front of the easy chair reading the book he'd laid out on the seat, much to Joey's amusement. He could never understand why Harry always put the book in pride of place instead of himself.

'You're always good for Auntie Annie, aren't you, Harry?' Annie asked.

Harry smiled up at her.

'I hope everything goes well at that poor girl's funeral,' Annie said quietly.

'As do we all,' Sali breathed fervently. 'I doubt we'll be long. I've a feeling it'll be a short ceremony. Megan's up and dressed but we made her promise to stay in her bedroom until we come back. We don't want her to tire herself.'

'I'll just go up and say goodbye to her . . .'

'Again!' Joey reprimanded Victor. 'You've been up there ten times in the last ten minutes. You'll wear out the stairs.'

'If we're going, let's go,' Billy said impatiently, picking up his hat. He shouted, 'Goodbye,' up the stairs as he walked through the hall.

Megan left her chair and tottered unsteadily to the window to watch them leave. Victor was the last out of the door. He looked back at the house, saw her and waved. She returned his wave and sank weakly on to her chair.

It was odd how she felt so at home with Victor and his family. Her hand went to her throat and she fumbled at her neck, automatically looking for her engagement ring. It was ridiculous; she had only worn it for a few months, yet she had become accustomed to having it. She was furious with herself for having to fight back tears – again.

She had Victor's love, and like he said, the ring wasn't important, only what it stood for. Their relationship was as strong, if not stronger than it had ever been, even though her injuries meant that they couldn't make love. She cried so easily these days. She really felt that it was high time she made more of an effort for Victor's sake.

Half an hour after the Evans had left to attend the funeral there was a banging on the front door. Annie lifted Harry and the book she had been reading to him from her lap and went to open it. The chapel minister, Mr Walker, Sergeant Martin and a small, wizened man she'd never seen before were standing on the doorstep.

'Miss O'Leary.' The minister doffed his hat.

'Can I help you, Mr Walker?' she enquired, glancing warily at Sergeant Martin.

'We've come for Miss Megan Williams,' the officer informed her flatly.

'Come for . . . she's ill.'

'She's in need of moral protection.'

'And we're going to see that she gets it,' the small wizened man yelled.

'I don't understand.' Annie gazed at the men in bewilderment.

Megan appeared on the stairs. She gripped the banisters tightly, barely able to stand.

'That's my daughter,' Ianto Williams pointed at her. 'You have her birth certificate, sergeant. She's not twenty years old. I am her father and she has to do whatever I say.'

The minister saw doors opening up and down the street and the neighbours leaving their houses. 'The law is on your side, Mr Williams but it would be better if we do this quietly,' he muttered anxiously.

Sergeant Martin took charge of the situation. 'Miss Williams, you are in grave moral danger. By flaunting yourself, you have roused and provoked an unknown man to attack you. I myself have seen Mr Victor Evans in your bedroom when you were attired in only a nightgown. The neighbours are aware that you and the bachelor, Victor Evans, share a bedroom at night. You are a minor living in sin, and in accordance with your father's wishes, you will be removed to a place where you can receive moral and religious guidance.'

Brusquely warned by Sergeant Martin to stay out of affairs that did not concern her, Annie grasped Harry tightly while the officer, Ianto Williams and Mr Walker half bundled, half carried Megan into a hired brake. Crying tears of frustration and rage, furious at her own helplessness, she stood on the pavement and watched the vehicle drive away less than five minutes after the sergeant had knocked on the door.

'Harry looked after the brake in confusion. 'Auntie Megan's gone?'

'She's gone, Harry, and I don't know what your Uncle Victor is going to say about it.'

'He has no right to say anything,' Mrs Robinson shouted from across the road. 'The Evans are a disgrace and an affront to decent people. First Lloyd Evans lives openly with a woman before marrying her, and now Victor does the same. I am afraid to tell people where I live. It's got so a respectable person from this street can't hold their head up for fear of being tarred with the same mucky brush as the Evans women.'

'Don't worry, Mrs Robinson.' Annie gave the fat middle-aged woman a contemptuous stare. 'No one would ever mistake you for a woman a man would want in his bed.'

'But Mrs Palmer told me that Lena had taken out a penny a week burial insurance,' Sali insisted, as she and Lloyd walked along the road towards Trealow cemetery with his father and brothers.

'She may have taken it out, sweetheart, but the companies never pay in cases of suicide. Their argument against doing so is that too many people might see it as the only possible ticket to a decent funeral.' He covered her hand with his as she tucked it into his arm.

'So who is paying for the funeral?' Victor asked.

'Mrs Palmer, but she won't be too much out of pocket. Betty told me last night that the men in the lodging house held a collection that has covered the cost of the coffin and the grave, and

Huw Davies insisted on paying the undertaker for his services and the carriages, which only leaves the headstone and the funeral tea. And because it's unconsecrated ground, the headstone will have to be small and simple.'

'This has to be the largest gathering I've ever seen for a funeral outside consecrated ground,' Billy Evans commented, as they approached the crowd waiting on the path that led to the graves.

'Every police officer not on duty must be here.' Victor scanned the twin lines of uniformed men lining the path from the gates to the newly dug grave outside the cemetery boundary. He recognized most of Mrs Palmer's lodgers among the hundreds in the line-up, but although the police presence was strong, there were few civilians. Three tradesmen who supplied Mrs Palmer were there, including Connie (who had driven over with her delivery driver in the cart, because with Annie absent she was reluctant to leave the shop for any length of time) and four colliers who had lodged with Joyce before the house had been taken over by the police. All sporting bruises, as he and his brothers were, picked up during the fighting that had erupted in the Empire Theatre.

Ten minutes later, the black top hat of the undertaker came into view as he walked slowly up the road in front of the hearse pulled by a matching pair of sleek black horses with black plumes fixed to their heads. A single mourners' carriage followed. Six police officers in uniform stepped out of the lines, all tall and well built with ginger hair. They bore a strong resemblance to Huw Davies and Victor assumed that he had asked his brothers to act as bearers. The undertaker opened the glass panel at the back of the hearse and supervised the removal of the coffin. The men shouldered it.

Huw Davies left the carriage and helped Mrs Palmer, Mrs Morgan and a girl down. She slipped her small hand into Huw's and Victor recalled Megan telling him that Huw had a young sister. The undertaker led the way, the bearers with the coffin followed. Huw, Mrs Palmer, Betty Morgan and Huw's sister took the position of chief mourners along with Father Kelly and the Reverend Williams, who walked behind the coffin as 'friends of the deceased', the position forced on them by the edicts of their respective churches.

As the cortège moved slowly down between the lines of police to the open grave, the officers lining the route joined it. The coffin was lowered on to the carefully positioned ropes beside the newly dug pit and the officers removed their helmets. They grouped together in an obviously rehearsed stance. Sergeant Martin faced them in much the same way that a conductor faces a choir and, at a signal from him, they began to recite the Lord's Prayer.

Sali was glad of the veil that covered her face and hid her tears when the men followed the prayer with two beautifully sung hymns, 'The Lord is my Shepherd' and 'Love Divine'. The silence that followed was punctuated by sobs from Mrs Morgan and Huw's sister. Father Kelly and the Reverend Williams exchanged glances. The Catholic priest nodded to the undertaker, who signalled to the gravediggers. Four men moved either side of the pit, lifted the ropes and began lowering the coffin.

'All have sinned, and come short of the glory of God. There is none righteous, no not one,' Father Kelly recited in his rich Irish brogue. 'But we should not forget that God so loved the world that he gave his only begotten Son, that whosoever believeth in him should not perish, but have everlasting life.'

The 'Amen' that followed resounded in the still air, muffling the sound of the coffin hitting the earth at the bottom of the grave. Mrs Palmer, Betty Morgan and Huw's sister each threw a rosebud into the grave and Sali dropped the posy of rosebuds she'd cut that morning.

'Well,' Billy Evans said as he limped alongside Sali and his sons back towards the road, 'that was some funeral service, but I don't think it could be said to be Catholic, chapel or Anglican.'

'It was beautiful.' Sali laid her hands over her stomach. She could feel her baby moving within her and, remembering Megan's story of how Lena had been orphaned, prayed that she'd be able to give it a better life than Lena's parents had given her. She stopped and looked back from the gate. Huw Davies was standing alone at the edge of the grave watching the gravediggers filling it in. 'He shouldn't be by himself.'

'He's not,' Lloyd reassured. 'Look behind him.'

Huw's father, brothers and sister were waiting for him.

'Let's go home.' Victor felt that he had never needed Megan quite as much as he did at that moment.

'The bloody minister must have planned this,' Billy swore angrily as Annie fought back tears. 'He knew we'd be at the funeral, that there wouldn't be a man in the house.'

'Victor,' Lloyd stood in front of the door, blocking his brother's path, 'where are you going?'

'To see Mr Walker to find out where her father's taken her.'

'You confront Mr Walker in this mood and you'll be spending the next ten years in gaol,' Lloyd warned.

Victor eyed his brother then turned on his heel.

'Joey, stop him!' Lloyd shouted, as Victor headed for the basement door.

Joey did his best, but at six foot, he was six inches shorter and three stone lighter than Victor, who picked him up and set him to one side before opening the basement door and leaving.

Mr Evans reached for his cap. 'I still haven't got the hang of this leg. You boys run on ahead to the minister's and try to stop Victor from doing something he'll regret. Sali, you stay here,' he ordered, as she exchanged the veiled hat she'd worn to the funeral for her everyday one. 'We can't risk you getting involved in anything in your condition.'

Sali looked at Annie, who was still tearfully clutching Harry.

'I shouldn't have let them take her . . .'

'You couldn't have stopped them, Annie,' Sali comforted her. 'Megan's father had the law on his side, a police sergeant to enforce it and Mr Walker as his witness.'

'What do we do now?' Annie asked.

Sali set her mouth into a thin grim line. 'We wait.'

'The minister isn't in,' Mrs Walker snapped when she opened her front door to see Victor filling her small porch.

Victor pushed his foot in the doorway when Mrs Walker tried to close the door. 'Then I'll wait until he comes back.'

'Not in this house, you won't, I don't allow strangers inside.'

'What time are you expecting him?'

'I'm not. Jenny?' Mrs Walker shrieked to her maid of all work. 'Go out the back door and run to the police station to fetch a constable. Tell him we have trouble at Mr Walker's house.'

'I need to see the minister urgently,' Victor pleaded. 'He has taken my fiancée . . .'

Lloyd looked up the hill and saw Victor shouting at Mrs Walker on the porch of her detached villa.

'You know what he's like when it comes to anything to do with Megan. We'll never calm him down.' Joey ran alongside Lloyd as he quickened his pace.

'I doubt that Mr Walker took her to his house. I'll see what I can do here. You go down to the station and see if they've already left Tonypandy by train.'

'They could have gone by tram.'

'Whatever,' Lloyd countered impatiently. 'Annie said they left the house in a hired brake. Someone must have seen them.' He charged up the hill towards Victor, who was still shouting at Mrs Walker. Lloyd lifted his hat and slowed his step as he walked up the steps to Mrs Walker's front door.

'I've sent for the police.' She tried to slam the door again, but Victor refused to move his foot.

'Victor,' Lloyd touched his brother's arm, 'I think Mrs Walker wants to close her front door.'

'And I want to see Mr Walker,' Victor repeated obdurately.

'I am sure that Mrs Walker can have no objection to us waiting on the road for her husband.' Lloyd smiled at the minister's wife.

Victor looked at the woman and realized he'd terrified her. He moved his foot and lifted his cap. 'I'm sorry, Mrs Walker but—'

The door slammed in his face.

'I sent Joey to the station to see if he can find out where the hired brake took Megan and her father.'

The anger that had sustained Victor ebbed and he sank down on the doorstep in despair. 'It's as Annie said. Megan's father had Sergeant Martin with him. That man does everything by the book.

The law is on their side. She's her father's daughter and he can do whatever he wants with her.'

'Whatever we think of Mr Williams, or however misguided he is, he must care for Megan and sincerely believed that he is doing what is best for her.'

'Do you really think that?' Victor questioned acidly. 'You heard Annie. The Sergeant said Megan was in need of moral protection. You know what that means. They could put her into a correctional ward in a workhouse and even if I find her I'd have no right to take her out. Not until she is twenty-one and perhaps not even then if her father has had her committed.'

'He could have taken her home.' Lloyd sat beside him.

'And pay for her keep?' Victor dismissed cynically. 'All he's interested in, all he has ever been interested in, are the postal orders Megan sends him.'

'Well, there won't be any more of those.'

'If I had money I could try to buy him off, but as much as he loves money I doubt he'd take it from a Catholic.' Victor rose to his feet and dusted off the back of his trousers when he saw the maid, Jenny, walk up the steps accompanied by a constable.

'We've had a report of a disturbance here,' the constable informed them officiously.

'We are waiting for Mr Walker. He removed a young girl from my father's house this morning,' Lloyd interposed. 'And we are concerned for her safety.'

'Constable.' Mr Walker opened his front door and joined them.

'Mr Walker,' Victor crossed his arms and looked at him. 'Mrs Walker said you weren't in the house.'

'I have just walked in through the back door.' He turned to the constable. 'Sergeant Martin, whom I'm sure you know, and I helped a young girl's father to remove her from Mr William Evans' house this morning because she was in a morally precipitous situation. Her father is her legal guardian.'

'How old was the girl?' The constable unbuttoned the breast pocket on his tunic and removed a notebook and pencil.

'Under twenty and she was in moral danger.'

'And she is now with her father?' The constable scribbled a note.

'She is.'

'Where?' Victor demanded.

'Somewhere where she will receive care and Christian guidance and you will never find her.'

'Victor!' Lloyd pulled his brother back as he towered over Mr Walker.

'I will find her, Mr Walker, and if she has been harmed or humiliated in any way, I will be back here to make you pay for what you did this morning.'

'You heard him, constable, he's threatening me,' the minister squeaked. 'His name is Victor Evans. He's a criminal—'

'I will do a lot more than threaten you if you've hurt Megan.' Victor advanced on the minister.

Mr Walker retreated and crashed backwards into the wall of his house. 'I'm injured, send for the doctor,' he cried, rubbing the crown of his head.

The constable put his hand on Victor's arm. 'You'd better come with me.'

'You're arresting him?' Lloyd looked from Mr Walker to the constable.

'Threatening behaviour and bodily harm,' he confirmed.

'Victor never touched Mr Walker,' Lloyd protested.

'But he caused him injury. That's bodily harm.'

'Take him away.' Mr Walker ran into his porch. 'And if any of you Evans's come round here again, I'll send for the police. I'll see the lot of you in gaol for corrupting that girl.'

Lloyd ran his hands through his hair. 'Dear God, Victor, I begged you to stay home.'

'You can't keep me away from Victor forever. I love him and he loves me—'

'Any more fuss from you, girl, and I'll put you in the workhouse and tell them to throw away the key,' Ianto Williams warned Megan, as they sat in a third-class carriage.

'Where are you taking me?'

'That's for me to know, and you to find out. But don't for one minute think that I didn't mean what I said about the workhouse. You're under twenty-one and I can do what I like with you.'

'I haven't even a change of clothes.'

'You won't need one where you're going,' her father interrupted ominously. 'Now sit quiet. I can't think for all your jabbering.'

Any hopes Megan had of running away from her father faded when they reached Cardiff station. A woman and two men were waiting for them. The woman and a man moved either side of her, grabbing her arms and holding her tight. Her father and the other man went into the waiting room. They emerged a few minutes later. Her father walked away without a backward glance. She was hustled down the steps that led from the platform and up another flight. A train was waiting. The men pushed her into a carriage. The woman sat beside her, a whistle was blown and they moved off.

'Gwyn Jenkins came up to the house. He told me that Victor is in court again tomorrow?' Mr Evans caught up with Lloyd outside the police station.

'Unfortunately,' Lloyd confirmed.

'This is one instance I can't send for Geoffrey Francis, unless he's prepared to defer payment until we start back in the pit.'

'Given the amount of work our family has put his way lately, I'm sure he'd be happy to do that. Victor's going to need a good solicitor. He didn't hit Mr Walker, but he did threaten him, unfortunately in front of a constable, his wife and me, so even I could be called as witness for the prosecution. And he frightened Mr Walker into backing into a wall. Apparently, technically at least, that constitutes bodily harm.'

'What about extenuating circumstances? He was looking for his fiancée.'

'Who is under age and in the guardianship of her father,' Lloyd reminded.

'So it's not looking good.'

'That's putting it mildly. Look, there's Joey, I sent him down the station to see if he could find out where the brake took Megan and her father. Any luck?' Lloyd asked his younger brother.

'They caught the Cardiff train, but as Phil station said, they could have got off anywhere on the way, Porth, Ponty, or even changed in Cardiff to get a train to Swansea. I heard about Victor, dull,' a constable passed them and Joey tempered his language, 'idiot. Magistrates court in the morning, I suppose.'

'It's become a family tradition,' Billy Evans agreed sourly.

'Sali must be worried sick. I'm going home.' Lloyd lifted his hat to a group of women who passed them.

'I'll call in the County Club on the way; we're hoping to hear something from management today on when the pits will reopen. I'll see you back at the house later.'

'If you like, I'll come up to the County Club with you, Dad.'

'I'm seeing to union business. There's no money for drinking,' Mr Evans warned.

'With Lloyd needing to spend more time with Sali, I thought I could take over some of his work,' Joey said.

'You volunteering to help the union?' Billy said in amazement.

'Yes.'

'Never let it be said that I turned away a volunteer. Let's go and quickly, before you change your mind.'

'I'll go down to Pontypridd tomorrow and see Mr Richards.' Sali dropped the last potato she'd peeled into a saucepan of water.

'My father intends asking Geoffrey Francis if he'll take the case, so there's no need to involve Mr Richards.' Lloyd looked around the kitchen. 'Where's Harry?'

'Playing on the mountain with Dewi and a gang of small boys. They called after you left and informed me that they were off to discover a new world. I told them that I hoped it would be an improvement on this one, made them a couple of jam sandwiches, gave them a bottle of water and sent them on their way.'

'I hope they succeed. This world is looking pretty miserable at the moment.' Lloyd sat on the easy chair.

'I thought it might be worth asking Mr Richards if he could try to find out where Megan's father has taken her. I had a long talk

378

with Annie after you left, went over everything she could remember and I have a feeling, from what the sergeant said about Megan needing moral guidance, they've put her into a workhouse.'

'And I think her father is too fond of money to put her somewhere where she won't be earning any money, but even if he has put her in a workhouse, there's nothing we can do about it, sweetheart. Her father's her legal guardian.'

'Housekeepers looking for staff go to workhouses to recruit girls.'

He gave her a small smile. 'Housekeepers like Mari?'

'Precisely, if we find out where Megan is.'

'Clever girl.' He patted his lap. 'Come here for five minutes.'

Sali looked down at her swollen body. 'The two of us are too big for you.'

'Rubbish.' He grabbed her hand and pulled her down as she tried to pass his chair. Wrapping his arms around her, he rested his hands lightly on her bump. The baby moved and he smiled. 'Did you feel that?'

'I'm pregnant not insensitive, Lloyd.'

'She's going to be a dancer.'

'Or a footballer.'

'It will be a girl, you mark my words.'

She fell serious. 'I only hope Megan will be around when he or she arrives in six weeks I was counting on her to help.'

Chapter 23

EVERY MUSCLE in Megan's body ached. She was in pain, completely exhausted but worst of all, she had absolutely no idea where she was. The men had pulled the blinds on their carriage windows so she hadn't been able to read the signs at the stations they'd passed through. And, as they hadn't left the train until after darkness had fallen and she had been hustled straight into a van, she hadn't been able to read any signs at their destination. They had driven for what seemed like hours, and now, as she stared up at the grey, forbidding mansion in front of her, she wanted to sink to the ground and cry.

There were bars at every window, and she counted four locks as well as bolts being drawn back when one of the men tugged at the bell pull on the front door. They stepped inside and the man who had admitted them proceeded to lock the door behind them.

'The girl Mr Walker recommended?' A woman in a matron's uniform walked down the corridor to meet them.

Megan had to strain to hear her. The noise level was unbearable; high-pitched screams, cries and moans echoed into the high-ceilinged hall that was lit by a single inadequate gas lamp. She clapped her hands over her ears.

'You'll get used to the noise.' The woman who had accompanied her finally broke her silence.

'Where am I?' Megan ventured.

'In an asylum.'

'My father has had me committed to an asylum?'

'You are not mad, are you?' the matron asked.

Megan shook her head.

'Good, because you will be employed here as a maid.'

'A maid.' Megan breathed a heady sigh of relief. She'd get days off, she would find out where she was and get a letter to Victor . . .

'We've paid your father in advance for your services. You will get time off but you will not be permitted to leave the building and the walled garden. There is no point.' The matron gave her a cold smile that failed to reach her eyes. 'It is over twenty miles to the nearest farmhouse, thirty to the village.'

The following morning Victor appeared before Porth magistrates, who listened to Geoffrey Francis's pleas and released him on condition that he stay away from Mr Walker's house, and pay a bail of fifty pounds, which to his shame, Sali arranged to borrow from Mr Richards against the ring that the solicitor hadn't, as yet, managed to sell for her. He returned home from the court morose, silent and determined to travel to the Swansea Valley to ask Megan's father what he had done with her.

'If someone doesn't go with Victor, he could end up on another charge of threatening behaviour, or creating a disturbance and assault,' Sali warned Lloyd, when Victor went upstairs to pack a spare shirt.

'We don't have enough money to pay one train fare to the Swansea Valley, let alone two,' Lloyd pointed out. 'And as Victor is determined to walk and get rides where he can, he's better off going alone.'

'If I wasn't pregnant you'd be going with him.'

'But you are pregnant, Sali,' Lloyd said logically.

'Sali's right,' Billy Evans said flatly. 'Victor can't be trusted to go alone.'

Although Lloyd was glad that his father was reasserting his authority and resuming his place as head and mentor of the family, he was concerned at the thought of leaving Sali. The baby wasn't due for weeks but the warm weather had taken a toll on her health. 'I can't leave Sali, and you can't go with him because you're needed to finalize the arrangements for the reopening of the pits with management. There's no use in Joey going because he's even more headstrong than Victor,' he added, glad that Joey was delivering goods for Connie and wasn't there to argue with him.

Sali glanced at Victor when he returned to the kitchen carrying his haversack. 'If you can wait until tomorrow morning, Victor, we'll use the carriage from Ynysangharad House to travel to the Swansea Valley.'

'The carriage? Sali, are you mad?' Lloyd exclaimed. 'It's fifty miles or more and even that depends on which part of the Swansea Valley Megan's father lives in.'

'We'll go over the Bwlch.'

'And where do you suggest we stay the night?' Lloyd enquired. 'Inns cost money and even if we manage to stay awake, the horses will be tired.'

'I'll borrow more money from Mr Richards. It is an emergency.'

Victor looked so miserable that for once Mr Evans decided to break the family's cardinal rule of not using Sali's money for the family. 'Whatever you borrow from Mr Richards, Sali, we pay back.'

'That won't be a problem when you are all working again, Mr Evans.'

'Time you started calling me Dad. And what about Harry?' he added, without giving her time to absorb what he'd said.

'He'll come with us – Dad,' Sali smiled. 'We'll make it the holiday we didn't have last year or this. You'd like to ride in a carriage to the Swansea Valley with your father, Uncle Victor and me, wouldn't you, Harry?' Sali asked her son. 'We'll see lots of things along the way. Farms, cows, horses, wagons, strange places we've never been to before.'

Harry knew something was very wrong with the way that his Auntie Megan had left the house. Since she'd gone, his Uncle Victor had been miserable and had stopped playing with him, but his mother was smiling for the first time since his auntie had left and that had to be good. 'Yippee, a holiday.' He smiled at Victor, but his uncle wasn't looking at him.

'Sali, I can't expect you to travel all the way to the Swansea

382

Valley in the carriage in your condition. Lloyd can come with me,' Victor protested

Billy studied Sali for a moment. 'You never moan or complain like most women in your condition. Tell me, how is that granddaughter of mine?'

'He's fine,' Sali teased.

'He's not going to like being called Isabella,' Lloyd chipped in.

'No more than I like being called Sebastian,' Victor complained.

'Seeing as you only hear it whenever the police arrest you or in court, let's hope you won't hear it too often again,' his father said wryly. 'Sali, if you're sure you're up to the journey, I think it's a good idea that you go with Lloyd and Victor. Joey couldn't go with you anyway because he has Connie's deliveries to see to in the morning.'

'Thank you for agreeing with me,' Sali said sincerely. 'A woman in my condition is bound to get more sympathy than either of you two.' She glanced from Victor to Lloyd. 'And before you say another word, I have more tact and diplomacy in my little finger than you two have in your entire bodies. Lloyd, why don't you go down to Pontypridd tonight, see Mr Richards, tell him what we want to do, borrow the money we'll need and arrange for the carriage to be here at six o'clock tomorrow morning. That way we can get an early start.'

'Here.' Victor put his hand in his pocket and pulled out a shilling. He gave it to Lloyd.

'What's this?'

'Train fare to Ponty.'

The next morning dawned, bright and clear, with a fine mist on the mountain tops that heralded a fine day. Lloyd had warned Sali that Mari was packing a picnic hamper, so she left what food there was in the house for Joey and Mr Evans. She secreted ten of the twenty sovereigns Mr Richards had insisted on loaning Lloyd, although he'd only asked for five, in her purse, checked the changes of clothes she had packed 'in case' and was waiting impatiently when the coachman, Robert, brought the carriage to a standstill outside the house at five minutes to six.

'We've a fine morning for our trip, Mrs Evans,' he greeted her as she left the house ahead of the others.

'We have, Robert.'

'It's a long time since the carriage has been further than Pontypridd so Mr Jenkins thought there should be two of us.' He pointed to the boy sitting alongside him on the box. 'This is Simon.'

'Pleased to have you with us, Simon,' Sali smiled.

Lloyd lifted Harry into the carriage, helped Sali in and took the seat beside her. Victor sat opposite them next to the window. He leaned back lest anyone recognize him, and rag him about riding in an expensive carriage drawn by thoroughbred horses. Harry had no such compunction. He pushed down the window and would have fallen out if Lloyd hadn't held on to him as they set off at a brisk trot.

It took them an hour and a half to negotiate the narrow roads of the Rhondda villages that led up to the steep mountain track road that wound up the Bwlch. Robert held the horses steady and when they reached the top, Sali insisted on stopping for a picnic. Robert lifted down the hamper Mari had packed for them and Sali spread out the cloth and set out plates of chicken and ham sandwiches, an enormous bowl of salad, one of Mari's veal and ham pies, and two apple tarts.

'This is some breakfast. Even if we get lost we're not going to go hungry.' Lloyd took one of the thick, pressed-glass tumblers Sali had filled with Mari's homemade lemonade.

Robert and Simon accepted Sali's offer of food, but insisted on sitting apart from them to eat. Sali didn't argue with them, and she stopped Lloyd from forcing them to reconsider their decision.

'You may believe in a classless society and equality, but they have to go back to Ynysangharad House.'

'And your brother and mother.' Lloyd brushed the crumbs from his suit and called to Harry, who was watching rabbits play around the grazing sheep.

'If we had the dogs, Uncle Victor, we could have rabbit pie.'

'That's my boy.' Victor was more animated than he had been

since they'd returned from the funeral to find Megan gone. Sali only hoped that their journey wasn't going to be as fruitless as she and Lloyd suspected it might well turn out to be.

'Ladies to the left, boys to the right,' Lloyd said, when Sali began to pack up the remains of the food into the basket. 'You all right, sweetheart? You look pale.'

'Only under this sunshine. Time we left if we're going to get to the Swansea Valley before nightfall.'

They pulled into the yard of an inn at six o'clock. Lloyd went in to check the address Sali had found among Megan's papers. When he returned, he asked Robert and Simon to take the hamper and valise into the inn before they walked the horses around to the stables.

He opened the door, and lifted Harry down. 'Apparently this is the nearest inn to Ianto Williams's farm.'

'I bet they would have told you that even if it wasn't.' Victor was obviously on edge now they had almost reached their destination.

'The landlord said it's only a mile up the road. I think that we should leave the carriage here and hire a trap from the inn. If Megan is at the farm they'd hide her as soon as they caught a glimpse of the carriage. Whereas the trap is at least local.'

'I've already met Mr Williams so I think I should go up there alone.' Sali brushed the creases from her maternity suit. 'He's always been antagonistic towards you, Victor, but he may talk me.'

'You can put that thought right out of your head, Sali Evans,' Lloyd declared firmly. 'You're not going up there alone and that's final. And unlike Victor, I haven't met the man so he's just as likely to talk to me as you.'

'A pregnant woman is less threatening.'

'I can be nice.' Lloyd straightened his collar and tie.

'If she's there . . .' Victor's voice trailed at the thought that Megan might not be.

'We'll try to spirit her away,' Sali promised, 'and if she's not, I'll do my very best to find out where she is.'

Just as the landlord had said, Ianto Williams' hill farm could be seen from the road, a long, low, grey stone building nestling into the curve of a horseshoe-shaped hill. The mountain behind it and the long slope that led up to it were dotted with sheep. Lloyd slowed the pony and trap to walking pace when they left the road for the rough track in an attempt to avoid the ruts and potholes, but he wasn't always successful and he was very aware of Sali's condition when she gripped the side of the cart whenever they negotiated the worse bumps.

'This isn't doing Isabella any good,' he commented after the wheel went over a particularly large stone only to sink straight afterwards into a rut.

'She's enjoying the fresh air.'

'Ah, you admit, she's a girl.'

'Not at all.' Her eyes sparkled in the golden light of the setting sun. 'Just tired of a futile argument. When Will arrives—'

'Will?'

'William Lloyd Joseph Victor Evans.'

'Poor soul. I'm glad she's Isabella.' He reined in the horse as they entered the farmyard.

'Let me do the talking.'

He saw two children standing in front of a chicken coop but it took him a few seconds to recognize them. 'Try to have a word with Daisy and Sam first, and ask them not to call me Mr Evans. If Megan's father overhears them, it might put paid to any chance we have of getting her out of here before we even start.' He tied the reins together, jumped down and walked around to help Sali to the ground.

'Mrs Jones.' Daisy ran towards her and Sali was appalled by the difference in the young girl. She'd grown since the last time she'd seen her but her dress was ragged and far too small for her. Sam's clothes weren't much better and full of holes. Both children looked thin, undernourished and filthy.

'Daisy, it's lovely to see you.'

'You come from our dad to get us?' Daisy questioned hopefully.

'No, Daisy, I'm sorry. I haven't heard from your father.'

'You lost?' A woman came out of the back door and Sali fought to keep her equanimity. She felt as though she were looking at

386

Megan, but a Megan who had been worn down by half a century of hard living. She was painfully thin and her skin was heavily creased and worn, like the leather in an old pair of shoes. Her eyes were green like Megan's but they were dull and lifeless, and although her hair had threads of the same marvellous red-gold they were vastly outnumbered by the grey and white hairs.

'I'm Sali . . . Jones,' Sali only just remembered that the surname Evans would be instantly recognizable after all the appeals Megan had made to be allowed to marry Victor. 'Mrs Sali Jones. This is my husband Lloyd. We are friends of Megan's.'

'She's not here.' The woman looked nervously over her shoulder.

'We were hoping that you could tell us where she is. As you can see,' Sali looked down at her swollen figure, 'I am going to need a nursemaid soon and my husband and I were hoping that Megan would be free to take the position.'

'She has a job.'

'Perhaps we could tempt her with extra money,' Sali persisted.

'My husband will be back from the fields any minute and he doesn't like strangers.'

'But we're not strangers, Mrs Williams. I met your husband when he came to Tonypandy to see Megan.'

'I told you she's not here.' Mrs Williams became quite agitated. 'Now go, before he sees you.'

Lloyd glimpsed movement out of the corner of his eye. Sali turned to see Ianto Williams walking down the mountain towards the yard. His trousers were still held up by string and tied beneath the knees and he was wearing the same threadbare jacket that he had been the last time she had seen him. She went to the gate to meet him.

'Mr Williams.' She extended her hand as he approached, 'I don't know if you remember me.'

'Mrs Jones, isn't it?' He looked pointedly at her swollen figure. 'You said you were a widow.'

'I was a widow, I remarried last Christmas.'

'They came to offer Megan a job, Ianto,' his wife broke in.

'She's got one,' he barked gruffly.

'That's what I told them, Ianto.'

'So good day to you.'

'Just a moment.' Lloyd wrapped his arm around Sali's shoulders. 'My wife and Miss Williams were good friends. She would like to write to her. If we could have her address—'

'No point, she's not in a place where she's allowed to have letters.' Ianto whistled to his dogs. 'Now get off my land before I set the dogs on you.'

Sali looked back at Daisy and Sam, as Lloyd helped her into the trap. He climbed into the driver's seat and turned the horse around. The last thing Sali saw was Daisy waving a handkerchief with a daisy embroidered on the corner. The small girl looked lost, forlorn and frightened, with Mr Williams and his dogs standing behind her.

'Ay, I remember Megan Williams.' The potman set a tray of three lamb dinners and a half-sized plateful for Harry on their table in the dining room of the inn. 'She was a pretty girl. But her father sent her away years back, to keep house for his brother-in-law in the Rhondda.'

'Then you haven't seen her lately?' Victor took the jug of water and filled everyone's glass.

'Not since we were in the same class in school. I missed her when she went. She was good too, not like the rest of us. Teacher said she could have gone far, perhaps even been a teacher herself. Nice girl as well as pretty. There was no one like Megan for smoothing over a quarrel before it got started. But then, that's Ianto Williams for you. He couldn't wait for his children to start earning so they could send money home. He took his two boys out of school to put them on a farm over Ammanford way. His girls are in Madame Patti's place.'

'The opera singer?' Lloyd asked in surprise.

'She owns the castle up the road towards Brecon, Craig y Nos. Mind you, after all the improvements she's made to the place it looks more like a mansion than a castle now. Money no object, or so people who've been in there say. The best of everything goes through her gates – food, furniture, carpets. Even her servants' uniforms are better than most people's best clothes. Her staff have their own cook and get three hot meals every day. I should be so lucky.' He dropped his voice when he saw the landlord glaring at him. He lifted the four plates from the tray and set them in front of them.

'Can I get you anything else?'

'No, thank you.' Sali reached for the pot of mint sauce on the table. 'Are our coachmen all right?'

'Eating mutton chops and drinking beer in the bar. They seemed happy enough with the room I showed them over the stables.'

'Thank you, you've made us very welcome.' After the man left, Sali looked from Victor, who was crushed, to Lloyd. 'So, what do we do now?'

'What can we do, except eat this, stay here tonight and go home tomorrow?' Lloyd leaned over the table and cut the lamb on Harry's plate into bite-sized pieces.

'You're sure that Ianto Williams told you Megan had a job?' Victor finally picked up his knife and fork but made no attempt to eat.

'I'm sure, Victor,' Sali replied.

'And you offered to pay Megan more money if she worked for you?'

'We did,' Lloyd said.

Pushing his untouched plate aside, Victor went to the dresser where the man who had served them was polishing cutlery. Concerned that the potman might feel intimidated by Victor's size and attitude, Lloyd followed.

'You have a problem, sir?' The potman looked warily at Victor.

'Not with the food. Do you know if there's been a hiring fair in Brecon in the last couple of days?'

'Yesterday, sir, so you've just missed it. There won't be another for six months.'

'What happens at these fairs?' Lloyd asked.

'Every worker who wants a job lines up in Ship Street, and the farmers come down and pick out the people they want – dairy maids, shepherds, cowmen, or whatever they're short of. They take them for six months or, if the workers are lucky, a full year.

389

But there's not many farmers willing to pay people through the winter months when there's so little work for them to do.'

'And the wages?' Victor questioned.

'Are agreed and paid in advance.'

'In advance? You're sure about that,' Victor said carefully.

'There's many a small farmer around here who has managed to build up a flock of sheep or add to a herd of cows on what he's brought in by selling his son or daughter's labour for six months or more.'

'Does anyone keep records of who goes where?' Lloyd glanced back at Sali and Harry. She pointed down to his and Victor's plates to remind him that their meals were getting cold.

'Bless you, no, sir, it's all done quiet like between the farmer and the people they hire.'

'How big are these hiring fairs?' Victor had seen Sali signalling to them, but he ignored her and his meal.

'Young Bill over there has just taken on a shepherd from Brecon. Bill?' The potman called, 'Were there many people at the hiring in Brecon this week?'

'Hundreds,' shouted back young Bill, who had to be at least forty.

Lloyd walked over to him. 'Can we buy you a drink, Mr . . .'

'Hughes. Ay, I don't mind if I do have another pint.' He drained his glass and handed it over.

'Did you see a girl at the hiring?' Victor opened his wallet and extracted a smaller version of the framed studio portrait of Megan that stood on his bedside table.

'Hundreds.'

'This one is special, pretty girl with long, red-gold hair.' Victor set the photograph on the table in front of the man. 'Her name's Megan Williams, she's from around here.'

'Place was teeming with girls, young man, but no pretty ones.' He picked up the photograph, studied it and shook his head. 'But then they get snapped up early, so even if she was there, it could be that she was hired before I arrived. Some of the farmers round Brecon don't see a soul from one year to the next unless they make an effort to go into town on market day. Pretty girl like this,' he gave Victor a sly wink as he returned the picture, 'is worth a lot, especially to the unmarried farmers and their farmhands. If you understand me.'

Lloyd gripped Victor's right arm to stop him from thumping the man, and they returned to their table and their meals.

'We have to go back to Tonypandy tomorrow. With luck, the pits will reopen in the next few days and we're not expecting more than twenty-four hours notice to start work,' Lloyd reminded his brother.

'I have to find Megan,' Victor insisted stubbornly. 'She hadn't recovered from her injuries. If she's not being looked after, anything could happen to her. And I can't bear the thought . . .' He turned his head, but not before Sali and Lloyd saw the torment in his eyes.

'You'll get Sunday off next week,' Lloyd sympathized. 'The trains run to Brecon, so we'll borrow more money from Sali and I'll go up there with you. We'll both ask around. Someone might remember seeing her.'

'One young girl among hundreds,' Victor whispered despondently.

'I'll ask Mr Richards to send someone to Brecon to look for her. We'll get copies of her photograph so he can show them to people,' Sali suggested. 'If she was there, Victor, someone is bound to have seen her.'

Victor left the table, his meal scarcely touched. Lloyd laid his hand on Sali's shoulder to stop her from going after him. 'He needs time to himself. I suggest we finish our meal and go to bed. We have to be away by six o'clock tomorrow.'

The following morning, Lloyd, Sali and Harry waited for Victor for five minutes before Lloyd went to his room to look for him. He returned with a note that had been left on his bed.

Gone to Brecon. Expect me when you see me, Victor.

'It's the noise the inmates make, they never stop, day or night, it makes no difference. Someone is always screaming at the top of their voice but then you've found that out. And we're miles from anywhere, so if you don't live in and learn to put up with the racket, there's no way you can get here to work here,' a fellow maid, Judith, confided to Megan as they knelt side-by-side scrubbing the kitchen floor. 'Took me years to get used to the din, but now I don't even think about it.'

'How long have you been here?' Megan wouldn't have liked to hazard a guess as to Judith's age. With her cropped mousy grey hair and blousy figure, she could have been anything between a careworn thirty and a young-looking sixty.

'Twenty years next month. It is September now, isn't it?'

'Twenty years!' Megan gasped.

'I came here from the orphanage when I was twelve. They needed a kitchen maid and the matron said I might do. I got promoted to full maid a year later.'

'And you've never left?'

'Where would I go?' the woman asked. 'I don't know a soul outside of this place and the orphanage, and I was too old to stay there. It's not so bad here, apart from the noise. The food's good, the work's not too hard and as I get full keep and my uniform, I save every penny of my wages. I get thirty pounds a year now, and that's on top of the nest egg in my chest.'

'You keep your money in your chest with your clothes, not in the Post Office?' On arrival Megan had been given two maids' uniforms, two yellow winceyette nightgowns, two towels and flannels, and a key to a lock-up chest, which served as chest of drawers, washstand and wardrobe rolled into one, and stood alongside her bed in the dormitory that housed five other maids.

'I haven't seen a Post Office since I left the orphanage. We used to walk past one when we were taken to chapel on Sundays, but then, I haven't been to chapel since I've been here. There isn't one for miles.' Judith dipped her scrubbing brush into her bucket of soda crystals and hot water.

'You must leave here sometime. On your days off.' Megan leaned back. Her head and the half-healed injuries on her thighs and stomach ached unbearably, but as her fellow maid said, apart from the floors, the work wasn't too hard, and they were only on duty for eight hours a day. Four hours less than she had worked in Mrs Palmer's lodging house on the lightest working day.

'We spend our days off in the part of the walled garden the inmates can't get into. There's no point in going anywhere else because there's nothing around here. Come on, once we've finished this we can break for dinner. It's my favourite today, beef stew, dumplings and apple crumble and custard.'

Megan's mouth went dry and her heart beat erratically. Would she be allowed outside the asylum on her day off? Even if they were in the middle of nowhere, if she walked for long enough, she'd surely see some sign of habitation and meet someone who could get a letter to Victor – that's if she could find paper and pen to write one, and borrow enough money for a stamp to send it.

Recalling her father disappearing into the waiting room on Cardiff station with one of the men who had brought her here, she had absolutely no doubt that her wages had already been paid in advance and she would never see a penny of it.

'I thought I heard someone come in.' Billy Evans limped into the kitchen to see Victor lighting the lamp Sali had bought to replace the one Jane had taken.

'Sorry if I woke you.' Victor turned up the wick and his father saw that his face was grey with exhaustion, his clothes filthy.

'You didn't,' Billy lowered himself carefully into his chair. 'I don't sleep so well these days.'

'Your leg?'

'The part they took off hurts like hell. The doctor calls it ghost pain but it feels anything but ghostly to me.' He glanced at the clock; it was two in the morning. You came back with no time to spare. 'First shift back goes down the cage in four hours.'

'I'll be ready.' Victor sat on the easy chair, pulled a chair out from under the table and propped his feet on it.

'You must be starving.'

'I've eaten today.'

'Not much by the look of you.' Even in six days Mr Evans could see a change in his son. Victor's cheeks had sunk and his clothes were hanging on him. He doubted if he'd eaten a decent meal since they'd returned from the funeral to find Megan gone. 'There's no need to ask if you had any luck. I can see it in your face.'

'No one I spoke to had seen anyone who looked like Megan.'

'It took you five days to find out that?'

'Brecon's a fair-sized town and the county is enormous I've never seen so many bare, empty hills, or so few people and houses.' Victor rested his head on the back of his chair and closed his eyes.

'You couldn't have gone everywhere.'

'All I know is that I didn't find her in Brecon town. But there are hundreds of remote farms in the county. She could be on any one of them, miles from the nearest village and Post Office, with no means of contacting me. I walked around to a few near the town, but it was hopeless. There are places out there that people know about only because someone who works there walked into town to visit the market ten years ago.'

'Lloyd and Sali were worried sick when you left the inn without a penny in your pocket.' Billy pulled his pipe from his dressing-gown pocket and stared thoughtfully at it. 'Sali wanted to go after you, but Lloyd pointed out that if you'd got a ride to the town you could have gone from there to almost any farm in the area. They could have spent a week looking for you without any success. How did you manage without money?'

'I left the inn on a brewery wagon and paid my way by helping the drayman unload his barrels at the inns. When I reached the town I helped a blacksmith for a couple of mornings and chopped a load of logs for a farmer I made enough for food and managed to get rides on a couple of carts. I doubt I walked more than fifty miles in the five days I was there.'

'Well, you're home now.' Billy left his chair. 'But a word of warning, boy, you're going to drive yourself and everyone around you crazy if you don't calm down.'

'I have to find Megan.'

'And we'll do all we can to help you find her. But there are better ways and means than charging round the countryside, living like a tramp.' Billy went to the door. 'You'll get an hour's sleep if you go up now.'

'I haven't washed in days. I'd only dirty the bedclothes. I'll stay here for half an hour then have a quick bath.' Victor stretched back on the two chairs.

'In cold water?'

'If I'm working at six it will wake me up.'

Chapter 24

SALI AND Lloyd rose at a quarter to four. Leaving the washstand in the bedroom for Sali, Lloyd picked up his clothes and, tiptoeing so as not to wake Harry, crept down the stairs. It was odd to resume a daily routine that had been disrupted by the onset of the strike almost a full year before. He went through the kitchen to the basement to discover that both stoves had already been lit in preparation to heat water for their baths after they finished their shifts.

'Good God, when did you get back?' Lloyd asked, when he walked into the basement to see Victor rising naked from a tin bath.

'Early hours, and before you start the cross-examination, no one I spoke to had seen or heard of Megan in Brecon and I've already had a dressing down from Dad for leaving you and Sali at the inn and going off without any money.' Victor grabbed a towel and began to rub himself dry.

Lloyd stepped outside, used the ty bach and returned to the basement. Stripping off his robe, he hung it on a hook, went to the tap, turned it on, picked up the soap and started washing under the stream of icy water. 'Was it you who lit the fires?'

'Yes, but only ten minutes ago, which is why I didn't bother to try to heat any water for my bath; by the time it's hot we'll have to be on our way.' Victor draped his towel over the rail in front of the stove and padded over to the row of pegs where Sali had hung their working clothes. All were clean and neatly pressed. 'Do you think Sali will mind me eating breakfast in these?'

'As they're a damn sight cleaner than what you wore to Brecon, no.' Lloyd watched Victor bundle his discarded clothes together and toss them on top of the linen bin. 'They look as though they need fumigating.'

'I slept rough.'

'So I see.' Lloyd rinsed off and dried himself before joining Victor in front of the clothes' pegs. 'Just as long as you remember to put on your tidy clothes tomorrow morning when these will be filthy. I don't want Sali doing any more housework than absolutely necessary.'

'Is she all right after that journey?' Victor asked, concerned that Sali might be ill on his account.

'She doesn't look well, but you know Sali. She insists she's just tired.'

'Not long to go now.' Victor pulled his moleskin trousers over his drawers and buttoned his flies.

'Five weeks, if all goes to plan.'

'And the father-to-be is getting nervous.' Joey ran lightly down the stone steps and hung his evening clothes on a peg. His robe flapped open as he dived out of the back door to the ty bach.

'Any woman looking over her garden wall will get an eyeful.' Lloyd fastened his trousers and pulled his flannel vest over his head.

'She'll only be interested if she hasn't seen it before.' Victor went to the mirror and brushed his wet hair straight back from his forehead. 'It feels strange to be dressing for the pit again.'

'Strange but good.' Joey banged the door shut behind him. 'I've had enough of being broke and getting arrested.'

Lloyd sniffed the air. 'I don't believe it. I smell bacon.'

'With eggs, sausages, lava bread, tomatoes . . .' Victor tied a kerchief around his neck. 'There should be plenty of tomatoes. I hope you've been picking them, Joey, and not letting them rot on the allotment.'

'I went up yesterday, and not only picked tomatoes, but also the last of your beans. I lifted a row of potatoes and cut a couple of cabbages and when I came back here I collected the eggs and cleaned out the chicken coop and dog run.' Joey finished splashing under the tap and turned it off.

397

'And he only needed four hours of continual nagging from Sali to make him do it,' Lloyd teased, hoping to make Victor smile.

'Rubbish!' Joey went to the clothes' pegs. 'If you two are dressing in your working clothes, so will I. Has Dad been down yet?'

'He came down and went back up half an hour ago.' Victor went to the stairs.

'If there is bacon, don't eat it all before I get there.' Joey managed to put his trousers on back to front in his hurry to get dressed.

'As if Sali would let him.' Lloyd fastened the last button on his shirt and followed Victor. His father was already sitting at the table eating; Sali was turning food in the frying pans on the stove.

'I didn't think we could afford a breakfast like this.' Lloyd looked suspiciously at Sali when she set plates piled high with food in front of him and Victor.

'I couldn't let you go down the pit with nothing in your stomachs so I opened a slate in Connie's on Saturday.' Sali lied to conceal the fact that she had used the leftover money Lloyd had borrowed from Mr Richards. 'We'll pay her back at the end of the week when you get your wages.'

'I've missed these breakfasts.' Joey breathed in theatrically, savouring the scent of the bacon. Sali set a full plate at his place at the table. He picked up his knife and fork and started eating before he even sat down.

Sali lifted the empty frying pans into the sink and went to the pantry to get the snap boxes she had packed the night before. She made tea and filled their tea bottles before filling their larger water bottles with fresh water from the tap.

She filled the kettle again and set it on to boil water for the dishes. Then she went into the pantry and lifted out the potato box and a cabbage, desperately doing anything she could think of not to look at the men. Everyone was relieved that the strike was finally over but nothing had really been resolved and she knew that Lloyd, his father, the strike committee and most of the colliers regarded the return to work as a shattering climb-down for them and an unqualified victory for the owners.

Lloyd finished his breakfast, left the table and carried his plate over to her. 'We'll walk out through the basement, sweetheart. Don't go overdoing it today. Father Kelly has more than enough volunteers to run the kitchens until the first wage packets start coming in, so please, put your feet up and rest after you've taken Harry to school.'

'I will.'

'Promise.' He stood in front of her and she smiled at him. 'I know that smile, it says, "Yes, I've listened to you, Lloyd, but now I'm going to ignore every word you've said." '

'There's not much to be done today,' she insisted.

'I mean it, take it easy, for Isabella's sake.' He kissed her before following Joey, Victor and his father down the stairs. Knowing that it would take the men a few moments to lace on their boots, Sali dried her hands in her apron, went to the front door and opened it. For the first time in almost a year the colliery siren was wailing, signalling the first shift of men to head for the pit and the cage.

Dawn had broken half an hour before and although it was the tail end of a warm summer, the light was cold and grey. All the men on the six o'clock shift were leaving their houses and the only sound that could be heard above the din of the siren was the steady tramp of their boots as they made their way down the road and the hill at the end of the street.

Joey walked around from the back of the house, his cap pulled low over his face, his haversack hanging at his side. Victor and Lloyd followed, walking either side of their father, whose limp seemed more pronounced than ever. Sali knew her father-in-law was concerned that management might not give him his job back, but it didn't seem appropriate to shout good luck. They all saw her at the door, but only Lloyd touched his cap to her as they passed.

No one spoke, no one uttered a sound, although women were standing in every doorway in the street. Hearing a noise behind her, Sali turned and saw Harry on the stairs. She held out her arms, and he went to her. Lifting him up, she continued to watch the men until the last one rounded the corner and disappeared from sight. Then she set Harry down and took him into the kitchen.

*   *   *

'Can you imagine the mess down there after nearly a year of neglect?' the management's representative shouted over the heads of the colliers who had gathered at the pithead in the hope of getting their jobs back right away. Billy, Victor, Joey and Lloyd pushed their way through the mass of workers and headed towards him.

'That's all the more reason to get as many colliers down there as quickly you can, Mr Stephens,' Billy said when he reached the official.

'Six hundred today—'

'Six hundred? There has to be four thousand men here,' Billy protested, looking around.

'Management has issued a statement. Within a month we hope to have seventy-five per cent of the twelve thousand strikers back in employment.'

'And the others?' Lloyd enquired.

'There are problems.' John Stephens couldn't meet Lloyd's eye. 'The strike ended so suddenly, Mr Thomas didn't have time to buy enough pit wood to effect all the repairs that are needed. Some of the faces aren't safe.'

'If they are not safe, then you need to get every repairman down there now, Mr Stephens, and, as I'm in charge of them, I should be the first down. Joey here is an assistant, and if the props need repairing, chances are the tram tracks need sorting by a blacksmith, so you'll need Victor.'

'We have falls that need clearing before anything else can be done.' John Stephens ran his finger nervously around the inside of his collar.

'Then I should be down there with my team clearing them.'

'Billy, a word.' John Stephens' immediate superior, Mr Thomas beckoned to him from his office door. Lloyd, Victor and Joey followed. Mr Thomas pushed the door to when they joined him inside.

'A man with one leg is a liability down a pit, Billy,' Mr Thomas began.

'I can walk.'

'Everyone can see you're limping, man.'

'So are three-quarters of the colliers in every pit by the end of their shifts.' Lloyd crossed his arms across his chest and eyed Mr Thomas. The official glanced away, unable to met Lloyd's steady gaze. He didn't have to say another word. Lloyd guessed what he was having difficulty in telling them. 'My father won't be taken back.'

'He's disabled—'

'And neither will I,' Lloyd added.

Realizing that it was useless to try to conceal the truth, or soften the blow with sympathetic words, the official opted to tell the truth. 'It's nothing personal, Lloyd. Both of you are good workers, the best we have, but management—'

'Regards strike leaders as troublemakers and they don't want them working in their collieries.'

'I thought you'd be glad of an opportunity to retire, after your accident, Billy. How old are you now? Fifty—'

'Retirement age is sixty-five,' Billy said. 'What am I supposed to live on for the next fifteen years?'

'You'll get compensation from the railway.'

'Betty Morgan has been told that she'll get five hundred pounds for her husband, I'll get one hundred pounds for the loss of my leg and fifty pounds of that went in medical bills. Are you suggesting that I should live on the remaining fifty for the rest of my life?' Billy demanded.

'Everyone knows that you and your boys have invested in houses. Several, or so I've been told. At ten bob a week rent, you'll earn more from them than you would if you went back underground.'

'And Lloyd? Are you suggesting that he should retire too?' Billy finally allowed his anger to show.

'It's not just me, is it, Mr Thomas?' Lloyd questioned softly. 'It's Joey and Victor too.'

'I'm sorry, I really am—'

'But the management of the Cambrian Collieries don't want the sons and brothers of union leaders working in their pits.' Lloyd kicked open the door. 'Thank you for letting us know where we stand.'

'I'm sorry, Lloyd, this is none of my doing, I'm just the messenger. I'm sorry, I really am. Perhaps you'd let the other strike leaders know—'

'That they're out of a job?' Billy questioned contemptuously. 'That's one bit of news I'll allow you to break to them, Mr Thomas. Mabon has well and truly sold us out. Other signatures might be on the agreement to return to work but we came back because he gave us his personal assurance that once the collieries were operational again, management would discuss our demands. They've no intention of even giving us a hearing, have they?'

'We'll never get a minimum wage, will we?' Joey questioned angrily.

'We?' Lloyd countered bitterly. 'We're not colliers any more, just four more men in the ranks of the unemployed. James Connelly was right when he wrote his *Workers Republic*: *"Apostles of Freedom are ever idolised when dead, but crucified when alive."* If you can remember that, Thomas, perhaps you'd tell it to the management the next time you lick their boots.' Lloyd turned on his heel and walked out of the door.

Sali was sweeping the kitchen floor when Lloyd climbed the basement stairs. He opened the door. She looked at him and knew something was very wrong.

'My father and brothers will be up in a minute. They're changing out of their working clothes. I wanted to tell you what's happened before you see them. I'm sorry, Sali. No one in this family has a job to go back to. No strike leader, or member of any strike leader's family, has work. I don't know how we're going to live or what we're going to do . . .'

A sharp pain ripped through Sali and she felt as though something was tearing inside her. She gasped and doubled up in pain. Crying out, she stared in horror at the pool of bloodstained water spreading over the flagstones at her feet.

Lloyd swept her up into his arms. Hearing her cry, Joey and Victor ran up the steps from the basement, followed by their father.

Mr Evans looked from Sali's features contorted in pain to the pool of bloodstained water on the floor. 'Joey! Run as fast as you can and get Mrs Morgan. If she's not at her house, she'll be at Joyce Palmer's. As soon as you've asked her to come here, fetch the midwife. Quick as you can.'

Victor ran after Joey and opened the door for Lloyd. He swept through it and carried Sali up the stairs.

'The parcel in the wardrobe.' Sali fought another pain, as Lloyd lowered her on to the dressing-table stool.

While she undressed and washed, Lloyd stripped the bed and after covering the mattress with layers of brown paper, remade it with an old pair of sheets Sali had set aside in preparation for the birth. As soon as she had put on her nightgown Lloyd lifted her on to the bed.

'Where the hell is Joey?' he said angrily, after settling her on the pillows.

Sali gave him a weak smile as the contraction eased. 'I have done this before, Lloyd. It's not that hard. You'll remind your father and brothers about Harry needing to be picked up from school. Everything is ready for the evening meal. All you have to do is put the beef in the oven at two o'clock. I bought it on Saturday as a special treat for your first day back at work, it's hanging in the meat safe in the pantry, and I've already peeled the potatoes and prepared the cabbage—'

'Will you stop fussing about food? We can take care of everything.' Concern for her made him uncharacteristically brusque. He gripped her hand. 'Sweetheart, please, tell me what I can do.'

You did enough eight months ago, Lloyd Evans.' Betty Morgan rolled her sleeves to her elbows when she came into the room. 'You all right, love?' She looked down at Sali in concern.

'It shouldn't be coming this soon.'

'You're eight months, aren't you?' Betty tipped water into the bowl on the washstand, soaked a flannel in it, and pressed it against Sali's forehead.

'The midwife said I had five more weeks to go.' Sali moaned softly as another pain took hold.

'It's high time you were out of here, Lloyd Evans.' Betty gave him a push. 'Go on, off with you, do something useful like look for the midwife.'

'No.' Sali reached out and grabbed his hand. 'Stay.'

'A man at a birth! I never heard of such a thing. He'll be about as useful as an elephant at a ballet.'

Lloyd crouched beside the bed and continued to hold Sali's hand. 'If Sali wants me here, Betty, I'm staying. And if you want this elephant to dance, you'd better find me some ballet shoes that fit.'

'Where the hell is Joey?' Victor paced the kitchen, as his father filled kettles and saucepans with water and set them on the range to boil.

'There now by the sound of it.'

'He wouldn't knock.' Victor went into the passage and saw that in his haste Joey had left the front door open. Sergeant Martin was standing in the open doorway.

'If you've come to arrest anyone, we're busy,' Victor snapped, as another cry echoed down the stairs.

'I'm sorry, is someone ill?'

'My sister-in-law is having a baby.'

'I apologize for breaking in on you like this, but if you could spare me a minute, I'd be grateful.'

Billy opened the door, took one look at the sergeant and shook his head in despair. 'Not you again.'

'Please, this really won't take more than a minute.' The sergeant then said the one thing guaranteed to galvanize Victor's attention. 'It is important, to Miss Megan Williams.'

'You'd better come in.' Victor led the way into the kitchen. 'Won't you sit down?' He pulled a chair out from the table.

'No, thank you, Mr Evans.' Sergeant Martin reached into his tunic pocket and pulled out a small, brown paper bag. He opened it and shook the contents on to the table. 'Can you identify those?'

The engagement ring I gave Megan, and the chain she kept it on.' Victor picked them up. The heart-shaped diamond glittered, beautiful and perfect, between the miniature gold hands, just as it had when he had given it to her. But although it was thick, the chain had been snapped clean in two.

'Where did you get them, sergeant?' Billy moved protectively closer to Victor.

'On a body we fished out of the river. But don't worry, they've been thoroughly disinfected.' Sergeant Martin's skin was still burning. He and Gwyn Jenkins had scrubbed themselves raw after stripping the clothes from what was left of Shipton and returning them to the river. Fortunately, the man who had found the body – caught in a slick of slaughterhouse waste on the bank below Tonypandy – hadn't recognized the remains of the police uniform. The sergeant had hated bending the rules. But Shipton was dead. Megan Williams was where she now belonged. It made no sense to investigate further when it would only bring the force into disrepute.

'Whose body?' Victor whispered hoarsely.

'We don't know,' the sergeant lied. It was naked and too far-gone to be identified, almost skeletal in fact. The chain and ring were caught up in the fingers. All I can tell you is that it was a man. We have no idea of age, looks or even hair colour. The skull was bald. But now that you've identified the ring I think we can say that we have found Miss William's attacker and close the case.' The sergeant walked to the door. 'I am sorry about your fiancée, Mr Evans. She was a nice girl.'

'Do you know where she is?' Victor demanded, his temper rising at the 'was'.

The sergeant shook his head.

'You were with her father when he took her from here. I have been searching everywhere.'

'She is a minor. The law is on her father's side. He and the minister assured me they'd send her to an appropriate place where all her needs would be met, spiritual as well as physical.' The sergeant almost added that girls who'd been used the way Megan Williams had, were better placed in an institution but there was something in Victor's eyes that stopped him.

'If you should happen to hear where she is—'

'Goodbye, Mr Evans.'

Joey barged into the kitchen to see Victor and his father,

standing staring at one another. 'The midwife went straight upstairs. Was that Sergeant Martin I saw leaving the house?'

'It was,' his father answered.

'Wanted to arrest the baby before it's born, I suppose.'

'No.' Victor showed him the ring.

'A cup of tea to go with the explanations, I think,' Billy said, as the kettle began to boil. 'My experience of babies is that they can be a long time coming.'

Victor and Joey were glad when it was time to pick Harry up from school. Sali's soft moans were worse than screams, because they knew she was holding back for their sake. When they returned with Harry they went straight to the kitchen. Billy shook his head and they retreated again, taking Harry for a walk over the mountain with the dogs.

The first sound they heard when they returned was a baby's cry echoing down the stairs and Victor smiled in spite of the misery that had gnawed like a cancer at him since Megan's father had taken her.

'I'm an uncle . . .' Joey charged up the stairs.

'You stay there,' Billy thundered, opening the kitchen door and stopping Joey in his tracks.

'I want to know if it's a niece or nephew.'

'You'll meet the newest Evans when you're invited and not before. All of you in here.' Billy reached for the teapot and caddy. 'I'll make another brew to toast the arrival.'

Betty Morgan came down half an hour later with a bundle of bloodstained linen and the slop bucket.

'They're all right?' Billy asked.

'The baby's healthy, and the mother must be mad after what she's been through because she told me to tell you that you can all go up, even Harry.'

'Is she really all right?' Billy asked.

'As all right as any woman can be living in this houseful of crazy men.'

'Boy or a girl?' Joey asked.

'Go on up and you'll find out,' Betty smiled.

*　　*　　*

406

The midwife was laying sheets in the cot that had been used for Lloyd, Victor and Joey. Lloyd was sitting next to Sali on the bed, both of them looking down at the tiny baby Sali was holding, dressed in the white knitted layette Betty had brought with her.

Sali held out the baby to her father-in-law and he took it gently in his arms.

'Isabella Maria Evans,' Lloyd smiled, 'and she has our mother's eyes.'

'And her black curly hair.' An overwhelming wave of emotion washed over Billy as he held the child. For the first time since he had lost his wife, he felt truly alive again.

'So what do you think of your new sister, Harry?' Betty Morgan asked, when Billy brought him back downstairs after Victor and Joey had gone into the garden.

'She's small as a monkey and ugly,' Harry said with startling honesty. 'All red and wrinkled.'

'I wouldn't let your mam or dad catch you saying that,' Billy warned. 'Take my word for it, for a baby, she's beautiful.'

'You said she's your granddaughter.' Harry looked thoughtfully at Billy.

'Yes,' Billy agreed. 'Your dad is my son, she's his daughter and that makes her my granddaughter.'

'But I'm dad's son and I call you Uncle Billy.' Harry pulled his stool up to the back window and looked out.

'Only because I was your uncle before your mam married your dad.'

'Then can I call you Granddad?'

'If you want to,' Billy answered casually, but his offhand tone didn't fool Betty. She saw the telltale flush of pride in his cheeks.

'Uncle Victor is cleaning out the chickens and dogs. I'm going to help him.' Harry jumped down from the stool and opened the basement door.

'Tell your Uncles Joey and Victor that your tea will be on the table in twenty minutes and I'll expect them and you back here with your hands and faces washed ready to eat it,' Betty called after him. 'Don't forget now.'

'I won't.' Harry frowned at Billy from the doorway. 'Dewi has two granddads and sixteen uncles.'

'But no sisters,' Billy reminded him.

'See you.' Harry closed the door behind him and went down the stairs.

'He might not be yours by blood, but that's a proper little character you've got there, Billy. And if you ask me, there's as much of you, Lloyd, Victor and Joey in him as there is his mam.' Betty took the plates down from the dresser and put them into the bread oven to warm.

'I'll not deny that we've all had a hand in his upbringing for the last year or so, but I hope there's not too much of Joey in him,' Billy said seriously.

'Do you know, I haven't heard a single word of gossip about your Joey since Jane Edwards disappeared.'

'Is that right?' Billy muttered from behind the paper he'd picked up.

'That's right,' Betty answered. 'Could it be that he's studying to become a priest or a monk? You know how keen the Catholics are to fill their monasteries. If I were you I'd have a word with Father Kelly on the subject.'

'Or it could be that you've no time to listen to the gossips now you're working more or less full time for Joyce Palmer?'

'More or less being right. Joyce is keen to give me more hours than there are in a day. I couldn't have come here today if she hadn't taken on another girl from the workhouse. But I could ask her to give me a couple of days off, if you'd like me to help out here until Sali is back on her feet.'

'I wouldn't want to put you to any trouble,' Billy said gruffly.

'No trouble,' Betty said blithely. 'That's settled then, I'll come in every day until Sali's fit again. To get back to Joey—'

'I thought we'd finished discussing him.'

'They were asking me in the Post Office if he's turned over a new leaf,' she continued unabashed. 'Apparently he's been seen going into the tea shop with the maids from Llan House.'

'Any maid in particular?' Billy asked, instantly on the alert.

'No, that's the strange thing. He's been seen with three of them

408

but then Mrs Williams would castrate him if he went out with just one. You know how closely she guards her girls. Like every woman she knows there's safety in numbers.' Betty set the knives and forks on the table, and laid a tray for Sali.

'About time the boy calmed down.'

'That's exactly what most of the fathers and husbands are saying in the Rhondda, Billy.'

'So they're even gossiping about the boy when there's nothing to be said about him.' Billy opened out the newspaper, turned the page, folded it back and looked through the For Sale notices, not that he wanted anything, or had the money to buy it even if he saw something he needed.

Betty saw him frown. 'You worried about your court case, Billy?' she questioned astutely.

'You heard that I am?' he growled.

'No.'

'Then why are you asking?' he demanded.

'Because I've known you over thirty years, and that bark of yours has never fooled me. I was told before your Joey found me this morning that you and the boys have been laid off. It's no surprise. Everyone knows that now the owners have had their way and got the men to crawl back to the pits for less wages than they were earning when the troubles started, they're going to look round for scapegoats to blame the strike on. With you, Lloyd and Victor due in court soon, you must be worried.'

'Not for myself.'

'But Sali, Joey and the children,' she guessed.

'With all of us out of work, and three of us likely to be put away, of course I'm worried, woman,' he retorted bluntly.

'You stuck your neck out for the colliers, Billy, they're not going to forget it.'

'You can't really believe that?' He set the newspaper aside. 'Management made it clear today that there's not going to be enough jobs for everyone, even when the pits get back to full production. So can you honestly see any miner risking his weekly wage to sympathize openly with me, Lloyd or Victor if we're put away?'

'Yes.'

'Then you're a bigger romantic than Ned ever was.'

'I never said I wasn't.' She smiled at the mention of her husband's name. 'I just let Ned think he was the only one with dreams.'

'Why?'

'Because I didn't want mine to overshadow his.'

'He was a good man,' Billy agreed crustily.

'He was. Do you remember a couple of months after Isabella died, I asked you how you were, and you said the worst thing was people never mentioning her name when they talked to you? It was as if she'd never lived.'

'I don't remember,' he lied, ashamed of the one time he'd lowered his guard and allowed his emotions to show.

'Whether you do or you don't, you were right, Billy. Even my sons, daughter, and their wives and husband, and my grandchildren try to avoid talking about Ned and I hate it. It's almost as though they are trying to kill him a second time by obliterating his memory.'

'If anyone is going to be remembered by the miners in this valley it's Ned.'

'I hope so. He would have liked that.' The potatoes started boiling and she pushed them to the back of the hob. 'Do me a favour, shout up to Lloyd and ask if he's going to give his poor wife and daughter a bit of peace and eat his dinner down here, with us.'

Chapter 25

'I DON'T intend to argue about this with you, Sali.' Lloyd took off
the jacket of the suit he'd worn to visit Geoffrey Francis, and hung
it over the back of the chair in their bedroom. 'It's common sense
for Victor, my father and me to sign over everything we own to
you and Joey before the court case tomorrow. And that's why we
asked Mr Francis to draw up the papers today, so we can all sign
them first thing in the morning.'

'You don't know what's going to happen in court tomorrow,'
she countered.

'Precisely.' He unbuttoned his waistcoat.

'You'll be tried by an impartial jury. After they've heard the
evidence they'll realize that none of you have broken the law.' Sali
glanced down at the baby at her breast. At six weeks, Bella, as
Lloyd had first called her, and she was now generally known, was
plump, contented and stunningly beautiful. She was as dark as
Harry was fair, with Lloyd's thick black curly hair, and deep navy
blue eyes, which Sali was convinced would soon turn the same
ebony shade as her father's.

'We're only taking sensible precautions. You and Joey may have
to sell a house, or given the way prices have fallen since the strike,
two, just to live if we are imprisoned for more than a couple of
months. In fact, you may need to sell two anyway, just to recoup
your losses.'

'What do you mean?' she asked warily.

'I'm not stupid, Sali, and neither are my family,' Lloyd said
quietly. 'We all know that you've been paying the household bills
since we've been laid off. And before you say another word on the
subject, there's no point in trying to deny it.'

'Connie's paying Joey wages,' she answered defensively.

'And although they are good for a delivery boy, the fifteen shillings a week he now brings home doesn't cover the cost of coal, lamp oil, chicken and dog food.' He gripped the back of the chair and looked at her. 'You promised you wouldn't use Harry's money to keep us.'

'I'm not. I've used a very small part of the eighteen hundred and fifty pounds Mr Richards raised when he sold my ring. And if I hadn't paid the bills, we'd owe money to almost every tradesman in Tonypandy, and they can't afford to carry anyone. The strike may be over, but it's going to take months, if not years, for people to clear their debts and that goes for the shopkeepers like Connie as well as the colliers. Besides, it's only temporary,' she protested. 'You'll pay me back.'

'And just when do you think we'll be a position to do that?' he enquired sceptically.

'When this court case is over and everything gets back to normal.'

'None of us will ever work in this valley again, Sali, and you know it.'

Sali flinched from the bitterness that had been eating away at Lloyd, his brothers and his father since they had been laid off. The colliery company had taken their pride along with their jobs, and nothing she could do or say could restore it. Unable to meet Lloyd's steady gaze, she glanced down; Bella's eyes were slowly closing. She pulled her gently away from her nipple and a bubble of milk appeared at the baby's mouth.

'If she's finished, I'll wind her,' Lloyd offered.

She knew that was the closest she'd get to an apology for his outburst. 'Take your waistcoat, shirt and vest off first in case she brings some milk back. It's easier to wash you than your clothes.'

Lloyd did as Sali suggested, leaned over the bed and tenderly took the baby from her arms. Supporting Bella's tiny body in his hands, he set her against his shoulder and gently rubbed her back. 'You're looking tired. My father's right, you left your bed and started running the house too soon after Bella's birth. Just look at what you've done today. Cooking, cleaning—'

'Sat and drank tea with you and your father this morning. Gossiped with Mrs Morgan and later on the midwife when they called to see how Bella was doing this afternoon.' Sali left the bed and poured water into the bowl on the washstand. Rubbing soap on to a flannel, she washed her heavily veined, swollen breasts. 'We have some decisions to make, and no matter how much you try to evade the subject, sooner or later we are going to have to talk about the money that Mr Richards transferred into my bank account after he sold my ring.'

'Not now, Sali,' he pleaded.

'Rather than just sign your houses over to me and Joey, why don't you sell them to me? I could put them in Bella's name as a nest egg for her. It would give you and your family a little capital. Give you all a breathing space until you find other jobs. It can be only a matter of time until you do.'

'If the court fines us, the authorities will take whatever money you give us.'

'You think they'll fine you that much?'

'I don't know. What I do know is that they can't take what we don't have. And that is why we don't want to own the houses – not even on paper.' Lloyd sat in the nursing chair Victor had carried up from their father's bedroom after Bella's birth. He wrapped the shawl Sali had crocheted around both himself and Bella, and bent his head so he could watch the baby as he continued to cuddle her on his shoulder.

'You really think you are going to be sent to prison, don't you?' She buttoned the bodice on her nightdress.

'Yes, and frankly, the way things are at the moment with all of us except Joey out of work, and him earning a boy's wages, I'd prefer it to paying out a heavy fine. What little we've saved as a family and invested in houses will be wiped out soon enough if we try to live on it for any length of time. And, although Harry's future might be assured, we've Bella to consider now.'

'The men in the unions will never stand for you and your father being made scapegoats,' she said firmly.

'With the collieries in production and over seventy-five percent of the men back in work, management know the other twenty-five percent won't risk losing their jobs before they get them to protest at the way the strike leaders are being treated. No more than any collier in work will dare to miss a shift to demonstrate outside the court. You will take over the houses in joint ownership with Joey, won't you?'

'I will,' she conceded, tired of the argument.

'And if I'm put in prison, you'll stay here, with Joey?' he pressed.

'You may not go to prison,' she dismissed, 'and even if you do, it may not be for more than a week or two.'

'And if it is?'

'I'll think about what to do if it happens.'

'That's not good enough, Sali. I'm the first to admit that Joey thinks before he acts, behaves like an idiot most of the time and, despite all the promises he's made to my father, incapable of keeping his flies buttoned around the wrong kind of woman, but he is family. And I know that he'll do everything in his power to look after you and the children. I trust him more than I trust Geraint.' Holding Bella close to him so as not to wake her, he left his chair.

'How about I solemnly promise to live with Joey, will that do?' She climbed into bed. 'Who knows, he may get an offer of a better paid job elsewhere.'

'No creating a job for him in one of Harry's companies,' he warned.

'After the way Geraint's behaved since he started work in Gwilym James, I doubt that Mr Horton or any of the other trustees would allow me to create another job for someone in the family.'

Lloyd laid Bella down on her side in the cot, tucked her long nightdress around her legs and tiny feet as she curled up, kissed her cheek, folded the shawl and pulled the bedclothes over her. 'I know that I don't have to ask you to look after Bella and Harry, but will you look after yourself?' he questioned seriously.

'That's the third promise you've coaxed out of me in the last two minutes. The room is freezing; come to bed.'

He slipped his braces from his shoulders, unbuckled his belt, and stripped off his trousers, drawers, sock suspenders and socks. 'I love you, Mrs Evans, never forget that, whatever happens tomorrow.'

'I want to go to court with you.'

He shook his head. 'You need to look after Bella, and I'll be better off by myself, no distractions.' He climbed in beside her, blew out the candle and wrapped his arm around her shoulders.

'I love you, Lloyd.' Her breath caught at the back of her throat, as he caressed the soft skin beneath her ear. 'Please, promise that you'll be sleeping with me tomorrow night.'

'I only wish I could.' He kissed her and one kiss led to another and another. 'I don't want to hurt you, sweetheart . . .'

'You couldn't, darling, not this way,' she whispered.

'You've just had Bella.'

'Weeks ago, and she'll soon need a younger brother to bully.'

'Sali—'

'Where's the man who told me there's no point in discussing things that can't be changed? Let's just make the most of what we have here and now, Lloyd. Please.'

Mr Richards slipped out of the back door of the court and walked down the corridor. He knocked at a door marked private and Mari opened it.

They're making the closing statements in five minutes, Mrs Evans.'

'Couldn't have come at a better time,' Mari said, as Sali buttoned the neck of her blouse. 'You look fine,' she reassured. 'Bella will be all right for a good four hours and not even the judge will let them rabbit on for that long.'

Sali left the room with Mr Richards. Constable Davies was in the corridor and he nodded to them.

Thank you again for arranging this, Huw,' Sali said.

'It was no trouble, Mrs Evans. But I warn you, the public benches can be seen from the dock.'

'It will be too late for Lloyd to complain about me being in court when I'm there,' she said nervously.

'I don't think he'd dare object in front of the judge,' Huw agreed.

Sali glanced at her watch as she walked with Mr Richards. Half past three. Harry would be home from school, sitting in Connie's living room, and knowing Connie's routine, eating tea with Antonia while Annie and Connie served in the shop downstairs. She crossed her fingers hoping that she and Lloyd would be able to catch the train back from Cardiff together with all his family, to walk up from the station, call in at Rodney's to pick up Harry . . .

Mr Richards opened the door to the public benches and Sali stared in amazement at the number of people who had come down from Tonypandy for the trial. Luke Thomas and all his friends were there, Beryl and Alun Richards, Betty Morgan, and the entire strike committee who had all been laid off the same time as Lloyd.

Mr Richards indicated two seats at the end of the front bench and she sat beside Joey. Mr Richards took the end seat next to her as Geoffrey Francis rose to his feet. The barrister glanced back at Lloyd, Billy and Victor, straightened his wig and faced the judge.

'Your honour,' he bowed to the judge, 'members of the jury. I beg your indulgence. Please allow me to establish the characters of the accused; refresh your memories as to the evidence against them and re-examine the events that took place at the pithead of Ely Colliery, Penygraig on Tuesday, twenty-fifth of July 1911.

'In addition to being the financial secretary of Number One District, Lloyd Evans is chairman of the Cambrian Joint Workman's Committee. Is it likely that he would have been democratically elected to such responsible positions by his colleagues if he were not well respected and regarded as highly trustworthy by his fellow workers, neighbours and friends?' Mr Francis fell silent for a moment, giving the jury time to absorb what he had said.

'You heard Lloyd Evans state under oath that he took no part in the stone-throwing and assaults on police officers that day. He, along with the other two defendants, have stated clearly and unequivocally that they went to the Ely pithead only because it was rumoured blacklegs were working there and every time rumours of that nature had arisen in the past, there had been instances of trouble between the police and the strikers. And it was solely with the intention of averting trouble, and none other, that the defendants went to Penygraig that fateful afternoon.

'You also heard Mr Lloyd Evans refute on oath that he did not say as, Sergeant Lamb has suggested, "I am not sorry that there have been riots as it shows that people are awakening to their rights." In fact, he said, "Riots had alienated and would alienate the sympathy of the general public from the men on strike."

'I am not saying that stones weren't thrown at the police. Some colliers did so, yet they are not on trial here. The police have failed to produce a single witness who saw any one of the accused throw a stone in the direction of the officers on duty on Tuesday the twenty-fifth of July at Ely pithead. Indeed, Victor Evans testified that he only stepped in between the police and his father because he thought an officer was about to injure his father, who had recently been disabled and had not recovered from his injuries.

'Only five days before the events at Penygraig, on the twentieth of July 1911, police fired at demonstrators at Llanelli killing nine people who were supporting the dockers and railwaymen's demands for a minimum wage of thirty shillings a week—'

The judge leaned forward, 'Stick to the facts of this case only, Mr Francis.'

'Forgive me, your honour,' Mr Francis apologized. 'Members of the jury, may I draw your attention to the second defendant. William Evans is president of the Glamorgan Workman's Baths and Institute, a member of the South Wales Miners' Executive Council, and although he would not like me to say it, severely disabled, as a result of the train crash on Monday, the twenty-third of January 1911 in which three of his and Lloyd Evans's fellow members of the South Wales Miners' Federation Executive Council were killed. He is an upright man and, like his son, well respected by every member of the community in which he lives. He testified that far from throwing stones, he did all in his power to preserve harmony between the two warring factions. He believes that the demonstrators went to Penygraig with the intention of peacefully persuading the blacklegs they thought were at the colliery to stop work. After hearing some of the evidence the police have given to this court, *I* believe the police imagined a great deal of what happened that day. And in some instances,' Mr Francis stared blatantly at Sergeant Lamb, 'made mistakes. During

417

the fighting that erupted after the police officers charged the lines of colliers, William Evans' younger son, Victor, helped his father into the Golden Age public house, not as the prosecution claims, to avoid arrest but to escape the constables who were chasing the protesters with drawn batons. And that is why Victor Evans is standing in the dock accused of assaulting a police officer.' He took a deep breath and pointed at Victor. 'Since when has protecting a sick, elderly man become assault?

'The local police sergeant, the Reverend Williams and Father Kelly, all highly respected and esteemed community leaders, have testified that they have always considered the accused to be the sort of men who would help to preserve peace. But, as Father Kelly added, "Now the authorities seemed to be very anxious to hit the men's leaders." I put it to you that is why all three men are on trial here today.

'There was much confusion at the pithead that afternoon, but Father Kelly was there. He testified that he saw all three defendants exhorting the men to be peaceable. He saw the police charge the pickets and,' Geoffrey Francis glanced at the judge almost daring him to object, 'in his opinion, incite the temper of the striking colliers. You heard Sergeant Martin state that he believed all three men were attempting to placate the colliers and break up the demonstration. Therefore I implore you, the jury, to bring in the only verdict possible if justice is to be served here today: Not guilty. Thank you, your honour.'

Geoffrey Francis looked from the jury to the people in the public gallery. Joey's attention remained riveted on his father and brothers in the dock, but he fumbled for Sali's hand. She caught it and held it tight.

The prosecuting counsellor rose to his feet and bowed to the judge. 'Your honour, members of the jury, I put it to you that you have before you three exceedingly cunning and clever men. You have heard the testimony of the police officers present at Ely pithead in Penygraig that fateful afternoon. The defending counsellor would have you believe that the police imagined what went on that day. Did they imagine the stones that were thrown?' He paused for effect. 'Did they imagine the injuries, some severe, that were sustained by police officers engaged in preserving the peace and preventing rioting, of which law-abiding citizens have had far too much in the Rhondda and Wales in the past year?' He raised his voice effectively. 'No one disputes that the police drew their batons. As to it being an incitement to trouble?' He shrugged. 'What are police officers who are faced with a hail of stones and missiles supposed to do? Stand and wait until they are hit and not lift a finger to defend themselves?

'These two men, father and son, are made in the same mould,' he indicated Lloyd and Billy, 'strike leaders. You heard Sergeant Lamb testify that Lloyd Evans stood on a position overlooking the colliery and shout, "We cannot go on always like this. If we cannot get justice by fair means we will get justice by others. We cannot allow the women and children to starve another winter."

'Mr Lloyd Evans' wife has just given birth to his daughter.' He looked to where Sali was sitting in the public gallery, and repeated, *"We cannot let the women and children starve another winter."* Need I say more, gentlemen?'

A red haze formed in front of Sali's eyes as she was forced to sit in silence and listen to the lies being said about Lloyd.

'I agree with the learned counsel,' he gave Geoffrey Francis a perfunctory nod, 'that the testimony of the three defendants differs in many respects from Sergeant Lamb's, but who are we to believe? Strike leaders and troublemakers who have incited their fellow workers to withdraw their labour and bring the coal industry on which the economy of the Welsh Valleys and indeed the whole of South Wales is based? Or a respected, God-fearing police officer and representative of authority?' He bowed his head. 'Your honour, members of the jury, I rest my case.'

Sali never remembered what she did during the half hour it took the jury to retire and bring in their verdict. She only recalled afterwards – sitting on the bench between Joey and Mr Richards, and Joey's hand trembling and growing cold in hers as they both tried to absorb the implications of the jury's verdict.

'Guilty on all charges with a recommendation for mercy.'

'What does that mean?' Betty Morgan whispered behind them.

'Silence.' The judge glared around the courtroom. He waited for the murmur of voices to subside before looking to the three defendants in the dock.

'William Evans, Lloyd, Evans, Victor Evans, you have had fair hearing and a judgement made on your crimes by your peers. I have taken into account the jury's recommendation of mercy. William Evans and Lloyd Evans, you have been found guilty of riotous assembling at Penygraig on July last. Thereby I sentence you, Lloyd William Evans, on that charge to one year's imprisonment with hard labour. William Wilberforce Evans I sentence you on that same charge to one year's imprisonment with hard labour.'

Banging his gavel for order, the judge waited until the uproar at his pronouncement subsided. 'Victor Sebastian Evans, I have taken into account the mitigating circumstances of the assault you perpetrated on the officer you wrongly assumed was threatening your father. However, as you have asked for another offence to be taken into consideration, that of threatening and inflicting grievous bodily harm on a clergymen, I sentence you to six months imprisonment with hard labour.'

Joey jumped to his feet and began shouting. To Sali's amazement, the other men and women on the public benches followed suit, ignoring both the judge's calls for order and the police officers moving in on them. Numbed by the prospect of losing Lloyd for an entire year, she stared down at the back of his head.

Lloyd's father and Victor continued to face the judge, but almost as though he had sensed her presence, Lloyd turned and looked directly at her. And in that single moment, she felt as though she had seen into his soul and the very heart of the love he bore for her and their children.

'I'm sorry,' shocked by the severity of the sentences Sergeant Martin apologized in advance to Sali and Joey, 'but I can't allow you more than five minutes and under no circumstances are you to touch the prisoners.'

The prisoners. The words seared into Sali's mind when she

walked into the waiting room ahead of Joey. It was bare with yellow distempered walls and a wooden floor. Lloyd, Victor and Mr Evans were standing in line, handcuffed and flanked by police officers. At a signal from Sergeant Martin the constables moved to the door behind them.

'We'll be fine,' Lloyd said unconvincingly to Sali. 'You look after yourself and Bella and Harry.'

'We'll come to see you as soon as they let us,' Joey said, fighting emotion.

Victor looked silently at Sali. She knew what he wanted to ask.

'I'll do all I can to find Megan, Victor, I promise. Take care of yourselves. Joey and I will keep a fine home for you to come back to. I love you, Lloyd. All three of you and you're not to worry about us . . .'

The outer door opened and they were hustled away.

Sali had never felt so exhausted and beaten in her life. Joey led her into the corridor where Mr Richards was waiting with Mari who was carrying Bella.

'I have arranged for the carriage to pick us up at a side door, Mrs Evans, to avoid the crowds. Half the Rhondda and all the Federation members are demonstrating outside the court building. It wouldn't surprise me if the police find themselves facing another riot after such injustice.'

'Of course, Mr Francis will appeal the sentences . . .'

'But he may not be successful,' Sali interrupted, guessing what Mr Richards was trying to tell her.

'No, he may not,' the solicitor reluctantly agreed, as the four of them sat in the coach that headed through Taffs Well towards Pontypridd.

Sali tried to put her thoughts in order. There were so many decisions to make. She had enough money to keep herself, the children and Joey in Tonypandy, but she knew that if she continued to pay the household expenses she would only succeed in hurting Lloyd and his father's pride all the more.

But as she tried to concentrate on practical matters, an image of Lloyd, Victor and Mr Evans travelling to Cardiff prison in a Black

Maria intruded into her mind. She pictured the indignities they would be subjected to. She had heard so many stories about what happened to prisoners when they were admitted to jail.

Stripped of their clothes, personal possessions and dignity, hosed down with cold water as they were forced to stand naked, locked like animals in a cell . . . What was hard labour these days – breaking rocks?

'Mrs Evans,' Mr Richards touched her arm, 'have you thought what you are going to do now?'

Sali bit her lip in an effort to contain her emotion and shook her head.

Mr Richards looked across at Mari, who was engrossed in nursing and protecting the baby against the movement of the carriage. Joey was slumped in the corner. His eyes were closed, but it was impossible to say whether he slept or not.

'Perhaps now is the time for you to consider moving back into Ynysangharad House. The trustees will cover all your expenses. You have no one to pay the expenses of your father-in-law's house.'

'Move in with Geraint? No, Mr Richards, it is out of the question.'

'Here, Mrs Evans.' He opened his briefcase and thrust a pile of envelopes at her. 'Put these in your handbag, I think you will find solutions to some of your problems in the minutes of the last two meetings the trustees held in your absence.'

'I had Bella—'

'That was not meant as a criticism, Mrs Evans; we were aware that you were indisposed and could not attend. I will do all I can to help Mr Francis appeal against the sentences but you must also fight, Mrs Evans. Not everyone will see the sentence your husband received as unjust. There are those who will try to use his criminal record against you, to discredit both you and the family you have married into.'

'Geraint,' she said wearily.

He patted her hand. 'Come and see me tomorrow afternoon when you have had time to think. We'll talk over things then. I will send the carriage to Tonypandy for you. Shall we say, two o'clock?'

'Harry will be in school.'

'I am sure that his education will be able to survive one afternoon off, Mrs Evans.'

She removed her handkerchief from her handbag, covered her mouth and looked out of the window. The sun had set and the gas lamps had been lit. Curtains were being drawn in the houses they passed and she imagined men coming home from work and washing, women carrying the food they had prepared to the table, a family sitting around, eating, laughing, talking . . . a sudden vision of Lloyd, and all his family, and the children sitting at the table in the kitchen of his father's house was so acutely real and painful that she blanched.

'Won't you at least stay in Ynysangharad House tonight, Mrs Evans?' Mr Richards pleaded.

'No,' said Sali, 'But I will read the minutes of the trustees' meetings and consider the future, Mr Richards. And tomorrow I will meet you in your office.'

Sali picked up Harry on the way home. Joey helped her and the children down from the carriage and opened the door. To his surprise a fire had been lit in the kitchen and a pleasant smell of cooking and baking filled the air.

'I've put one of my meat and potato pies into the oven for you, Sali.' Joyce Palmer untied her apron, lifted it over her head and folded it into her shopping bag. 'Mrs Rodney sent up some bread and other essentials, and the kettle's boiled for tea. The whole of Tonypandy's heard about the sentences and, like everyone else, all I can say is it's an absolute disgrace that good men should be punished for fighting for their rights. And that is just what my Aled would say if he were here. I can't stay. I have my lodgers to see to. There's an apple pie and a jug of custard in the warming tray, don't let them go to waste.' She tickled Bella under the chin, and smiled at Harry. 'Gorgeous baby you have there, young man, you must be really proud of her.'

'Thank you,' Sali shouted after her as she bustled out.

423

'Sit down, Sali.' Joey adopted a paternal attitude that she found difficult to take seriously in spite of her misery. 'I'll dish out the food.'

'You see to Harry and yourself,' she said. 'I'll bath Bella, feed her and settle her down first.'

'Sali—'

'Don't worry, Joey, I'll eat. I promised Lloyd that I'd look after myself, and I will.'

Sali and Joey sat in the kitchen after Sali had put Harry to bed. The baby hadn't stirred in her day cot in the corner, and Sali didn't expect her to until she woke for her midnight feed. It was so quiet that the ticking of the clock resounded like gunshot into the still atmosphere. She started at the slightest sound, half expecting Lloyd, Mr Evans or Victor to walk through the door, even though she knew that was impossible.

She read the minutes of the meetings that had taken place in her absence, re-read them, considered the implications of the decisions that had been taken and set the papers on her lap. She looked across at Joey. He had said very little since they had left Cardiff and hadn't referred to the trial once, but she could discern the same bitterness in him that she had detected in Lloyd, Victor and Mr Evans, for all that Joey had found a job – albeit one more suitable for a boy than a grown man.

'We have to talk, Joey.'

He looked up from the book he wasn't even pretending to read. 'What's there to talk about?'

'The future.'

'The future is I go to see Mr Francis tomorrow and ask him to sell one of the houses and hope we get enough money from the sale to live on for the next couple of months.'

'No, it isn't,' she said determinedly. 'The future is we move out tomorrow.'

'To where?'

'Ynysangharad House.'

'Lloyd said—'

'I know Lloyd and your father's views and I went along with

424

them before I read these.' She lifted the papers from her lap. 'Ynysangharad House is Harry's, the trustees have been wanting me to move in there for some time and we'll do just that because temporarily it is going to be very convenient for our new jobs. Gwilym James is opening a new store in Tonypandy. The company is going to need new staff, lots of staff. People who have been trained to do shop work.'

'I'm not even a decent delivery boy.'

'You are young, good-looking, bright and charming. You were a brilliant repairman and I'm sure that given time you will become an excellent sales assistant, assistant manager and, given your knowledge of Tonypandy and the training you will receive from the manager of the Pontypridd store of Gwilym James, eventual manager of the Tonypandy store.'

'Lloyd also said no made-up jobs,' he snapped.

'It won't be. Look at this.' She thrust the copy of the minutes Mr Horton junior had written and pointed to a section Mr Richards had underlined: 'A conservative estimate is twenty trained staff to start in the Tonypandy Department Store within two months, training to be carried out in Gwilym James department store, Pontypridd.' 'We'll be lucky to have you.'

'And this house?'

'We'll close it up and ask Betty Morgan to keep an eye on it.'

'You have it all worked out, don't you?' he said bitterly.

'No, I don't, Joey,' she said honestly, 'but what I do know is that we can't sit back and feel sorry for ourselves, or allow your father, Lloyd and Victor to worry themselves sick about us when they need every ounce of energy to look after themselves. Good things aren't going to happen unless we make them.'

'After what happened today you can talk about good things?' he mocked.

'The first good thing I want to happen is Lloyd, Victor and your father's release from prison. And I intend to start fighting for that with every means at my disposal first thing tomorrow. Which is one of the reasons I intend to see Geoffrey Francis, after I've met Mr Richards.'

'I'm with you there.' He finally began to show some signs of enthusiasm.

'Tell me, do you hate the idea of working in a department store that much?'

'What would an assistant manager earn?'

'Trainee assistant managers in Gwilym James, and that's what you will be next Monday morning if you decide to take the job, receive one pound ten shillings a week. I've done no favours for my brother, and although I hate to say it after recommending him for the position, he's not a particularly good assistant manager, but he still gets the going rate of three pounds a week. The manager of the Tonypandy store would get more than four pounds a week.'

'That's more than I would have earned in the colliery even if we had been given our pay rise. You really think I could do the job?'

She saw the excitement in his eyes and breathed a heady sigh of relief. If she could sort out Joey it would be a start. 'There's only one way to find out. But I warn you, the training won't be easy. Mr Horton, the manager of Gwilym James, is a stickler and a tartar. If he catches you flirting with the staff or customers he'd probably put you in the modern day equivalent of the stocks,' she said not entirely humorously, 'and you'll have Geraint to contend with. He hates me, but he hates Lloyd and all of you more.'

'I met him – once.'

'Then you know what I mean. So, what do you say?'

'Anything has to be better than moping around here trying to pay the bills on fifteen shillings a week. But what about you?'

'I have some ideas of my own,' she said lightly. 'It's high time I became more involved with the businesses Harry will own one day.'

'You have the children.'

'And I have Mari and a full staff to run Ynysangharad House and you to help me face Geraint when I move in there.'

He fell serious. 'This is a gamble, Sali. I may not be up to doing what this Mr Horton wants of me, but you do know that even if I make a go of it, my father, Lloyd and Victor will never work in a shop. Especially one Harry will inherit.'

'I know, Joey,' she agreed, 'but let's take it one step at a time.

As soon you wake up tomorrow, go down to Pontypridd and ask them to send the carriage up early. I'll have everything packed by the time you come back. Now we've made the decision, the sooner we move the better.'

'You understand?' Sali looked from Mr Jenkins to Mari and the housekeeper.

'Mr Geraint and Mrs Watkin Jones aren't going to like it,' the housekeeper warned Sali.

'This isn't their house for them not to like it,' Mr Jenkins pointed out.

'I agree, Miss Sali, it's an ideal solution,' Mari said. 'You, Master Harry and your husband's family will occupy the main house and Mr Geraint and your mother will move into the separate wing. It's been closed for about five years but I check it periodically and I've seen no sign of damp or decay. It shouldn't take more than a day or two to air the rooms once we get the fires lit. Do you want us to air the separate dining and drawing rooms there as well?'

'Please, Mari. Given that I have two young children, I wouldn't want them disturbing my mother or Geraint, so I think we should run the two households as entirely separate entities. I will occupy the master bedroom, Mr Joseph the blue room, and you'll need to prepare two — no three — other bedrooms for my father-in-law, Mr Victor Evans and his fiancée Miss Williams and hold them in readiness. If their appeal is successful, and we hope it will be, they could be with us within a few weeks. Bella will of course sleep in my room and you can put a bed for Master Harry in the dressing room off my room until he gets used to the house. Then he can move into the nursery.'

'Yes, Miss Sali.' Mari beamed. She had considered Sali to be her mistress ever since Sali's twelfth birthday when she had taken control of her late father's house after her mother had fallen prey to hypochondria. But it had been a long time since she had heard Miss Sali give so many orders and so decisively. 'Will you and Mr Evans be in to lunch?'

'We will, Mari. An early one at twelve o'clock, please, as I have a meeting with Mr Richards before the trustees' meeting. Joey will take care of Harry while I am out. Perhaps they could both explore the house.'

'I'll tell cook.' The elderly housekeeper, who hated change, hurried away to break the news to the rest of the staff, that new management had taken over the running of the household and there was no saying what might happen.

'It is good to have you and Master Harry in residence, Mrs Evans.'

'Thank you, Mr Jenkins,' Sali said gratefully to the butler. 'It is good to know that you approve of our being here.'

Chapter 26

'YOU'RE EARLY, Mrs Evans.' Mr Richards glanced up from his cup of tea and roast beef sandwich when his clerk showed Sali into his office at one o'clock.

'I am sorry, Mr Richards, but after studying the minutes of the meetings you gave me yesterday, I thought we had a great deal to discuss.'

'Can I get you anything?'

'I've just eaten a substantial lunch at Ynysangharad House, Mr Richards, but please, don't let me stop you from eating.' Sali took the plate and cup he had set aside and placed them back in front of him. 'Joey and I have just moved into Ynysangharad House.'

The solicitor sat stunned, as Sali outlined the changes she'd put into motion in the house in the course of one short morning. 'You approve, Mr Richards?'

'The trustees have been trying to get you to move in for months—'

'And now I have. Now, about these minutes.' Sali removed her gloves, opened her handbag and took out the papers. 'It says here that the solicitors have found a property in Tonypandy they consider suitable for a Gwilym James store and you intend training staff with the intention of opening it within two months.'

'That is correct. However, two months may be a little optimistic. In my experience carpenters can be slower than their estimates, especially when it comes to fitting out a store.'

'And you think that you'll need approximately twenty new staff to begin with, and probably more long-term.'

'We will.'

'You know my husband's younger brother, Joey?'

'A collier.'

'He was a repairman, but until we moved out of Tonypandy this morning he was working for Rodney's.'

'So he has experience of working with customers.' Mr Richards brightened a little.

'He has. He also knows everyone in Tonypandy, and, because he wasn't exactly at his best yesterday, you might not have noticed that he can be very charming. What I would like to suggest is that he start training in the Pontypridd store as an assistant manager. Mr Horton will soon find out whether he is suitable for a position in Gwilym James. If he is, he could be transferred to Tonypandy when it opens.'

'As manager.'

'He wouldn't be experienced enough after only two months' training, Mr Richards.'

'Then as a full assistant manager under Mr Watkin Jones.'

'No, Mr Richards, as a full assistant manager under Mr Alfred Horton.'

'You know something, Mrs Evans, I believe that for Master Harry's sake, you should take a more active part, both in the businesses he owns, and on the board of trustees.'

'Thank you for your confidence in me, Mr Richards. Do you think that I can count on the support of the trustees from this firm when I put these suggestion to the board this afternoon?'

'I most certainly do, Mrs Evans.' He smiled and rang the bell on his desk to summon his clerk. 'I most certainly do.'

Mr Horton positively bristled with pride as he looked around his fellow trustees. Like Mr Richards he had listened in muted silence when Sali had proposed bringing down men from Tonypandy to train as assistants for the new store, but his entire attitude to her idea had changed to enthusiastic endorsement when she suggested that when the store opened, his son manage it.

'It will cost Gwilym James a ridiculous amount in extra wages with no return until the Tonypandy store opens, Sali,' Geraint commented disparagingly. 'This store will have assistants positively tripping over one another in their eagerness to please customers. It will create havoc and put people off from shopping here.'

'Do you agree, Mr Horton?' Sali addressed the manager.

'Not at all, Mrs Evans. In fact I can think of several projects that I have been meaning to undertake for some time that could be facilitated by the addition of extra staff. Reorganization of the stockroom and displays, a thorough stock take, and if I might be so bold as to suggest that we hold a pre-Christmas sale. With extra staff, albeit trainees available, we wouldn't need to hire any temporary assistants . . .'

Realizing that Mr Horton would regale them all afternoon with ways of utilizing the extra staff if he allowed him to monopolize the meeting, Mr Jenkins interrupted. 'Shall we take a vote on Mrs Evans' proposal that we actively recruit staff for the Tonypandy store in Tonypandy. And secondly that we train them in this store? All in favour?'

Sali looked at her brother, but Geraint was the only trustee who failed to raise his hand, at either motion.

'Carried with one abstention.' Mr Jenkins made a note on the sheet of paper in front of him.

'I would like to raise another matter,' George Owens, the director from the Capital and Counties said after the motion had been noted. 'Some of you may be aware that Mr Hardy is putting the Mason and Hardy department store in Cardiff on the market next year. I have met with Mr Hardy. He informed me that he intends to retire in June when the present lease on the premises expires, and as neither his, nor the late Mr Mason's sons are interested in running the business, he feels that both the staff and customers will be best served by a change of management. The store is operational, profitable and fully fitted. I put it to the committee that we should consider purchasing both the lease and the store.'

'Could we afford to finance the opening of a new store in Tonypandy as well as take over Mason and Hardy's in Cardiff, Mr Owens?' Mr Jenkins enquired.

'It would reduce the trust's cash holdings to below two thousand pounds, Mr Jenkins, which in my opinion would be a far more satisfactory situation. Money should be used to make money and I believe both of these ventures to be as sound as any I have seen. And don't forget, Mason and Hardy's is already a profitable store.'

'Would we change the name from Mason and Hardy to Gwilym James, Mr Owens?' Mr Horton asked.

'That is for the trustees to determine, Mr Horton. However,' Mr Owens gazed intently at the men gathered around the table, 'I believe these things are best done slowly. Do we all agree that at present, Mason and Hardy's is not run to the same,' Mr Owens paused, 'shall we say, high standards as Gwilym James?'

The nods around the table precluded a vote.

'But it is fully staffed and stocked, and we would be taking it over as a going concern. What I suggest is, that we invest the profits in the modernization of the store. When, and only when, we are satisfied that Mason and Hardy is of comparable quality to Gwilym James, will we change the name. I think now is the time to take a vote on whether I initiate further enquiries along those lines, Mr Jenkins.'

Mr Jenkins rested his elbows on the table and pressed his fingertips together. 'All in favour?'

For once Geraint was the first to raise his hand, and Sali realized that he was hoping to be made manager of the Cardiff store.

Mr Jenkins again noted the proposal and the vote. 'Carried unanimously.' He removed his pocket watch from his waistcoat and opened it. 'Lady and gentlemen, it is almost four o'clock. Does anyone wish to raise any other pressing business?'

'I do, Mr Jenkins.' Sali looked down the table and wondered how she had ever found the board of trustees intimidating. After all, they were being paid to administer her son's estate. 'I will try to be brief, gentlemen. I don't doubt that you are all aware that my husband, his brother and father have been imprisoned.'

Geraint tilted his chair back and stared at the ceiling. She ignored him.

'I do not propose to go into the rights or wrongs of the case or make excuses for what I consider to be a severe miscarriage of justice. Suffice to say their legal advisers are working on an appeal.

432

However, to get to the point, this morning, my children, myself and my brother-in-law moved into Ynysangharad House.'

Geraint sat upright, slamming his chair down on all four legs.

'I am certain that I speak for all the committee, Mrs Evans, when I say that we are pleased to hear that you have done so.' Mr Jenkins smiled at her before looking to Geraint, who was staring at his sister.

'I have asked Mr Richards to find a tutor for Harry, hopefully one who can start immediately, meanwhile I will supervise his education. I do not want Harry to be tutored as an only child, so I have decided to look for half a dozen children or so around Harry's age who can be taught alongside him in Ynysangharad House.'

'Very commendable.' Mr Jenkins nodded. 'Do you have any children in mind, Mrs Evans?'

'No, Mr Jenkins, I had hoped that yourself and the committee could assist me. If any of you know of children Harry's age who live within easy distance of the house and who would like to be educated alongside my son I would be grateful if you could ask their parents to contact me. It is my intention to turn the library into a schoolroom.'

'The library!'

'Yes, Geraint, the library.' Sali looked her brother in the eye. 'Do you have any objections to my son using *his* library as a schoolroom?'

'None at all.' He looked down at his hands.

'I also wish to inform you that I met with Mr Horton prior to this meeting and he has agreed to take my brother-in-law, Mr Joseph Evans, as one of the trainee assistant managers destined to be employed at the Tonypandy store. The last thing Mr Evans would want is any favouritism to be shown to him because of his relationship to me. Should he prove unsuitable, he will be dismissed. I discussed some ideas of my own with Mr Horton.' She looked at the manager. 'In the future I hope to take a more active role in Gwilym James and possibly the Market Company as my Great-Aunt Edyth did. Mr Horton has agreed that I should supervise the buying of stock for the Tonypandy store. As I have been living there for the past few years I am acquainted with the goods the colliers and their wives need. Mr Horton is arranging for me to have an office here, on the top floor. Should any of you wish to contact me, I will be working here every Monday, Wednesday and Friday from two o'clock until five in the afternoon. The remainder of the week I will work in the study in Ynysangharad House so I can be close to my children.'

'I am sure that the entire committee welcomes your news, Mrs Evans.' Mr Jenkins looked around the table. 'Any other business? No? Lady, gentlemen, I declare this meeting closed.'

'May I speak to you alone for a few moments, Geraint?'

'If Mr Horton will excuse me,' Geraint replied sullenly.

'Of course, Mr Watkin Jones.' Mr Horton left the room.

Sali touched Mr Richards's arm. 'I hope you will come back to the house with me for tea. I'd like to discuss investments with you?'

'I will wait in the carriage, Mrs Evans.' The last to leave the conference room, Mr Richards closed the door behind him.

'Investments?' Geraint sat back in his chair.

'Mr Richards sold some jewellery for me. I intend to invest the money.'

'You've sold Aunt Edyth's jewellery! Her will clearly states that it is yours for use only in your lifetime and is to be left to Harry.'

'I am aware of the terms of Aunt Edyth's will. Her jewellery is in the bank. I sold the engagement ring Mansel gave me, which I think you'll concede is mine.'

'And you've moved yourself and your brother-in-law into Ynysangharad House and arranged a job for him here?'

'That is what I wanted to talk to you about, Geraint.'

'Have you realized what you've done, Sali?' he railed. 'You have put Mr Horton and me in an impossible position. You have asked him to try to turn a filthy collier into a competent sales assistant, who will have to deal with ladies and gentlemen. And you're asking me to live with the man . . .'

'No, I am not.'

'Pardon?'

'Let's deal with the position I have put Mr Horton in first, shall we? I asked him to consider Joey, not as an assistant but as a potential assistant manager for the Tonypandy store. But then, that is no more than I would do for any member of my family, Geraint. Even you.'

Taking her barbed remark as she'd intended, Geraint remained silent.

'About our living arrangements,' she continued. 'I have spoken to Mari and the housekeeper and organized you and Mother's move into the annexe. Joey, the children and I will be occupying the house and given the tension between us—'

'Which is of your making. Marrying a common criminal—'

'I am not arguing with you, Geraint, I am informing you of the arrangements I have made. I am not prepared to allow Harry to be brought up in a strained atmosphere, or witness any bickering between you and me, or you and Joey, and given your attitude towards Lloyd and his family there will be some.'

'You think I would be impolite—'

'I think there would be sharp words and arguments. Harry is not used to either. I have ordered Mari to run the annexe as an entirely separate household, although you will have your meals supplied from the kitchen of the main house. I don't believe it's fair to expect the estate to go to the expense of hiring any extra staff, so Mari will assume housekeeping duties in the main house; Aunt Edyth's housekeeper, one maid and the nurse will assume duties in the annexe.'

'And Mr Jenkins?'

'Mr Jenkins and Robert will continue to work in the main house. If you want any extra staff you will have to pay for them out of your wages.'

'You know what I earn here. I can't afford—'

'Your finances are your own affair, Geraint. For Mother's sake I will continue to allow you both to live in the house, rent and expense free. But I expect you to remain in the annexe unless you are given a specific invitation to visit the main house. If you want to use any of the carriages, you will have to clear it with me first.'

Geraint pursed his lips sullenly.

'You have nothing to say?'

'What about Gareth and Llinos?'

435

'When they come home from school they will live in the annexe with you and mother.'

'You humiliate us by forcing us to live in the cramped annexe, while you and a common collier lord it in the main house, and when your husband comes out of prison—'

'That common collier is my brother-in-law and soon to be your colleague. As to Lloyd moving in, I haven't dared think that far ahead, Geraint. The annexe has four bedrooms, a bathroom, dining room, drawing room and kitchen, in my opinion, hardly cramped quarters. I think you are forgetting that Mansel and I decorated and prepared the annexe to be our home only six years ago. As for humiliating you, you haven't paid a single penny towards your own or mother's keep since you moved into Ynysangharad House on a "temporary basis" that has lasted over a year. Joey, however, has already offered to pay his keep from his wages.'

'He wouldn't earn enough to pay his keep in a place like Ynysangharad House,' Geraint sneered.

'Ten shillings a week is the going rate in the Rhondda for lodgings and that is what he will be paying. It will cover the cost of his food. Now if you'll excuse me, I don't want to keep Mr Richards waiting.'

'If you two boys can tear yourself away from killing your men,' Mari shook her head at the lead soldiers scattered around the nursery fort, 'I'll show you your bedrooms.'

'Later, Mari.' Harry made a booming noise and knocked over another of Joey's officers.

'Come on, Tiger, it is not polite to keep a lady waiting, or not do as she asks.' Joey picked him up and swung him on to his back.

Mari smiled, as Harry wrapped his small arms around Joey's neck. 'You two are close.'

'We're in the same gang,' Harry informed her seriously.

'This will be your room until you decide whether or not you want to move into the nursery, Master Harry. It's next door to your mother's and there's a door between the rooms, so if you need her in the night you don't have to go out on the landing.'

Joey looked around the dressing room, then opened the

connecting door and gazed at the master bedroom. He whistled appreciatively at the sight of the mahogany four-poster, matching wardrobes, dressing table, washstand and desk. Two upholstered chairs stood either side of a sofa table in front of a huge window that overlooked the gardens. A Persian rug covered most of the floor and white silk drapes on the bed and windows and a white silk bedcover lightened the impact of the furniture. 'So this is how the other half live.'

'It is a nice room,' Mari concurred, 'and it's been crying out to be used since Mrs James's death. I'm glad that Miss Sali has decided to move in here. You're in the blue room.' She led the way along the landing and opened another door. 'I hope it will do you.'

'Do me?' Joey untangled Harry's arms from around his neck and dropped him on the bed. 'It's bigger than the whole of the upstairs in my father's house in Tonypandy.'

'I'm going to set the soldiers up for another game, Uncle Joey.' Harry jumped down from the bed and ran back down the landing.

'Thank you.' Joey gave Mari one of his most charming smiles. 'I'll feel like a prince sleeping in here.' The drapes at the window were blue, the bed wasn't a four-poster but the rest of the furniture was the same standard as that in the master bedroom, and there was a desk, table and chairs at the window. The toilet ware on the washstand was Doulton — he recognized it because his mother had loved good china and had frequently taken him around the china departments of big stores before he'd been old enough to protest.

'The maid's unpacked your things and put them in the wardrobe. Your case has been taken to the box room.'

'I could have done that,' Joey protested. 'I'm not used to being waited on hand and foot.'

'Get used to it,' Mari warned. 'Because the last thing my staff, especially the younger maids, need is an over familiar member of the family when he's as young as you, and,' she gave him a stern look, 'who can turn on the charm whenever he wants to.'

'Sali's been talking to you.'

'Miss Sali didn't have to say a word. Mrs Williams—'

'Llan House, I forgot. You're sisters, aren't you?'

'She said you were good-looking and personable, and she was right on both counts. She also said that you couldn't be trusted around pretty girls. Well, don't try any of your antics on any of my staff or Mr Horton's in the store. The first hint of any trouble and you'll be out and not even Miss Sali will be able to save you. You want to play with anyone,' she paused, as Harry called him again from the nursery, 'I suggest you restrict yourself to playing soldiers with your nephew.'

Not wanting to give herself too much time to think about Lloyd or build up hopes that his appeal would be successful when it might fail, Sali immersed herself in work. She contacted Mr Richards every day to check on the progress of the appeal that he was working on with Geoffrey Francis. She taught Harry and the sons and daughters of the estate workers Mr Jenkins had rounded up for his 'class' in the mornings. She fed and played with Bella and Harry, spent three afternoons in the shop meeting manufacturers' representatives and discussing policy and shop fittings for the new Tonypandy store with Mr Horton. She visited Mason and Hardy's in Cardiff, and approved of the buy-out, which was ratified by the trustees.

She also made daily duty visits to her mother, always before Geraint came home, and rarely saw her brother outside of the store. The running of the house she left entirely to Mari, who saw that apart from the meals, which were delivered from the kitchen in the main house, the annexe and its occupants were regarded as entirely separate from the main household. She paid a short visit to Gareth and Llinos when they came home from school for the Christmas holidays and, mindful of the staff's workload during the holidays, invited them and Geraint to Christmas dinner, which turned out to be a subdued affair, in sharp contrast to the two Christmases she had enjoyed with the Evanses. And a week after Christmas, she left Bella and Harry with Mari, and she and Joey set off to make their first visit to Cardiff prison.

Sali crept close to Joey and took his arm, as they joined the crowd waiting outside the jail. It was a grey day and the wind whipped icy needles of sleet beneath their umbrella no matter how close to their heads Joey held it. She turned up the collar of her coat, pulled her hat down and glanced at the people around them. One young woman was barefoot, the child she was carrying wrapped in a tattered blanket.

Joey put his hand in his pocket and slipped something into the woman's hand. Sali pretended she hadn't seen him. The one thing she had learned about all the Evans was they hated to be thought of as soft touches and although Joey had a pound a week left over from his wages, she knew he was saving as much of it as he could. Most of their tenants were so deep in debt after the strike that their rents were slow in coming in and Joey was acutely aware that even when Lloyd, Victor and his father were released, he was the only one with a job.

After an interminable ten minutes, locks were drawn back and they all filed through a small door set in the high gates, into an open inner yard. Two warders stood behind a table and searched all the bags and parcels the visitors had brought in for the prisoners. After the food and books she had brought for Lloyd, Victor and Mr Evans had been confiscated for distribution 'at the governor's discretion', she was separated from Joey, taken through a door into a side room in the main building and patted down by a female warder before being allowed back into the main corridor.

Joey joined her at the door to the room set aside for visits.

A warder held the door open and chanted, 'Sit at a table as soon as you are inside, no touching the prisoners, no handing any objects whatsoever to the prisoners. Sit at a table . . .'

'They only sit four,' Joey whispered, when they were inside. 'Take those two in the corner.' Joey sat across the aisle from Sali on one of the rough wooden benches set either side of the heavily scarred deal tables. The first thing that struck both of them was the lack of oxygen in the air, and the smell. A foul overpowering stench of unwashed bodies, clothes worn too long, faeces and urine.

Whispers occasionally broke the silence as they waited and, after another ten long minutes, the convicts eventually began to file in.

Sali covered her mouth with her hand when she saw Lloyd. His head had been shaved and his cheeks were covered in dark stubble the same length as his hair. As he moved towards her she saw that he had lost an alarming amount of weight. Victor who walked behind him didn't look any better, but her father-in-law was obviously very ill. Hunched and grey, he tottered and stumbled towards them like an old man, and she felt that he had aged ten years in a month. He started to cough when he and Victor sat at Joey's table, and his breath was harsh, grating as he drew in the foul stinking air.

'Don't be fooled by the uniform, Sali. Underneath these imposing clothes, I'm the same old me,' Lloyd joked as he sat opposite her.

'You look . . .' Words failed her.

'Like a convict?'

'Lloyd . . .'

'If you don't keep a sense of humour in here, you'll go insane. How are Harry and Bella?'

She looked into his eyes and saw that he was hungry for news of the children and, if anything, was missing her even more than she was him. But then she could immerse herself in the children and work, whereas he . . . she didn't want to begin to imagine what his days were like within these grim, grey walls.

She forced an insincere smile, and realized he had seen right through it. 'They're both fine. Bella can roll around the floor of the nursery now, and Harry is enjoying his lessons with his new friends.' Unable to keep up the pretence, she fell serious. 'I'm so sorry, Lloyd. I didn't know what to do after the trial. Then I read the minutes of the trustees' meetings I had missed and saw a chance for Joey. I moved because I thought it solved a lot of problems. Joey has a job with prospects. I don't have to worry about money, the house, shopping or even the children. If we'd stayed in Tonypandy . . .'

'You don't have to apologize, Sali.' He clasped his hands together to remind himself not to touch her. 'I'm proud of you for not sitting back and crying, which is what most women would have done if their husbands had been locked up. I got your letter and I

440

wholeheartedly approve of every decision you made, especially kicking Geraint out of the main part of Ynysangharad House. I agree that you can't abandon your mother but you've been feather-bedding him for far too long.'

'You don't mind? I thought you'd be furious.'

'Our marriage is a partnership, sweetheart. I know I can be stubborn to the point of pigheadedness at times, but I am proud of you and the way you've dealt with the strike, the trial and now this.' He looked at their miserable surroundings. 'I wish I could have written to tell you just how proud of you I am, but there's a stupid rule, no letters for the first month. You made all the right decisions, Sali, especially for the children and Joey. I saw the letter he wrote to Victor. He's enjoying his new job.'

'I don't know what kind of collier he was, but he's a superb salesman. Mr Horton said Gwilym James's china sales have doubled since he put him in the department. As soon as the Tonypandy store opens he'll be going up there as assistant manager.'

'I read your letter and Joey's, so I know what you are doing with yourselves. But how are you, Sali? Really?' he said earnestly.

'Missing you, grateful at the end of every day because it's one day less that we have to spend apart.' She stretched her hand towards him. A warder shouted at her and she withdrew it. 'I see Mr Richards every day. He and Geoffrey Francis are working hard on your appeal . . .'

'I know. Geoffrey Francis is allowed to visit us.'

'Lloyd . . .'

'No lying, Sali, and no false hope, please. We've always been truthful with one another, don't change that now.'

'You were wrong about the men not daring to support you. You may not have seen them but thousands of colliers gathered outside the court in Cardiff to protest after you were sentenced. And there have been demonstrations all over the Rhondda at your imprisonment. All the unions are agitating for your release. Mabon has asked questions about your sentences in Parliament and they are allowing your appeal without costs. Every Labour politician, and even some Liberals are saying how unjust your sentences are. The unions have offered to support us—'

'You said no,' he broke in.

'I told them that Joey and I are earning enough to keep the children and ourselves. Working in the business gives me something to do and it stops me from thinking about you every single minute of the day.' She saw a warder glance at his pocket watch. They were running out of time. 'Mr Richards has done all he can to find Megan. We haven't found her. But tell Victor we are still looking and haven't given up hope. Your father is ill.' She eyed Mr Evans in concern, as he burst into another coughing fit.

'He's spent most of his time since we've been here in the infirmary. He only left there today because he wanted to see you and Joey, and by the look of him he'll be back there tomorrow.'

'Lloyd, what is hard labour?' she asked quietly.

'Work, no different to any other,' he said lightly. 'Let's not talk about me, or politics or the appeal, let's talk about you and the children. I want to know every tiny little thing that you do, starting with when you get up in the morning.'

So she sat and wove him a tale of their days in Ynysangharad House and pretended not to see the pain and despair in his eyes, as she described a family life he was no longer part of.

'How is Lloyd?' Joey asked, when he and Sali were in the train on their way back to Pontypridd.

'He didn't want to talk about much except the children and me. I could see that he is worried about your father. That cough of his sounds dreadful.'

'He said it sounds worse than it is, but I'm not convinced.' Joey propped his umbrella in the corner of the carriage where it couldn't drip on them. 'Do you think that we should write to the governor to say we're worried?'

'The governor and our MP. I'll do it tonight.'

'Victor is climbing up the wall because there's no news of Megan.' Joey sat forward and sank his face in his hands. 'I'll be honest with you, Sali, I don't know how they are going to survive the next eleven months – or any of us come to that.'

'We'll survive because we have to, Joey,' she said finally. 'We have no other choice. Do me a favour?'

'If I can.'

'Put a smile on your face before we reach Ynysangharad House. Harry is so bright and sensitive. Sometimes I think he picks up on our worries even before we're aware of them.'

Mr Richards was right; the carpenter had underestimated the time needed to fit out the Tonypandy store. It opened in March, not January as the trustees had intended, and Sali and Joey invited every friend, neighbour and all the families of the union men Mr Evans knew to the opening. The store was packed, and Sali's thoughts turned to Lloyd, Victor and Mr Evans and how proud they would be if they could see Joey, in his brand-new black wool, three-piece suit and wing-collared shirt presiding over the celebrations with Mr Horton junior.

'We showed the lodgers where the kettle is, put a tray of shortbread on the dining-room table and told them to fend for themselves for once,' Betty said to Sali after she and Joyce Palmer had fought their way through the crowd to where Sali was helping dispense lemonade and sweet biscuits to the first customers. 'Tell me, how is Harry?'

'And little Bella?' Mrs Palmer added.

'Not so little any more,' Sali smiled. 'I'll bring them up for a visit, but I can't promise when. I don't know where my time goes but I never seem to have enough of it to do everything I want.'

'Neither do I,' Mrs Palmer agreed. 'I've been meaning to write to you. Can we go somewhere quiet?'

'I'll ask the assistant manager if we can borrow his office.' Sali waved to Joey. He waved back to her from the middle of a crowd of local girls. Judging by the way they were all talking to him at once, Sali assumed he'd been missed. 'Can I borrow your office?' she mouthed.

He nodded. Sali handed Betty and Joyce two glasses, picked up a jug of lemonade and a glass for herself, and led the way. She closed the door and breathed a sigh of relief. 'I wanted the opening to be successful, not bedlam.'

'You can't blame people for coming. We've needed a shop like this in Tonypandy for some time, if only to convince people that not everyone has given up hope of prosperity returning to this valley.' Joyce sat on one of the two easy chairs Sali set in front of the desk. 'And it will be nice not to have to go into Pontypridd to buy clothes.'

'What will be even nicer is having a department store down the road that we can call into and look around any time we've a spare five minutes. No one else is investing in the Rhondda, Sali, especially with the colliery owners point blank refusing to make any improvements in the colliers' pay and conditions. Businesses are going bankrupt at a rate of knots. Even the farm went yesterday. Everyone is wondering when the next strike will take place.' Betty took the second chair.

'Surely no one wants another strike.' Sali cleared a pile of manufacturers' catalogues from the desk to make room for the lemonade and sat in Joey's chair.

'No one wants one and there's no denying that it will take us a few years to get over this one, but there'll be another, mark my words. Did you know there've been four deaths from accidents underground since the men have gone back?' Betty held her glass while Sali filled it.

'I've heard,' Sali said sadly.

'It'll take everyone years to pay off the debts they've incurred in this strike before the union can seriously consider calling another,' Joyce observed. 'You watching Joey, Sali?' she asked, seeing Sali look through the glass window of the office.

'Those girls have me worried. I hope Joey doesn't go back to his old ways now he's working here.'

'Is he moving back home?' Joyce sipped her lemonade.

'Not for the moment. Mr Horton's son lives in Pontypridd and they travel up together. Harry misses Lloyd and the family a great deal. Joey and I think it would be too much if he moved out as well. Not that they see that much of one another. Joey's been working twelve hours a day since he started in the shop, but Harry gets up to eat breakfast with him every morning, Joey reads him a story every night and,' Sali made a wry face, 'it's easier if we travel down to the prison together. And because prisoners are only allowed to send one letter a month Joey and I share the news.'

'How are Mr Evans, Lloyd and Victor coping?' Betty enquired.

'Lloyd and Victor are just about managing. Mr Evans has spent more time in the prison infirmary than out of it. He's had pneumonia twice since Christmas.'

Mrs Palmer nodded sagely. 'He loved his wife very much. Sometimes it's easier to let go than keep fighting.'

'We hope that when he comes out—'

'Any news of the appeal?' Betty interrupted.

'Not yet. Mr Francis has warned Joey and I that there's no hope of a quick release for any of them. Not even Mr Evans, although he's pressing a case to get him released on the grounds of ill-health.'

'Do the prisoners hear the news in prison? If they do, they must have been happy last Friday,' Joyce said brightly.

'When the minimum wage act was passed by Parliament? I don't know,' Sali said thoughtfully. 'I hope they heard about it, but as Joey said, it's only a beginning. You do know that all the Labour MPs refused to vote because the government wouldn't agree to set the minimum wage at five shillings a day for a man and two shillings a day for a boy.'

'I didn't know Joey was interested in politics,' Betty said good-humouredly.

'His interest has developed since his father and brothers have been imprisoned. I don't want to be rude, Mrs Palmer, but I should go back out there soon. You said you wanted to see me?' She was anxious to change the topic of conversation. The longer she and Lloyd were apart, the harder she was finding it to keep up a brave façade.

The nights were the worst, especially since Harry had moved into the nursery suite, because before, when she hadn't been able to sleep she had opened the connecting door between the dressing room and her bedroom and listened to his breathing. She still had Bella, but even the presence of her baby daughter wasn't enough to dull the ache engendered by Lloyd's absence from her life and her bed.

'I packed all Lena's things into a suitcase. Huw Davies was transferred back to Pontypridd shortly after her funeral.' Mrs Palmer gripped her glass and stared down at her lemonade. 'As you know, Lena left a letter for Huw and the engagement ring he gave her. I asked him if he wanted anything else. All he took were two photographs and a scarf to remember her by. He insisted on giving me the ring and I wondered if Megan would like it, together with the rest of Lena's possessions. Everything Lena owned was suited to a young girl, her clothes were all practically new and Megan was probably the closest friend she'd ever had. Do you know where Megan is?'

'Unfortunately not. My solicitor, Mr Richards and I have looked everywhere we can think of. But we haven't found any trace of her.'

'I've never seen two people more in love than Victor Evans and Megan Williams. And I'm sure she'll contact Victor just as soon as she is twenty-one. You will take Lena's things, won't you, Sali?' Joyce pleaded and Sali saw that she simply wanted them out of the house.

'Yes, I'll take them. As you say, Megan will be twenty-one in August and I'm equally certain that she will contact Victor then.' Sali sat back in Joey's chair and smiled.

'What is it?' Betty asked.

Sali left the chair, and kissed and hugged both women. 'Thank you, Mrs Palmer. You have just given me the most wonderful, marvellous idea.'

'You will pick up those things today?' Joyce asked, bewildered by Sali's behaviour.

'Just as soon as we've closed up here for the night.'

Mrs Palmer and Betty Morgan exchanged mystified glances, but Sali was in no mood for explanations. She didn't know if her idea would work. But it was a better alternative than sitting back and waiting for Megan to contact them, which was the only other option.

Chapter 27

IT HAS to be worth a try, Mr Richards,' Sali pleaded, after stopping off at her solicitor's house on the way home. Not wanting to tell Joey her idea in case it didn't work and she raised his hopes to no purpose, she had left him in the carriage. 'The one thing we do know about Megan's father is that he loves money. If we advertise in a Swansea Valley newspaper asking that Megan write to your firm because she has been named as beneficiary in a will, he is bound to contact us.'

'He may well do so,' Mr Richards agreed guardedly, 'but what if he refuses to divulge her whereabouts?'

'He'll tell us where she is if you say that the legacy can only be paid out if Megan signs for it in person, and that you have to witness her signature.'

'Have you thought she might be happy where she is, and won't want to leave?'

'I don't believe for one minute that she wants to stay away from Victor, but if that is the case, we can at least be sure that she is well and happy.'

'And if her father has sold her labour for a twelve-month and they demand she fulfil her contract?'

'I'll buy her out of it.'

Sali was so full of her plan, Mr Richards didn't remind her that that if Megan had an employer who refused to allow her to be bought out of her contract, they would have every legal right to demand she stay. He picked up his pen, looked at Sali, and asked, 'How exactly would you like this advertisement worded?'

Sali didn't tell Joey about the advertisement Mr Richards had placed, in case Megan's father didn't reply. And, as first one, then two, three and finally four weeks passed, she was glad that she had kept her plan a secret between Mr Richards and herself. She even began to wonder whether or not Megan's father could read. Mr Richards contacted the newspaper and arranged for the notice to be inserted in the weekly paper for another two weeks, on the premise that few papers were actually bought in the rural areas, but passed from farm to farm and could easily get lost along the way.

Two weeks after the final insertion, when Sali had almost, but not quite, given up hope of Mr Williams contacting them, Mr Richards knocked on the door of Sali's office in Gwilym James. One look at his smiling face was enough to send her spirits soaring.

'The appeal—'

'I warned you not to expect to hear anything for months.'

'Then you've had a letter from Megan's father!'

'It's about the sale of the farm at Tonypandy – you asked me to look into it.'

Trying to hide her disappointment, she said, 'Yes. Please, sit down, Mr Richards.' She indicated the chair in front of her desk. 'Is it for sale?'

'I don't know where your information came from, Mrs Evans, but it was accurate.' He took the chair she offered him. 'Mr Adams was about to go bankrupt. His farm, including the five-bedroom house, barn, cowshed, stable and workshops, over seventy acres of land – hillside, valley and woodland, about half classed as good grazing – has debts of around three hundred pounds against it. I looked over the place with a surveyor this morning. A few of the buildings are in disrepair, and there are areas where work needs doing but essentially it is a sound proposition. The surveyor suggested that given the downturn in the Rhondda's economy and the uncertainty of the future, four hundred pounds may be considered a good price for the place, which will give Mr Adams a clear hundred pounds. However, a note of caution, the place went bankrupt once, it could do so again.'

'Mr Adams had a mortgage. He couldn't sell his produce to

make the payments because the strikers had no money,' she said logically.

'That is true but several things can go wrong with a farm. The crops can be blighted, the animals fall sick, the price of feed can go up, that of produce can fall.'

'But with good management it might become a paying proposition,' she suggested optimistically.

'It might,' he replied, cautious to the last. 'Would you like me to make an offer?'

'Pay what it's worth, Mr Richards. It would be perfect for my brother-in-law, Victor – and Megan Williams, if we find her,' she added despondently.

'If you are free, we could look at it now. I have a carriage waiting outside.'

'I've seen it, Mr Richards. I have walked up there many times with Victor, Joey and Harry.'

'And been inside the house?' He looked at her enquiringly.

'Only the kitchen.'

'If you don't mind me saying so, Mrs Evans, you work too hard. A trip out would do you good.'

Sali thought for a moment. 'That might be an idea. We could call in at the Tonypandy store and see Joey afterwards. I'd like to make him a proposition.'

'The house is lovely and it's in a beautiful spot. You may be able to see the collieries, but you are so far away from them, they don't matter. The air is fresh, clean, free from dust, and smells entirely different. The way you feel air should.' Sali stood on the doorstep of the farmhouse and looked over the fields to a patch of woodland on her far right and the valley with its ugly black collieries and slag heaps beyond.

'It's a nice spot,' Mr Richards agreed. 'And I can see why Mr Adams will be glad to give it up. Aside from his debts, the place is a lot of work for a young man, let alone one of seventy, with a wife in poor health. Are you sure that you want to buy all the existing stock and machinery at valuation? It could push the price up by as much as another hundred pounds.'

449

'I am sure.' Sali looked around the farmyard and almost wished that Lloyd had the same interest in animals and market gardening as Victor. She could imagine living in the generously proportioned farmhouse with its tiny parlour and massive kitchen, looking up from her sewing and seeing him turn the pages of his book, as they sat either side of the range every evening after they had finished work for the day. Spending her days cooking, cleaning, washing, helping Lloyd with the farm, bringing up Harry and Bella . . .

'I'll see to the paperwork as soon as I get back to the office. Whose name do you want to put on the deeds?'

'That's why I want to call into the store and talk to Joey. He and I own all of Mr Evans's and the boys' houses. If I buy six of them from the Evans's it will give Joey six hundred pounds to buy the farm and the stock, and Victor, if he wants the place, a hundred pounds operating capital. In exchange I can put the houses in Bella's name. Then, if Mr Evans and Joey agree, they can give or sell the farm to Victor.' She looked around the farmyard one last time. 'Victor spent every spare moment he could up here. I think he'd want it, and if we don't buy it now we may not get another opportunity for years. If I'm wrong, and Victor doesn't want it, there shouldn't be a problem renting it out. Should there?' she asked anxiously, suddenly wondering if she was taking too much upon herself.

'None at all, Mrs Evans,' Mr Richards assured her. 'There are always people looking to rent farms.'

'Did you ask Mr Adams if the farmhand would stay on to look after the stock until someone takes possession?'

'Yes, and he can.'

'And you'll make the offer today?'

'If you give me five minutes I'll go back and talk to Mr Adams now.'

'I'll wait in the carriage for you, Mr Richards.'

'You've bought the farm for Victor?' Joey dropped the pen he was using to mark entries in the purchase ledger and stared at Sali and Mr Richards.

'Do you think he'll be pleased?' Sali removed her gloves and twisted them nervously in her hands.

'Given that he's spent all his free time up there since he could walk, and there are plenty of outbuildings that he can turn into a smithy, I think he'll be over the moon. It will also solve the problem of him finding a job when he comes out of prison. You're really buying it?' he reiterated, as if he couldn't quite believe her.

'Yes, but I don't want to register it in my name because that would complicate matters. Your family owns a dozen houses quite separate from Lloyd's. If you agree to sell me six at a hundred pounds apiece—'

'You already own half of them,' he pointed out.

'Only on paper,' she contradicted. 'If you sell me six for six hundred pounds, Mr Richards will arrange to have the deeds registered in Bella's name as an investment for her, and in return you will have the money to buy the farm, the stock and machinery and have enough left over for Victor to start running the place. Mr Richards can register the farm in your name and when Victor comes out, you, your father and Victor can decide who should own it.'

Joey frowned. 'It sounds to me like you're giving us money and Lloyd would hate that.'

'I am not giving you money,' she argued. 'Your houses are worth a hundred pounds apiece and I am buying them off you.'

'I'm not stupid, Sali. I know that the strike's forced property prices down,' Joey said seriously. 'If they came on the open market now, we'd be lucky to get fifty pounds apiece for them from an investor.'

'The prices have already risen to seventy, and we're expecting them to recover fully in the next year or so.' Mr Richards spoke with all the authority of a solicitor accustomed to purchasing property for his clients.

'Provided there isn't another strike,' Joey said caustically.

'Bella will have the rents as interest,' Sali determinedly ignored the mention of another strike.

'Tell me, what do you really think of Sali's plans, Mr Richards?' Joey asked the solicitor earnestly.

451

'I think Mrs Evans' idea is an eminently sensible one.'

'She's not giving us money?'

'On the contrary, she is making an investment for her daughter and freeing you enough capital to purchase a farm that could provide your brother with a comfortable living. No one has a crystal ball, Mr Evans, and there may well be more trouble coming to this valley, but there are also a lot of natural resources. Long term, I don't think an investor here will lose out.'

Joey hadn't had many personal business dealings, but for reasons he couldn't have begun to explain, he trusted the solicitor's judgement. 'In that case, go ahead and make all the necessary arrangements, Mr Richards.'

Sali kissed Joey's check. 'See you back at the house for dinner?'

'Just as soon as I've made a note of all the incoming stock, checked the sales figures, put the takings in the night safe and closed the store for the night. It's Mr Horton's night off.'

'It seems like your brother-in-law takes his duties here very seriously, Mrs Evans.' Mr Richards closed the carriage door behind them and rapped the roof with his cane, signalling the driver to move off.

'He does, and he carries them out well. You know how reluctant Mr Horton senior is to praise anyone, and even he said that Gwilym James was lucky to have Joey as an employee.'

'And what is going to happen when the manager of Mason and Hardy's retires from the Cardiff store next Christmas?' he enquired drily.

'As it happens, I was speaking to Mr Horton about that very matter earlier in the week.' It was warm in the carriage and Sali unbuttoned her coat. 'We both thought that as Mr Horton junior has made such a good job of managing this store, he should receive promotion to the same position in the Cardiff store.'

'And Mr Evans could be promoted from assistant manager to manager of the Tonypandy store?' Mr Richards suggested.

'Joey's proved that he's up to the job, and he knows Tonypandy, the people and their shopping habits.'

'And the three managers of Gwilym James's three stores would, as senior members of staff, sit on the board of trustees, one of the new managers effectively replacing the assistant manager, Mr Watkin Jones.'

Sali gave Mr Richards an artful smile. 'That thought, Mr Richards, never once crossed my mind.'

'How long will it take to finalize the purchase of the farm and the houses, Mr Richards?' Sali asked, as they drove back to Pontypridd.

'A few weeks.'

'Two? Three?' she pressed.

'Shall we say that if everything goes according to plan, a month at the most. There is something else that I wanted to discuss with you.' Mr Richards pulled an envelope from his inside pocket. 'I have been corresponding with Mr Williams for two weeks but I didn't tell you, because he was extremely difficult and at first I seriously doubted that he would give us any information as to the whereabouts of Miss Williams.'

'And?' Sali's heart thundered against her ribcage.

'He has finally given me the address of the asylum where his daughter is working as a maid. But only after I wrote to him three times, informing him that I had to see her in person to effect the transfer of her inheritance. He has demanded that her legacy be sent to him, which, as Megan is under twenty-one, he has every right to do.'

'An asylum?' Sali's eyes rounded in horror 'Where, Mr Richards?'

'The middle of nowhere, or so it would appear. I looked at a map before I went to your office.' He extracted the letter from the envelope and studied it. 'The nearest town is Llanidloes, but she is thirty miles outside it. The asylum is called Ty Bryn.'

'How much did you tell Megan's father her inheritance was?'

'Fifteen pounds.'

'I suggested fifty,' she protested.

'And I thought fifteen sufficient.'

'Then we must go there at once.'

'I was afraid you would say that, which is why I suggested we look at the farm this afternoon. I have made arrangements to leave

453

tomorrow. I have booked train tickets for my clerk and myself and wired ahead for a carriage to take us to the house. You cannot go, you have your baby.'

'Mari can look after her for the day. I'll take your clerk's ticket.'

'It may not be possible to travel to the asylum and back in one day,' he warned.

'Then Mari will have to look after Bella for two days, Mr Richards,' Sali countered impatiently. 'You can have no idea how happy this makes me.' She frowned. 'Just in case there is a mistake or we can't get Megan out, let's keep this as a secret between ourselves for a little while longer. But,' she smiled broadly, 'if we do manage to bring her back, just imagine the look on Victor's face the next time we visit, if Megan is with us.'

'I don't understand. Why you have to go to Mid-Wales with Mr Richards at a day's notice, Sali?' Joey said at the dinner table that night.

'Because he wants me to meet a man who has a gold mine that might be a good investment.' It was an idiotic story but after inventing it on the spur of the moment, Sali had no option but to stick to it. 'You don't mind taking care of the children, do you, Mari?' She turned to the housekeeper who at her insistence ate all their meals with them except when they had company.

'Not at all, Miss Sali.' Mari looked at her even more suspiciously than Joey had.

Sali looked at Harry. 'You don't mind me going away for one night, do you, Harry?'

'Tell you what, it's half day tomorrow, so when I come home from work I'll take you riding on your pony,' Joey promised.

'Yippee!' Harry shouted.

'That's settled then.' Sali spooned the last bit of gooseberry fool from her dish into her mouth. She hated lying to Mari and Joey, but then, if tomorrow worked out the way she hoped it would, it would be worth it.

'Megan, you have visitors,' the matron announced from the

doorway of the sluice room where Megan was leaning over the sink washing out floor clothes.

'Visitors!' Megan had woven so many dreams around a moment just like this; she couldn't believe it was actually happening.

'Your father wrote and asked us to allow you see them. They are waiting in the small office at the end of the corridor. At the end of the day I will expect you to make up the time you will lose speaking to them.'

'Yes, Matron.' Megan left the floor cloths in the sink and went to the bathroom next door. She washed her hands and face, rolled down the sleeves of her uniform and buttoned her cuffs. Wishing there was a mirror so she could check her hair, she made her way to the small office, not daring to wonder who might be the other side of the door. *Them.* One just had to be Victor . . .

She knocked and opened the door.

'Mrs Evans, we have to make a decision as to what to do next,' Mr Richards remonstrated, as Sali and Megan continued to hug one another wordlessly. But while Sali remained dry-eyed, Megan couldn't stop sobbing.

'I am sorry, Mr Richards.' Sali helped Megan into a chair. 'We have to talk, Megan. First, do you want to leave here?'

'I have been trying to think of a way to get out ever since I came here. But we're locked in, just like the inmates. Even the delivery vans come through two sets of gates that are locked after them before they are unloaded. And I've stood by those gates. You can see for miles and miles and there's not a house in sight. Not even a farmhouse.'

An agonizing scream tore through the air from one of the upstairs wards.

Megan shuddered. 'Did you hear that?'

'I heard it,' Sali confirmed. 'And I don't know how you've stood it here.'

'I've wanted to leave since the minute I arrived. I've been so frightened. There are maids here who arrived thirty years ago and more as children. I thought I'd end up like them. That no one would ever find me . . .' Megan began to cry again.

'Don't worry, we'll get you out,' Sali promised. 'Mr Richards,' she turned hopefully to the solicitor, 'I'm sure you'll be able to persuade the matron that I need Megan to be my nursemaid more than she needs her to be a ward maid here.'

'I wish I had your confidence, Mrs Evans.'

'Come on, Megan.' Sali pulled the girl to her feet. 'Let's get you out of here.'

'I am sorry, Mrs Evans, it is quite out of the question,' the matron said. 'Miss Williams has been paid for a year's service in advance as a trainee maid. Twenty pounds . . .'

'Which I will reimburse you, Matron,' Sali interrupted smoothly.

'It is not the money, Mrs Evans. You have seen this place. There is neither a town nor even a village for miles; it is not easy to get girls to work in such a remote location. We need Megan to work here.'

'Thirty pounds.' When Sali saw the matron wavering, she added, 'it is imperative that my solicitor and I get Megan to Cardiff tomorrow to claim her inheritance. A delay could cost her the legacy.'

'I see . . .'

'Forty pounds,' Sali said recklessly. 'But only if we can leave within the next ten minutes. You can get two maids to take Megan's place for that amount of money.'

'I have to find them first.'

'Fifty pounds and that is my final offer.'

The matron turned to Megan. 'You may go to your dormitory. Change out of your uniform and dress in the clothes you were wearing when you arrived. I will send one of the ward sisters up to make sure that you leave all of your uniform behind. Including your shoes.'

'I'll never be able to repay you.' Megan dried her tears in the handkerchief Sali handed her, as their hired carriage headed down the long drive that led from the front door of the asylum to the first set of gates.

'Not a word to Lloyd, Victor or any of the Evanses about the money I paid to get you out.' Sali looked intently at Megan. 'Promise?'

'I promise,' Megan answered solemnly.

'If you really want to repay me you can start by laughing instead of crying.' Sali listened hard. 'Do you hear that?'

'What?' asked Mr Richards.

'Silence.'

Sali pushed down the window and looked out at the countryside, as the lodge keeper unlocked the gates. The surrounding hills were bathed in the soft golden light of the setting sun. The sun itself, an enormous red-gold ball, the colour of Megan's hair, was sinking slowly behind a copse of oak trees that crowned a rise to their left.

The driver walked the horses slowly on, the gates clanged shut behind them and the lodge keeper ran on ahead to open the second set of high gates.

'Thank you.' Megan took Sali and Mr Richards's hands. 'I couldn't have borne it there much longer. How is Victor?' she asked, as the second gates closed behind them.

'We have a lot of catching up to do. Mr Richards, I don't suppose there's any chance that we will be able to get back to Pontypridd tonight?' Sali asked hopefully.

'None at all, Mrs Evans, but there is an early train tomorrow. And I did see a respectable looking hotel in Llanidloes.'

'Then I suppose we had better go there.' Sali squeezed Megan's hand. On the way I'll tell you what's been happening to Victor and his family. But I warn you now, it's not good news, although he was comparatively well the last time I saw him.'

As the hotel only had two spare bedrooms, Megan and Sali shared one. After they had eaten dinner with Mr Richards in the dining room, Megan had a bath while Sali arranged for the local dress shop to open so she could buy a few essentials and a new dress for Megan. Afterwards they sat up half the night talking, and although Megan had no news beyond the boredom and monotony of life in the asylum, Sali had plenty to tell her about Victor's trial and imprisonment.

But the plans she and Joey had made to buy the farm, Sali kept to herself. She knew Lloyd and his family's pride too well. If anyone was going to tell Megan about the farm, it should be Victor, and only after its purchase had been cleared with everyone in his family, especially his father.

They reached Pontypridd late the next afternoon; Mr Richards hired a carriage at the station to take them to Ynysangharad House and left them to go to his office.

Mari met them at the door. 'They're at the Athletic Ground in Tonypandy.'

'Who are?' Sali asked, taking Bella from her.

'The Mr Evanses. Mr Francis turned up here first thing this morning to tell you that the Home Secretary intervened in their appeal without any warning. They were all released from Cardiff prison at midday. The Federation arranged a demonstration to welcome them home. You should have seen Mr Evans's face when he discovered you weren't in the house.'

'All of them have been released.' Sali sank down abruptly on one of the hall chairs and cuddled Bella. 'Harry . . .'

'Wouldn't leave Mr Lloyd, so they took him with them. Mr Jenkins,' Mari called to the butler,' would you ask Robert to bring the carriage around to the front of the house, please?'

'I have already done so, Mrs Williams.'

Sali looked at Megan. 'If you want to wash and change before seeing Victor, all your clothes are upstairs. Mari, will you show her, please?'

'Mr Victor will be pleased to see you, Miss Megan. He asked after you as soon as he walked through that door, although none of us could tell him anything about you.' Mari shook her head at Sali. 'You and your gold mines, Miss Sali. Come with me, Miss Williams.' Mari led the way upstairs.

Sali looked down at Bella, then at her own clothes.

'As your daddy's being given a hero's welcome the least I can do is look presentable. Wouldn't you agree, darling?'

The baby looked back at her wide-eyed, as if she'd understood every word.

'And you'll stay here with Mari. Just for a little while, and then I promise you that Daddy and I will be back and we'll bath you and put you to bed.' Carrying the baby, Sali raced up the stairs after Megan and Mari.

Thousands of men, women and children had gathered at the Athletic Ground. The coachman, Robert, did his best to forge a path through to the platform at the front for Sali and Megan, but it was hopeless. The people who had gained prime positions weren't about to give them up for anyone, not even Lloyd Evans's wife.

Sali could see Lloyd, Victor and Mr Evans sitting on the dias with men she recognized as union officials and local dignitaries, including the MP for the Rhondda. She couldn't see Joey or Harry, but she knew they wouldn't be far away.

The MP, Mr Brace, took the megaphone from the official who had welcomed Lloyd, Victor and Mr Evans home. He began to speak and his deep, rich, voice carried loudly and clearly over the crowd, even to the back where she and Megan were standing.

'These men have suffered martyrdom for the sake of the cause, and for the cause of humanity. They were called upon to pay a heavy penalty, not for what they had done, but because the judge and the court panicked over the industrial situation in Wales and indeed in Britain.

'Lloyd, William and Victor Evans have suffered punishment not under penal laws but as men who had been called on to make a sacrifice on behalf of and in the interests of you.'

He pointed into the crowd, and Sali and Megan were deafened by a burst of cheering and applause that lasted for several minutes.

'As to the minimum wage act, I cannot find words to express my disappointment at the decision regarding the payment of the lower paid men. We have never argued their case from the economic standpoint, but the case of human necessity. Every underground worker is entitled to five shillings a day. They have not been given it. But today we have won a small victory. Our martyrs have been freed. We have lost the battle, and we have more work to do, but with men like these,' he indicated Lloyd, Victor and their father, 'we will win in the end. Even if the fight carries on beyond our lifetime, we *will* win.'

During the cheers that greeted the end of his speech, he turned to the men sitting behind him. Mr Evans shook his head and laid a trembling hand on Lloyd's arm. Sali realized just how frail her father-in-law had become.

Lloyd left his chair and stepped forward. 'On behalf of my father, my brother and myself, I thank every one of you for this rousing reception. And I agree with Mr Brace, they may have beaten us now and it may take years, but in the end we will win.' He lifted his head and Sali felt that he was looking directly at her. 'Thank you.'

A councillor rose to speak, but people were already beginning to drift back towards the entrance to the field. Sali saw Luke Thomas with his wife and children.

'Mrs Evans,' he tipped his hat to her, 'you must be feeling happy.'

'Yes, I am, Mr Thomas, thank you. How are you?' She smiled at Mrs Thomas and the children.

'Emigrating,' Luke said shortly. 'My brother's paid our passage to Australia. There's work there and hopefully I'll soon earn enough to pay him back.'

'I am sorry.'

'So are we, Mrs Evans. It's hard on my mother, I am her only daughter, but,' Mrs Thomas shrugged her shoulders, 'what can you do? There's nothing for us here now that Luke can't get his job back.'

'Good luck, to all of you.' Sali offered Luke and Mrs Thomas her hand. They shook it warmly.

'We tried, Mrs Evans, and,' Luke waved in the direction of the platform, 'for all the fine words, we lost. I know when I'm beaten. Say goodbye to Billy, Lloyd, Victor and Joey for me?'

Sali turned and watched them walk away.

The end of the speeches signalled the end of the meeting, and Sali, Megan and Robert found themselves caught up in the crowd that was pouring out of the ground. Robert fought and bullied his way through, guiding them back to the carriage he had parked close to the entrance.

'They have to pass this way, Mrs Evans. May I suggest you'd be safer looking out for them from inside the carriage?'

The last thing Sali wanted to do was sit in the carriage when Lloyd was so close but she looked back at the throng streaming out of the field and realized Robert was right.

He opened the door, folded down the steps and helped first her, then Megan inside. They sat opposite one another on the bench seats, glued to the windows, watching the people pass the coach. After what seemed an eternity, Sali spotted Victor, who towered over the men around him, flanked by Joey, Mr Evans and Lloyd, who was carrying Harry on his shoulders.

Sali saw that Megan had seen Victor but she placed her hand over Megan's as she reached for the door handle. 'You don't need an audience for your reunion, or to alert any gossips who'll write to your father. Sit back so Victor can't see you. I'll send him in.'

Megan moved further into the coach. She couldn't take her eyes off Victor as he strode towards them. Sali had warned her that he had changed, but she wasn't prepared for the convict haircut, or the amount of weight he had lost.

Sali opened the door and jumped down on to the road as the men drew close. 'Can I offer you gentlemen a ride?'

'Mam,' Harry leaned towards her, Lloyd lifted him down and all three embraced. For a single blindingly emotional moment, nothing existed outside of each other for Sali or Lloyd. She lifted her head to his and he kissed her, not caring that thousands were witnessing their reunion.

'Time to go home, I think,' Victor said drily, when people began to stop and point.

'Home or Ynysangharad House?' Billy Evans asked miserably.

'Ynysangharad House, because all our things are there and the house here isn't aired. We have a lot of things to talk about and many decisions to make, Dad, and we need your help to make them.' Sali kissed her father-in-law's cheek. 'Victor, get in the carriage.' When he hesitated, she added. 'Please.'

Victor opened the door and Joey went to follow him.

Sali held him back. 'Not you. We're all going to take a short walk around the Athletic Ground.'

'What are you up to?' Lloyd asked.

She raised her eyebrows as they heard the unmistakeable sound of crying coming from the carriage. Lloyd looked at Sali. 'You didn't?'

Sali took her father-in-law's arm and his. 'How about a race to that post, Harry? Who do you think will reach it first? You or Uncle Joey? My bet's on you.'

'Well?' Victor asked Megan two weeks later. They walked out of the farmhouse into the yard.

'All I've done since I've left the asylum is cry.' Megan brushed the tears from her eyes. 'It's ridiculous. I've never been so happy.'

'You like the house?'

'Like it? I love it. And we can do so many things to improve it. Those alcoves are crying out for shelves and if we have light curtains at the windows and distemper the walls in white the rooms will be so much brighter. And we can strip the paint from the upstairs floorboards . . .' He was grinning at her and she realized that she was getting carried away. 'Too many things at once?'

He hugged her. 'I'll try to finish as many as I can in the first week, Megs, but it may take a little longer to get the place the way you want it.'

'I don't care if it takes us a lifetime.'

Victor looked down the hill to where his father was walking with Lloyd, Harry and Sali, who was carrying Bella. It said something for the state of his father's health that he was leaning as heavily on Lloyd's arm as he was on his walking stick. 'Our Lloyd married a woman in a million. She acts as if we're the ones doing her a favour and she has sorted out your life, and found work for Joey and me.'

'But not for Lloyd.'

That's something he would never allow her to do. He has to find his own way. And Sali is wise enough to realize that.'

'I wonder what he'll do.'

'I have no idea, but whatever it is, knowing Lloyd, he'll make his mark somehow.' Victor stood at the entrance to the farmyard and looked through the yard to the hills, fields and valley beyond. 'We may own this outright thanks to Sali's conniving, but the last owner went bankrupt,' he warned. 'Everyone knows there's more trouble coming to the valley. The war between the colliers and the owners isn't over . . .'

'It is for us, Victor.'

'No.' He shook his head. 'Not with the father and brothers I have. Don't ever ask me to walk away from my own kind, Megs.'

'I won't,' she promised.

'And we'll have to live on what we produce.'

'There's enough fruit and vegetables in that garden and orchard to keep a street of colliers and their families for a year. Someone,' she glanced slyly at him, 'is going to have to go to market and open a stall.'

'Or we could sell our surplus to Connie.'

'That might be easier,' she agreed.

He swung her off her feet and kissed her before looking to the field beyond the yard. 'There I think, don't you?'

'What?' she asked, mystified.

'Remember that farmhouse you told me you imagined us living in?'

'That was a dream. I didn't expect you to take me seriously.'

'You wanted a duck pond.' He smiled. 'I'll start digging it out tomorrow. We'll put it there.'

'I love you, Victor Evans.'

'Enough to live in sin with me here until the twenty-fifth of August nineteen twelve?'

'Yes. We're going to have a good life here. I can feel it. If only my father doesn't find us . . .'

'Don't even think it,' he said, allowing his anger to show.

'Victor—'

'I don't want to talk about the ranting of a crazy old man, Megs.'

For all of Victor's dismissal, they both fell silent and recalled the letter that had been sent to the house in Tonypandy four days after

Victor's release from prison. Someone had recognized Megan at the Athletic Ground and that someone had wasted no time in writing to her father.

'*Don't think that you can get away with this my girl. You are not twenty-one until August. Four months is a long time and the law is on my side . . .*'

'He won't find us here, Megs,' Victor reassured her in a softer tone.

'And if he does?'

'I'll not lose you a second time.' He turned and looked at her. 'That is one thing that I will promise you, my love.'

Note

I HAD hoped to make *Winners and Losers* an unbiased reflection of the 1910–11 miners' strike but it has proved a difficult task. Myth has overlaid the facts and I discovered that anecdotal evidence frequently incorporated events that occurred during the 1926 strike. Therefore, I found myself relying more and more on contemporary newspaper accounts, most of which were clearly prejudiced.

Until I began my research, my only knowledge of the Tonypandy Riots was from family legend. Welsh industrial history never featured on the syllabus at either my primary or Grammar school in Pontypridd in the 1950s and 1960s and it is difficult for us now to comprehend the effect the miners' withdrawal of their labour had on the establishment in 1910.

Miners' wages, substantial in the mid-nineteenth century, had been steadily eroded by the conglomerates who had bought the pits from the entrepreneurs who sunk them, until miners found themselves working in dangerous conditions for a wage that didn't allow them to provide the basic necessities for themselves and their families. It was hardly surprising that they became socialists, Marxists and Communists before the Russian Revolution. But the Workers' Rights they demanded were seen as a threat to the social order by the ruling and upper classes. If newspaper reports are to be believed, even the king had a hand in trying to settle the dispute. He and the queen certainly visited South Wales during the strike.

The miners' demands proved infectious. In October 1910 local shopworkers asked for a minimum wage, the freedom to live off the premises and shorter hours. Fearful that it was the beginning of a workers' revolt, the authorities panicked.

There were bloody and violent clashes between police, soldiers and miners. Soldiers from the Somerset Light Infantry, armed with fixed bayonets, were employed to break up demonstrations. Police were issued with four-foot wooden batons, and the miners, never ones to turn the other cheek, fought back with ripped-up colliery palings and buckets of stones. Tempers were lost and injuries sustained on both sides.

Contemporary reports from the *Rhondda Leader* paint a picture of a society on the edge. Headlines in October/November 1910 shriek *Red revolution — Streets at mercy of mob — Terrible bloodshed*. There are tragically true reports of women and children dying from starvation, headmasters canvassing for donations for the feeding centres they had set up in their schools and blacklegs being dragged from their houses and beaten on the streets. In December 1910 Rhondda church leaders accused the police of entering the homes of innocent people, assaulting them, their wives and children, and destroying their few possessions. Keir Hardie MP asked questions in the House of Commons about unprovoked police assaults on strikers and their families to no avail.

In retaliation against the charges of police brutality, the police charged strikers with every offence on the book: card-playing in the street, obstruction, intimidation, theft, swearing, drunkenness, and sheep stealing.

In the same month the authorities finally capitulated and tried PC James Thomas of Penygraig for clubbing a striker in his own home. The prosecution failed. In August 1911 Mabon (William Abraham MP) again appealed for an inquiry into charges against the police but the Home Secretary declined to 'put police on trial'.

All the major events portrayed in *Winners & Losers* actually occurred. The train crash at Hopkinstown on the morning of Monday, 28 January 1911 killed eleven passengers, including three miners' leaders: Councillor Tom George from Ferndale, Councillor W. H. Morgan from Treherbert and Councillor Tom Harries from Pontygwaith. All three were miners' checkweighers. (The checkweighers' calculations formed the basis for the colliers' wages and they were chosen by both management and workers for their honesty.) Miss Margaret Davies (age ten of the Commercial Hotel, Ferndale), Thomas John Hodges (a butcher, Ferndale,) Thomas Ivor Hodges (age nine, his son), Reverend W. Landeck Powell, (Caerphilly), Hannah Jenkins (age sixteen, Morgan Street, Trehafod), Idris Evans (age eighteen, Tonypandy), Edward Lewis, (a horse dealer, Llwynypia), and Lodwig Hughes (a colliery engine driver, Mardy) were also killed. Seven people were seriously injured and taken to Cardiff Infirmary.

The Australian premier, Andrew Fisher visited Tonypandy in July 1911, but after reading his speech to the miners I cannot help feeling that his visit was prompted less by a desire to help the situation than in the hope of recruiting citizens for his country. The cost of the strike to the establishment was certainly greater than it would have been to meet the miners' demands. The total expenditure on extra policing alone was put at the then enormous cost of £95,030 in September 1911.

Eventually, and perhaps inevitably, the miners were broken by their families' suffering. They went back for no gain. The settlement partly negotiated by Mabon eventually brought about his downfall. Rightly or wrongly the miners believed their leader had sided with Leonard Llewellyn and the collieries companies.

Billy Evans, his three sons – Lloyd, Victor, Joey – Megan Williams, Sali Jones, Joyce Palmer, Lena, and all the police officers are creations of my imagination. The Reverend Williams, founding member of the Mid-Rhondda Central Distress Committee, Captain McCormack of the Salvation Army and Leonard Llewellyn are actual historical figures.

Billy, Lloyd and Victor's arrest and trials are based on those of the miners' leaders, William John (thirty-two) and John Hopla (thirty-one), checkweighers of the Glamorgan Colliery, Tonypandy and members of the Cambrian Combined Joint Committee. They were tried at Glamorgan Assizes, Cardiff in November 1911 (after the strike had been settled) for riotous assembly. Found guilty they were each sentenced to one year's hard labour. John Hopla's brother Henry, was tried and found guilty of assaulting a police officer and sentenced to nine months hard labour.

The sentences led to miners' demonstrations all over the Rhondda. The Federation of Mineworkers pledged support for their families, and when Mabon asked the Home Secretary in Parliament if he was aware of the sentences, Mr McKenna (who succeeded Winston Churchill in the post) decided that the men were entitled to appeal without cost to themselves. As a consequence, six months later, their sentences were halved. William John became a Rhondda MP and served his constituents for many years. John Hopla's health broke during his imprisonment and he died shortly after his release.

Revolutions are rarely reported accurately, especially when they fail, and the events surrounding the Tonypandy Riots are no exception. Some people believe the past has no relevance today. I would disagree. I think the story of the far from 'ordinary' self-taught, working-class miners, who prized education and knowledge and built libraries from donated pennies in the hope of advancing their families is inspirational. And, on a more personal note, I want my own children to know about their great-grandfather, Harry Glyndwr Jones, who went down the pit at the age of eleven and worked his way up from collier boy to colliery repairman, and their great-uncle, collier Owain Glyndwr Jones, both of whom took an active part in the 1910-11 and 1926 strikes.

I am proud of my Welsh roots and all the Welsh men and women who dared to fight the establishment the only way they could and with the only weapon at their disposal – the withdrawal of their labour.

Catrin Collier
October 2003